Love Auction
Too Risky to Love Again

A Novel By

Sharon Carter

Published in the United States by SC Publications
Memphis, Tennessee

First Edition, February 2020

ISBN: 978-1-7342038-0-6

For my husband and mother. Thank you for believing I'm a talented writer. Love you both so much.

Chapter 1

Sage Sullivan yelled across the room, trying to get Cindy's attention. It was crowded and chaotic at the center on a warm, sunny Saturday morning. McMorris Community Center—MCC—was a nonprofit organization that helped financially distressed people. They provided food for homeless families, job programs, counseling, assisted financially, and helped orphaned children. The job program assessed people's skills to help place them in a suitable job, paving the way to their financial independence.

MCC was active with many vendors in the city and received its funding from some of the local businesses in Bayville. Cindy Robinson had founded the center. Her staff put together marathons, bake sales, and auctions to help raise money. The center was hosting an auction the following month and would be auctioning some of Bayville's most beautiful women and handsome men. The fundraisers were always successful. People were generous, which was good, because without their help, the center wouldn't survive.

MCC had been named after Cindy's aunt, Alice McMorris. Cindy had always admired her aunt. Alice opened her door to help anyone in need. She was a loving person who would give anyone the clothes off her back if she could. The center was celebrating its fifteenth anniversary. It was crowded with guests and noisy with the band and laughter. There were arts and crafts, games, live music provided by a local band, as well as a large food buffet. Sage, a volunteer at the center, was trying to get Cindy's attention to discuss some details with her. As she waited, Sage noticed a man with Cindy wearing an expensive blue suit, similar in style to what her husband had worn. His eyes were a deep ocean-blue. Sage had lost her husband in a horrendous car accident two years before. He'd been the love of her life, and she still grieved for her husband. The man, probably a benefactor, noticed Sage looking him over. He seemed to like what he saw too. He smiled at her and turned his attention back to Cindy.

"Fiddlesticks! What was that?" she thought, tearing her eyes away. You know that deja vu feeling you get like you know a person, or you've seen someone before? But she didn't know this person. He wouldn't be on her radar anyway. He looked totally full

of himself—a man who probably thought highly of himself.

The benefactor with Cindy had noticed Sage instantly. She had been assisting the children and reminded him of his mother, whom he'd lost years ago to breast cancer.

"I don't mean to be rude, but who's the beautiful woman in the kid's section, glasses on top of her head, long curly charcoal hair?" he asked. He was lusting after a woman who reminded him of his late mother. "*Stop it old perv,*" he thought.

"*So, he's into my best friend,*" Cindy thought.

"Ah, that's Sage. She's a good friend of mine who volunteers on weekends. She's an absolute doll with a beautiful spirit. We've been blessed to have her helping at the center. She works for Bayville's Protective Children Services," Cindy said. "I'm so grateful for your large donation, Mr. Brimmer. MCC very much appreciates you." Cindy smiled up at him.

"You're very welcome," he said, still watching Sage. "Anything to help those in need."

Why couldn't he stop watching her? He knew from experience with his ex-wife, watching her shouldn't be an option.

"I hope to see you at the auction on June 1st."

Cindy was hosting a dinner date auction as a fundraiser for the center. She had recruited single women and men who were sure to have people bidding for the opportunity to have a date. She knew that Mr. Brimmer would fetch a pretty bid. She also realized that she needed to confirm with Sage if she was going to be a part of the auction. She was sure Mr. Brimmer would bid high after what she'd seen.

"Not sure if my schedule allows it. I am a very busy man," he admitted, looking at his gold Rolex. He wasn't being rude; he had a meeting with Gaines and Blackwell along with lawyers in half an hour. What he wanted to do was go to the beach and breathe in the fresh ocean air then hit the waves. That would be heavenly. He worked too damn much and didn't have enough excitement in his life. He looked at Sage again and thought, "*She's too young.*"

"I'm going to head out," he said to Cindy, handing her his business card.

"Thank you," she replied, accepting the card. "Thanks so much. I'll walk you out."

R&B music played over the PA system; the band was on break. Children and adults were dancing and laughing, having a good time. Several children ran straight by them, but that still didn't distract him from inspecting Sage as they walked out. Her cat-like emerald eyes, full bow-lips, high-cheekbones, and curvy body had him mesmerized.

Sage looked up, feeling his eyes on her. Her eyes blinked owlishly as she looked around for a moment to see what was so darn interesting. Then she realized it was she who was so fascinating. She touched the tip of her nose briefly, thinking something might be there. She was relieved he was on his way out. She wondered why he had been staring at her like that—his blue eyes examining her. She resumed helping one of the children.

Cindy walked over to Sage when she came back into the center.

"Hey chick," Sage spoke happily. "This is a huge success," she said, noticing all the fun everyone was having, her eyes beamed with joy. "I'm so glad I decided to come out this morning."

"You and me both. I'm so glad you could help. So, that was one of our biggest donors," Cindy divulged, briefly taking hold of Sage's hand. "He couldn't keep his eyes off you. He wanted to know who you were."

Sage turned quickly to give Cindy her full attention. "I hope you didn't tell him anything about me, Cid," she stated.

"Of course not. I only told him your first name. But if you like, I could give him your number," she said facetiously.

Sage frowned. "Now Cid, don't you dare," Sage said, shaking her finger at Cindy. "That man isn't my type, and even if he were, I still wouldn't be interested. Men like him think they are entitled to everything. I can't stand men like that," Sage finished, turning her nose up.

Cindy knew it was a defense approach. Sage wasn't usually presumptuous, especially about other people.

"I know you don't date, and I know he's most definitely not your type. But if you did, he would be the right choice. He's well off. You do realize he's one of Bayville's hottest bachelors? I think he was married once upon a time. And, he's one of our big donors," Cindy boasted. "The man isn't anything you would expect. He's very nice and especially to us."

"I'm not interested in your hot donor-bachelor. I noticed from the tailored suit he's got the Benjamin's," Sage said.

Benjamin was Sage's brother-in-law, and he was most definitely full of himself. She also noticed several other things which she dared not to admit to herself. Luke was the only man who'd held her interest at first glance, and he died.

"So, you did notice how sexy he was?" Cindy giggled, placing her arm around Sage.

"I do have eyes," Sage said, taking the reading glasses from her head. "Make that four," she expressed, waving her glasses at Cindy. "Like I said, I'm not interested in your donor."

Cindy decided to change the subject. If she wanted Sage to participate in the upcoming auction next month, it was best not to antagonize her.

"Are you going to be a part of the auction next month? I need a smart, beautiful, successful woman like you to auction off. You'll bring in the big bucks, and I've been your good friend for the past two years." Cindy grinned, pulling Sage away from the children. The band had resumed playing, and it was a little too noisy, so they headed to the garden.

MCC had a small private garden area which came in handy. The staff, along with the people they assisted, helped maintain the garden. The garden had fresh fruits, vegetables, and a few fruit trees. The ladies sat on a bench in the shade of an apple tree.

"This garden has come into its own," Cindy commented, touching an apple.

"It is really beautiful and peaceful here. And Cid, I told you I would participate in the auction if you didn't have enough women," Sage said. "I don't mind helping for a good cause. So, how many women do you have so far?" Sage inquired.

"Not enough," Cindy answered, honestly. Men were always easier to recruit than women. "I'm going to be in the auction myself. Lord knows I need a date. I've been going through a dry spell."

"Well, I'm not doing this for a man. That's the farthest thing from my mind,"

Sage objected. "I'm doing it for the children and my good friend."

"Oh, thank you, thank you," Cindy said, hugging her.

"Welcome, welcome," Sage chimed, hugging her back. "What are friends for?"

Sage went to the gym to meet Sarah Jones Crawford, one of her oldest best friends, at 2 p.m. They'd been friends since their freshman year in college. Sage worked out at the gym not far from her two-story home. If the lights were in sync, it took her less than twenty minutes to get there. When she arrived, Sarah was already on a treadmill, which meant she was a little late. Sage got on the treadmill next to her.

"Hi Sage," Sarah greeted, and then resumed walking. "How was your morning at MCC?"

"Sorry I'm late. Traffic. It was fabulous. I had a good time," she reported as she stretched her legs. "You should have come. You would have enjoyed it too."

"I was a little too tired from last night. I had a date."

"Oh, and how did it go?" Sage could tell it hadn't gone well by Sarah's expression.

"Not well. The guy kept talking about his two cats and his boring job as a banker. Trudy and Beth are his pride and joy," she smiled, rolling her eyes. "The guy even showed me pictures of them in his phone. Showing me how he dressed and had this special song he plays just for them. That weirdo," she fumed. "What a waste of my valuable time. It took me two hours to get my hair right."

"Sorry you had to go through that," Sage commented. "I could have told you he wasn't a match for you. He's a banker. Bor--ing!" She thought Sarah would be a good match with Parker. "You like guys with enthusiasm. Maybe the next one will be better," Sage assured.

"I haven't given up hope. I know my future husband is searching for me just as I'm searching for him. I'm waiting for you to start dating." Sarah glanced at Sage for a moment, then looked straight ahead—she knew her friend was still living in the past.

"I'm good. I don't need a date. I'll leave that to you. Hopefully, you'll find your Mr. Right soon," Sage said, starting up the treadmill.

"Yep, totally," Sarah agreed. "And so, will you."

"Whatever, chick," she laughed, throwing a towel at her.

Sage was thinking about the man at MCC that morning. He had a tall, well-built body and beautiful blue eyes. She was unsure of what made her think about him. Men like that couldn't be trusted. He was wealthy. He had to be into something illegal.

She knew not to judge a person by their appearance but found herself still making assumptions about him. Sage didn't understand why she was behaving so out of character. And besides, perhaps he'd worked hard and accumulated his fortune perfectly legally.

Sarah and Sage worked-out for two hours. After the gym, they headed downtown for a smoothie. The best smoothie place was on Rippleridge Dr. where there was always a lot going on. Of course, Bayville always had something going on. It boasted a beautiful skyline with its skyscrapers, nice parks including a large waterpark, several museums, art galleries, and theatres both for live performances and movies. The city buzzed at night with its restaurants, jazz clubs, R&B clubs, and country theatre. The best views were from the restaurants lucky enough to be on the top floor of the skyscrapers. The light fest was spectacular. The population was not quite a million, and people loved living in Bayville. It truly had something for everyone. But like every other city, it had its fair share of crime too.

Parker Richards had been protecting and serving the public for five years. A year ago, he'd been promoted detective second grade for Bayville Police Department—BVPD. Parker had left Bayville for college, and after graduation, he'd moved to Miami. After three years of working for the Miami-Dade police department, he realized he missed his hometown and moved back. This was one of those nights he'd missed so much in Miami. This time of year, it was too hot, and there were way too many tourists. Getting a smoothie in Miami meant waiting in ridiculously long lines full of drunk college kids. Berry House Blends was Parker's favorite place to get a smoothie. It was busy, but not so busy that you couldn't get served within a reasonable amount of time.

Parker pulled his blue 1968 Shelby into a parking space at the smoothie shop. He was lucky to find a spot as this was the busiest time of day. As he stepped from his car, he saw Sage and Sarah sitting outside, enjoying their smoothies, talking, and laughing. He'd known Sage since junior high school.

"Hey, Parker is on his way over, so play nice," Sage said, knowing Sarah didn't care for him. Sage thought that Sarah's angst toward Parker had to do with pent up energy—the kind that could only be exhausted in the bedroom.

"Hi, ladies," Parker said, taking a seat.

"Hello, Park, how's it going?" Sage asked.

"It's going okay. I noticed the two of you and decided to say hi." He looked in Sarah's direction. He understood why she didn't care for him—he'd broken her best friend's heart.

"Hey," Sarah said, dryly.

"So, how did it go at MCC?" he asked Sage.

"It went really well. Great turn out. I even volunteered to be auctioned off," she chirped proudly.

"What! I don't believe it," Sarah said with a grin. "Awe snap," she continued, snapping her fingers, "You are down for some man bidding on you? And having dinner with you when he wins?"

"Wait one freaking minute," Sage cringed, shaking her index finger slightly. "I'm doing this for the kids, not for a man," she emphasized. "I don't need to date."

"It wouldn't hurt you to start dating," Parker said, matter-of-factly.

Sarah was dumbfounded by Parker's words. She had to force herself to focus on her smoothie so she wouldn't say anything. Dating was a sore subject for Sage. She was still hurting over the death of her husband. A death she still blamed herself for. Sage and her husband had had an argument just before the accident that had killed Luke. Sage never said what the argument was about, but Sarah suspected it was about Sage's pregnancy.

"Sage, I'm sorry if I stepped out of line, but you are still very young, and he's been gone two years now. I just want my friend to be happy again." He placed his large hand on her small one, giving it a gentle squeeze.

Sage pulled her hand away angrily.

"I would love to see my best friend that way, too," Sarah added, looking at her with compassion.

"Awe fiddlesticks," Sage snorted irritably, using a word she'd picked up from her mother years ago to keep from swearing. "Parker, stay in your lane. You weren't pleased when Luke and I started dating," she huffed. "I'm cheerful. I have my health, family, and good friends. I'm fine the way my life is now. I don't need anything new," she muttered as she stood. "I'm gonna head home. I don't want you two double-teaming me. In fact, it's adorable to see your new-found union on something. I'll talk to you both later."

Sage went straight home after she left the smoothie shop. She wasn't in the mood to hear her friends tell her she needed to forget Luke and move on with her life. She was upset with Sarah and Parker. They had never seemed to agree on anything, but when it came to Luke, she didn't want their opinions—whether they agreed or not.

Lucas Luke Sullivan was the love of her life. He practiced law at Randolph and Smitz, one of Bayville's top law firms. She met him in her second year at Penn State. He was in his last year there.

"Hi sexy, mind if I join you?" He had whispered to her. The words rang in her ears as though he'd just spoken them. She had looked up from her books to find a gorgeous, 6'3" man with a muscular body, chocolate eyes, and brown cocoa skin. He also had nice, full, kissable lips. She couldn't say no to his request. Sage and Luke had been distracted from the assignments. They had spent most of the time in the library studying each other instead of their coursework. It had been love at first sight for both of them.

Sage sat in her study, thinking about Luke. It was her favorite room in the house. It had white high gloss marble floors, wall to wall bookshelves, with a ladder that moved across the expanse of shelving. A large bay window overlooked the garden with an overstuffed couch in front so she could sit and enjoy the view. Another couch was by the bookshelves, and her large cherry wood desk was in the center of the room. While it was her favorite room, Sage loved her home. The inside had been remodeled with modern appliances and fixtures, but the outside had maintained its appearance from the glory days of Victorian architecture homes.

Sage felt safe here with her memories of Luke. The room was her sanctuary. It was also where she wrote her short stories. For the most part, she'd always written mysteries, but since Luke had died, she dabbled with romance stories. Her romance stories had taken the place of real romance in her life. Sage didn't feel the need for the real deal—her stories were enough.

She hadn't told anyone about this side of her—that she loved writing. It had been a well-kept secret. The only other person who'd known was Luke, and he was gone. Sage didn't feel she had the talent to write, but Luke would read her work and encourage her to have them published. Even with Luke's encouragement, Sage had never let anyone else read her work. She was waiting for the right time. When was the right time? She wasn't sure.

"Luke, one day, I'll get up the nerve and let someone read them. And get them published. I promise," she muttered as if he was in the room with her.

One hour and thirty minutes later, Sage woke up on the couch. She hadn't realized she was so exhausted. At least she hadn't woken up screaming from her nightmares. Sometimes she still had dreams about the deadly crash. That night was etched deep in her mind.

Sage could barely move, fastened in the wrecked car by her seatbelt. She was coughing and barely able to breathe. The acrid taste of smoke and the gas fumes overwhelmed her, and the pain was excruciating. She remembered calling out his name as she looked upon her husband's body with his head through the windshield, feet hanging in the front seat. Sage knew he was dead. At that point, the darkness overcame her. Sage regained consciousness in the hospital. Her injuries were not life-threatening, but she'd sustained a broken arm and pelvis, as well as a severe whiplash.

Sage had gone to physical therapy after she was discharged from the hospital. A year after the accident, she had stopped going because she didn't feel it was doing her any good. She'd only started going because her friends influenced her to go. Working at MCC had helped more than the therapy had. It showed her there were so many people who endured hardships every day and had no one in their corner. Sage did. Her family and friends were there for her if she needed them.

Sage got up from the couch stretching catlike, making a purring sound as she wiped the sleep from her eyes. She went to the kitchen and put on a kittle to make tea when the phone began to ring—it was her landline hanging on the kitchen wall. She and Luke must have been one of the few people who still had a landline. Luke had it installed for business purposes, and Sage had left it there not wanting to make changes in her life. She had tried to keep most everything the same as it had been when Luke had been alive. She didn't want or need more reminders of his absence. She knew the caller was either her aunt or her sister.

"Hello," she answered.

"Hey, Sugar, how are you this Saturday evening?" her aunt asked. "No hot date tonight?" She had tried to fix Sage up several times.

"Hi Aunt Katie, I'm well. I'm about to have tea. What is my aunt up to later? Do you have a hot date?" Sage asked with a smile. "Are you performing at Club Latey tonight?"

Katie was Sage's maternal aunt. Sage's mother had been killed in a gruesome accident, and she had gone to live with her. Sage blamed her father and hadn't had anything to do with him since. She lost her mother and then her husband to the same fate. What were the odds? She felt she had been dealt a bad hand by the Universe. She decided she wouldn't ever fall in love or let a man get close to her ever again. It would only end up in heartache and pain. She hadn't stopped crying for her husband each time a memory washed over her. She still sometimes cried for her mother. Sage was always replaying the crash in her mind. The 'what if' game. What if we hadn't been arguing that night? What if he just had his seatbelt on? Would he still be alive?

"No date, Sug," Katie answered. "I'm taking a break from men, and I'm not performing anywhere tonight."

Her aunt always said she was staying away from men until she found someone new. She'd lost her husband a long time ago and hadn't met a man that could equal her late husband. But that didn't keep her from trying to set up Sage. She wanted her niece to get back out there and start trying.

"Have you talked to Lora lately?" Katie asked.

"I spoke to Lor a few days ago. Why, Auntie?"

"Nothing, I was just making sure you girls weren't quarreling over your father again."

Lora Tate was three years older than Sage. She was an obstetrician married to Benjamin Franklin Tate, a veterinarian. They had two children, a son Benjamin Franklin Tate Jr., age six, and a daughter, Lilianna Tate, age two. They lived in Atlanta, Ga. Oh, they had a dog too—one of those little house dogs. His name was Wiener Tate because of his shape.

"If she doesn't mention him to me, I wouldn't quarrel at all with her," Sage answered. "I don't care to know what he's doing. I've been over him since Mommy died twelve years ago. She won't leave it alone," she said angrily.

"Sugar," Katie said in her southern twang, "your sister and I mean well. You must move on and forgive. Forgiveness is for you, not him. You think just because she got behind the wheel of her car upset it's his fault. But it isn't, Sage. It was my sister, your mother. She should have thrown his ass out. I'm not angry with your father." She wanted to say she was angry with her sister but didn't. "And you shouldn't be either."

"I hear my kettle going off. I'll call you later, Aunt Katie."

"Okay, Sug," she replied, knowing her niece was dismissing her. "You have a good night." She knew her niece wasn't going to call her back—talking about the past always upset Sage.

"You too, Auntie. I love you."

"I love you too, Sugar." Katie heard the kettle in the background. "Make sure you have some good hot tea. Bye, Sug."

"Bye," Sage smiled as she hung up the phone.

Chapter 2

Two days later, Sage was up to her neck in case files. The Nicole-Marie Fulton case was a tough one. The child had lost her mother, Gloria Fulton, eight months before. It was a drug deal gone badly, according to Parker. Nicole had been hiding in a closet when the police found her. Still, no one had been charged with Gloria's murder.

Sage had placed the child with the Grissom Family. They had a little girl around Nicki's age. Sage thought she would fit in with them, but she'd received a call from the family asking her to remove the child, which they had every right to do if it wasn't working out for them or the child. She prayed that Nicki would give them a chance. Sage had her reading glasses on as she squinted, looking over the file, hoping it would help her find someone else to place Nicki with. Sage held her pen close to her lips, biting on the top nervously as her eyes scanned several pages. According to her file, Nicki was an only child. Her mother had also been in the foster care system. There was no information on the father or any other next of kin.

"Hey, save the pen top," Sarah addressed, grinning at her from the doorway. "It's going to be alright." Sarah walked into Sage's office, closing the door behind her. She and Sarah had their own offices as they each managed their departments—they were the best caseworkers at the agency.

"It's this case I have in front of me. It's one Parker brought to me. The Grissom's may not keep Nicki. I was reading over the file to see if I overlooked anything," she explained, gliding her finger down a page.

"That's the little girl who was hiding in the closet with her dead mother's body on the floor," Sarah said, taking a seat. "She called 911 after she realized no one was in the room. She's a smart little girl. I hope they caught the bastard who did it."

"Yeah, you and me both," Sage agreed. "I'm praying I'm wrong, but I think they'll be calling me later today or at least within the next two days to tell me to remove her."

"I know you've gotten attached to her. Why won't you consider taking her in if all goes south with the foster parents?" Sarah suggested.

"I can't be a foster parent, Sarah. I'm barely at home. I work long hours here sometimes, and I help at MCC. You should know, you're here at this office with me."

There was a soft knock at Sage's door. One of the caseworkers peeped her head in her office.

"Hi, Rebecca," Sage greeted with a smile.

"Sorry, I see you're busy. I'll come back later." She started to back out the door.

"Give Sarah and me a few minutes. I'll be with you shortly," Sage said, courtly.

"Thanks," Rebecca replied.

"Now that she's gone, I think this little girl would be what you need. You have both suffered losses. You could help each other heal. You've thrown yourself into work far too long, Sage. You need to balance work and home life. If it weren't for your good friends, you wouldn't go out, period. You must focus on the present, not the past. Let this little girl be your present and future. Experience a new kind of love. One that may help you move forward with your life," Sarah stressed.

"Fiddlestick," Sage squeaked. "We discussed this a few days ago—you and Parker being on my case. I know this is close to home for you. It's one of the reasons you chose this profession, and I admire you for it. But I'm content with my life the way it is. My life is fine," she finished, placing her glasses on her desk.

"Sure, if you say so." Sarah stood and stepped closer to the desk. "I know differently. You used to be carefree, enjoying your life. The accident changed you, and his death did, too."

"I have work to do," Sage said, dismissing Sarah. "I'll talk to you later." She put her glasses back on and buried herself in the case file, hoping Sarah would get the hint and leave. She did.

Nickolas Brimmer sat at his large desk on Tuesday evening, staring into space. He hadn't thought about a woman that way in a long time. He hadn't known why she was getting under his skin. He loosened the blue silk tie around his large neck. He had a private investigator investigate Sage's background. In fact, he did this with every woman before going out with her. She'd lost her husband two years ago in a fatal car crash. He was an attorney who'd worked for the firm that handled some of his legal matters. Her husband worked on some of the mergers for companies he'd acquired. He bought companies that were failing and turned them around.

His marriage of two years caused him to keep women at arm's length. He had nothing to offer them except a good time and sex. And he did that quite well and lavishly. Every woman he went out with was given a token of his appreciation—usually in the form of expensive jewelry. Nick had purchased a diamond necklace for the last woman who'd piqued his interest some ten months ago. That necklace had cost a cool 30Gs. He'd really wanted to connect with her, but there was no spark. Nothing. He'd felt bad and hadn't wanted the woman to feel used, so he'd bought her the necklace.

Nick was contemplating exploring the feelings he'd suddenly developed for Sage simply from watching her. Sure, this was lust. She was stunning in the pink cashmere top that hugged her lovely breasts, and blue denim jeans that fit her sculptured perfect butt and thighs. She'd completed the outfit with a pair of white flip-flops. He wanted her, true. However, it was more than the burning desire of lust, which was normal in any attraction. He wanted to get to know her—really know her. He hadn't felt that way in any of his previous relationships.

"She's too young for you. She'll only be trouble," he complained to himself. She would be trouble because of the last woman he had feelings for. He married her, and she'd turned out to be a snake. Nick went to the large office window and studied the view of downtown Bayville. He had a huge picture on his wall of the beautiful skyline. He had painted it when he was 18 many years ago. His uncle had brought him to Bayville on a business trip. Nick had fallen in love with the city and had relocated to Bayville after college. His mother, Megan, had been an artist when she was alive.

She'd died of breast cancer when he was nineteen years old. The painting that hung in his office was the last acknowledgment from his mother that he was an artist.

His mother used her talent to inspire disadvantaged children. Megan loved seeing a child's face light up when he or she got what she was explaining. Most of all, Megan loved being Nick's mother. She wanted more children, but his father didn't. Nick wasn't as close to his father as he was his mother. He'd been named after his father, and that was the extent of their relationship. His father was a Marine, who traveled most times, going to different cities and continents serving his country proudly. He and his mother didn't travel with him like other families did when they had a family member in the service. His mother preferred staying in San Francisco, making a home there, and Nick was glad she had. Nick lost his father when he was thirty years old. His dad liked the action of being a soldier and died doing what he loved. He'd left him a modest inheritance that Nick invested wisely.

Nick had an Uncle Simon, his dad's brother, which he'd been close to. Simon had never had children of his own and took the young Nick under his wing. He'd been the greatest influence in Nick's young life, making him the man he was today. Unfortunately, Simon smoked and died of a smoke-related disease four years after Nick's father had died. Now Nick had no close family—he missed that in his life.

Nick compensated for his loneliness by working long hours. His large penthouse was empty, so there was little point in going home. He'd wanted a big family, but his marriage didn't last. He was grateful that he and his ex-wife hadn't had children—the woman was selfish and completely self-absorbed. Nick had been blinded with his love for her and hadn't seen who she really was until she showed him. His best friends had tried to warn him, but he didn't listen. Five years ago, he thought he was married to the perfect woman. He would have and did, do anything to make her comfortable, until he found out she was seeing other men. He closed his eyes at the memory. She thought Nick had left town on business. He'd forgotten important documents for the meeting he was going to and returned home to retrieve them. As he walked up the winding staircase, he'd heard her say, *"Baby, don't stop,"* she moaned. *"Harder, baby,"* she grunted. *"Right there."*

Maybe it was the universe that interfered with his sham of a life. It took pity on him and showed him who he was really married to.

Nick immediately forced the door to his large bedroom open and found another man fucking his wife. It had ripped his insides out to see his wife's ass posted in the air, faced downward, allowing another man to ram into it, begging the man not to stop. Nick stood there in the doorway, shell-shocked at first. Then he moved like a bolt of lightning, pulling the man's naked body out of his bed, and started to beat him. He beat the man so severely, it looked as though he'd gone twelve rounds in the ring. In Nick's state of rage, he'd meant to kill him. His rage was lethal.

Nick hadn't gone alone to pick-up the documents. Paul Writhers, his best friend, was waiting in the car for him. Paul began to worry when Nick didn't return within five minutes. He'd gone up to the penthouse and found the door open. Paul walked in and heard Nick's wife screaming upstairs and the sound of furniture being broken. He'd taken the stairs two at a time and arrived at the bedroom door to find Nick beating the life out of a naked man. Paul pulled his friend off the man, threw the man his clothes, and told him to get out. Nick cleaned up after the fight and had instructed his wife to get out. She'd tried to cajole him into staying together, but he'd been betrayed and crushed—he was done.

The man had pressed charges against Nick, and he'd been sentenced to attend an anger management program for six months and put on a one years' probation. Nick wasn't a violent man; it was seeing his wife with another man that had sent him over the edge. Nick couldn't believe his lovely wife had betrayed him that way. He was heartbroken. He was lucky that was all he got. The judge must have taken pity on him knowing what kind of man Nick was and what he did for a living, which was helping people.

Nick cursed at the memories as he opened his eyes and moved away from the window. He had to engross himself in his work to stop thinking about the woman he'd seen across the room at MCC. *"She's bad news. Stay away from her."* Nick looked at the file he had on Sage one more time before he tossed it into the trash. He'd made up his mind not to get involved with her no matter how much he wanted her or how drawn he was to her.

Nick leaned back in his big chair and laced his fingers behind his head. His hair was well-groomed and a midnight color, with the first hints of grey showing at the temples. His greying hair gave him an even more distinguished look. He was happy about the decision he'd made not to pursue Sage. His thoughts were interrupted when the door to his office flew open. He looked up to find his secretary and best friend in the doorway.

"Hello, Paul," he greeted.

He'd asked his secretary to cancel his appointments and not allow anyone to see him—Nick didn't want to be disturbed.

"I'm so sorry, Mr. Brimmer. He wouldn't listen to me." She looked at Paul for a moment then back at her boss.

"It's okay, Staci," he assured.

"Hi, buddy," Paul said, dropping down in a chair. He noticed Nick wasn't his usual self. His smile seemed forced. "What's going on, Nick-O?" He'd always referred to him as Nick-O, from the time they'd met in college.

"Nothing much... work. What about you? You still heading to Portland?"

"Shit yeah. I want to know what's going on with the hotel chains there. You buy, and I make sure all of our businesses are making money."

Nick and Paul had been best friends for twenty years. Fifteen of those years, they'd also been business partners. They were brothers from another mother. Paul was still watching Nick, who was giving off a frustrated vibe. This could only mean one thing.

"Okay, tell me her name," he demanded with a smile.

"What?" Nick looked up from the computer. "I don't know what you're talking about," he answered, shaking his head.

"You sure about that? Fuck! Come on man, I know you. I've been your friend a long time."

Nick leaned back in the chair, scratching his brow, "I can't get a damn thing past you," he cackled.

"Of course, you can. Not certain things." Paul laughed, gliding his hand over his champagne blond hair. "Now, what's her name?"

"Sage Sullivan," Nick replied as he reached down and removed the file from the trash and handed it to Paul.

"Fuck," Paul gasped, with a whistle as he looked at the photo of Sage. He read over her file for a moment then looked at Nick. "She's fucking gorgeous. I can see why you have ants in your pants. I also see why you are taken by her. There have been two tragedies in her life, works for BPCS, and she was married to Lucas Sullivan. He worked on some mergers for us at Randolph and Smitz. And you want her." Paul smiled again, getting up from the chair with the folder in hand.

Nick turned to face him. "I don't know what I want. I got this feeling I can't shake. I threw that file in the trash, so I can forget about her. I don't want to feel this way about a woman I haven't met. Why her? What's so special about her?" He turned back around, looking out the window and ran his hands over his head sighing. "Hell, I've been with plenty of beautiful women, and none of them have had this effect on me."

Paul could see many special things about her, and how a man could easily be head over heels about her. Those emerald cat-like eyes staring at you, her beautiful light caramel skin, and her sexy body. He'd bet money the photo didn't do her justice.

"Look at her," Paul prompted, holding up the picture. "For Fuck's sake... look, man!"

Nick tried to turn his thoughts to the sights, sounds, and smells of downtown Bayville rather than think about her or even look at the pictures of her. In spring, the view in the morning lit by the sun was breathtaking. He loved being able to see from a bird's-eye view. Nick felt the muscles in his neck tense as he curved slowly around to look at the picture. "And what's your point?" It was a rhetorical question— he knew those points. Still, he shouldn't involve himself with any of them.

"Come on, Nick-O," Paul entreated, waving the picture in front of his face. "The woman is captivating." He looked at the picture again himself. He was gawking a bit too hard.

Nick snatched the photo from his hands. "Stay away from her, Paul," he warned.

Paul laughed. He knew Nick's jealousy over a woman all too well. He'd almost killed a man. Well, to be fair, the man was doing his ex-wife in his bedroom. "I simply looked at the pictures. I know you want her," he chuckled, hitting him on the back. "Hell, go after her. I know you think all women are like your ex, but they aren't. You were dealt a bad hand. It looks like things are looking up for you now."

"Maybe," Nick said, staring at her picture. She was married only for a short time. And the man she was married to seemed like a man of integrity as far as he could tell.

"Don't take too long looking at her pictures. Some other guy just might beat you to her," Paul said, placing the folder on Nick's desk as he headed to the door.

Nick didn't like the idea of another guy touching her. His blood boiled, and the muscles in his jaw twitched at the thought. He didn't know this woman to possess any kind of feelings for her. Why was he feeling this strong primal emotion toward her?

"Sure, Paul," Nick said, placing the picture back into the folder. "Whatever you say. I'm not going after her, and neither are you," he warned.

"I get the message, Nick-O." Paul opened the door, and as he stepped out, chided Nick with, "Tick tock, tick tock."

Nick sank back into his chair. "I've been there done that. No need to repeat history." He tossed the folder into the trash.

Parker was on his way downtown to the tallest of all the buildings. It gave you the feeling of touching the sky in its height, opulence, and everything around it. It featured large black panes of glass on its round architecture. The sun reflecting on the panes of glass only enhanced its beauty. He was working on the Nicole-Marie case and it had led him in that direction. That's what he called it—the little girl he found in a closet. The memory of finding her with her mother's dead body only a few steps away still haunted him.

He parked his Shelby on the lower level of the building's parking garage. As he headed to the elevators, Parker noticed some of the names on the reserved parking spaces. A few other professionally dressed people were waiting for the elevator. There were two men in designer suits with briefcases in hand, and a woman dressed in a two-piece button down, cream jacket with a matching skirt hinting slightly of her thighs. He couldn't forget her or her perfect straight blondish hair draping off her shoulders or the expensive heels on her feet. He wasn't sure of the designer, but he knew it was more than he could afford. Parker was out of his element for sure.

He got off the elevator on the 30th floor knowing the big-wigs had to be on that floor. He noticed a lot of expensive paintings in the halls. "*Sage would love these,*" he mumbled. Even the receptionist desk was exquisite. A good-looking brunette, probably thirtyish, smiled at him as he drew near.

"Hello," he stated. "I need to speak to Paul Writhers. I'm with BVPD." He showed her his badge.

"Could you tell me what it's in regard to?" she challenged.

"No, it's police business. I need to speak to him privately."

"If you'll have a seat in the area to your right, I'll see if he can see you." She picked up the phone and dialed her boss's extension.

"Yes, Margret, I'm about to head out of the city."

"I know, but a detective from the BVPD wants to see you," she informed in a low tone.

"Police department," he blurted, sounding puzzled. "Did he say what it's about?"

"No sir, he wants to see you."

"Okay, send him in, Margret."

"Sure, Mr. Writhers," she complied, hanging up the phone.

"Sir, Mr. Writhers will see you now."

"Thanks," Parker said, following the woman to the door. She knocked lightly.

"Come on in, Margret."

She opened the door, allowing Parker to enter the exquisite office. Parker envied the office that must have cost a pretty penny. It was simple yet luxurious. Even the chairs near the desk were corporate rich.

"Can I get you anything Mr. Writhers?" Margaret asked politely.

"No thanks, what about you, Detective?" Paul queried, getting to his feet.

"Nothing, thanks. I'm good. I'm Detective Richards," Parker introduced himself, extending his hand to Paul.

Paul shook his hand. "That'll be all, Margret."

"Please sit, Detective," he gestured with his hand. "I'm not sure what brings you to my office."

Parker took a seat in a chair in front of his luxury, stylish dark-brownish desk. "Where can I get this matching set from?" he teased.

"I think it was an order from one of those fancy places online," Paul answered, shrugging his shoulders. "I had the place decorated. Told her to go all out."

Parker glanced around the room before taking out his notepad and pen.

"I'm working on a case, and it concerns one of your properties. You see, I'm investigating a case where a mother was found dead in her apartment or someone else's apartment. A six-year-old girl was found a few feet from her mother's dead body." He didn't disclose the few drugs he'd found in the closet.

"Damn, that has to be tough on the child," Paul said with concern. "I'm not sure if I can help you, Detective. What does this have to do with me? Especially, causing a woman's death and leaving her child without a mother. I want the bastard caught, but I'm not sure where I fit in." Paul grimaced, looking baffled. "We do keep security guards on our properties. I'm sure they have cooperated with your department."

Paul remembered the tragedy that occurred about eight months ago. He and Nickolas couldn't believe what had happened. Those apartments were for the rich, but you could never assume anything when it came to people.

"Yes, they have been forthright. But I'm missing something. I don't understand how a well-protected building could miss such a heinous crime."

"I agree with you, Detective, and that's why we have beefed-up security for the building by adding more cameras to make our tenants safer. We want to provide top-notch services for our clients. But the mother wasn't a client. For fuck sakes, that apartment should have been vacant. Despite that, there was furniture from a previous tenant. Nick lived in that unit but didn't appreciate the view. So, I know you assume it's an inside job. Again, where do I fit?"

"I'm glad you asked. Those apartments offer some great views of the city. Some can run you sixty-grand a month or more depending on the space. I want to borrow the one that's vacant. I need to catch a killer. During the initial investigation, it appeared to be one person who pulled the trigger, but the killer must have had an accomplice."

"Let me make sure I'm following you. Are you saying for sure someone in our building is responsible for a child losing her mother?" Paul asked, rubbing his jaw.

"Maybe. I want to stay in your building to investigate. But as a tenant, not as BVPD. How do you feel about that?"

Parker had been coming up with dead-ends on this case. No one was coming forward with any information, and the best way to find his killer was to stay in the building and get to know some of Bayville's elite. He knew the killer was there.

"It'll be fine with us. At least, they'll have police protection under their noses." Paul smiled.

"I'm thrilled you're onboard with this." Parker stood. He was pleased Writhers didn't mind him using the apartment. He had him figured wrong. He thought the man would turn him down. However, he should have known he wouldn't, given his generosity to charities in the city.

"I'm heading out of the city tonight on business, but I'll let my business partner, Nickolas Brimmer, know about this matter. I'll make sure management knows you are coming onboard. They'll only know you are a new tenant. Nothing more. Of course, you won't be charged." Paul laughed, knowing Parker probably couldn't afford the apartment.

"Good to know," Parker bantered. "Those apartments are more than my yearly salary."

"Hell, I think the lowest one is twenty-five thousand a month. But they do come with excellent views of our lovely city. You can't beat that," he praised.

"I guess not. I'm going to head out, and thanks so much for allowing me to use the apartment," Parker said, heading to the door.

"Not a problem. I want the SOB caught. If you need anything, don't hesitate to give me a call." He moved toward the door, handing him a business card.

"Thanks again," Parker shook his hand, taking the card and went on his way.

Chapter 3

Sage had stopped by to visit her aunt on her way home from work. After she left there, she decided to go by Parker's. When she arrived, she discovered he'd moved. She could have saved herself the trip if she'd called him first. Sage called Parker to get his new address and headed to the outskirts of the city. When she pulled up to the building, she thought it had to be a mistake. The man at the gate had to call Parker to let her inside. There was no way he could afford to live there on his salary. She pulled into a vacant parking spot and got out of her car. She gazed up at the grand structure. The building was massive and had a ton of security. She wouldn't mind living there herself. Her heels clicked the concrete as she headed inside. The entrance had magnificent artworks on the walls—the kind that cost a fortune. No wonder there was so much security everywhere. A receptionist area was in front of the elevators where a tall, chubby man was seated. Sage informed him of who she was on her way to see. The man rang

Parker's apartment, informing him of his visitor. He was on the 10th floor. The man walked her over to the elevator. Sage was in awe of the whole place. It was like living in a mansion, something of a Scottish style, and her best friend lived here.

On her way to Parker's apartment, she saw someone watching her as she approached his door. Whoever it was, disappeared back into their apartment when she was at Parker's door. She knocked softly. Parker opened the door with a big grin plastered on his handsome face.

"What the hell, Park?" she asked, grinning up at him.

"Come on in, and I'll tell you everything." He pulled her inside the apartment.

Nick saw the woman go inside of Parker's apartment. The cop Paul told him about. He didn't know she had a boyfriend. He should have known she wouldn't be single. The report didn't mention anything about a boyfriend. He needed to get rid of his private investigator. He wasn't as good as he thought he was. Nick went to the bar to pour himself a shot of whiskey. He threw the first shot back quickly and poured another. This one, he took to his studio. He had plenty of his artwork there, including some he hadn't finished. Well, in his mind, they were missing something. He had some of his mother's art in the room, but they were mostly covered. He missed his mother even now. He wasn't a momma's boy. Heaven forbid that because his dad wouldn't want his son weak. But he knew if she were alive, she wouldn't want for anything.

He sat the whiskey down on the stand near the bare white canvas. His mind was on her. The woman next door. The one he couldn't seem to escape. He was so drawn to her, like a magnet drawing her into his world. It was like the woman had cast a spell on him.

Her image was still on his mind as he opened some paints and dabbed some on his pallet. He thought about the woman next door, moving his brush gracefully on the canvas. Making a face of a woman he vaguely knew, but in some way, he did. Her charcoal curly hair flowing down her back. Her beautiful heart-shaped face, high cheekbones, her emerald cat-like eyes, her small pointed nose, and her full-bow lips. He continued to paint her. She had on a dress that framed her perfect hourglass figure. Nick knew for sure she would haunt his dreams again that night.

He put down the brush, taking a drink of his whiskey, staring at the image he was in the process of creating. The sunlight was hitting his canvas in the right spots, as if it knew where to shine its splendid light, taunting him. He wondered who the man was she was making love with at that moment. He knew if she was with him, she would be naked next to him in bed because he would have taken her and satisfied her completely. *Shit*! He dismissed the thought. It only made his blood thicken to think about another man with her. He put the drink down, focused his energy, and went back to work, taking his frustration out on the canvas, creating something beautiful.

Two hours had passed before he was finished with his masterpiece. He didn't realize how much time had gone by. Nick, wearing only his black shorts, stood back with his powerful arms crossed over his bare muscular chest, observing the painting of the beautiful goddess he had created. He could only imagine what it would be like to be with her. He was relieved that she was in a relationship. It meant she was off limits. Nick had no choice but to stay away from her.

His heart had been brutally beaten by his ex-wife. He didn't need women except for bedmates when he needed relief from his main vein. Nick's thoughts were interrupted by his cell phone ringing. He covered the painting, raced out of the room, and picked his cell off the desk in his office. He saw it was his friend Royce Pierceton.

"Hi Roy," he answered, taking a seat.

"Did I get you at a bad time?"

Nick wanted to say, yeah. He wasn't finished watching the painting of her. "No, man. What's up?"

"You have any plans for a Friday night? I have tickets to the theater, and I have a date for you if you are game. The woman I'm going with wanted to see 'Paris in Spring.' I don't want to go, but the things we do to make someone feel lucky. I really like her."

"Sure, you do," he acknowledged with amusement. "You like them all."

"She's different. She has that charm and appeal I'm into," Royce chuckled.

"Er, what the heck. I'm free. Is her friend good-looking?"

"I'm your bro. I wouldn't set you up with a beasty. You know I'm known for hottie ass," he boasted.

Nick doubted there would be any connection... because of her, the woman who was next door. *Damn, she's probably gone. Two hours had gone by.* She had to have done something to him to make him this way. Was it the electric stare she had given him? Or those full lips he wanted to taste so damn badly? He didn't know. He couldn't figure out what. Because, for one, she had a boyfriend. And, two, she was way too young. Then there was three: he had never dated another woman outside of his own race. Not that he wouldn't. He thought he favored only redheads.

"You don't have to sell her, Roy. I'm in. What time should I meet you all there?" He glanced at the clock on the wall—it was five-thirty.

"You can meet us at 7:30 p.m. The show starts at eight."

"I'll be there."

"Thanks, Nick."

"Don't mention it. I'll see you later." Nick hung up, ending the call.

"They don't care that you are living here, rent-free, in one of their expensive apartments? One that can bring in money for them?" Sage asked, getting up, looking at the marvelous view out on the terrace.

"I'm here to do a job. This is the apartment I found Nicki in," Parker sighed, walking out onto the terrace.

Sage shifted her gaze, glancing at Parker. She couldn't believe this was the actual place. Nicki's mother wasn't wealthy. There was no way she could have afforded a place like this. From what she could tell before coming up to the apartment, the whole building was... well-guarded. "You think the killer lives here?" she asked.

"I'm not sure." Parker couldn't disclose any information about the case. Sage was already struggling to try to find the child a new home, and he wasn't going to share everything with her.

Sage moved away from the terrace, staring at a beautiful picture that hung on the wall. It looked like it was expensive, as did the other artwork. The frame alone looked expensive. She reached up and touched it with her fingertips, tracing the outline. It was cool to the touch. The picture was a woman and her son. The artist knew how to capture the images. It appeared as if they would come to life.

Parker called her by name to get her attention as he moved beside her, caressing the small of her back. Sage turned and looked at him.

"Sage, you were in your own world just then. It is a beautiful picture," he conceded, gazing at the artwork.

"It's more than a picture, Park. It's art." She looked back at the painting. "Whoever created it is an extremely talented person."

Sage loved art—anything highly abstracted, formulaic portraits, and landscapes. She also was a fan of contemporary art. The type of art from the 1960s to the 1970s that displayed artists who broke the old rules of viewpoints, color, and bravura. She remembered going to art shows with her father and getting lost in the artwork and sculptures. She missed doing that with him. She shook her head, dismissing the thought. "I was admiring a bit too much," she smiled.

"Mm-hmm, like you wanted to get to know them," he joked, moving to the refrigerator. "You want something to drink? Sorry, no cherry coke. I have mineral water, juice, Powerade, and I'm not sure what this fancy stuff is. It was here when I moved into the place."

"Mineral water is fine." There was more art on the walls. Sage began to walk around the apartment. "Sarah and Cindy are going to flip when they find out about this," she bubbled, her eyes filled with delight. "Our detective is living this extravagant lifestyle."

"Nope, I'm here to catch a killer. That little girl deserves justice for what they did to her mother," he explained, handing her the drink.

"Thanks." She took the drink and continued eyeing the artwork. "I know, and I hope you find out who did it. Nicki deserves justice for her mommy. Some no-good, low-down dog took her mother from her. They deserve to die." Sage was angry. Sarah was right—she had grown very fond of the little girl. "You should enjoy this place, too, as you are on the hunt to catch this animal. You deserve it. I don't remember you taking a break from your job," she said more calmly.

"As I recall, I don't remember you taking a break either. You are always trying to save them all, which is understandable." Parker caressed the side of her face. "You need to take care of yourself, babe." He used a term of endearment that he'd called her since high school.

"I don't mind doing what I can to help the children who need me. I guess I get that from my mother. She was a workaholic, always trying to save them all. Sometimes I wished she had been around us more. Giving us more memories of her... being with my sister and me. It felt like she cared about them more than she did us."

Parker pulled her into his arms, comforting her. Sage had tears in her eyes. "It's okay, babe. I remember your dad being there for you and your sister. He was there for most of your cheerleading gigs. I loved to see you in your outfit at the games," he said, trying to get her mind off her mother.

She hit him playfully on the back, laughing. "I remember you chasing all the pretty girls in school."

He released her, laughing with her. "Uh-huh, I was quite the ladies' man back then," he jested.

"Whatever!" Sage took a sip of her water and shook her head at him. She remembered all the girls chasing him in high school and the ones in college, too. She had gotten hurt in the process and gotten pregnant, but she hadn't kept it. Nobody knew this except Sarah. Even Parker didn't. He was on a basketball scholarship and didn't need to be tied down by her and a baby. She wasn't ready to be a parent at the time anyway. She was only nineteen. Still, she regretted her decision.

"I'm about to head home, Mr. Lover." She smacked him on his well-built butt.

"It was good having you come over to my new digs." He finished the juice, tossing the bottle in the trash.

"This place is dope-a-mattic. I can't wait for another invite," she grinned, showing her white smile.

"I'm glad you love it, and anytime, babe."

Parker wanted to ask Sage if it was okay to go out with Sarah. He had wanted to date her since he moved back to the city, but Sarah was always nasty with him. What happened with him and Sage was long ago. He believed she was over that, but he saw this look in Sage's eyes a few minutes ago. He didn't think it was such a good idea. Parker opened the door for her and escorted Sage downstairs to her car.

Nick was on his way out of his building when he saw her and the boyfriend heading to her car. The boyfriend kissed her chastely on the lips, then opened her car door. She was laughing and looking at him with such admiration as she slid her sexy body in the car. He wished he was the man in that moment. Jealousy reared its ugly head. *No, keep away from marked territory.* He walked quickly toward his silver F-type SVR Jaguar to stop the abnormal feeling.

"That's the guy who gave so generously to MCC," she pointed toward Nick.

Wonder what he's running from or to? "Cindy says he's one of MCC's biggest contributors. I didn't know he lived in your building."

"He doesn't just live here. He and Paul Writhers own this building and a lot more," Parker interpreted, looking in the direction she had pointed. "They seem like good guys. They buy up failing businesses and make them better somehow."

"Whatever, guys like that have major power egos." Sage started the engine, remembering her husband used to do mergers for companies. She frowned, wondering if he had ever worked for him. That had to be that deja vu feeling when she'd first seen him. Sage didn't remember her husband ever mentioning the man's name. Even if he had, she wouldn't have remembered anyway.

Sage went home after leaving Parker's, driving the Audi R8 Luke used to drive most of the time. Before the accident, she used to drive fast, now she was afraid to speed. She felt close to Luke whenever she drove the car. Sage sat in the car, looking at the house. It was a lovely home she and her husband had purchased three years ago. It was in a well-established neighborhood. The Victorian had been built in the 80s. It was dark gray with white trimmings with shutters on all the windows. On the front porch was a swing and potted plants of different varieties. Sage wasn't sure what types of plants they were but liked the beautiful colors each one of them offered. She loved the deck. There were six large cushioned rocking chairs on the deck interspersed with tables. She hadn't had anyone over for drinks since her husband died—she usually went out to visit her aunt and friends.

Sage got out of the car, picked up the mail, and looked around. She noticed her neighbor Mr. Vengo across the street. He checked up on her from time to time. He'd been good friends with her husband. He was the first to welcome them to the neighborhood. She waved at him then opened the door, stepping inside, placing her keys and mail on the table near the foyer. Sage listened to her messages then headed to the winding staircase; she paused before walking up. Pictures of her family lined the walls. This was the part of her day when she really missed Luke. She would hurry upstairs, change clothes, and try to get dinner started. She wasn't a good cook. She could only make soup from a jar and a damn good sandwich with the right fixings. Luke oversaw cooking the meals unless he was working late. Nowadays, she sat in the large kitchen, wishing. She hadn't made up her mind to sell the place yet. It was the only connection she had with Luke besides his car. This was their home.

Luke had decided to move to Bayville because he wanted Sage to be closer to her family. He was originally from Louisiana; however, he liked Bayville and what it had to offer. They were going to have two children—a boy and a girl. Or maybe three if she could handle the pain. Childbirth was scary and painful. Her sister could attest to that. It was so lonely for her now. She only heard a creaking of the old house, which sometimes freaked her out. She slept with the light on in the hallway when that happened. She was in her bedroom, taking off her sweaty clothes and heard the phone on her antique dresser ring.

"Hello," she answered.

"Hi, Sage, how are things with you?" her sister asked.

"I'm doing okay. How are you and the family doing? I know BJ and Lila have grown like grass-weeds since the last time I saw them."

"Yes, honey. You know, you should come for a visit. I know they would love to see their favorite aunt. I want to see you, too. Has anything exciting happened since the last time we spoke?" That was her way of asking if there was a man in her life, which she doubted. She prayed her sister would move on soon.

"I'm going to visit real soon. I promise. And Lor, it's only been a few days since we last spoke. Nothing exciting to tell you. Sorry, sis. What about on your end?"

"If you call Wiener running through the house, knocking over my furniture exciting, then that's excitement for your ass." She laughed. "Oh, BJ lost a tooth the other day. I'm thinking about going back to work in the fall. I'm not sure if I want to go back full-time or part-time."

"Well, you see, you have more exciting news than I do," Sage spoke happily. "That's great you want to go back, Dr. Tate. Have you spoken to Ben about it?"

Her sister loved her job just as much as their mother had. She knew her sister would be the one to follow in their mother's footsteps and become a doctor. She was surprised her sister had taken a year and a half off. She was still involved, but from the home-front only. Sarah wanted to be more involved in her children's lives than her mother had been with them.

"Of course, I have. He's fine with it. Hey, I saw Dad two weeks ago. He asked about you." She changed the subject, waiting for Sage's reply. Lora has always tried to persuade Sage to talk to their dad no matter how upset her little sister got with her.

"You know I don't give a damn about your daddy," Sage retorted crossly. "Why do you discuss him every time he visits you? I hate him. He can die and go straight to hell."

"Sage, you can't mean that. He's your daddy, too," Lora sighed.

"*Argh*, I do, Lora. He killed Mommy."

Sage closed her eyes for a moment, thinking about the pain her father had caused the family. The day her mother died was devastating. It had altered their lives forever.

"I know you blame him for our mother's death. He didn't kill Mommy. She was killed in a car crash, Sage. She was angry and upset. She got into the car then drove off. Daddy tried to stop her, but she wouldn't reason with him."

"Fiddlesticks," Sage screamed at the top of her lungs. "Because the bastard cheated on her, Lora, that's why she wouldn't reason with him. He hurt her. He betrayed our mommy. How can you talk to him? How can you stand the sight of him? If he hadn't cheated on Mommy, she would still be here. I would have a mother. You would have a mother. The kids would have a grandmother. I don't want to talk about him. I love you, Lor. Tell Ben and the kids I said hi. Someone is at my door," she lied. She didn't want to discuss their father anymore. The more Lora tried to defend him, the angrier she became.

Sage hadn't seen her father since her mother's funeral. Their father's name was

Cooper Taylor. He was Caucasian. Deborah Jennings-Taylor was their mother. She was multiracial. African-American, Caucasian, and Puerto Rican. Their parents had met about thirty years ago. Their father was a stockbroker until his wife's death. After he lost Deborah, he couldn't concentrate on the job anymore. He moved to Phoenix and started working for a nonprofit agency.

Deborah had been a pediatrician. She loved her job helping children. That was why Sage chose a career in helping children and her sister practiced medicine as an obstetrician. Deborah was a bright, caring woman—friendly to everyone and loved by many. When she was killed in the crash, everyone took it hard. Sage took it the hardest. Cooper blamed himself for her death. It was like his youngest daughter always said: if he hadn't cheated on her, she would be alive. He believed that himself. He hated himself for it. Sometimes he wished he hadn't confided in the girls and told them the truth about what had happened.

He always tried to contact Sage by phone and email, but she wanted nothing to do with him. He was her favorite, but now she hated his guts. He did get to know her husband a little. Of course, Sage didn't know that. Luke kept that away from her. He hoped that one day they would reunite again.

As a child, Sage adored her father. He was number one as far as she was concerned. He was her pick. Lora was her mother's favorite. They were the perfect American family, or so Sage used to think. Her perfect world with her parents crumbled more than twelve years ago.

Chapter 4

Another work week was over, and it was time for Sage to pick up Nicki. She had worked hard to find the child a new home but was getting stonewalled at every turn. She decided to take the child to MCC. It wasn't a bad option for Nicki. Cindy and her staff had one of the best orphanages for children like her. Sage was still disappointed in herself for not being able to find her a home. Nicki wasn't giving the Grissom family a chance. She wasn't getting along with their daughter, and acted out constantly, misbehaving. Sage called the Grissom's to let them know she would be by to pick up Nicole-Marie at 4:30 p.m. Sage was sitting at her desk when Sarah knocked on her door. Sage waved her in.

"Hi, no luck finding anyone?" Sarah asked.

"No," she replied, hanging up the phone. "I'm going to take her to Cid. They run a good program. I know Nicki will be taken care of," she grumbled, thumbing through another case file.

Sarah observed her for a second. She wanted her friend to take Nicki. She didn't want to seem pushy, but she knew this would be good for them both.

"Hey, remember what we talked about before?" she asked, closing the door, taking a seat in front of her desk.

Sage looked up from her file. Of course, she remembered. She also remembered telling her it wasn't a good idea. She worked too much to consider that. Who would keep an eye on her while she worked? And she didn't know the first thing about being a mother. She would have to read the latest books, go to seminars, and whatever else there was about rearing children. Why was she even considering it? They'd both suffered losses. They would be good for each other. At least, that's what Sarah seemed to think.

"I understand your passion for wanting me to keep her. I don't have room in my life for her. I wouldn't be good for her." Sage placed her glasses on her desk. "That's what I do Sarah, find someone who is better qualified to take care of these children. Nicki needs two parents in her life. Not someone like me—an amateur."

"You wanted children. You and Luke wanted them. You were so excited about being a mother, Sage. That little girl needs you, and you need her. I saw you with Nicki before. She adores you."

"I remember once-a-upon time I wanted children with my husband. We tried, and it didn't work out. I don't want to be a single mother, Sarah. I know you mean well but drop it. I have to go pick up the little girl in a few minutes."

Sarah got up from the seat. She knew it was a losing battle right now. Sage had to do things on her own. "Are you ready for the little get together Parker is having tonight?" She questioned, changing the subject.

"Yes, you won't believe where the man is staying. It's badass with a bit of dope-a-mattic."

"I bet," Sarah giggled. "I can't believe the man invited me."

"I can believe it. You and Parker would be great as a couple." Sage brightened. She knew Sarah didn't think of Parker in that way.

Sarah grimaced at her. "No way...no how," she said, shaking her head in disagreement. "Parker and I are like 'grease and water,' 'Night and day.' We don't mix that way."

Sage belly laughed. "Okay, but all I'm saying is pinned-up energy. The current between the two of you is electrifying. And let's not forget that day you and Parker double-teamed me. A new-found union. I could hardly believe it."

"I'm going to go back to my office 'cause you are making no sense whatsoever at this second." Sarah walked out, closing the door without saying another word.

Sage snickered as she gathered her things to leave for the day.

Sage headed to the Grissom's home to pick up Nicki. When she arrived, the child was excited to see her. She greeted her with a big hug, which Sage reciprocated. Sage collected Nicki's belongings and loaded them in the Audi. She belted Nicki inside, then spoke with the Grissoms for a few minutes. They said how sorry they were again. They did their best to help the child but couldn't get through. They hoped this wouldn't put a damper on the next time they wanted to invite a child into their home, which it wouldn't anyway. They had a right to remove a child from their home if it wasn't working out. After Sage was in the car and on her way to MCC, Nicki finally talked to her.

"Nicki, you know I can't keep you. I don't have time to be a mommy to you, honey. I work most of the time." She glanced over at Nicki.

"But I can take care of myself. I'm a big girl. I can bathe and dress myself. I don't need much, Ms. Sage. I promise I won't be a problem," Nicki pleaded, looking at her with large sad eyes.

Sage peered at her, then focused her attention on the road. She was a beautiful, smart little girl with the same curly mane as

Sage, a skinny, oval face with a half-full top lip and full bottom lip. She had a small pointed nose with hazel eyes. Her complexion was a slightly lighter tone than hers. She reminded Sage of herself at that age.

Sage hated to see those eyes so sad. She wanted to take her home and care for her when she looked at her that way. It did something to her heart. But she wasn't in any position to take care of a child. Was she? She did have her aunt if she needed a babysitter. So, what was her excuse for not wanting to take care of the little girl? Was she afraid of loving someone else or was she afraid of change? Or was it a bit of both?

"Nicki, I know you wouldn't give me any trouble, sweetie," she said, touching her cheek slightly. "Baby, you need someone who can give you their full attention. Wouldn't you like that?"

"What I like is you," she bawled. "Please keep me, Ms. Sage," she begged.

It was killing Sage to see the little girl cry for her. *Fiddlesticks*! It was heartbreaking. Nicki's tears rolled down her cheeks. Sage touched her face with the backside of her hand and wiped her face. She glanced at her once more before deciding to turn around and head home. She would keep her for tonight then, go to MCC tomorrow. She had to call her boss to let him know she would be keeping her tonight.

Sage arrived home at 5:15 p.m. She took Nicki's things from the trunk, then opened the door and let Nicki out of the car. The two of them walked up the steps holding hands. Sage liked the way her little hand felt in hers. They were small, soft hands— hands she could get used to holding.

"You have a porch swing! And a lot of pretty flowers!" Nicki expressed excitedly. "Wow! This is way cool!"

"Thanks, sweet girl." Sage unlocked the door and led Nicki inside.

"Woo-wee! I like your house, Ms. Sage," she said, looking around animatedly. "You have a lot of neat pictures on the walls."

"Thanks, Nicki. I love good art. Maybe one day soon, I'll take you to an exhibit." She smiled down at her. Sage remembered when she was about Nicki's age, her dad introduced her to the art world. She fell in love instantly and had been ever since. "Are you hungry? I could make some sandwiches?" she asked, squeezing her little hands.

"Nah, I'm okay. I don't need much. I'm gonna live here with you, and I won't be any trouble at all." She beamed, happily at Sage with cheery hazel eyes.

Sage didn't want to disappoint her, but she was going to take her to MCC tomorrow sometime.

"Listen, Nicki," she said, kneeling beside her. "I'm letting you stay this one time. I can't keep you." She drew Nicki close and hugged her. "The people at MCC can take care of you until I can find a good home for you," she cajoled, stroking her back warmly. Sage pulled out her cell, continuing to comfort Nicki as she dialed Martin's number.

"Hello," he answered.

"Hi Martin, it's me, Sage."

"Oh, hi, Sage. What can I do for you?"

"I'm keeping Nicki for tonight. Could you please let the judge know for me?"

"I'll let Judge Myers know, but you have to come in and sign some paperwork on Monday. The usual stuff you have dealt with before. You know the routine."

"Okay, I'll do that." She stood, taking Nicki by the hand, leading her to the kitchen. She knew the little girl had to be hungry.

"Thanks, Martin. I better get her settled in. I'll see you on Monday. Have a good weekend." She rang off.

Sage was in the kitchen with Nicki having dinner. She had made turkey sandwiches and heated up a can of tomato soup. She gave Nicki apple juice while she enjoyed her Cherry Coke and her cheesy Cheetos Puffs.

She had made up her mind to let her aunt babysit for her while she hung out with her friends tonight. Parker had invited them to a cocktail party. She couldn't believe that either. Parker and cocktail party didn't sound right in the same sentence. He was dinner-and-a-movie type guy. If her aunt wasn't entertaining for the evening, she would ask her to keep Nicki. She knew her aunt would love the idea of caring for a child.

Sage heard the phone ringing.

"You enjoy your dinner while I take this phone call," she urged.

Nicki nodded her head, agreeably.

Sage grabbed the receiver from its base.

"Hello," she chimed.

"Hi, sister-girl. What are you up to?"

"I'm having dinner. Why?" she asked curiously.

"Hi Sage, it's your Aunt Katie," her aunt echoed with pleasure.

"Hi, Auntie. You two aren't trying to double-team me, are you?" Sage asked, laughing. "Because that's been happening lately."

"No," they answered in unison.

"Auntie, I need a favor. My friends and I are hanging out tonight. I need you to watch Nicki for me," she blurted out quickly.

"Watch who?" Her aunt sounded baffled. "Who's Nicki? You have a kid I don't know about?"

"Yeah, who's Nicki?" Lora inquired.

"No, Auntie, Lor, I don't have any kids," she answered, even though they both knew she didn't. "Nicole-Marie Fulton is staying with me tonight, and I need a babysitter, Auntie. Will you babysit for me or do you have someone coming over tonight?"

"No, I have no one coming over. I told you, I'm taking a break from men. Tell me about Nicole-Marie Fulton."

"Well, Nicki is a six-year-old girl who I'm taking care of tonight."

Sage stepped into the other room, so Nicki couldn't hear her.

"She's one of my cases. Her mother was murdered, and she has no other relatives. I've been trying hard to place her, but no luck so far. I'm taking her to MCC tomorrow."

"Oh, my goodness... how awful," her aunt lamented. "Is she a troubled child? You know, sometimes kids don't cope well losing a parent. You are a prime example of that," she sighed.

"She's a little sweetie. She isn't any trouble. I'm letting her spend the night with me. I'm not sure if I should go out tonight. And I cope just fine, Auntie."

Her aunt ignored her last comment.

"I think it will be alright if you leave her with me for a little bit. Go out with your friends. Enjoy yourself. I'll take real good care of Nicki."

"I know you will, Auntie. You took great care of me. Thanks."

"Hey, when do I get to meet my little niece?" Lora asked.

"She is a foster child, Lora. Didn't you hear any of the conversation?" Sage asked, exasperated.

"Of course, I heard you, but you would make a terrific mother. Why don't you keep her instead of giving her to someone else? She would be good for you. You are already attached to her."

"Have you been talking to Sarah because she suggested the same thing? I don't have time to be a foster mother," she whispered, rubbing her temple. "I wouldn't be good at it. I've never even cared for a cat or dog."

"Yes, you would," her sister laughed. "What do animals have to do with it? Give yourself a chance. Keep her," Lora beseeched.

"Well, you two, I have to go. Nicki needs me. I'll see you about 7:00 p.m. Auntie. Bye, you two." Sage signed off.

Deep down, Sage wanted to keep Nicki. However, she didn't want to become a single parent. Her life was a mess as it was. She didn't need to add Nicki to make matters worse for the child or herself.

Sage dropped Nicki off at her aunt's house around seven that evening. She assured Nicki she would be back to pick her up around eleven or eleven-thirty. She was glad Nicki bonded with her aunt quickly.

She didn't have to worry about her while she was out.

Sage explained to Nicki she would be staying with her aunt for a few hours because she had made plans to hang out with her friends before that evening. Nicki didn't like the idea of being left behind. She wanted to spend time with Sage. Nicki was afraid Sage wouldn't come back for her. However, Sage explained to her she would be back. She didn't intend to leave her with her aunt. Nonetheless, Nicki felt abandoned. Sage glanced at her facial expression and felt compassion for her. It pained her that Nicki was feeling that way. She wished she could take her in, but she knew that would be a bad idea. She wasn't ready to be a mother and didn't have a husband. Sage believed strongly in two-parent homes.

Sage arrived at Parker's around 7:30 p.m. She had to go through all the security as she had the first time. She couldn't wait to see the expressions on Sarah and Cindy's faces. She knocked on Parker's door, who answered almost immediately.

"Hi Parker," she hailed happily. She had a bottle of red wine in her hands.

"Hey, is that for me?" he asked, grinning kissing her on the cheek. "You look beautiful as always."

"Yes," she walked inside, handing him the bottle. "You look nice yourself. I see I'm the first of your guests."

He closed the door, moving behind the bar. "You know I'm having this cocktail party to get to know some of the neighbors," he interpreted as he mixed her a drink.

"I know, but it's still fun getting to know some of your rich neighbors." She neared the bar where he was, taking the drink he offered her. "Mmm," she gushed, "you still know how to mix great drinks."

"I guess so," he responded.

A knock came from the door.

"You want me to get it?" she asked. "It can only be Sarah and Cindy. They said they were going to be riding over together."

"Sure, go ahead," he answered, wiping down the bar. He made drinks for Sarah and Cindy, as well.

Sage opened the door swiftly. "Get in here, you two," she said loudly.

Sarah and Cindy walked in, looking around in amazement.

"Can you believe it, girls? Our Parker is living among the rich and famous," Sage reported.

"Parker, what the fudge, man?" Cindy gazed around the huge room, looking in all directions.

"Yeah Park, what the fudge is right? Have you hit the lotto or something?" Sarah gawked, taking it all in.

"No, you two," he chuckled, handing them both drinks. "This has to do with work. You know, the Nicole-Marie case," he said, taking a drink of his whiskey. "This is police business, nothing more. I found the little girl's mother's body in that bedroom." He pointed at the closed door. "Nicki was found in a closet in the same room. I have to find out who killed her mother."

They all took a seat on the dark gray couch. Parker took a seat across from them on the teal sectional.

"How is the case coming along?" Sarah asked seriously.

"I can't give you all the details, but that is why I'm having this little get-together. I want to get to know some of the neighbors. And by the way, all of you look lovely." He eyed Sarah, staring a little longer than he should have.

Sage and Cindy looked at one another. They knew something was brewing.

"So, how many guests are coming?" Sage asked.

"I'm not sure," he stated, taking a drink. "I hired someone to cater this thing for me. Scott should be over in a little while. He asked about you Cid."

"Not interested in your partner, Park," she scolded, rolling her eyes. "He's such a horn dog."

They all laughed.

After an hour had gone by, the caterer had come over getting things set up. The group sat around talking and laughing until the guests started to arrive. Soon, the apartment was filled with wealthy and interesting people. Nick and Paul had arrived later in the evening. Parker greeted them with smiles, offering food and drinks. He was making sure they were well taken care of because he valued their help. They had people spread the word about the cocktail party.

Nick wasn't going to miss this for the world. He knew *she* had to be there tonight. The woman who had been clouding his mind and dreams. When he spotted her, she was wearing a fitted blue thigh-high dress with a pair of black heels. That dress fit her body like a second skin. He wanted to run his hands all over her... touching her... feeling her soft body. Getting to know the body he had taken the time to paint on canvas.

He had painted her the way he saw her that day at MCC with the pink cashmere top, blue jeans, and flip-flops. And there was the other painting he had done of her in a floral, thigh-high dress. But tonight, he had another image of her. Almost naked—in his mind. She was showing shoulders, long neck, slender arms, nice thighs, and long legs, and her long, bouncy, curly charcoal hair. He stopped ogling her when she looked his way.

Sage noticed the man that she had seen at MCC watching her with his extraordinary blue gaze again. He tried to play it off by talking to one of the guests, but she knew he had been looking her way. She looked his way from time to time catching his stalking stares each time. He was dressed in a black buttoned-down collared shirt with navy blue dress pants. Everything fit his muscular body perfectly. Even his perfect raven hair was in place. This was the first time she'd noticed a man who piqued her curiosity since the death of her husband. What could possibly be interesting about him? She mused, taking a sip of her wine, trying not to be obvious.

"For goodness sakes, would you stop watching me," she grumbled. *If he stopped gawking at me, I wouldn't pay him any mind*, she thought. She moved behind a tall guy with blondish hair to hide. He was good-looking with a muscular body, but she wasn't concerned with him. It was the man across the room she was concerned about. The man looked down at her when he felt her bump into him.

"Hello beautiful," he flirted with a toothy-white smile that had a small gap between his teeth. You wouldn't notice it unless you were up close to him, which she didn't mean to be.

"Er, hi. I'm so sorry," she apologized, embarrassed she'd bumped into him.

"No need to apologize, beautiful." He drank from his glass. "Who are you trying to hide from?" He asked with a gleaming smile. "My name is Paul Writhers," he introduced himself, extending his hand.

"Nice to meet you, Mr. Writhers," she replied, shaking his hand. She knew who he was. He was one of the owners of this building. "My name is Sage Sullivan."

Paul thought of the pictures he'd seen in Nick's office—they didn't do her justice. She was a very stunning woman. And that curvy body was doing a waltz all on its own.

"It's nice meeting you, Sage. Call me Paul if I may call you Sage." He released her hand.

"Yes, of course, you can. Are you enjoying the party?" she questioned.

"I like socializing with other people. I get to meet more exciting new people. Like you," he announced, shifting a little to see where Nick was. As he figured, he was watching him and Sage. "Do you mind if I introduced you to a good friend of mine?" he asked, looking toward his friend. He was standing near the door with a champagne glass in his hand, talking to a woman with dark brown hair.

"I don't think so," she declined graciously. "He seems busy enough. And besides, I've taken up enough of your time.

You enjoy the party," she ended, hurrying away from him because she didn't want to spend any more time around the man who was gawking at her.

Sage was safely tucked away in the kitchen. A sigh of relief came over her as she leaned over the cream countertop on her elbows. Her wine glass was still in her hand. The flat-screen TV was on Sports Center. It wasn't too loud, but she hadn't heard the man enter the kitchen. Her mind was preoccupied in thought. "*What gave him the right to stare at me like that*?" she mumbled softly.

Nick stood there a moment, watching her converse with herself before moving next to her. He wasn't sure if he should approach her, seeing that she did have a boyfriend.

Sage jumped a little when she found the man who was stalking her standing in the kitchen. She thought she had ditched him. His friend must have said where she was.

"It's quieter in here," he spoke with a nice baritone voice. "You don't mind if I stay here with you for a little while?" he queried. Nick could smell her spellbinding scent standing this close to her. She smelled of tropical fruits and fresh flowers. He wanted to pull her close into his arms and lose himself in her.

"No, I don't mind," she confessed, meandering away from him. "It's not my place."

Her pores were sweaty. A tingling sensation spread all over. He was standing much too close to her. She moved to the opposite side of the long counter. She wanted as much space between them as possible. His nearness was already affecting her senses.

"Fiddlesticks!" What's going on with me? She pondered again. *No, no, no, freaking way can I be attracted to a guy like that. It has been two years since Luke,* she thought. *I won't betray him. Not even with the likes of you!* She screamed to herself.

"My name is Nickolas Brimmer," he stated with a warm gaze. He wondered why she moved so far from him. *Perhaps, she's bothered by me.* This was probably a bad idea. He shouldn't have listened to Paul. He wanted to be next to her. Was it the cologne he was wearing? He hoped it wasn't giving off a bad vibe. He had purchased it online a few months ago. As expensive as it was, it shouldn't make a woman run.

"Hi, I'm Sage," she introduced herself, not taking her eyes away from the TV. "I saw you at MCC two weeks ago. My friend said you are a generous man," she focused on him.

"I am. I don't mind helping others. I enjoy it. I have plenty," he commented, observing her, hoping he was scoring some points. "My friend and I buy businesses that are failing and make them profitable again. We become partners with those who want to hold onto their businesses. I saw you talking to him earlier, my friend Paul. He's a good guy."

Was he trying to set his friend up with the woman he wanted? She did smile happily. She seemed to like him. Pump your brakes. *Don't endorse Paul. You want her yourself,* he thought.

"Yeah, Paul seems like a nice guy. I did accidentally bump into him," she replied. "I love helping others as well. I work for Bayville's Protective Children Services—BPCS—in the downtown area, and I also volunteer at MCC sometimes on weekends." Why had she volunteered information about herself? *He's trying to make me like him. It won't work, mister.*

"Yes, I know," he said, taking a drink of his champagne. "Your friend Cindy told me you worked there." He didn't want to scare her off. He already knew a lot about her from the private investigator. "When I noticed you helping the children, it reminded me of my late mother," he added with sadness.

Great, was he now using his dead momma for sympathy from me? "She must have been a wonderful woman." Sage thought about her mother at that moment, then dismissed it because she wasn't about to open to a stranger about her past no matter how sexy he was. She twisted toward the TV as if she was tangled in what was going on. *Old man, just go away. Can't you see I'm ignoring you?* She thought. She could still feel his blue stare on her. If his eyes were lasers, they would burn the dress right off, showing her bare skin. He was sending chills up and down her spine with that hot gaze. Sage noticed he had joined her on the other side of the counter, which she wished to God he hadn't.

"Yes, my mother was a wonderful woman, who I miss every day of my life. Did your boyfriend always want to be a police detective?" he asked, derailing the conversation with his large chiseled body turned toward her. "He seems like he loves what he does. I mean, he's getting to know a lot of the people in this building."

He placed his glass on the counter, pretending to be concerned about Parker's career choice. Truth be told, he was jealous of the guy. He had her—the woman he wanted, and she was off-limits to him. He sensed she was supposed to be his, but how was that possible when she belonged with another man? It took all his being not to reach out and touch her.

Boyfriend? Parker? She smiled to herself, thanking the universe. When she came to visit Parker the first time, she thought she saw someone watching her. It was him. The door to the kitchen opened, and Parker entered the kitchen.

Thank God. Saved in the nick of time.

"Hi babe, how's it going?" he asked, walking over to her. "I see you have met Nick," he said, smiling, looking in his direction. He was probably trying to get at his friend. He would be pleased if she did start to date.

"Yes, I was just speaking to your girlfriend about you," Nick added, wishing he hadn't interrupted them.

"Sage isn't..." Sage cut off his words with a pinch to his side and a penetrating glare, meaning go with it or else. "I hope my girl spoke only good things about her man," he said, looking down at her, stroking her cheek.

"She was about to," Nick said, moving away from them. "I'm going to head out. Really nice party. I hope you took in a lot of information, Parker," he said, walking toward the kitchen exit.

"I did. You all have a lot of fascinating tenants," he beamed with laughter.

"That we do." Nick turned, eyeing Sage. "You both have a good night." He left the kitchen.

"What was that about, Sage? You know we are only friends. Why did you tell him differently? He's interested in you," Parker said, placing both hands on her shoulders.

"I know, that's why I want you as my boyfriend." Her face held a devious grin. "I don't want him all in my grill," she emphasized. "I want that man nowhere near me." She pulled away from Parker, biting on her lower lip, playing with a strand of her hair. "I don't need his behind, even if I were interested in a guy. He's not my type. The man I loved left me," she said sadly.

That wasn't accurate for sure. She'd been living alone for two years. Stuck in the same place. She needed to find love, not run from it. Or at least, try to find it. The man seemed like a stand-up guy, Parker thought. He was divorced and a tad older, but he didn't buy into what the internet said about him. Parker had also run both their names in the police database. The only thing that stood out about Nick was an assault charge. The judge saw fit to put him on probation. He couldn't be that bad. And he gave to charities. After all, he and Paul were letting him use the apartment rent-free.

"Nick seems to be a good guy. You don't have a problem with his age or skin tone, do you?" he asked, leaning up against the counter. "From where I was standing when I first walked in here, you two seemed quite cozy. I thought he was about to lean in and take those shimmering lips of yours," Parker teased.

"I'm not prejudiced. I'm living proof of mixed parents. And his age wouldn't be a factor if I were into him, but I'm not," she objected. "For the record, he wasn't about to kiss me. I would have smacked the piss out of his ass."

Parker held up both hands. "Whoa, I'm just calling it as I saw it. No need to be offended."

This was a good opportunity to ask her was it okay for him to date Sarah. "I have something I need to ask you," he said, moving next to her.

Sage looked at him curiously, speculating on what he was about to say. "Okay, what?"

"I was wondering if it was alright for me to ask Sarah out. I know you and I have a history, and she is our friend. Hold up, let me rephrase that," he grinned, "she's more your friend than mine."

Sage stood somewhat on her toes, wrapping her arms around his neck, giving him a bear hug. He hugged her.

"Parker, this is wonderful," she squeaked, letting go of him. "I think you two would be great together. I think she feels something for you as well. However, there is only one way to find out," she suggested.

"Yeah, I know. I have to get up the nerve to ask her." He ran his hand over his wavy brown hair.

"You, Detective Parker Richards, are a very sexy brown-skinned man with those cocoa brown eyes. And that six feet three-inch muscular bod, baby--," she snapped her fingers. "You have nothing to worry about. Sarah would love to go out with you. I have this feeling."

"Okay, I need your confidence right about now," he laughed, thinking about how he was going to get the woman who seemed to never be in the same room with him, to go out on a date.

Chapter 5

It was a beautiful sunny Saturday morning the following day when Nicki woke up in the bed next to Sage. She rubbed her small hands over her eyes, wiping away her night sleep. She didn't want to wake Sage, so she quietly crept out of bed. She wanted to show Sage she could take care of herself and only needed a place to stay—a place she could call home. She went to the closet where Sage had stored her belongings and took out her favorite red top along with her blue shorts. She figured if she was quiet enough, Sage would keep her.

Nicki tiptoed to the bathroom and laid her belongings on the bathroom counter. She used the chair to turn on the faucet then squeezed toothpaste on the toothbrush and began brushing her teeth. After she was done, she placed her toothbrush beside Sage's, then ran water for a bath. The Jacuzzi tub was low enough for her to manage it herself. She placed her hand in the water, testing it to see if it was warm. It was. Nicki undressed and climbed into the tub.

Sage woke up to the sound of water splashing. She grabbed her robe and headed for the bathroom, where she found Nicki taking a bath. It was lovely to see her playing in the water. Sage didn't know the girl was old enough to bathe herself.

"Well, good morning, pretty girl," Sage complimented with a sunny smile on her lovely face.

"Morning, Ms. Sage. I'm taking a bath. I can bathe myself. I know you probably didn't know that," Nicki spewed, playing in the water.

"No, I didn't know, but let me help you out." Sage moved toward the tub, grabbed the towel, and began to wash her gently. "Nicki, I don't want you doing this by yourself. You may have been hurt. How did you know the water was warm enough?"

"I watched Mommy do it all the time," she spoke sadly. "And Mrs. Grissom ran the water in the tub for me all the time, too. I was careful. I'm sorry. I didn't mean to do something I shouldn't. Don't send me away, please," she protested.

Nicki looked at her with big, wanting hazel eyes. She wanted Sage to be her new mommy. She wanted to belong to someone. She wanted someone to love her. She hadn't felt love from anyone except Sage.

"Nicki, we talked about this yesterday. I will take you to MCC today. I'm not licensed to take care of you. I'm not married, sweetie. And besides that, I'm your caseworker."

Nicki peeked sadly at her. Sage didn't meet her gaze as she continued to wash her, because if she had, she would have been tempted to keep her. Sage couldn't stand to see Nicki's sad eyes gazing at her.

Nicki watched television while she ate her bowl of cereal. Sage had cut up an apple and gave her orange juice to go along with her cereal, then started the coffee before going back upstairs. She began to make up her bed with her mind musing over Luke. They had planned to have a baby before the accident. She was keen on the idea of having a little person who resembled her or him or them both. However, that seemed like ages ago. A little girl sat at her kitchen table, needing a mother. She wanted the job, but she was unsure of herself.

Sage put on a pair of yellow thigh shorts, a sleeveless blue top, and her blue open-toed wedge-heel sandals. Her toenails were polished bronze. She wouldn't dare wear open-toed shoes without her toes being polished. Satisfied with her outfit, she went to the mirror, pulled her hair into a high ponytail, leaving out a few loose strands, put on a little makeup, grabbed her purse, and went back downstairs.

Nicki was finished eating her cereal and had begun to flip through the TV channels.

"You haven't found anything interesting, baby-girl?" Sage asked.

"Naw, I haven't." She shook her head. "There aren't any decent TV shows on for a little kid like me," she complained as she continued to flip through the channels.

Sage laughed. The child was truly smart for her age. She made herself a cup of coffee, watching Nicki as she tried to find something stimulating to watch. Sage placed her favorite heart-shaped coffee mug on the counter. It was decided—she would keep Nicki until Monday morning.

"Nicki, I'm going into my study for a minute. Be right back."

"Okay, Ms. Sage."

Sage took the phone from her desk, dialing Martin's number.

"Hello," he spoke drowsily.

"Sorry to wake you, Martin."

"No prob, Sage. Is everything alright?"

"Yes, I'm letting you know I'm keeping Nicki until Monday morning. I hope that's alright," she voiced.

"Sure, it's fine. Sage, if you want to keep her as in becoming her foster mom, I'll inform the judge. I'll back you if that's what you want."

"I'm only doing it this weekend, Martin. I'm not sure if I'm cut out to be a mom." She had come to love the child, but becoming a mother was a full-time job, and she didn't have that to offer her.

"I think you are, but if you change your mind, you have my support."

"Good to know," she uttered. She liked her boss. He was good to work with; he wasn't the micro-managing type, which was great. "You have a great day, Martin, and thanks."

"You too, Sage," he yawned.

Sage decided to head out with Nicki to have some fun. She entertained Nicki with shopping in the mall and bought her new outfits. Nicki's eyes lit up every time Sage picked something out for her. Nicki rode the pony ride in the mall three times and a few other kiddy rides. Sage imagined it would be like this if she kept Nicki. They would hang out together like mother and daughter, enjoying each other's company.

Wait, was she really thinking about keeping her? Nicki? It would be a huge change in her life. Was she ready for that? She'd kept the same routine for the past two years. Having a child in her life would be a drastic change—life changing. Perhaps Nicki was what she needed in her life. Sage and her husband did try to have children but were unsuccessful. She still didn't know if it was her fault, they couldn't have children. She wasn't tested to be sure. It probably was because of what she had done all those years ago—having an abortion. It was her punishment from God because she'd destroyed a life. It had to be. And now, this beautiful little girl needed a mother in her life. She could be her mother if she stopped rationalizing her situation. *Thanks, Universe. I'm undecided,* she thought.

She took Nicki to the beach around four that same day. It was a nice day, and the sky was now partly cloudy with a breeze blowing off the ocean. The smell of the sea air was spectacular. Sage loved coming to the beach. It was a simple, beautiful escape from life for her. Sage and Nicki walked the shoreline hand in hand. Nicki was talking up a storm telling her about the last time she'd visited the beach.

"Do you like collecting seashells, Ms. Sage?" Nicki asked curiously. "My mommy and I collected them when we came together." She stared at the shell in her hand.

"Of course, I do lovebug." Sage stopped walking, nudging her cheek. "Do you know if you put a shell against your ear, you can hear the ocean calling you?" she burst happily.

"I thought you could hear the ocean? I didn't know it would call my name," Nicki snorted.

"Oh, yeah," Sage said. "Hear the ocean."

Sage picked Nicki up, spinning her around in a circle. They both enjoyed it until Sage got dizzy, and they crashed onto the sand.

"No more spinning around for now, kiddo," she exclaimed, standing up. She reached for Nicki's hand, grabbing her sandals, and they began walking again.

They stopped to observe the ocean. It was so blue and beautiful. It reminded her of Nick's eyes. *Fiddlesticks, where had that come from? I'm not interested in that man.* She dismissed the thought.

Nick was at the beach, enjoying the waves. As a kid, Nick had practiced his skills on skateboards as well as the water. He would practice on sidewalks, empty pools, playground slopes, and parking lots with friends. Muscle memory was key for him. However, he wasn't a pro at the sport, but he wasn't sloppy at it either. He hadn't been out in the water in a while, but it was better than thinking about a woman he couldn't have. And besides, he had done enough work at the office—he needed a break. Paul had spurred him into that.

He had been out in the water for almost an hour when he came back up on the beach. Low and behold, the first person he saw was the woman who'd been entering his thoughts lately. His main vein seemed to feel her presence. He had to think of something disgusting to keep it at bay. "Stinky, sweaty, dirty drawers," he whispered. "Stinky, sweaty, dirty drawers," he repeated.

Sage was in yellow shorts showing off those nice hips, thighs, and beautiful, sculpted legs. She had a short-sleeved blue top exposing her toned arms, and it was cut lower to her breasts. "Damn, stinky, sweaty, dirty, drawers." She was a vision—a goddess. Her long, curly, charcoal hair was in a high ponytail as the wind took control of it. There were loose strands elegantly framing her gorgeous face. She was having fun with the little girl who looked more like her daughter. But she didn't have any children according to the file he had on her. At least, he didn't think she had, because his file had also failed to disclose her boyfriend. He headed over to her.

Sage noticed the man with his surfboard walking toward her and Nicki. At least he looked to be coming toward them. When she drew nearer, she realized it was him—the old man. He was a walking dream carrying that large surfboard under his nicely built arm. Wow! He looked so damn sexy with that board. His body showed off tons of muscles, with water dripping off his black hair. His hair was perfect, even wet.

She licked her lips, wetting them as her eyes lingered on him. Were her panties moist? *Fiddlesticks!* Even the hints of gray at the temples were attractive. That dark, blue, wetsuit fit his tall frame just right. Nick's ripped, muscular arms and chest flexed as he carried the board. Him pushing the wet hair off his forehead was sexy. Yes, he was a sex symbol. Sage wondered if he knew it. An image of Luke appeared. She felt guilty thinking about the man that way. He was old enough to be her father. If not father, certainly an uncle. She composed herself.

"Hi Sage," he addressed, smiling at her.

"Hello Nickolas," she said, holding Nicki's hand.

"You two enjoying this nice day, I see," he breathed, moving the hair off his forehead. He glanced at Nicki. "And who might you be?" he asked, bending down slightly close to her.

"Hey, I'm Nicole-Marie Fulton," she replied. "My friends call me Nicki."

"My name is Nickolas Brimmer. My friends call me Nick. You like collecting seashells?"

"Yes, Ms. Sage helped me collect this one. Are you Ms. Sage's boyfriend?" she quizzed innocently. "That would be great. Nick and Nicki," she poked his arm and then herself.

Sage coughed, almost choking. She didn't realize Nicki knew about such things already. She would most definitely have to give her the sex talk soon. Sage remembered how uncomfortable that talk had been with her mother. The Dreaded "S" Talk.

Nick chuckled at her comment. He wished it were true. All three of them like the three musketeers. He stood up straight, eyeing Sage. She had a look of disgust. He knew what Nicki implied was awkward but not disgusting. Was it?

"Nickolas isn't my boyfriend, lovebug," Sage corrected, staring down at her. "He's a.... a new friend."

"Oh," Nicki sang. "Ms. Sage, is it alright if I go over there to collect more shells?" she pointed where she wanted to go, releasing her hand.

"Sure, don't go too far. I want to be able to see you," she called after her, making sure she understood.

"Okay, I won't," she yelled, running to find more shells.

Nick and Sage looked at each other for a moment, then spoke at the same time.

"No, you first," he proposed, wanting to reach out and touch her lips. He wanted to see what they felt and tasted like. Her luscious pink, lips were shining as if daring him to kiss them.

"I want to apologize for Nicki assuming you were my boyfriend. I didn't know she was old enough to know about that type of thing." Sage bit her lower lip, anxiously.

He laughed. "I didn't mind her thinking that. I don't mind at all. She's a pretty little girl." He gazed in Nicki's direction. "She's the child whose mother was killed in our building about eight months ago, right?" he said sadly as he turned his eyes back on Sage.

"Yes," she answered, observing Nicki. "Parker is working hard to find her mother's killer. That's the reason he hosted the cocktail party—to get to know some of the people living in your building."

She had to indicate the boyfriend. *Damn, he's lucky.* "Yes, I know. I hope he catches the SOB soon. I couldn't believe he suspected someone in our building. That's what Paul thinks." He moved his hair off his forehead.

"I don't know. He hasn't said as much to me," she replied, continuing to watch Nicki, making sure she was close. Nicki was occupied, digging in the sand. "Parker keeps his cases confidential. We don't talk about his work." She saw a couple walking by holding hands as she looked back at Nick. She wondered what it would be like to hold his. *What the fudge?* She said to herself, dismissing the terrible thought. As a matter-of-fact, she missed a whole lot of things if she were honest with herself.

Stop it, he's not your type. He's older. Much older.

God, I want to grab her. She's standing there, biting her lower lip, talking to me. She's taunting me and doesn't even know. Tempting me, he thought. *Those cat emerald eyes looking up at me so wantonly. If only she didn't have a man, dammit.*

Or was he imagining her looking at him in that way? Because just moments ago, she hadn't. It was the look of repulsiveness. He looked at his wristwatch. It was almost six. He was meeting up with Paul and Royce at seven.

"It was nice running into you," he said, staring at her as if it would be the last time, he saw her. He almost palmed her shoulder but positioned his board against him, so he wouldn't make a bad move. How could he be captivated by her? Another man's woman. He remembered how awful it was to be cheated on by someone you loved. He wouldn't be the sides in any relationship. Not that this goddess would even do such a thing. Or give his old ass the time of day. She had to be unique.

"Err, good chatting with you," she said, relieved. "Come on, Nicki," she called, waving her hand at her.

"Possibly, I'll see you again at MCC or in the apartment building."

"I hope not." She didn't mean for that to slip out, but she didn't need to be reminded of her attraction to him—even if it hurt his feelings. And she had. She saw it in his eyes. She didn't have time to correct herself anyway, which was perfect timing, Nicki was beside her now.

"Hey, don't you want to come eat with us, Nick?" she asked.

What are you up to, young lady? Is she trying to hook us up? Sage considered.

"Nicki, he has plans." She squeezed her small hand casually. Sage mouthed sorry to Nick.

"I can't, sorry, sweetie," he apologized, looking at Nicki. He wished he could have dinner with the two of them, but he knew it wouldn't be right. He would only be intruding on another man's woman. *Lucky, lucky, man,* he thought. *Damn, she didn't want to be near me. It hurt to hear her say it so boldly.*

"It's okay," she said, holding tightly to Sage's hand. "Bye-bye, Nick." She waved.

"See ya," he smiled, going on his way, disappointed he couldn't join them. Disappointed she didn't want him.

Nick met up with Paul and Royce at his bar and grill. They all were seated in a large booth near the back with a window view. The bar wasn't crowded at that time of the evening. Nick had purchased the restaurant from the previous owner, who was ready to retire. He'd kept on the same staff as he didn't see the need to replace them. Nick wasn't the type of guy to put employees out of jobs. Since taking over a year ago, he'd made minor changes to the establishment by installing better lighting and remodeling the bar area. Eventually, he would change the booths to tables. The business had increased. He gave his employees promotions and raises. He'd learned from his uncle how to keep good employees, among other valuable lessons.

"How is business in Portland?" Nick inquired, taking a drink of sprite.

"It's picking back up. I'm going to make another visit there in a month. I've been making some changes in how we are running the hotels. We have valet parking now, and we've increased the size of the parking lot. Parking was hectic for our customers. I implemented these changes last month. I'll make sure Margaret gets the report to Staci, so she can pass it onto you." He took a drink of his bourbon whiskey.

"Okay, I look forward to that. How's it going on your end with business, Roy?" Nick asked, picking up a fry, biting it.

"It's going great. I can't complain. Life is good." He smiled. Royce's family owned a stake in land, properties, oil, and hotels. His family owned software technologies, which Nick and Paul were invested in. "Did you like the woman I introduced you to?"

"She was okay." He raised the burger to his mouth, taking a bite. "The usual type I prefer," Nick professed, chewing his food.

"Just okay." Royce surveyed him with sharp eyes. "The woman was gorgeous."

"Nick only has eyes for Sage. He hasn't elaborated on anything about her to you?"

"Nope, who is she?" Royce queried.

"Didn't you see her today, Nick?" Paul asked. Nick had told him about the encounter before Royce joined them. "And you didn't ask her out?" Paul shook his head, taking a drink of his bourbon whiskey.

"She has a boyfriend, and he lives in our building."

"What girl?" Royce demanded impatiently. "I didn't know Nick was seeing anybody. He went to the theater the other night with two other ladies and me. And they both were smoking hot, hot."

"Hey, you invited him instead of me?" Paul scoffed, putting his whiskey down.

"He's going through a rough patch. You're always out with the ladies," Royce grinned. "You probably were out then."

"Right you are," he boasted loudly. "I'm fine with not getting serious. I leave that to you and Nick-O."

"Y'all still didn't answer the question," Royce said.

"May I get you anything else, Mr. Brimmer?" their server asked.

"No, thank you. You're doing a fine job," Nick reassured her.

She nodded appreciatively, heading to the next booth. Paul resumed the conversation.

"Oh, Nick-O did a full investigation on her. He didn't tell you?" Paul eyed Nick for a second then resumed talking to Royce. "She's this green-eyed beautiful black woman. Nick seems to be into her completely. Who he hasn't asked out yet."

"I'm not going to ask her out," he glared at him. "I've told you she has a boyfriend... the detective in our building," Nick divulged.

"Wait, that's Parker's girlfriend? Because he never indicated to me, he had one, and we've become buddies since he's been staying at Breckville Towers. If she's his girlfriend, he would've said it. I can't see him not boasting about a woman like her."

"Paul, he did say it. Remember the cocktail party, that's when he said it. I was in the kitchen with her alone, and he walked in when we were conversing. Just let it go, Paul. I'm not about to date a woman who is obviously in a relationship. And he's a detective," he said with a sneer.

"Nick, she's into you, man. I saw the way she looked at you that night," he confirmed. "I wanted to introduce her to you, but she ran scared. I know this because she was watching you when we bumped into each other. That's why I told you where she was. Trust me, she's into you, Nick-O."

Nick had been busy sipping Sprite, so he hadn't heard everything Paul had said. Sage wasn't interested in him. She didn't want him in that way. He saw how offended she was when the little girl asked if he was her boyfriend. Hell, it was on her face how disgusted that sounded. And the woman flat-out told him she hoped not to see him again. It still stung to know that.

"She doesn't sound like Nick's type. Don't get me wrong, I've dated plenty of times outside of my race. I've never seen Nick do it," Royce professed, looking curiously.

"This will be a first for him stepping into the wild side. This is one-woman Nick isn't going to let get away. Am I right, Nick?" he took a drink from his glass.

"She has a nice rack, and let's not forget that fat-ass and those cat-like green eyes and her mouth. Makes me want to go after her myself." He guffawed when he saw Nick's expression.

"Don't punch his lights out yet," Royce sniggered. "You have to get the girl first."

Nick hadn't comprehended how heated he had gotten to hear his best friend talk about her. Sage wasn't his woman. Why was he upset at Paul? He surely was acting like she was his. And she had no idea.

"Let's get off this subject, guys. We came here to talk sports, not women." He threw his balled-up napkin at Paul.

"Okay, Nick-O, we'll drop it until next time," Paul promised. He knew his friend wasn't going to walk away from her. He had seen how his best friend had watched her the night of the cocktail party.

Chapter 6

Sage enjoyed having Nicki for the weekend. It was a blessing for her in some ways. She missed having someone in the house. It made her understand her life wasn't fine at all, like she told her friends. Sage thought maybe everyone might be right about her keeping Nicki. They needed one another, but Sage needed to convince herself.

She didn't want to drop her off this morning, but she had no choice—she couldn't keep her. It wouldn't be fair to Nicki. Sage had been deprived of her mother's attention when she was a child, and because of that, she didn't think she could be a good mother to Nicki. Her mother hadn't been present as she should have been in her life or her sister's. When they needed her, she was always working. She wasn't the mother Sage needed. Deborah was great to her patients, but her girls lacked her attention and support. Sage wouldn't condemn Nicki to that kind of life. She had to take her to MCC until she could find her a permanent home.

Nicki started crying at the center. Sage promised she would come back later to check on her. Sage hated to see her cry. She wanted to draw her up and take her home, but she knew she couldn't. Sage informed Cindy she would call to check on her.

Sage hurried out of the center because she couldn't bear the pain. She had tears in her eyes herself. In the car, Sage let the tears fall. Back in her office, She sat at her desk in a fog, thinking about Nicki. Had she made the right choice leaving her there? Should she keep her? That was her number one question. It was a huge responsibility to be a parent. Sage's thoughts were interrupted by her phone ringing.

"BPCS, Sage Sullivan speaking," she answered softly.

"Hi, babe. How are you this morning?" Parker asked, a happy tone in his voice.

"Oh, hi Park."

Sage wasn't in the mood for happiness right now. Why was he so freaking chipper? It bugged her because she had taken away Nicki's happiness this morning, leaving her at MCC. Every child deserved to be happy. However, every child wasn't. She knew all too well because of her job.

"What's wrong?" he asked with a worry voice. "Does it have to do with Nick?"

"Fiddlesticks," she cried bitterly. "Heck no, it has nothing to do with him. Why would you even think that? It's about Nicki," Sage said with a frown.

"I was only assuming that because of what I saw in the kitchen. You two were into each other. Then you made me be your fake-ass boyfriend. So, what about Nicki?" he asked, changing the subject.

"I had Nicki this weekend. My aunt took care of her while I was at your little party. I'm debating if I should become her foster mother. Sarah and my family think it would be a good idea," she told Parker, the doubt obvious in her voice.

"You know it doesn't matter what I or anybody else may think. It matters what Sage Sullivan wants."

It would be a good thing to do. Sage needed change in her life, though this was a huge one.

"Thanks, Park," she said, smiling. "Now that you gave me good friendly advice, have you talked to Sarah?"

Someone knocked at her door.

"Hold on, Park. Come in," she called out. Martin stepped into her office.

"Oh, hi, Martin," she attended, covering the receiver.

"Sorry to interrupt. I didn't know you were on the phone. I'm going to have to step out for the day. You and Sarah will oversee the entire office. I have that all-day meeting to attend," he announced, looking at the time.

"Sure, no problem, Martin. Sarah and I can manage," she assured him.

"I know you both will. I'll see you all tomorrow," he said, then left her office.

"Okay, I'm back," she continued. "Where were we? Oh, have you spoken to my chick?"

"No, I haven't spoken to her, and you better not say anything to her. Promise me, babe, you will not speak to her about this," Parker almost begged.

"Sure, agreed," she vowed, crossing her fingers. If she got the chance, she would ask Sarah how she felt about Parker.

"Okay, good then. I'm not going to waste any more of your time. Remind yourself that it's what you want, not what someone else wants for you."

"I know, thanks again, Parker. Enjoy the rest of your day," she added, feeling more positive.

"You too, babe, bye."

After she got off the phone with Parker, Sage sat at her desk, thinking about what he'd said. It was what she wanted—she wanted Nicki to be a part of her life. It was what she and Nicki needed. Sage truly believed she'd messed up years ago by having an abortion and regretted that decision. Sage knew she would be the best mother possible to Nicki and was thrilled thinking about it. She didn't know why she was debating back and forth in her mind about it. When it came to Nicki, she was the right choice for the child—not anyone else. That was probably why the child liked her so much.

Even when they first met, there was a connection between them. Nicki admired her immediately, and Sage admired her also. She would have to talk to Lora about being a mother because she had no idea how to be one. Sage thought she lacked maternal instincts. How do you get that? She had no earthly idea, which meant she needed to do a lot of online research.

Thinking about things to research, she needed to see what the web offered about Mr. Nickolas Brimmer. She hadn't gone online to investigate him. If she needed anything on him, she could go to Parker. However, she didn't want him to think she was into the man, 'cause she wasn't. He was someone who intrigued her.

She had found herself thinking about Nick more often than she needed to be. And God, the man was so damn wonderful. Mr. Wondaful, that's who he was. He helped people and enjoyed doing it. How could she not be attracted to that? She applauded the man for that. But it didn't hurt that he was so good-looking either. It was a plus. Just thinking about Mr. Wondaful did things to her she hadn't felt since her husband. It felt wrong to be thinking about another man this way. And he was much older than she was. Old man. He was old enough to be her uncle on her dad's side of the family, which she hadn't spoken to anyone on his side of the family in years. Her sister must keep in touch with them all.

She pushed her glasses on her face, logged into her computer, and began to search for information about Nick. She found out the man had been married to a beautiful, red-headed woman. They had split five years ago when he had caught her cheating on him. It also revealed he almost killed the man and was sentenced to two years of anger management.

That's what happens when you have money and power. *"Like I thought before. He's full of himself. The bastard."* You don't get to go to jail. You go to therapy and get a slap on the wrist. But the man had sued him and won. He was awarded five million dollars. *"Good for you."* His attorneys must have settled out of court.

Sage also discovered he went through a lot of women. And he had a certain type— big-breasted redheads. When he was finished with them, he broke it off by giving them expensive gifts. *"Shallow, arrogant, bastard."* She shook her head as she read the articles about him. Now she knew for sure he wasn't her type at all. Sage closed her eyes for a moment. Why would she have feelings for a man who was a waste of her time to begin with? Well, not feelings...

attraction. He went through women like they were things and gave them jewelry to make them go away. *"Shallow, arrogant bastard."* It had to be the other way around. Some of the sites accused him of cheating on her. She had an affair of her own when she found out about his infidelity. *"Unbelievable how some men behave."* She pushed up from the chair, getting ready to leave for the day.

Sage went to MCC after work. She had assured Nicki she would stop by to see her. Sage knew it would be difficult for her being in a new place, so she wanted to make sure she was alright. She had called Cindy to check on her earlier. Cindy informed her that Nicki wasn't communicating with anyone. She kept to herself mostly.

"Hey, you," Cindy greeted as Sage stepped into her office. "How are you?"

"Hi Cid, I'm doing well. Working hard mostly. No complaints though, I enjoy helping the children. Sorry I haven't been able to come by and give a helping hand since the celebration. What about you?"

"I know you're a busy woman. I'm just glad you agreed to be auctioned off," she spoke happily. "And I'm doing okay. I've added more people to my counseling team and staff. Many of these adults need structure in their lives, especially the children. When they leave here, I want them to at least have a chance in life. You know, if you ever want to come back to counseling yourself, you can. I have three new counselors, and they are good at what they do."

"Nah, I'm good." Sage shook her head, frowning slightly. "You all do great work here. Just know you can't save them all, Cid. You're doing your best." She smiled, hoping to convince her she didn't need therapy anymore.

"Tell yourself that, honey. You try to save 'em all, too." Cindy grinned. "Which is great. Speaking of saving, Nicki isn't doing well, Sage. She's not talking to anyone. Not even to the kids. She's isolating herself from everyone. She asked for you. She's been crying for you."

Sage closed her eyes, gasping lightly, and sat mute for a moment.

"What am I going to do about her?" she asked, looking at Cindy.

"Have you thought about keeping her, Sage? I think it would be good for both of you. You could help one another heal in the process."

"You know, I have been thinking about it. I have come to love Nicki. I have been debating this over and over in my head. Even more so today. Should I keep her? And I've been coming up with poor excuses not to keep her." Her biggest fear was failing horribly as a mother. "I'm afraid I may not be enough for her."

"Yes, you are. All she needs is your love and support. The rest will come to you. believe in yourself. I believe in you."

Sage thought for a moment before answering. No more excuses. "Okay, I have come to this conclusion. The same one I came to before I came here. Yes, I will keep her. Could I take her home tonight?" she asked.

"I don't see why not. You are a very capable woman. But you'll have to see Judge Myers—she has to approve this."

"Of course, I know. Martin conveyed something about it before."

"You know the auction is less than two weeks away. You haven't chickened out, have you? Because I'm really counting on you," Cindy begged, pointing her finger at Sage. "I know it will be a big success with all the helping hands we have with this program."

"No, I won't let you down. I won't flake out. I swear," Sage pledged, holding up two fingers.

"Okay," Cindy sang happily. "I'm going to get your little daughter ready for you to take home." Cindy stood. "This is really good for you, Sage. For you both."

Sage stood up too. "I hope I can be a good mother to her. I don't know the first thing about it," she sighed.

"You are doing something right because that little girl loves you. Nicki is going to be ecstatic she is going home with you. I'm proud of you. You are making progress," Cindy said as she opened the door.

"Hey, don't tell her she's coming home with me. Let me tell her," Sage said, smiling.

"Sure, you got it," she said, as she left to find Nicki.

Sage sat again and began to think if what she was doing was a smart move. She didn't know the first thing about being a mom and would have to call her sister and get all the latest tips and what-nots. She was happy and scared at the same time. Nicki was going to be her foster daughter. Her daughter.

"I'm going to be a mom," she blurted out softly.

Ten minutes later, Nicki and Cindy came to the office. Nicki was enthusiastic to see her. She jumped up and down excitedly.

"I knew you'd come back for me. I prayed you would." She ran up to Sage and jumped onto her lap.

"Whoa, sweetie. I told you not to tell her, Cid." She laughed and wrapped her arms around Nicki. "I knew I would come back for you, too." She stroked her cheeks lovingly.

"I didn't say a word. This one is a smart cookie," Cindy beamed.

Sage already knew that about Nicki. She stood with Nicki in her arms and gave her a big squeeze before putting the little girl down.

"Thanks so much, Cid. I'll call you soon." She took hold of Nicki's hand.

"You two take care of each other," she said, handing Sage Nicki's bag.

"We will," Nicki commented joyfully. "Thank you, Ms. Cindy. You made my wish come true."

"Oh, sweetie," Cindy said, patting Nicki on the back, "that was Ms. Sage's doing."

"See you later, Cid," Sage said.

Sage and Nicki left her office together, fortunately heading home. In the car, Nicki was happily talking. She wanted to know if she would have toys, books, and paints.

"Ms. Sage, will I have my very own room for real?" She looked at her in amazement.

"Yes, baby. You will have your own room. I'll have to buy you some toys one day this week or next week, depending on my schedule. What are your favorite toys?" She glanced over at her then back at the street.

"I love dolls. I like to comb their hair and dress them up. I like painting. I get my drawing skills from my momma," she said sadly. "She could really draw. One time she drew a picture of this pretty sunset. We were at the beach. It was a really fun day. I really love books. I also love swings. You get to go really high in those," she said energetically.

"You can't go high in the one on the front deck, but I could get you one. I'll make sure you have plenty of dolls, paints, books, and other toys to keep you occupied," Sage said as she pulled up in her driveway.

"I don't care if you don't get me a swing, Ms. Sage. I'm just glad I'm living with you."

"So, am I." Sage caressed her face. "Okay, Nicki, let's get your stuff out of the car."

"Nicki," Sage called after her. "Don't run up the staircase like that. You could fall and hurt yourself."

"Sorry, Ms. Sage," she yelled back, then started walking.

When Sage was finally upstairs with her stuff, she found Nicki in her study.

"There you are," she said, breathing heavily.

Nicki was looking around the study at the many books Sage had. She might as well have called her study a library because of all the books. She had books on cooking, home repairs, mysteries, inspirational, and decorating. She started collecting books for her own personal use but then started to collect many varieties such as Jane Austen, Diana Palmer, Sue Grafton, Edgar Allen Poe, Charlotte Bronte, and many other famous authors.

"Wow! Ms. Sage," Nicki exclaimed, looking around at the books. "This is so cool."

"Well, little Miss Missy, you can come into my study and read some of these books. I'll make sure I add some books for you to read to the collection," she said.

"You will?" Nicki asked, running up to her.

"Sure, I will, baby-girl. Now let's go get something to eat. I know you are starving." She reached for her hand.

"I sure am," Nicki said, accepting her hand.

When they were in the kitchen eating, Sage's cell rang. She grabbed her phone and looked at the number. A smile spread across her lips. It was her aunt.

"Hello," she answered happily.

"Hi, Sage, how are you?"

"I'm great, Auntie. I have some news. I am now Nicki's foster mother. I have to make it official with Judge Myers first, which shouldn't be a problem."

"That is such wonderful news," Katie said. "I'm delighted you decided to keep my great-niece. How is she?"

"We are having a little dinner right now. She's fine," Sage answered, gazing over at Nicki. She was eating her turkey sandwich, flipping through the channels. "I'll need your help if that's alright with you, Auntie?"

"Yes, Sugar," she drawled.

"I know you get off work at two-thirty every day." Her aunt worked at a small accounting firm. "I would be honored if you would pick Nicki up after school and let her hang out with you until I get off work."

"Not a problem at all, Sugar. I would be honored to keep her for a while each day. She can help me in my garden. I'll keep her whenever you have a date. I'm at your service, Sugar."

"I'm not dating anyone, Aunt Katie." Sage rolled her eyes in annoyance. "I'm not seeing anyone, nor do I desire to see anyone."

"I was only letting you know all you have to do is ask, and I'm here," her aunt said, wishing that day was here.

"Sure, whatever, Aunt Katie. Thanks so much for agreeing to babysit for me. You are a lifesaver."

"That's what I'm here for, Sugar. Now you give Nicki a hug and a kiss for me. I love you," she said, right before hanging up.

That meant her aunt was there to support her. Her aunt was her rock. "I love you," Sage said, even though her aunt was no longer on the phone.

She wished she was more like her aunt sometimes. She was a lively, colorful woman. Katie didn't mind going out with men trying to find someone to connect with. Sage held her in great esteem for that. Sage hoped one day she would find happiness with a man. However, right now, that wasn't in the cards for her. She was satisfied with Nicki. Her little girl. Eventually, she was going to adopt her.

Later that night, Sage woke from her sleep when she heard Nicki screaming. She turned on the light next to her. Nicki was having a nightmare. Sage called her name softly, pulling her into her loving arms. She called her name until Nicki opened her eyes, realizing it was a bad dream. She wrapped her little arms around Sage's waist.

"You want to tell me about your dream, sweetie?" she asked, stroking her back, planting a kiss on top of her head.

"No," she cried, holding onto Sage tighter.

"Okay, baby, I'm right here," she continued to caress her back. It was a little after one in the morning. Sage had nightmares and understood what Nicki was dealing with. She wondered if this was a one-time thing with Nicki. She had stayed with her before, and Nicki hadn't had any nightmares. The Grissoms hadn't discussed any problems with nightmares either. But if it was a reoccurring thing, she knew Nicki needed therapy. Nicki went back to sleep about ten minutes later.

Sage didn't go back to sleep immediately. She laid in bed, thinking. Maybe she saw her mother's killer and was afraid to say.

She was found in the closet hiding. If that was true, Nicki would need her support and care. She would need protection. What if the killer saw her? Was that possible? She sat up in bed, frightened. But if that was so, wouldn't the killer have gone after her too?

Maybe she was making too much out of the situation. It could be a little girl missing her mother. She lost her own mother tragically. She and Lora came home from school after practice to find her aunt at their home. It was unusual for her to be there during the school week. They would see her over the weekend sometimes, or if they invited her to any school activity, they participated in. Which was rare because their aunt had her own life. Back then, she was always on the go—ready to conquer the world. Her aunt sang in nightclubs and still did on occasion. She volunteered at her church and helped with their many bake sales and church functions. So, when Sage saw her that day, she knew something was wrong. But she wasn't expecting to find out her mother was no longer among the living. Tears rolled down her face. She took tissue from the nightstand, wiped her face then drifted off to sleep, dreaming of Nick. *"Get out of my head, old man,"* she complained before falling to sleep completely.

Chapter 7

Sage was working at her desk on Tuesday morning, thinking about Nicki and her nightmare. She needed to speak to Parker to determine if it was possible Nicki might know more. She had a feeling last night wasn't Nicki's first nightmare. Sarah came through her door, closing it behind her. She was grinning from cheek to cheek.

"You are keeping Nicki." She clapped her hands together.

"Yes, I am," Sage announced. I made up my mind after I went to the center. Really, before I went to the center." Her eyes twinkled. "I love that little girl. I will adopt her."

"Yippie! My friend is making a change in her life. Way to go, new momma." She high-fived her. "I'm so glad you are keeping her. Parker said something to me about it yesterday." Sarah blushed at the thought of Parker.

"You and Parker talking? Spill," Sage said as she sat on the edge of the desk.

"Well, Parker came to my office yesterday. It was after you left for the day.

He wanted to talk to me, and I sort of agreed to go out with him."

"That's great." Sage gave Sarah a hug. "So, it was pinned up energy and a lot more," she bragged.

"Yes, Sage," Sarah agreed.

"I'm glad you really like him because he really likes you. He told me he would ask you out. And to think, the man was nervous about doing so."

"You're not upset with us?" Sarah looked at her seriously. "Cause if this will affect our friendship, I will call it off, Sage."

"Chick, no way. I'm delighted for you both. My closest friends dating is good."

"Okay. I think you should tell Parker about the baby. I want to go into this with him without secrets. I told him if he talks to you first, I will date him," she said.

Sage went numb for a moment. She dropped her chin, closing her eyes. It would only make him upset with her. Look what revealing that secret had done to her and Luke. It destroyed her life ultimately. She wished she hadn't told her husband. He would be alive if she had kept that secret.

Sarah got up from the chair and placed her hands on Sage's shoulders. She could see her friend was in pain. Sarah didn't want her friend to feel that way, but she couldn't be with Parker with that huge secret between them. Sage looked up with glassy eyes. The memory of her husband was on her mind.

"Oh Sage, I'm sorry," Sarah murmured, touching her back. "But I can't be with him knowing this—your secret."

"I know," she sniffed. "It's what caused my husband's death. I told him about the baby that awful night. He was so angry with me that night. I should have told him at the beginning of our relationship, but I didn't," she sobbed. "I will tell Park. I don't want your relationship built on a lie." Sage felt her life was built on a lie ever since the accident.

"Sage, you know Luke loved you very much. There wasn't anything that man wouldn't do for you. I saw the way he was with you even in college. Don't you dare think your marriage was built on lies because it wasn't." She took hold of her hand. "You withholding that doesn't make your marriage a lie. He truly loved you, and you loved him."

"I'm being punished for what I did, Sarah. I shouldn't have had the abortion. That's why I couldn't have my husband's babies. It was God's punishment for me," she said sadly.

"That's not true. Would God give you Nicki if he was punishing you? I don't think so." Her grip tightened on Sage's hand. "You've been given a second chance."

"Perhaps you are right. You're truly a great friend. Thanks, Sarah," She said, hugging her friend.

"I'm only saying what is true, Sage. Your husband loved you completely. Now you go to the ladies' room and wash your face," she instructed.

"Okay, and thanks again."

Sage left the office to take an early lunch. She needed time to think about breaking the news to Parker about the baby. How was she going to tell him about the baby she aborted years ago, after their break-up? She didn't think she would ever have to tell him. She wanted to keep it buried, but her best friends wanted to explore their feelings for each other.

Sage was glad her friends had come around to dating one another. She needed to talk to Parker about Nicki as well. She wasn't sure if Nicki was safe, but her gut was telling her she was. It had been eight months since her mother's death. Surely, Parker would know if Nicki wasn't safe. He would have her in police custody if he thought she wasn't. So, she had to have it all wrong about the nightmare.

She was at Capricorn not too far from work, buried in her thoughts. She loved sitting outside to eat most of the time. The temperature was seventy-five degrees, and the winds were blowing. It wasn't too breezy for her. Sage was seated at a table with a large pink umbrella, sipping on Cherry Coke—her favorite bad addiction.

Nick couldn't believe it when he saw her sitting alone outside the restaurant. She had a bleak look on her lovely face. He speculated on what might be wrong. What could have her in this space? Her long hair was blowing with the wind. She was a beautiful painting, though he wasn't going to paint her again. He already had her many different images in his studio. All four of them staring at him every time he entered the room, reminding him of what he couldn't have. He didn't like the distressed look on her face. He shouldn't go over. She had made it known to him she didn't want to see his face. However, he wanted to see hers. So, he headed over to her table to see if he could help.

"Hi Sage, mind if I join you?" he asked charmingly.

Sage looked up from her Cherry Coke, gazing into the eyes of the man she wasn't expecting to see. *Shallow, arrogant bastard.* He was a grand statue, standing there scrutinizing her. He was dressed in a black, expensive suit with a light-blue dress shirt and a black tie around his large neck. Why was he invading her space? She didn't need him standing there, looking so goddamn deliciously handsome. Freaking Mr. Wondaful.

"Oh, hello Nickolas," she acknowledged, pointing to the seat. He took a chair across from her, setting his briefcase beside him.

"Are you alright?" he asked with interest in his baritone voice.

"Yes." She straightened, forcing a smile.

"Sage, you look like something is wrong. I don't mean to pry, but if I can help, I don't mind," he offered.

Sage pulled back. She felt a bolt of lightning flowing from him. He was awakening parts of her that had been in a siesta for a long time. She didn't need that happening to her now. She had Nicki in her life. No time for this. His shallow butt! Not that she was looking for anything. Her chance at love died two years ago. No duplication required.

"I'm sorry," he said, withdrawing his hand. *Fuck, this was a bad idea.* "I shouldn't have touched you." But he couldn't help it. She was in his brain, constantly taking up too much damn space, totally muddying his mind.

"No, you shouldn't," Sage agreed. She didn't expect that—the feeling of something stirring inside of her. "I've got something on my mind, that's all. Why are you acting so concerned?" She rolled her eyes at him in aggravation, remembering what she'd read about him.

"I'm not acting at all, Sage. I'm very concerned about you," he stressed.

"You don't have to be. I'm a big girl," she guaranteed.

Nick was trying to charm his way into her life by being concerned. She didn't need his attention. In fact, she didn't want whatever he was trying to give. She wasn't going to be a part of his games. She didn't have time for him or his shenanigans.

Fuck off!

"Sage, let's stop pretending with each other. That's why you pulled away from me just then. You feel it, whatever this is between us. I'm not alone in this. It started for me when I first laid eyes on you at MCC. I know you have a boyfriend. I've been telling myself that since he walked into the kitchen, searching for you that night. I've been trying to keep away from you. By chance, I ran into you at the beach. You told me point blank you don't want to see me, which hurt my feelings, by the way. Then I find you out here, looking upset about something. You can trust me." He stroked her cheek. He couldn't help it. Just a sample. He was like a drug addict. An obsessed addiction he couldn't shake. He wanted to touch her again. He needed to touch her again to feed his desire for her.

"Nick, don't," she hummed. "Just go. Never touch me like that again. I don't need your help. Stay away from me. I don't need a man like you near me. Have I made myself clear? You are a father figure that keeps popping up. I don't want another daddy."

Fiddlesticks! Shallow, arrogant bastard!

Nick stared at her for a second. There it was, that look of revulsion. He couldn't believe she was serious. Here he was, offering her a helping hand. But she sneered at it like it was nothing. *Wow, is that what she really thinks of me?* He thought. Most women couldn't get enough of him. It didn't matter if they were younger or women in his age group. Even much older women. He had to let them down easily by buying them expensive gifts. She was anything but most women. That was probably why he couldn't stop thinking about her.

She sat across from him, looking savagely beautiful. Her orange, strapless dress stopped short at the thighs, accompanied by a small gold chain around her neck. It had a symbol on it he couldn't make out. A white short-sleeved jacket hung on her chair. No, he couldn't fathom why this stunning woman resisted him. No matter how disgusted she may be with him, she felt what he did when he touched her. She probably did see him as a perverted old man or father figure, but there was want in her eyes. He stood and bent down slightly, to pick up his briefcase before he moved beside her.

"Sage, I will not touch you again," he whispered close to her ear, hoping to get a response from her. "Not unless you want me to, sweetheart. Let me be clear, I want you."

Nick wanted to run his tongue down the length of her ear and suckle her lobe. But there was no need. He got the reaction he was looking for.

Sage wondered if Nick knew what effect he'd had on her? Did he know what it had done to her body? She shivered as if being cold, but she wasn't. An involuntary sound had slipped from her mouth, when his baritone voice spoke softly in her ear before he kissed her cheek tenderly. It was a touch that wouldn't be forgotten. He'd lit a fuse to start a fire inside of her with his moist breath and words. *Fiddlesticks!*

"I have no intention of being your daddy unless you're screaming big daddy when I make you scream from pure pleasure. I want to be much more, Sage. Much more," he growled near her ear.

She didn't think she could feel pleasure from another man. Luke had been the only man in her life who made her body react to this degree. Sure, there was Parker once upon a time. Still, he hadn't given her pleasure with his words. The evidence was in her panties. It was terrifying and wonderful at the same time. Her first instinct told her to flee. She couldn't deal with whatever this was. She had no place for whatever it was in her life. She was in love with Luke and she vowed not to allow anyone else to get that close to her ever again. It hurt too much.

Nick stood, smiling satisfactorily. If he heard her correctly, she moaned his name softly. He knew that it had created the desired response from her body, no matter how she said she felt about him. He glanced down at his Rolex, walking away, not saying another word. He did what he meant to do. Hopefully, Sage would be consumed with thoughts about him that night—dreaming of him making love to her.

Sage's day drifted by quickly because she had a lot of work to do, which didn't stop her from thinking about what happened on her lunch break. She couldn't believe the man had the nerve to come to her table and act all concerned for her. *"BS, he wasn't concerned. All he was looking for was a helpless woman he could get in the sack,"* she thought. And she wasn't that. She was an independent woman and didn't need a man to save her. Why did he appear in her life anyway? Was the universe trying to tell her something? She wasn't interested in him and wished he would leave her alone. *"Shallow, arrogant bastard,"* she spoke aloud. She couldn't get him out of her ear. Those words he said to her, and he'd purposely mouthed them to her like that. He had to know the effect it had. *"Oh God, I crooned his name. Fiddlesticks."* Sage sat back in her chair, thinking about how he'd pleasured her with his spoken words. *"I won't get involved with another man. You hear me, universe?"* she spoke softly aloud. *"You took the love of my life away from me. I don't need someone else showing up,"* she spat in an angry whisper. She went back to finishing up her work before heading to see Judge Myers.

An hour later, Sage had seen Judge Myers about Nicki. The Judge gave her permission to take care of Nicki for six months then she would evaluate her. The judge said that after those six months were up, she would see if Sage was a permanent fit for Nicki.

Sage called Cindy and Sarah to inform them of the news. They were proud for them both and told her they would stand by her side when it was time for the evaluation. She entered her aunt's house to give her and Nicki the good news. She found them outside in the garden.

"Hi, you two," she greeted happily. "I have great news. Judge Myers said I can keep Nicki for six months, and then she'll evaluate me again to see if I could be a permanent placement for you." She pointed at Nicki, who got up from beside Aunt Katie and ran over to Sage.

"For real?" she asked enthusiastically. "I get to stay with you forever?"

"Yes, lovebug. Isn't that marvelous?" Sage bent down, giving her a hug.

"Mm-hmm," she hummed, hugging her neck.

"This calls for some good old-fashioned lemonade," Katie said, getting up from the plants. "And some strawberry shortcake."

"Yay," Nicki cried gleefully, clapping her small hands together.

After spending an hour at their aunt's house, Sage and Nicki spent two hours in the study. Sage worked on a story, and Nicki worked with her paints and pad at the research table. They were busy as bees until it was time for bed. It was indeed a good day for them both.

Sage still had to speak to Parker about two matters. Nicki seemed to be adjusting okay, but the nightmare she had still bothered Sage. Nicki didn't want to talk about it, and Sage didn't want to force the issue with her. She was finally in a good place with her. They were in bed, watching a friendly kiddie show on TV when Sage's cell phone rang.

"Hello, Lor," she answered. "I'm glad you called."

"Hi, Sage," her sister spoke drowsily. "When were you going to tell me about Nicki? I'm so glad for you. You are now a mommy," she yawned happily.

"I was getting around to it. The judge decided in my favor today. I get evaluated in another six months to see if I can keep her permanently. I must confess," she whispered, "I'm a little terrified as well. What if I can't be the mother she needs? I don't know the first thing about being a mother. Is there a manual on raising kids, because I need it?" she sighed.

"You'll get the hang of it. There is no right way to be a good mother. You learn as you go. All mothers do. You'll be a great mother to her."

"Thanks, sis," she said, watching Nicki. She was into the show at the foot of the bed.

"I knew you would keep her permanently," she yawned again.

"Yep, you best trust and believe. How are the kids and that hubby of yours?"

"They are good. BJ can't wait to see you. And now he has a little cousin his age," she said with glee. "I'm sorry, Sage. I'm a bit tired."

"We can't wait to visit either. I know BJ and Nicki will be the best of friends. You sound like you need plenty of rest. I love you, Lor. Get some sleep."

"I love you too. Take care. Bye."

Sage moved down to the end of the bed with Nicki. She prayed she would be a good mother. The first thing she was going to buy was some parenting books to add to her study. She needed all the help she could get.

Chapter 8

Nick was in his office, trying to focus his attention on work. He was looking over the merger contracts between Blackwell and Gaines. The two men weren't ready for an agreement. They wanted it re-written to benefit each of their interests mutually. Nick was finding it hard to look over the merger. He had Sage on the brain. He hated himself for having no self-control yesterday. His main vein seemed to awaken from its state of rest whenever he was near her. It was a bad idea to even think about being with her in the first place. She was in a relationship with the detective. Nick kept telling himself that but couldn't make it stick in his brain. He'd been in and out of relationships with women since his divorce—that is if you could call them relationships because he wasn't in them long. The longest relationship he'd had was two months top and, he'd broken it off. He wasn't about to commit to another woman and get his heart ripped out of his chest. It had been hell getting over his ex-wife.

Nick and his ex-wife had dated for two years before he married her. In that time, he hadn't seen any signs that she wasn't right for him. If he had listened to his friends, he would have saved himself the grief. They had warned him she was a little bit too flirtatious toward them. Nick had chalked it up as part of her character to be overly friendly. If you called rubbing your best friends' chests sexually or kissing them briefly on the lips being flirtatious, which it wasn't. That was his sign; he'd refused to accept it because he thought he was in love with her, and that behavior would stop after they were married.

She was a beautiful five-foot-nine-inch redhead. He'd always favored redheads. She had a small frame, thin lips with gray eyes, and a sharp, pointy nose with a square face. She had used him until that awful day he caught her cheating.

"Never again will I let another woman do that to me," he protested, loosening his tie, angry at himself for lusting after another man's woman. He went to the refrigerator to retrieve an orange Gatorade. He walked over to the window taking in a deep breath. What was wrong with him? She wasn't even his usual type. Yet, he couldn't fathom why this woman had such a huge effect on him. Yesterday he wanted her so damn badly and leaning down whispering close to her ear hadn't helped either. It only made

matters worse for him. When he returned to work, he had to really focus his attention on "disgusting, stinky, dirty drawers," when she popped into his mind. He had to take several cold showers to cool off after he arrived home. *"Damn you woman for making me feel this way,"* he spoke aloud as he stared out the window. He finished his Gatorade and returned to his desk to work again. He pressed the intercom to get Staci on the phone.

"Yes, Mr. Brimmer," she answered.

"Could you come in here for a moment?"

"Yes, sir, I'll be right there." Staci came and sat at his desk with her pad and pen in hand, ready for dictation.

"Where's the other file on Blackwell and Gaines? Did you make the necessary copies I needed?" he asked. "Also, get me the information Paul has on the hotels in Portland. He mentioned he would have Margret get the info for you to get to me."

"Of course, I'll get right on that." She studied her boss. He didn't seem his usual self. He was usually optimistic, but lately, he'd been down about something. She'd worked for him for the past three years, and she could pick up on his moods. "Are you okay, Mr. Brimmer? You don't seem yourself."

Nick looked up from the file. He wasn't himself. His mind had been preoccupied with Sage. "I'm sorry, Staci. It's this merger," he lied, hoping she believed him. She didn't need to concern herself with him, but he was glad he had someone concerned for him. He had no family except Paul and Royce.

"Okay, sir. I hope the two men come to an agreement soon," she said.

"Yeah, me too," he answered, leaning back in his chair.

"Is that all, Mr. Brimmer?"

"Yes, and thanks."

"No problem, sir. I'll have this information in less than fifteen minutes," she insured.

"No, not to rush, Staci. Just have it by the end of the day."

"Okay, sir." She closed the door lightly behind her.

Nick closed his eyes, still leaning back in his chair, fantasizing about Sage. He knew it was a very bad idea, but it wasn't like it would come to pass. These were lusty thoughts that wouldn't see the light of day. He removed one hand from behind his head and adjusted his crotch. He was thinking about her giving him a private dance. His hand rested on his crotch, squeezing himself, wishing it was her touching him. He'd been with plenty of women, and none of them made him feel like he was drowning. Drowning with his emotions for her, and she was the only one who could save him.

He heard pounding coming from his door, bringing him back from where he shouldn't have ventured. He straightened up in his seat, pretending to appear busy.

Paul came in and took a seat.

"What's going on?" Paul asked.

"Work, man," Nick answered, putting on a phony smile. He pushed thoughts of Sage out of his mind and main vein. "What's up with you? Aren't you heading to Vegas to look at a property?" Nick asked.

"Shit, yeah. You should come with me. I plan on going next weekend. We should make it a guy trip. We haven't all been to LV in two years, which proves we've been working to goddamn hard around here."

Nick snickered because Paul was right. "I don't know. I'll have to get back to you on that."

"Come on, Nick-O. We need this, man. What could be better than LV? Oh, wait. This doesn't have to do with the green-eyed bombshell, does it?"

"Hell no," Nick replied grimacing, "Why would it have to do with her? I've told you that woman doesn't want a damn thing to do with me. I've flung her out of my mind," he fibbed. He straightened, pretending to look busy.

"Oh, I didn't know you were thinking about her." Paul knew his friend wasn't being truthful. "From the way you tell it, she doesn't know you exist anymore." He said that to get a reaction out of him.

"Trust me, she knows." He stopped playing around with the paper, looking at Paul, thinking about yesterday. Sage could deny all she wanted, but there was something between them. That jolting touch proved it.

"I'm only messing with you. You should get up the nerve to ask her out and stop thinking about her," Paul countered, getting up from the chair.

"I'm not going to ask another man's woman out," Nick stated seriously.

"I'm just saying. I'll get back with you about Las Vegas. Tick tock, tick tock." Paul left laughing as he shut the door.

Sage decided to drop by Parker's stake-out place after work. She told her aunt she would be a little late picking up Nicki because she needed to speak to Parker alone. This was the same place Nicki's mother had been murdered, and she wasn't about to bring her back to that horror.

Parker heard her knocking on the door and invited her inside. "Hello babe," he stepped aside to allow her to enter. "How have you been?"

"I've been great now that I have Nicki in my life." She was dreading the conversation they were about to have.

"Do you want something to drink?" he offered.

"Yeah, thanks. Mineral water, please."

"You know Nick asked about you yesterday," Parker said, getting two bottles of water from the fridge. "He wanted to know why you were upset. I'm not sure what he was talking about, but I played it off."

Sage turned toward him, accepting the water. *Why would he appear to be so freaking concerned about me to my fake boyfriend anyway?* She thought. *Damn him! He needs to mind his own business and keep out of mine. Shallow, arrogant bastard!*

"He does know I'm your girlfriend, right?" she inquired, taking a sip of her drink.

"Yes, he's convinced you are my lady," Parker winked, sitting down beside her.

"Good, let's keep it that way—at least until you and Sarah are official," she answered, clearing her throat before speaking again. She didn't have time to worry about Nick finding out Parker wasn't her boyfriend. She came here to talk about other things. One thing specifically, she hated to bring up.

"So, tell me, babe, what's eating at you?" he asked.

Sage stared at the bottle of water for a minute. She needed to ask questions about Nicki first—find out if she needed to be worried about her daughter.

"A few nights ago, Nicki had a nightmare. It made me wonder if she's in harm's way. Could the killer be after her?" she looked at him earnestly.

"No, babe. Nicki is safe. Whoever killed her mother didn't know she was in the closet. When I found her, she was tucked away where I wasn't even aware of her presence. She came out when she heard all the racket. There is a trap door inside the closet for a small child to fit inside. The previous owner obviously stored something of value they didn't want found. It probably saved Nicki's life. There's no need to worry." He kissed her forehead.

The thought of someone harming Nicki made Sage's blood hot. Who would do such a thing to hurt an innocent child? "Thank God." A sigh of relief escaped her lips. "Thanks, Park." Now that she knew her daughter was safe, she had to talk to him about the other matter.

"Something is still bothering you. What is it, Sage? Does it have to do with Sarah? I think she has decided against me. I did ask her to consider dating me, but I think she's going to decline," he said, disheartened.

"Parker, Sarah wants to go out with you. It has to do with our past—you and me. That's why she's hesitant about you," Sage finally admitted as she stood.

Parker stood removing the water from her hands, placing the bottle on the table.

He could tell she was distressed about something. But what from their past could have her this way? He was the dog in their relationship. He cheated on her, and it cost him his relationship with her. He was jealous of her relationship with Lucas at first—the man who'd taken his woman away from him. That was how he felt at the time. However, he knew it was his own doing that cost him Sage.

"Sage, what is it? I'm an idiot. I know I hurt you back then. I've paid for it, baby. I lost you." He stroked her cheek.

She twisted away from him. Sage didn't want to tell him about the child she aborted. It pained her to think about it all over again. It would forever haunt her— what she'd done all those years ago. She didn't know how he would react to the information. She lost her husband two years ago because of this deep, dark secret, and now she might lose him, too.

"Sage... Please, babe."

Sage had tears in her eyes. "Let go of me, and I'll tell you," she sniffled. He released her, and she faced him. "The night my husband was killed, I confessed something to him. Something I should have told you about eight years ago. I've kept this secret from you for a long time." She bit her lip, tasting the salt from her tears.

Parker tried to comfort her, but she brushed his hand away. "Baby." He looked at her compassionately. "What else did I do to you?" He ran his hand over his head. "Just tell me already." He sounded frustrated.

"After we broke up, I found out I was pregnant." She chewed her bottom lip.

He stared at her in complete bewilderment. "Huh?" he asked confused. "What?! You were pregnant, and you didn't bother to let me know. I could have been there when you miscarried our child. Why didn't you tell me, baby?"

"I didn't let you know because I was angry with you. I was confused. I didn't want you to be obligated to the baby or me." She moved away from him. "You were with other girls. I didn't want to ruin your life— or mine. We were young. I wasn't ready to be a mother, and you most certainly weren't ready to be a father. I aborted the baby," she whispered.

"You did what?" he snapped, his mouth set in a hard line. He glared at her then closed his eyes in disbelief. As he opened his eyes, his head was pounding as he stared at her. His mouth was on the verge of erupting words he might regret. "You got rid of my child because you weren't ready to be a mother. God, how could you? You knew I would have wanted the baby regardless of what you thought. That's why you didn't let me know. How could you destroy a life? Our baby?"

Parker was outraged. The muscles in his jaw jerked. He wanted to grab her and shake her for what she had done.

"If it hadn't been for Sarah, you wouldn't have told me. You would have continued to keep the secret." He glowered at her with two fiery eyes.

"I'm sorry, Parker." Tears streamed from her eyes, blurring her vision. Her blouse was damp from her salty tears. "I know I did a horrible thing. Please forgive me," she pleaded, reaching for his hand, but he rejected her.

"Sage, I need some time alone. I can't talk to you right now. Go home," he demanded, angrily. "I don't want to see you right now." He turned away from her.

She didn't know he would be upset enough to ask her to leave. Well, truthfully, she knew he would be angry with her. What she didn't realize was that he would be so cold. But he had every right to be. She had committed a ghastly act. An act she prayed God had forgiven her for. Sage collected her purse and walked slowly to the door. She twisted around, glancing at him. He still had his back to her.

"I'm sorry, Parker. I hope you can forgive me." She opened the door, walking out with her head downward, closing the door behind her.

Sage hurried to her car, not wanting to run into any of his new neighbors.

Especially Nick. She sat in her car and cried for a minute. She had to calm down. Sage understood why Parker was so furious at her. Hell, her husband had been angry. He was beyond angry. He blamed her for not being able to get pregnant. The memory of him saying, *"You can't have my babies because of what you did."* It hurt knowing that was how he felt. Those were the last words the man she loved had spoken to her before the crash. Honestly, he was probably right. She had never told anybody that part of the night. After she calmed down, she drove to her aunt's house.

Nick saw Sage crying and ran toward her car. He wanted to go after her, however, he didn't. He knew she wouldn't want his help or need his help. *"Keep out of it, old man,"* he mumbled. She made that crystal-clear yesterday. He wondered what had happened between her and Parker. He knew it had to do with her boyfriend. He asked him yesterday what was going on with her when he ran into him on the elevator. Parker had claimed it was a girl thing. You know how women get emotional over nothing. Nick wouldn't get involved with her. He waited a few minutes to see if she would go back inside her boyfriend's apartment, but she didn't. She drove off. He turned on his heels and headed inside the building.

Nick and Paul were playing pool. They sometimes played competitively, placing bets. The money went to the charity of the winner's choosing.

"So, you saw her yesterday, and she was upset, and she comes out of Parker's place crying a few minutes ago. Not sure what that's all about. I don't think she's his girlfriend," he remarked, hitting the ball, missing the shot. He picked up his bourbon and took a drink.

"You're wrong," Nick asserted, positioning himself to sink a ball. "I made it known to her that there's something going on between her and me. She doesn't want to own it. She probably thinks I'm an old pervert," he articulated, chalking his stick, moving to make another shot.

"Why would she think that? You are a striking, good-looking guy. No homo," he jested, with a half-smile.

"Gee, thanks. And good to know. It's the way she looks at me sometimes—like I revolt her," he said, making another shot. "The woman told me to stay away from her. She said I was a father figure that keeps popping up. She doesn't need another daddy. Can you believe that?" His mouth curved into a smile.

"Fuck, man," Paul laughed," "that's a bit harsh. And no, I don't believe what she told you. But trust me, Sage really likes you,

Nick-O. Sounds like a defense mechanism to me."

"You sure about that?" He sank another ball. "I know I made her feel something yesterday." He missed the shot and leaned against the wall, waiting for Paul to take his shot, thinking about her. The way she'd shivered from his mouth near her ear—the sound that had escaped her lips. He wanted to kiss her but didn't. Knowing her, she would have slapped him silly, or punched his lights out—well, would have tried to anyway.

"Nick, you know she's vulnerable. Her husband passed away two years ago. I saw that in the investigator's report," Paul said, hitting a ball, banking a shot. "She isn't the type of woman you usually date... short-term. She's the long-term kind," he said, making another shot.

Nick hadn't realized until now that he did pick shallow women who weren't looking for the long-term. They only wanted what he could give them materially mostly—expensive dinners, hotels, and gifts. The wine-me, dine-me, fuck-me type women. Sage wasn't like that. She was giving, kind, and loving. She didn't mind helping people—she had a genuine heart. The way she was with Nicki proved that. He'd been keeping his distance from women for so long that he'd forgotten all women weren't like his ex. However, she had a relationship with Parker. He had already gone too far yesterday.

"Thanks for reminding me," Nick grinned. "I do tend to go with the short-term type." He picked up his drink and threw back the last of it. "I think we'll call this game even, and we both contribute to our charity of choice."

"Cool, but we both know you had this game won," Paul said, placing the stick in the rack. "You might want to get your facts straight before you think about letting her go. I saw the paintings of her. They are some of your best work so far. Don't know why you won't do an art show."

"I don't have time for that. I'd rather focus on other things." Nick placed his stick in the rack, lifting the glass from the bar.

"Suit yourself. It's a shame to have all that beauty in the one room and not share it with the world." He drank the last of his drink. "I'll see you tomorrow, Nick-O. I have a date in an hour."

"Okay, see ya, and have fun." Nick took his glass and headed for the kitchen.

"Will do."

They aren't sure who killed the little girl's mother yet. So, you should be in the clear. But they have this cop living in the building. He's a detective. The kind that sneaks around, not minding his own damn business. He had this cocktail party two

142

weeks ago, inviting neighbors over—he wasn't gonna go. Fuck, no!

The man on the fifth floor was sitting at his massive dusty desk at Breckville Towers on a Wednesday evening. He was thinking about his old girlfriend—the one who'd been murdered. No one suspected him, and he was going to remain in the clear.

He'd met Gloria Fulton about a year ago at a bar on Fifth and Sixth Ave. on the westside of Bayville. He was out that night because he was angry with his folks. They wanted to introduce him to one of their friend's daughters. He didn't see the point of them meddling in his life. They hadn't done so when he needed them, and he wasn't interested in their friend's possessions.

Fifth and Sixth Ave. wasn't the best part of the city. It was called poor town. Mostly low-income people lived in that part of the city. MCC tried to come and help as many people as they could, but it wasn't enough. He applauded Cindy Robinson. The woman had spunk. She and her staff did the best they knew how to fix the problems for people who thought their lives were meaningless. Gloria seemed like a beautiful creature. She wanted too much from him in a short time though. He couldn't give her what she wanted, and she had that little brat, as well, and the one she was carrying to be his family. There was no way he wanted to be tied down with her and a baby, and some other man's brat. He recalled the argument they had.

"Gloria, I don't want to have children right now. I thought you agreed it was best we didn't." He frowned. *"How do you know it's mine? He stomped angrily across the room.*

"That was before I got pregnant, you asshole. And this is your baby. I love you," she cried. *"Why do you have to be like this? I thought you loved me."* She wiped her eyes.

"I do, and I'll love you even more once you get rid of whatever you're carrying." He smiled, coming over to her, caressing her cheeks.

"I'm not going to have an abortion," she roared furiously. *"I'll take care of this baby and Nicki all on my own. I can't believe you would treat me like this—like I'm your whore instead of girlfriend,"* she sniffed. *"I have to go. I'll see you around, I guess."*

He couldn't let her have that baby. Not his child. If it was his. "I'll call you later."

"Whatever, Max, you fucker," she screamed, slamming the door shut.

That was the last conversation they'd had. He had plenty of things he had to do with his own life. He still lived with his parents but basically had the apartment to himself. His parents stayed gone on business most of the time. He believed his father controlled every aspect of his mother's life—even when it came to him.

His mother never had time for him. He was only twenty-six. There wasn't time for him to have a family, let alone another man's child. He did get the chance to make Gloria feel special with his knife.

Max wanted to be a brilliant artist. Nick thought his work was showcase worthy. Nick wanted to connect him with one of the art galleries in the city. Max had seen some of Nick's work. Nick hadn't told him why he didn't want to showcase his own work. He had recently seen paintings of a stunning woman. Max wouldn't mind having a piece of that. She was his usual type, vulnerable with long, black hair, green eyes, and the body-build he preferred. He always picked women who, in some way, reminded him of his mother.

Those eyes, sexy high-cheekbones, bow-lips shining like rays of light, and that sexy hot-fucking body of hers had the power to make a man do things he wouldn't normally do if he wasn't careful. He believed Nick had fallen under her spell. He had to be with all the recent paintings of her. The copper was her friend—or boyfriend. He had seen her running from the copper's door earlier. Nick had also come out after she passed by his door. It was perfect timing when he walked out of his penthouse, heading out of the building. Thought he was going to go after her, but he changed his mind. He went back into his penthouse.

Max was online, searching for anything he could find on the copper. Nothing on him. Probably because he was a detective and preferred to keep his personal life private. Max thought if he knew something about Parker, he would have an advantage. He pushed up from the desk, paperwork flying everywhere, and went to his large room, where he kept his most valuable artworks. His work of his many women over the past. Well, that's what he thought. He lifted the covering off one, standing and admiring it. It was a painting he had done months ago of Gloria. He always kept this one covered. He didn't want anyone to find out he knew her. He kept her a secret from his parents and everyone he knew. She wasn't exactly parent worthy. She wasn't his equal. She was poor. Plus, she had that brat. If only you would have kept your mouth closed, Gloria, and had the abortion, you would still be here by my side. We could have done something great together. She was going to nursing school. She wanted to be an R.N. He wanted her to pursue her art career. He loved her work. In fact, he had some in that very room, he mused as he stared at the painting. He came back from his thoughts when he heard his doorbell. He covered the painting to see who it was. He guessed it was Nick. He only had one other person he considered a friend. However, Nick was more than that.

He was more like close family, and Max hadn't spoken to his cop friend in a while. His friend had assisted him in disposing of Gloria for a large sum, of course. He needed him to find out information about the copper in his building. Max came from his wandering thoughts when he opened the door; it was Nick.

"How's it going, Nick?" Max asked, inviting Nick in.

"Alright, Max," he answered. "Have you thought about what we discussed?"

"Sure, I've thought about it," he answered.

Maxwell Turner was an odd sort of guy who kept to himself a lot. He wasn't a social person. He only knew Nick because of his parents. They owned some stock in a few of Nick's companies. He was like a big brother to him. He looked up to Nick. He was an artist the same as him. Max admired how Nick took failing businesses and put them back together stronger and better. He was sort of like him. He didn't like being around a lot of people either. Not unless it was absolutely necessary.

"So, are you ready for me to make that call?" Nick probed again, taking a seat on the sofa. He wanted Max to do something with art, not take his talent for granted.

"Still thinking about it," Max said, going to the fridge, taking out two beers. He took a seat across from Nick, opened his beer, and took a drink. "I saw you earlier. I thought you were going to see what was going on with the girl. She's fucking hot." *Can't wait to paint her,* he thought. *Can't wait to get to know her. Can't wait for a lot of things—with her.*

Nick opened his beer. He could see that Max was interested in her. He had to act cool because this was a guy who saw him as family. He liked Max, but when it came to her, she was off-limits. She didn't know it yet, but she was going to be his. It was only a matter of timing. At least in his mind, she would be.

"Yes, she's beautiful. She was married once. He was killed in a car accident."

"Shit, that's fucking terrible. That must really suck for her. Was that why she was crying?" he inquired.

How in the hell did he know that? He must have been lurking around. I didn't see him though, Nick supposed. "I'm not sure, but her husband died two years ago."

"You know her, Nick?" Max looked at him curiously, drinking the beer.

"No, not really. Met her at the cocktail party," he burped. "You weren't there that night. Why? Everyone was invited. You would probably have had a good time."

"Nope, that's not my sort of thing. You know I don't do too well around a bunch of strangers. I like keeping to myself. I assumed you knew her because of the way you went after her when you saw her crying." Max's eyes glistened.

Damn, drop it! Nick thought.

"I was only concerned." He noticed the crazed glim in Max's eyes. "And I didn't go to her directly. Did you do another painting?" he asked, hoping to change the subject.

"Yep, I'm working on something. What about you? Do any more paintings of the mystery woman who you don't want me talking about?" Max grinned, showing uneven teeth. He was still a nice-looking guy with black preppy hair and gray eyes, and muscular six-foot frame.

"No, Max, and she has a boyfriend." Nick hated he showed the painting of her. Max had come over one day after he'd finished it. He snooped around his place as if he were looking for something. Wonder what? "He's the new tenant in the building. I wouldn't try to put any moves on her if I were you." Nick forced a smile.

"Not to worry, Nick. I wouldn't go after a woman you are interested in. Though she is much younger than you are. But I do understand why you want her, man. She's smoking hot."

"Like I said, she has a boyfriend. Aren't we going to watch the game? Or talk women?" Nick asked, picking up the remote and switching on the TV.

"Sure, Nick," Max laughed.

Parker went to Sarah's place after the heated argument with Sage. He couldn't believe she had aborted their child. Back then, he was a ladies' man and had hurt Sage in the process. He should have been a good boyfriend to her. Sarah had been trying to get him to go talk to Sage. She had been there for Sage through the whole ordeal.

"Park, you need to stop sulking. What Sage did was a while ago. Eight years to be exact. You have to forgive her and move on. She forgave you, remember?" Sarah urged. "You hurt her deeply back then. I was there when she cried herself to sleep because you cheated on her. You knew loyalty and trust meant everything to her." At this point, she was beginning to wonder if it was a good idea to be in a relationship with him. She knew what he had done to her best friend. Could she allow herself to trust a man like Parker even though Sage said he had changed?

Parker rose from the table, walking over to her. He took hold of her, bringing her up against his tall, muscular frame. He raised her chin to look in her eyes.

"I'm not the same man, Sarah, in spite of what you think." He kissed the corners of her mouth. She moaned from his touch. "I'm not that man anymore."

"Don't, Parker," she moaned softly, trying to move away from him.

"Baby, I love kissing you," Parker groaned. "Mmm, so mouthwateringly sweet," he sang, tasting her lips, suckling them with his mouth. He drew back, stroking her cheeks with his large hands, and stared into her deep brown eyes.

"Parker, I want to believe you. Sage was a mess after you hurt her. You were her first love. I was there to help pick up the pieces. It was her decision alone to abort the baby. It took her a month after finding out she was pregnant to figure out what she would do. She was scared, and the thought of her being a single mom terrified her, Parker. I'm sure you knew her home life, living with her parents. Her mother barely had time for her. She probably assumed she wouldn't be good at it either."

Parker released Sarah, walked near the kitchen window, and peered out. He had been a total jackass to Sage. He didn't know how much he had hurt her until now, listening to Sarah tell him what Sage went through because of him. He understood why she didn't want to take another chance with him after she got with Luke. But that was a lifetime ago. He wanted this beautiful woman, who was acting halfheartedly to be with him because she knew the man he once was. He cursed under his breath, running his hands over his curly brown hair. He faced Sarah.

"I'm going to prove to you I've changed, Sarah." He walked back to her, took her hands, and kissed her temples. "I must go see Sage. I had no idea that I hurt her so badly. I was a young idiot wrapped up in myself. I should have been better to her, and I wasn't. Not only did I lose her, it cost me our unborn child. I was a selfish, bastard." He squeezed his eyes shut for a second, trying to get rid of the image of Sage being alone, scared, and hurt.

Sarah stroked his jaw affectionately. "She's over it all, Parker. You have to forgive yourself and her." She tilted forward on her tip-toes, kissing his lips.

He took hold of her, seizing control of the kiss. His tongue entered her mouth, tasting her sweet liquid. He could kiss her forever. She tasted so, so, so good. He grunted, pulling away from her.

"I'll be back, baby." He dropped another kiss on her lips. "When I come back, be half-naked like I found you." A devilish smile curved his lips.

She shied away with a smile, moving her honey-blonde hair away from her face, biting her lower lip.

"Goddammit woman, you're so damn sexy. You know that." He grinned and walked out the front door.

Sage was in her study, working on one of her stories. It was ten-thirty, and she had put Nicki to bed around nine. She couldn't sleep, not after the day she had. She had finally told Parker about the child she aborted years ago, and now, he didn't want to see her. He'd kicked her out of his apartment. But what did she expect, she had kept a huge secret from him? And it would still be a secret if he and Sarah weren't interested in one another.

He'd broken her heart back then. Parker was her first real love, and she hadn't deserved to be cheated on. It had crushed her spirit. If she'd thought rationally back then, she might have had babies with Luke. Her life would be totally different. Her thoughts were interrupted by the doorbell.

Looking through the peep-hole, she saw Parker standing there. She was stunned to see him after he'd spoken so roughly to her. She opened the door, rushing into his arms for a big hug. He scooped her up off her feet, wrapping his arms around her waist, comforting her.

"Are you okay, Park?" she asked as he placed her back on the floor.

"Yes, baby. We need to talk." He stroked her cheek gently. "Where is Ms. Nicki?"

"She's in bed," she replied. "You want tea?"

"No, babe," he said, gripping her hand.

"Come on." She led him into the living room, where they sat on the couch.

"Sage," he whispered.

She turned to face him. "Yes?" she waited on him to say something.

He looked into her emerald eyes. He had always loved looking into those lovely eyes. He was upset with her, but he knew in his gut, it was his fault she broke up with him. It was his fault she aborted the baby. If he hadn't been such a big shot with the girls back then, their son or daughter would be alive. He should have been a better boyfriend and given her his heart completely. However, it was too late. What had happened back then couldn't be changed, and he understood that. After he calmed down and analyzed the situation, he realized it was partly his fault. Thanks to Sarah's help, he had to come to terms with it.

"Babe, I'm upset with you. You know that." He breathed. "I understand why you didn't tell me. I was an immature bastard. I'm sorry about that. I should have been better to you. I did love you back then. I know I carried on as if I didn't. I loved you, Sage. I wasn't ready to settle down with one girl. I thought being with you would change me. Me, being a selfish bastard cost me you and my unborn child," he stated harshly. "I guess I was so mad at you because I figured we would be together with a child. I know that isn't true. We weren't meant for each other. We are destined to be only friends." He cradled her cheek softly.

"Park, don't blame yourself for what I did. I alone aborted my child. I should have been stronger. I shouldn't have been so selfish. I destroyed a life, and I pray God has forgiven me. I hope you will forgive me. Don't beat yourself up about this, because it wasn't your fault." She squeezed his hand. "You have been a great friend to me. You can be a pain sometimes, but you have been there for me when I needed you. Thank you."

"I don't mind being there for you. You'd do the same for me, babe." He smiled. "We are there for one another. I know I had some part in your decision. I'll get over it. It takes time." He placed his large hand on her shoulder. "I'm sorry for going off on you earlier."

"Apology accepted," she uttered happily.

"Now, I have to convince your best friend I'm not the selfish bastard she thinks I am," he disclosed, disappointedly.

"Park, you have to change her mind about you. Look at the two of you," she said with a huge smile. "Who would have thought you would be into each other? Convince her you are a changed man. You no longer have the wandering eyes. She's the only one for you. If that's true, you'll figure out how to change her mind." She stroked his jaw.

"You're right," he said, getting to his feet. "I'm going to head out. I'll talk to you later." Parker kissed her cheek. He hoped she would find true happiness soon. He believed Nick was the man to make that happen.

Chapter 9

The last week of May went by quickly for Sage. It was finally June first, the night of the auction. It was held in the large conference room at MCC. There was plenty of good food, wine, and music for everyone to enjoy. Cindy wanted this year's auction to be better than the last. She was sure it would be as she looked around at her staff and volunteers, and all the work they had done. Cindy was pleased her friends, and some of the staff had agreed to be auctioned off.

A few of Bayville's finest also graced the crowd with their presence. Bayville's mayor was in attendance with some of the city's council leaders. A few members of the Rockfill Playhouse were there to put on a small show. The Bayville Boys and Girls Choir were in attendance to perform as was the Church Hall Band.

The hall was decorated like a beautiful ballroom with strings of fluorescent lights flowing across the room. The stage was decorated beautifully with strings of silk yellow, and a white tapestry ran across the high ceilings. A huge chandelier hung in the center of the stage area. It would be used to light the handsome men and gorgeous women who'd graciously agreed to be auctioned. The tables and chairs were decorated in an elegant, white silk cloth, and the chairs had yellow bows tied around the back of them. Candles glowed in glass votives, splashing a prism of colors throughout the room. Fresh cut flowers served as centerpieces. There were stylish plates, silverware, and napkins also placed on the tables. It was most definitely a place for big spenders tonight, and that's what Cindy and her staff wanted. Without the helping hands of these good people, MCC wouldn't thrive.

Sage was walking around, mingling with the guests. Her nerves were working overtime because she had to be auctioned off. She was trying to distract herself, but it wasn't working. Her Aunt Katie and Nicki were there. This was Nicki's first auction-ball, and she was so excited for Sage. To her young heart, Sage was a beautiful princess waiting to meet her handsome prince. Sage spotted her aunt and Nicki in a corner talking to one of Aunt Katie's friends. She also saw her neighbor, Mr. Vengo. He smiled and waved at her. She ran into Ron and Jenny Crawford and spoke with them for ten minutes before she saw Paul Writhers and stopped to say hi to him.

"Hello, Paul," she hailed.

"Why, hello beautiful," he said, kissing her cheek. "You look amazing."

"Thanks, so do you. Are you enjoying everything so far?" she asked.

"Yes. Cindy and her people outdid themselves," he complimented.

"You know Cindy?" She hadn't realized he did.

"I met her at the cocktail party," Paul answered.

"Oh, of course. Have you seen her tonight? I'm sure she would want to know a handsome man mentioned her."

"No, I haven't. Maybe I'll find her when things get under control." He saw Nick on his way over to Sage. "I'm going to head over to the bar. See you later."

"Okay, have fun."

Sage was about to grab a wine glass from a tray when suddenly, she felt someone take hold of her elbow. She turned and held Nick's blue eyes. He stood there looking like a million bucks. The man was dressed in an expensive tailored, black tuxedo with a white dress shirt and a black silk tie. His raven hair was combed toward the back of his head. *Wonder how much mousse it took to get it so perfect?* Even the few gray strands on his temples laid perfectly. His luminous white smile was flawless. *Shallow, arrogant bastard.*

He'd seen her from across the room talking to Paul. The gown she had on clung to her immaculate body taking his breath away. It was a shimmery red mermaid gown that had a slit coming up her thigh. It showed off her bosom and sexy back. Sage complemented the dress with a diamond necklace, earrings, and a bracelet on her dainty wrist. Her curly hair was in an updo hairstyle with few long, curly strands framing her face and nape of her neck. On her feet were a pair of shiny red stilettos. Her makeup was light. With her unblemished skin, she didn't need much. Her pretty lips were a glossy, reddish, beautiful glow. He was awestruck for a minute before walking over to her.

"Hi Sage, you look incredible." He had a grin plastered on his face.

God, could you wipe that goofy smile off your face? I can't stand him, she said to herself, hoping her body and mind agreed with her. "Hello Nickolas, you look handsome." She looked away, hoping to find Parker. He was busy making goo-goo eyes at Sarah. Well, the jig was about to be up if it already wasn't. "I didn't know you liked this sort of thing."

"I don't mind helping my fellow man." He continued to eye her warmly. "I think I commented it to you before."

"You might have, but Nickolas, if you'll excuse me, I have to go," she said, about to walk away from him, but he caught hold of her waist, pulling her back in place.

"Not so fast. Why are you trying to get away from me? I only want to talk. Is it so bad to hold a conversation with me?" He studied her.

"I didn't say it was, I..." She was caught off guard when he skimmed her cheek. She blinked. "I told you never to touch me," she said in a low, angry whisper.

He slanted down close with his mouth pressed against her ear. "Tell me why, sweetheart?"

Sage felt her body somersault. *What does he think he's doing?* He was being so disrespectful to her—making her body behave like a foolish schoolgirl in public. She wasn't having it. No way! No how! *Leave me alone! Shallow, arrogant bastard!*

She turned to walk away again but was looped back around. She was shocked. Mr. Wondaful was toying with her in a room where everyone could see. What the hell was wrong with him? Didn't he remember she had a boyfriend? Well, pretend boyfriend, who was occupied now.

Awe, Fiddlesticks! Universe, save me!

"Nick, I don't know what you are up to, but you had better back off," she growled.

Her aunt and Nicki approached them.

"Hi, Sug, who's this handsome man?" Her aunt smiled wickedly.

"Hey, Aunt Katie, that's the handsome prince. He's the one who was at the beach, isn't he, Ms. Sage?" Nicki asked.

Nicki had made matters worse. Sage didn't want to introduce her aunt to Nick. And when had she started shortening his name? Her aunt would only get the wrong impression about them because there was nothing going on between them. Boy was this bad timing. And Nicki outright gawking at Nick like he really was a handsome prince.

Nickolas decided to introduce himself. "My name is Nickolas Brimmer, but you can call me Nick," he announced, taking hold of Katie's hand, shaking it delicately. "I see where Sage gets her beauty from," he flattered.

Sage held back a low groan. He was making matters worse for her also. Her aunt was going to grill her later about him.

"My name is Katie Jennings. Sage is my lovely niece, and this is my pretty little niece Nicki," she said, patting Nicki on the cheek softly. Katie was happy that Nicki had inadvertently revealed something Sage was clearly trying to keep from her.

"Yes, I've met the little lady before. We met at the beach several weeks ago. And how are you, Nicki?" He kneeled to her level.

"I'm okay. I can't wait until Ms. Sage meets another handsome prince tonight. She's getting auction," she declared happily.

Nick rose with a broad grin. Katie laughed. Except Sage, who didn't find it amusing. She hoped he wouldn't bid on her for goodness sakes. She didn't want to have dinner with him. She didn't want to be alone in the same room with him. Nick was too old for her anyway, and he wasn't even her type. Luke was the exact opposite of Nick, and Luke was her type. He was a tall, handsome brown-skinned man. Why was she having these feelings for this Nick? Guilt was slicing through her like a sharp blade.

"Nicki, why don't we head over with your Uncle Parker and Auntie Sarah," Katie said. She could tell there was something going on between Sage and Nick and didn't want to intrude.

"You don't have to go, Auntie," Sage said, anxiously wanting her to stay.

"Say by-bye, Nicki." She took hold of Nicki's hand.

"By-bye, Ms. Sage," Nicki said, waving at her. "Bye, Nick." She waved.

"Okay, baby." Sage waved, wanting to take hold of Nicki's hand and leave with them. *Awe fiddlesticks*! Not fair, Aunt Katie.

"See you later, cutie," Nick responded.

"You know your eyes and mouth flutter when you're nervous, baby." Nick noticed, stroking her arm. "I know I said I wouldn't touch you unless you gave me permission, but I can't help it, love." *Yep, there's most definitely something between us. She can stand there and deny it. But I see it all over her.*

Sage crossed her arms over her breasts defensively, biting on her lower lip. She surveyed the crowd momentarily. Everyone was having a great time. Cindy was talking to Nick's friend Paul. She seemed to be engaged in a good conversation from her body language.

"I'm not your sweetheart, love, or baby, Nick. Don't call me that. I'm not interested in you." She shook her head at him. "You and I don't have anything to offer one another. Stop this cat-and-mouse game you're playing with me. I have to go and find Parker."

"I know he can't be your boyfriend because he's hugged up with someone else." He looked in Parker's direction, and so did she.

Well, the jig's up, Sage thought to herself.

"Baby, don't be afraid of me. Now that I know you don't have a boyfriend; it's going to be hard to get rid of me." He grinned boyishly.

She scrunched up her face. "Listen, you," she said incensed. "I'm not afraid of you. I want nothing to do with you, but you can't get it through your thick head. I've told you I don't need a daddy figure. Go find some other woman who'll let you have your way with her 'cause I'm not the one. You shallow, arrogant bastard."

He never thought himself to be a shallow, arrogant bastard—more of a suave, generous man with sex appeal. Nick pulled her up against him, her feet almost dangling off the floor. His face was so close to hers he could smell her sweet peppermint breath mixed with wine. She tried to twist away, but his hand held her face in his palm. "You know that's not what I am to you. Be honest with me," he expressed, staring into her eyes.

She chewed on her bottom lip. Her gaze fell to his chest. Absolutely, she understood. That's why she chose to try to ignore it. She heard the auction about to get underway. "I have to go." She wiggled unsuccessfully to free herself.

He held her briefly before lifting her chin meeting her eyes with his, then lightly touched her lips, watching her. Her eyes fluttered.

"I'll see you up there," he said.

Without a word, Sage hurried away from him, hoping he would leave her alone. She wasn't going to be a notch on his belt. He could forget about it. She had her dignity intact.

She found Cindy with the other women and men being auctioned off. Parker and

Sarah decided to pass on the auction. They would make their contribution to MCC in other ways.

"I can't believe I let you talk me into this, Cid." Sage was pacing back and forth, feeling like a mass of nerves. She could feel tiny beads of perspiration on the sides of her face—even her palms were sweaty. Sage needed a drink of water to quench her thirst.

"What's got you rattled?" Cindy asked suspiciously.

"Nothing," Sage fibbed. "I'm just feeling a little queasy, that's all."

"I saw you and Nick together. He's going to shell out the big bucks for you tonight." Cindy laughed. "And it's for a great cause. You can use a hot date in the process."

"I don't want him bidding on me," she shrieked. "Can you make sure he doesn't? Let him bid on anyone else but me. Please, Cid." Sage stopped pacing, taking her hand.

"You know that's impossible. Everyone is free to bid on whomever he or she chooses to. Sage, he's really a good guy. He has to be with as much money as he donates to us."

"Whatever, Cindy!" Sage snapped. "The man is a womanizer. A shallow, arrogant bastard. Do you hear me?" She pouted, throwing up her hands. "Fiddlesticks," she shot out.

Sage heard the auctioneer calling her name. She took in a deep breath preparing to walk out on the stage.

"Go make that money, honey," Cindy said teasingly, smacking her on the butt.

Sage rolled her eyes at her because she knew she was doomed to go out with Nick. When she was on the stage, men in the crowd whistled at her. She was a little intimidated by all the admirers but walked a model's walk on the catwalk, head held high with her hips swaying. She walked like she owned the runway. Sage couldn't see into the crowd because of the bright lights, which was fine with her. She heard the auctioneer spitting out numbers faster than she could account for.

The opening bid was ten thousand dollars. Did he say ninety-five thousand? She stood brightly, wondering what kind of men were at a bidding war over her besides the obvious one. The last number she heard him say was one hundred thousand. Going once, going twice, sold! The gavel hit the stand. She couldn't believe someone shelled out that much money for her. Her gut told her it was Nick. She walked off the stage, not knowing who won the bid.

Maxwell Turner made it his business to be at this event. Nick commented he was going to be there, so Max assumed she would be as well. He didn't know she was being auctioned off. He couldn't be in the bidding war over her. He wanted to but knew it wouldn't end well for him. He had been watching her most of the night. Every move she made, he was there. He couldn't believe he was in the same room with her, breathing the same air. His dick jumped in his pants with excitement. His desire for her was growing stronger by the minute.

He wanted to take her someplace quiet and rip that tight-ass dress off her hot-ass body, tie her up to his bed, let hot candle wax hit her gorgeous body, his hands slithering over her body, pleasing her every need for him—giving her what she wanted. Max wanted to take his special knife and slide it up and down her body, making him ejaculate. He knew for a fact Sage wanted this—wanted him. He caught her watching him a few times while talking to Nick, but she played it off as if she hadn't seen him. He wanted to walk over and snatch her away from Nick but was afraid of what Nick may think—them being like bros and all. She was the woman of his dreams, and he wasn't going to allow anyone to stand in the way of that. Not even Nick. He had to take his time and plan to show up in her life.

At the end of the night, Sage recognized one of her husband's colleagues from Randolph and Smitz. He was talking with Nick. Did her husband's law firm do business with him? She still didn't remember. It was possible. She shook the strange feeling, looking for Cindy. She would know for sure if Nick was the man who won her as a date, which would happen sometime within that month or next. She found Parker and Sarah sitting at a table and joined them.

"Hey, you two." She smiled at them. "You both need to knock it off," she said, laughing happily. "There is so much love around here, it makes me want to gag." She stuck her finger near her mouth. "I'm really elated for the both of you—earnestly. You make a wonderful couple." She touched their hands.

"Thanks, babe," Parker said, not taking his eyes off Sarah.

"I thought for a moment you and Nick were going somewhere to talk." Sarah turned, looking at her. "Anyone can see the man likes you. And you like him, also. I saw him pick you up off the floor."

"Whatever, chick. I don't want the womanizer near me. I want him to keep his distance from me. Do you know who won the bid for me?" she asked, looking at them.

"Ah, not really, Sage," Sarah said. "Sorry." She shrugged.

"We weren't paying any attention." Parker took hold of Sarah's hand, placing a kiss in her palm.

"I bet." Sage brushed the side of her nose. "I pray it wasn't Nick." She coiled to find Nick watching her, standing near her chair.

God, can I catch a break from this man? Look at him standing there, gawking at me like I'm a hot fudge sundae. Please tell me you didn't win me, she hoped.

"Hey baby, I'm your dinner date for whatever day you choose." He grinned, his tall frame hovering over her.

Fiddlesticks. Thanks a lot, universe.

"Didn't I tell you to stop that? I'm not your baby. I'm not your anything, Nickolas." She stood defensively, with her arms resting over her breasts. Her eyes blazed with anger.

"What's up, Parker?" Nick asked with a grin. He knew Sage wasn't dating for sure now. It was obvious Parker was with the woman his arm was draped around.

"Who's your lovely date?" Nick queried.

"I'm enjoying my date, and this is Sarah Jones Crawford," Parker spoke happily. "She's my girlfriend."

"Nice to finally meet you, Nick." She glanced Sage's way. Sarah could see Sage was uneasy with Nick in a good way. Sarah knew Sage really liked Nick and wasn't sure why her friend didn't want anything to do with him. The man was handsome, rich, and nice. Who cared if he was older? A very good combo, if you asked her. "How long have you known my best friend?" she asked, sipping champagne.

"Not long," he said, caressing Sage's cheek. She knocked his hand away rudely. "She's afraid of me." He winked at her.

Sarah and Parker watched Sage squirm in the presence of Nick. They were tickled to see a man make her react that way. Parker and Sarah exchanged a glance, knowing it would only be a matter of time before Nick and Sage were together.

"I don't fear you," Sage said, annoyed.

"Sage, may we speak in private? You and I need to talk." Nick wanted to pull her into his arms, but he realized right now wasn't the time.

Her aunt and Nicki came waltzing up to them before she could answer him.

"Sugar," her aunt drawled, "if you want, Nicki can spend the night with me. It's fine."

"I don't mind at all, Ms. Sage. You found your prince again," she said, looking at Nick. "I'm glad it was you, Nick," Nicki giggled.

Everyone laughed at her comment except Sage. Nicki was really trying to match her up with Nick. It was obvious Nicki was extremely naïve when it came to Nickolas Brimmer.

"Hey, Nicki and I are going to head home now," her aunt stated. "I'm a bit tired, and I know Nicki is, too." They both faked yawning.

What the heck were these two up to? "Nicki, are you sure you want to go home with Auntie?" Sage asked. Now she'd be out of excuses for not spending time with Nick.

"I'm sure." She walked over to Sage, who picked Nicki up, giving her a hug and a kiss on the cheek, then planted her back on the floor.

"No hug for me, Miss Nicki," Nick asked, kneeling to her level. She came running over to him and squeezed his neck. "Thank you, Nicki. You be good for your aunt. I'll take great care of your Ms. Sage." He stroked her head gently.

"Come on, Nicki," Katie said, reaching out her hand for Nicki to grab hold. "We'll see you tomorrow." She kissed her niece on the cheek, whispered something only Sage could hear, and then walked away with Nicki leaving her with Nick. She prayed Sage would give the man a chance.

"We're about to head out also, Sage," Parker said, helping Sarah with her shawl.

"See you later," Sarah said, embracing her. "Have fun. You deserve it," she whispered close to her ear. "Get rid of the cobwebs." Sarah guessed Sage's aunt had probably spoke something similar in her ear. Sage made a face at her.

"Later, babe," Parker said, and the pair were gone.

Everyone had abandoned her with a man she understood was a womanizer. She cursed mentally. Truthfully, Sarah was right, as was her aunt. Sage needed to have some fun. If sex was his game, she was interested tonight.

"Well, let's go to your place," she said, sashaying her body. "I'm sure this is what you are after." She moved closer to him, standing on her tiptoes and muttered in his ear. "Pussy," she coaxed.

Nick felt his main vein jump at the word. She was making a bold move. He couldn't believe she was being this straightforward with him. He wanted more than her body. She was a woman he saw himself settling down with. She was thinking of a fling, perhaps. But those weren't his intentions. He wouldn't tell her that now because he didn't want to frighten her off. She was already flighty. He grabbed her around the waist, carting her close to him, escorting her out of the building. He opened the door of his silver F-Type SVR Jaguar, allowing her to enter. Then he joined her on the driver's side.

"Buckle-up, sweetheart," he smiled over at her. "It's going to be a bumpy ride," he joked mischievously, pulling off quickly.

Max watched as she got into the car with Nick. He wanted so badly to take her from him. But, how could he? She didn't even know he existed until that brief eye contact earlier, giving him the green-light that she desired to know him. He'd spent the entire evening stalking her. "But she will know me very soon," he vowed with a wicked gleam, looking in their direction as Nick was racing off the parking lot.

In the car, Sage sat with one hand gripping the seat and the other gripping the door. Her feet were positioned as if she could stop the car herself. Perspiration was beading on her forehead, and her palms were sweating bullets. She presumed her heart was moving with the sports car's speed. She prayed he would slow down the beast.

Nick glimpsed over at her. He saw fear on her face. He was being insensitive. It had slipped his mind that she'd been involved in a deadly car crash.

She was holding onto the seat and the door as if her life depended on it. He should have known she was terrified of speeding. Not that he was speeding. He was only doing sixty, but in her mind, he was probably doing ninety.

"I'm so sorry, sweetheart," he apologized, touching her face lightly, slowing down the Jag.

Sage touched her forehead, wiping away some of the sweat, thanking the universe the man slowed the contraption down. Her body began to relax. He had some jazz music playing.

"I like jazz," she said softly, looking straight ahead.

A smirk creased his mouth. She was relaxed. "Good, we both have that in common." He glimpsed at her, then back at the highway. "I also like pop, soft rock, and R&B."

"I do also, and I like to listen to classical music. It helps me when I'm working on my writing." Oh God, she told him about her writing. She didn't mean to. He was so damn easy to talk to.

"Oh? I didn't know you were a writer," he said, continuing to look ahead. Nick was glad she was opening-up to him. "Are you a published author?" He gazed at her for a moment, then turned his eyes back on the road.

"I didn't mean to tell you that," she spoke nervously, playing with a loose strand of her hair. "But no, I'm not published." She bit her bottom lip.

She was so sexy, sitting there teasing him, playing with her hair and biting her lower lip. He wanted to pull over and experience the sweet pleasure of her lips. "I'm glad you did. What do you write?"

"I write mystery stories, but I've been dabbling in the romance department. I haven't experienced any in a very long time." *Stop opening yourself up to this womanizer. He doesn't deserve to know a freaking thing about you,* she chastised

175

herself. *Don't forget you are with him for sex only. Remove the cobwebs as Sarah suggested. Have fun like auntie said. You don't have to get to know him.* "This isn't the way to Breckville Towers," she realized, changing the subject, shifting toward him.

Nick noticed she'd redirected the subject. He would bring romance back into her life, along with everything she'd been missing and more. "No, this is the way to my house. You're safe. Nothing to worry about. I won't let anything happen to you, sweetheart."

His eyes raked her entire body for a second. That slit up her thigh was so inviting. He wanted very much to run his hand up and down her softness, then let his hand dive between her thighs, exploring her sweet spot. He turned his attention back to the highway. He couldn't wait to get her naked and worship her body.

"Did you ever do business with a law firm by the name of Randolph and Smitz? I saw you talking to one of my husband's old colleagues," she wondered, looking his way only a moment. She got the feeling he had.

"Yes, I've done business with them. I still use their services sometimes." He hoped her knowing that wouldn't matter.

"Did you work with Lucas Sullivan on anything? I don't remember him mentioning you."

"Yes, I did a few times, but we didn't get to know each other. It was strictly business." He trusted having worked with her husband hadn't scared her off.

And there it was again, the guilt, cutting her up into tiny pieces. How could she be considering being with him? He worked with her husband. It didn't matter they didn't get to know each other. What was she thinking, getting into the car with this man? She'd seen him... what... four times at most? And now she was going home with him. She shouldn't be thinking with her body. Hell, she hadn't had any in a long while. DICK. It had been so long; Sage didn't know if she could still perform. Way too long.

She looked his way. He was so handsome for a white guy. She hadn't been with one before, even though her dad was white. Sage favored the brathers. Nick would be her first white man. She was probably his first chocolate candy, she mused, smiling to herself. She was about to find out what it was like to be with a white guy.

She continued to stare at his profile. Running her finger across her bottom lip, then slightly touching her tongue over her bottom lip. She was getting turned on watching him. She darted her eyes out the window when he angled his eyes on her for a moment, then back on the road. *You need to stop, girl,* she thought. *Are my panties damp? Damn.*

Nick could sense her eyes on him. He hoped she was as worked up as he was. She ran her finger and tongue across her lips. God, he couldn't wait to taste them. Her for all that mattered. Her glorious sexy body. And she was all his. This Beautiful Goddess. *Where have you been?*

He pulled up into his long, winding driveway on the outskirts of the city. Nick didn't come out to the house often. It was huge and made him acutely lonely. The house had seven bedrooms and five full bathrooms, and that didn't include the living room, dining room, kitchen, study, library, and a few other rooms. He'd planned to sell the place but decided not to. He purchased the house after his divorce with the intent of living there, but he and Paul bought Breckville Towers. He decided to stay in the penthouse instead and use this house when he wanted complete solitude.

Sage was impressed with the massive house. She guessed how many wild parties he'd thrown there. It was lovely in its majestic stature. The grounds to the front were well-manicured with different varieties of flowers and tall trees. The trees appeared to be over a hundred years old. She could see herself living in a place like that. Wait. What the fudge?! What the hell was going on? Was she thinking marriage? No way! No how! She dismissed the thought.

Nick turned the motor off, shifting somewhat to look at her. He could tell she loved the house. She hadn't noticed his hand on her thigh until he glided it upward. He had startled her.

"Sorry," he apologized. "You ready to come inside?"

His words had a sexual tone to them. Or was she horny as hell? Her body was way overdue for a tune-up. "Sure."

He got out and opened her door. She slid out, taking her handbag from the seat.

"This place is huge and lovely," she remarked, eyeing everything, trying to take it all in.

"Thank you. I bought it a few years back. I don't really stay here." He took her hand as they walked to the door. "After Paul and I purchased Breckville Towers, I decided not to move in completely. It has furniture. We won't be sitting on the floor." He smiled at her, brushing an errant curl from her face, holding her close to him. He had to find out at that moment what her lips and mouth felt and tasted of. He took hold of her face.

"Sweetheart, I need to kiss you," he groaned, taking her mouth.

The kiss was sweet for a few seconds, but when she opened and gave him entry, it became fiery. A burning desire overcame them like a forest fire consuming all the oxygen in the air. They both groaned and moaned each other's name. Two cosmic stars coming together to form one body. He had to stop. He couldn't take her like this. He wanted their first time to be in bed. His bed. He needed to explore every sweet inch of her body. He pulled away from her.

He ran his hand over his jaw. "You are so deliciously sweet. I want you desperately," he groaned.

Sage blushed, nibbling her lip.

"Damn, sweetheart, stop looking at me like that. Sucking your lip before I have them again." He hurried, taking the keys from the electric box, and opened the door, allowing her to walk in.

Sage let herself become taken entirely by him. She couldn't control the damn thing—her body. It reacted to him like he was the owner, but her love died two years ago. Her temple had belonged to him, and she had shared it with no one except him. Now she was enjoying this. Whatever 'this' was. She let his kiss over-power her. She moaned for more without shame. She wanted him—every beautiful muscle of him. She was disappointed when he backed away.

Sage stepped inside, forming the letter O with her lips. It was even more impressive inside. The high ceilings and marble floors in the foyer, the two magnificent staircases coming together in the center. This was a house ready to be extoled.

"I thought you didn't live here?" She strolled inside, eyeing everything, stopping at the staircases. "You made it seem like the place was completely empty."

She laughed nervously. She didn't understand why she was anxious about him. Wasn't she betraying Luke? Just being with this man was a betrayal. Thinking all those damned naughty thoughts for the past several weeks was a betrayal. God, help her—she wasn't sure how to step away now. She couldn't seem to stop outside the house. She would have given herself to him right outside his door if he hadn't bagged off.

He moved like a lion stalking his prey. She was so stunning, and she didn't know the power she had over him. His hands trailed down her delicate spine, slowing, resting on her perfect butt.

She was edgy, standing there, with her hands resting about her waist. Her body a bundle of nerves, eyes blinking almost incessantly, and her lips on fire.

"There is nothing to be uneasy about, sweetheart," Nick assured, towing her away from the stairs. Hell, if he were honest, he was nervous too. He was with the woman who overrode his thoughts daily. What was going to happen when they shared each other's bodies? He began to take the pins out of her hair, letting the curls shape her lovely heart-shaped face.

"Sage, I have one question," he requested, removing the rest of the pins from her hair.

"What is it, Nickolas?" she breathed.

"Do you mean for me to have you? Do you want me to make love to you? Us making love?" he asked, staring at her intensely.

"Yes," she crooned. "God, yes," she sighed.

Chapter 10

Nick lifted Sage off her feet without warning, carrying her up the winding staircase to his bedroom. He couldn't believe he was about to have this woman. The woman he thought was out of his league because she had a boyfriend. The woman he thought was disgusted by him and wasn't. Tonight, he would make sure she was his. No other man would ever satisfy her.

He opened the door to his huge bedroom and set her down near the bed. He caressed her face with his large hands staring into her eyes. "I love looking into your eyes." He kissed her eyelids, then made his way to her ears, speaking softly in what sounded like French.

His tender kisses were churning something inside of her body that she couldn't contain. She moaned, moving her hands to explore his chest, tugging at his shirt, and pulled it out of place. Sage had to admit, she wanted this man regardless of the age difference. It was out of her hands with the way he was making her feel. Desire burned all over her body—a flame only he could extinguish.

Boy, did he have a sexy physique. She felt his muscles contracting as she moved her hands over his chest. Nick groaned under her sweet touch. He unzipped her dress as he kissed her slender neck and eased it off her shoulders.

"Baby, I need to see you," he whispered, his voice coarse with desire.

"Nick, I want to see you," she said in a soft whisper.

"Then let's help each other out of these confinements," he grunted.

Sage stepped behind him, boldly running her hands slowly up his back, then taking hold of his suit coat.

"Take it off," she commanded. Nick did as she instructed while Sage moved around him, observing his sex appeal. The man was a striking Greek statue that made her mouth water. Running her tongue over her lips, she demanded he remove his shirt. He tossed it with his suit coat.

"Does that work for you, love?" he asked.

"No, the t-shirt needs to come off," she commanded, enjoying the control. It was turning her on even more. She lauded his broad bare back a few moments before coming around the front. His abs contracted as she traced them with her fingertips.

"Nick, do you know how sexy you are?" she asked, gazing into his eyes. What she saw was pure desire. It frightened her because it wasn't Luke. She was about to step back, but he caught her waist, drawing her in. She coiled away from him.

"Look at me, Sage," he said in a raspy voice.

She curved slowly, looking up at him. Yes. It was still there in his blue gaze. She was entirely alone with Mr. Wondaful. What had she been thinking coming out here to his house alone? She didn't know him. All she knew was her body ached to be with him. Her eyes dropped to his chest. Nick lifted her chin, placing tiny kisses at the corners of her mouth.

"Sweetheart, I know this is scary for you. It is for me, too. I haven't given myself fully to a woman in a very long time." He kissed her mouth slowly. Seductively.

Sage moaned from his intoxicating kiss. She wished she could believe him but didn't. He was a player when it came to the opposite sex. She wasn't about to let herself get caught up into feeling anything for him. It was sex—pure and simple. The man she truly loved was gone. She wasn't here looking for love, just some fun, and sex. She had to keep reminding herself that he was a s*hallow, arrogant bastard.* Deep down she understood it wasn't absolutely true.

"Nick, I'm here to have sex. That's it. Nothing more. The man I loved died two years ago. After tonight, this won't happen again. I won't allow it," she asserted.

"Then we'll make this a night you and I will never forget," he said, lifting her off her feet, taking her to the bed. He removed what remained of his clothes. She had to admit, the man was going to be hard to forget, but she didn't need this whatever it was—not now. Only SEX.

Nick slid the dress off her body discovering she wore red lace underwear. He stared at her perfect body with its lovely curves. She was breathtaking—his beautiful goddess. On this night, he would make sure of that, no matter how much she tried to dismiss what was happening between them.

He climbed on the king-sized bed, spreading her legs wide. He kissed a trail of kisses from one thigh to the other. She moaned softly, looking at him while biting her lips, and resting on her elbows. He settled his head between her thighs, inhaling her sweet feminine scent, and moved her panties to the side. He ran his long tongue up and down her pussy. Sage cried out from the pleasure. Her head fell back, eyes rolling back into her head. She had forgotten how good it felt to have a man between her legs. Nick looked up at her, knowing this was his PUSSY—and he imprinted his name there.

"I'm going to love you, wanting you to come back for more and more," he declared, continuing to glide his tongue over her sweetness, tasting her. He moved her folds, taking hold of the kernel of flesh with his mouth, sucking it and licking it, loving on her intimate jewel with his hot mouth. She cried out loudly, laying down, relishing what he was doing to her. She took hold of his head, letting him know not to stop.

"Oh gwad," she cried.

Nick wasn't going to stop anyway. He was enjoying this as much as she was— tasting the juices ejecting from her hot core. He fed on her greedily, not leaving anything untouched.

"You taste so damn good, love," he grunted.

Sage panted his name holding onto his head. He placed a finger inside of her, moving it in and out as he licked and sucked on the clit.

"Damn Nick," she hissed. She was lost in this sensual feeling. This feeling she hadn't felt before. What was he doing that she hadn't known? Not even with Luke. He had done this to her, but something was different with Nick. How was she going to forget this—him?

Her eruptions exploded like a volcano. He was licking, sucking, swallowing all of it. He withdrew his head, removing her underwear. He pulled her to him, released her bra, removing it from her soft skin. Her gorgeous breasts were free for him to suckle, taste, and caress. He gawked at them for a moment. She had breasts women paid plastic surgeons for. They were perfect. His head went to them, taking his time, indulging each one. Sucking, nibbling, licking the brown buds. Sage was moaning and whimpering from the deliciousness of his mouth. She wanted very much to have her way with him.

After he released her breasts, she was now finally in control. She pushed at his chest to get him to sit down on the bed. She ran her tongue on the outside of his ear, tracing it slowly, making him grunt and finally into the ear, whispering sexual rants. "I don't know any French, sweet darling," she said against his ear.

He loved the endearments she whispered sexually. "No... need, baby," he roared loudly, enjoying the sensual pleasure.

She moved gracefully to his large neck, peppering wet kisses down the length of it. She didn't stop until she reached his muscular torso, then licked and sucked his pink nipples. He watched and groaned as she moved her pretty mouth over his chest, her beautiful round ass cocked up in the air for his enjoyment. She took hold of his shaft as she kissed her way between his strong thighs, planting a few kisses there. Then she ran her tongue up and down his shaft, sampling him like her favorite ice cream. Nick was thick, long, and wide.

"Mmm," she teased. He groaned deeply. She continuously licked him wet, then took him deep down her throat. His growl thundered, loudly calling her name, clenching his teeth. He didn't know how much longer he would last. The muscles in her throat clamped around him, causing him to jerk up, pulling her to him. At the rate she was going, he would have exploded. He couldn't tell she hadn't done this in a while.

"Not fair, Nick," she said, licking her lips.

"I know, baby. I can't last with you doing that." He breathed heavily and took a condom from the nightstand.

"Allow me." She took the condom, sliding it onto his erection. "Go easy with me. It's been a while."

"I won't hurt you," he promised, kissing her deeply. He ran his finger between her folds, making sure she was nice and wet. And she was. He slid inside of her halfway at first, still kissing her, making sure she was ready to receive him.

She held back a cry deep in her throat when he entered. It was a good pinch at first. She wanted this man to go into her deeply. She kept reminding herself this was the only time and last time for them to be united—their bodies one flesh. She better enjoy every moment.

She placed both her hands on his nice round-built ass, giving him permission to enter her deeper. He obliged her, pushing himself slowly inside of her, feeding her inch by inch until he was completely inside. She received him, grabbing his butt harder. His thrusts were slow at first. He looked down at her to make sure he wasn't hurting her, then began to roll his hips thrusting inside of her faster. She was moaning and moving her hips with him.

She ran her hands up his wide back, enjoying the movement of their bodies—his powerful form moving above hers. He was deep inside of her feeling her latch onto him. God, this glorious goddess—his goddess. She expected him not to want this. Not want her. She was fooling herself if she thought that was going to happen.

He stopped his movement, flipping her onto her stomach, her nice round butt high in the air for him, head held down, and her hands stretched out in front of her. He bent down slightly, running his tongue up and down her pussy, stroking her, tasting her for several moments. Then he went back inside of her, thrusting into her, making her moan out his name. He smiled with the satisfaction of knowing she did belong to him. He pumped harder and faster, moving his hips, giving her more of what she wanted. He groaned her name thunderously when she held onto his manhood tighter. She could feel herself creaming on him.

"Don't stop, Nick," she panted. "I need this. I need you," she whined.

And he didn't until they both released in heavenly bliss. He laid on her back momentarily, then moved, taking her with him. He removed the condom, tossing it into the trash. He positioned her on his chest, holding her close to him, placing a kiss on her forehead. He heard soft snoring sounds escaping her lips. *She snores.*

How had he let himself become so consumed with her so quickly? He had made the mistake once allowing himself to get involved with a woman. Why was he doing it again? Hadn't he learned already? Wasn't his previous relationship enough backlash? He remembered the headlines on the TV news and the internet. *"Business Tycoon Brutally Beats an Innocent Man."*

He couldn't go to certain places because some people bought into it, making him the bad guy. The media hadn't reported the complete story. He wondered if Sage had researched him. He hoped to God she hadn't. Nick wanted that part of his life left in his dark past. He pulled her closer to him, moving her curls away from her face, kissed her lips, closed his eyes, and joined her in dreamland.

Nick woke early with an erection. Sage was lying with her ass pressed against him.

He began to kiss her neck, coaxing her to wake. She climbed on top of him, riding him, pleasuring them both. When she felt her orgasm shredding through, she cried out in pure delight, her candy rain oozing down him like a warm shower.

He held her in place, moving her hips, filling her up. When he felt her gripping him, he soon found his explosion ripping out of him. He grunted her name loudly. She laid her head down against his chest, enjoying his heartbeat. He rested his hand on her back, caressing it.

"Sweetheart, I can't let you go. You have to know that," he whispered, running his fingers through her hair.

She didn't respond because she knew he didn't have a choice. This was the only time he would have her. She needed to have sex with him—well, it took more than once—so she could get him off her mind, once and for all.

Nick had fallen asleep again. Sage eased out of bed, not wanting to wake Nick. She washed up quickly, then called a cab before he noticed she wasn't in bed. She knew it was wrong of her to leave him like that, without saying goodbye, but it was for the best. It would only make the situation worse if she woke him. He'd already stated the obvious to her—he couldn't let her go. Sage was trying to make it easy on them by quietly slipping out. She looked over at Nick sleeping peacefully. His chest was moving up and down as he snored. She moved silently out of the room, closing the door lightly, and hurried down the staircase and out the door.

She'd had sex with him. *God, how could you? You are Luke's girl. His wife only. Fiddlesticks! You performed like you were his. And yet, you slept with him. More than once*, she berated herself.

She was in front of the house, walking along the driveway, regretting having slept with Nick. *I should have just gone home.* She closed her eyes, covering them with her right hand in shame. "*I'm so sorry, Lucas,*" she whispered. She uncovered her eyes when she heard the cab coming.

Nick reached over to pull her close, but she wasn't there. "Sage," he called, moving toward the bathroom. He had a feeling she had gone. She had left him without saying a word. He put on the robe that hung on the back of the bathroom door and went downstairs swiftly. He heard a car pull up outside. He opened the door quickly, however, she was already inside the car before he could stop her. He yelled out her name, but the cab sped off, leaving him standing in his driveway.

"Fuck," he cursed angrily, going back inside, slamming the door shut. The woman acted as if he were a piece of meat. She took what she wanted then disposed of him. He was angry with her for leaving. They needed to talk about this. He wasn't imagining their feelings for each other. She was running scared of him. But he was afraid of his feelings for her, as well. He wasn't running; his arms were outstretched for her. He wanted to give her all of him. Nick knew she was different from the woman he had married. She loved one man and had given herself to that one man. Until death did them apart. He wasn't about to give up on her.

Nick went into his studio and uncovered the nude painting he'd done of Sage weeks ago. He gawked at it. *"Sweetheart, I'm not letting you go."* He ran his hand over the face of the painting as if it was her. He had a chance to see her again. Alone. He was going to make sure there was no way for her to run and hide. He had won her at the auction. He would make a date with her that she would never forget. He turned on his heels, walked out of the room, and slammed the door in frustration.

Sage heard him yell out to her and told the driver to move quickly. She knew he would only try to stop her. She wasn't about to let him sway her into staying. She didn't need him in her life. He was a one-night stand. That's what she wanted—nothing more from him. No strings attached. Her priority was Nicki, and Nick would only be a distraction. He wasn't meant for her. He wasn't her type. Neither was she his according to the websites. He was a father figure. Okay, a sexy father figure. A shallow, arrogant bastard she'd slept with. Certainly, the sex was the best she'd ever had. So, what?

After the cab dropped her off, Sage took a shower, letting the warm water wash over her, erasing the memory of last night and early morning. She grasped it was going to be hard. The man had worked his magic over her body, and it seemed to come alive for him. Sage's body had betrayed her—the damned traitor. It behaved like he was the key-master to her body and soul. At his command, he could unlock her body, making it do whatever he desired. That was the way it had behaved last night and in the early morning hours. She ran her hand over the glass, wiping the steam from the window. How was she going to get over him?

Sage stepped out of the shower, dried herself off, and rubbed her favorite lotion on her skin before glancing at herself in the mirror. *"I won't give into him. Not again."* She talked to her body as though it were listening. She prayed it was.

Sage picked up Nicki later that day. When she arrived, she hadn't expected her father to be at her aunt's house.

"*Fiddlesticks, fiddlesticks!*" she muttered harshly. She had to calm down. The blood in her body was at a boiling point. Her head felt like someone was sticking needles in her temples. The last time her aunt tried to make her connect with him, it hadn't ended well. Sage wondered why her aunt was doing it again. But this time, Aunt Katie had involved her daughter Nicki. Sage wasn't going to make a scene in front of Nicki. What did her aunt expect from her when it came to her father? He had the nerve to show his face. Here and now.

"Nicki, I want you to go into the kitchen. Your aunt and he need to speak to me in private." She pointed at her father like he was a total stranger.

"I didn't do anything wrong, did I?" She looked at Aunt Katie then at Sage's father.

"No, sweetie. We grown folks need to talk. I'll give you some grapes while we talk." Sage took hold of Nicki's hand, leading her into the kitchen. She eyed her aunt and father severely as she and Nicki went to the kitchen.

After she had given Nicki a snack, she made her way back into the living room. She heard her father and aunt whispering as she approached. Their words were vague. Sage stood silent for a moment. Her blood was still boiling, but her head was clear. Still, she couldn't believe her aunt had him there with her daughter. Even though Nicki was joyfully talking to him, he had no right to be near her daughter.

"Why have you come?" Sage asked, glaring at him.

"Sage, I need to tell you something. I need to speak to you both. I need to tell Lora, too." He looked at her aunt briefly before turning back to her. "That's why I came to your aunt's house. We need to talk," he said, looking at her, wanting to give his daughter a hug, which he doubted would happen.

"Cooper, you and I don't have squat to talk about," Sage spoke crossly. "You and I haven't had a respectful conversation since my mother's death. I don't know what could be so important to make my aunt break her promise to me."

"Please, don't blame your aunt." He tried to stroke her arm, but she rebuffed him.

"I know my aunt has a soft spot for you, and so does my sister Lora. I'm not going to allow you to worm your way into my life or Nicki's. That child has been through enough."

Katie came over and took Sage's hand. Whatever her father had to say was serious. She could tell by his appearance. She hadn't noticed when he came over a few weeks ago, but he looked thinner. His eyes appeared tired and had deep, dark circles. She hoped that he wasn't about to tell them he had a life-threatening disease.

"Sug, I think you need to listen to your father." She stroked Sage's cheek tenderly, helping her to calm down.

Sage slowly looked her father's way. He was worried about something. She hadn't really paid attention until her aunt came over to her. Her aunt looked nervous for what he was about to say. He said he needed to tell her sister and aunt, which meant it wasn't good.

She began to watch her father, who had aged a little more than she remembered. He had more gray hair and wrinkles around his eyes, though he was still a handsome man. He wasn't like she remembered him when she'd last seen him. That was before Luke died. She remembered she was out having lunch with Sarah. They were at Bay Ray's Vegan Shack, checking the place out. At the time, it was a new restaurant near the beach district.

Her father and husband hadn't spotted her that day, and Sage had made sure of it. She observed them from afar. She could tell they had been getting together for a while without her knowing. Her husband had gotten to know his father-in-law. She never mentioned it to her husband. Now, looking back, she was glad her husband didn't listen to her when it came to her father. He was her only living parent. To make it easy for him to tell her, she moved next to him, taking his hand.

Cooper was surprised his baby-girl took hold of his hand. Was she trying to show him love? Love he hadn't been privileged to experience from her for a long time. It was refreshing not seeing hatred coming from her.

"Sage, two years ago, I had colon cancer. I thought I had it beat," he declared. "Baby-girl, I went to the doctor for a routine checkup. It's back."

Sage looked at him, dismayed. She couldn't believe what he was saying. Was he trying to be cruel because she had been for so long? This couldn't be true; he wanted to reconcile.

He's making it up!

"I can't believe you would make this up. How can you be so mean?" she asked brittlely. "You want to reconcile with me so badly that you would actually make this up," she said, shaking, with tears stinging her eyes.

Cooper took hold of her, comforting his little girl for the first time in a very long while.

"Baby-girl, I'm not making anything up. I love you, and I wouldn't hurt you like that. I'm telling you the truth."

He glanced into the eyes of disbelief. She didn't want to believe him. He could understand why. She'd lost her mother years ago, and she was now afraid of losing her father—the man she'd hated for so long.

The one parent she had left in life was telling her he may die. Could he beat cancer's butt again? Only time would tell. Time could be a cruel, mean, evil bastard.

Katie was shocked at his declaration, as well. She figured it wasn't good. But cancer? She had tears in her eyes. Cooper was the brother she loved dearly. Even after her sister's death, she'd remained close to him. She knew her sister's death was an accident. She hoped her niece would now come to her senses and let her father into her life again. She wrapped her arms around them both.

"He's lying, Auntie," Sage said again, raising her head, looking at her aunt. "He's lying," she repeated harshly, sobbing, not wanting to accept the truth.

Katie grabbed her niece and hugged her tightly. She couldn't believe it herself. Cooper had cancer once before and hadn't told anyone. She knew it was true. She looked his way as she was comforting her niece. He had a painful expression on his face. She knew something was wrong with him, but she didn't think it was cancer.

"I know this is hard, Sugar." She caressed Sage's back sadly. "We'll get through this—us as a family. Your father needs us all," she soothed, watching Cooper, reaching for his hand.

Sage released her aunt and went into her father's arms. She raised her head, staring at him for a long moment, then laid her head on his chest. Her father wrapped his loving arms around her with tears in his eyes. He knew this was only the beginning of their reconciliation—sorry it took the big "C" to make it happen.

Chapter 11

Sage was in a funk at work on Monday morning after hearing the devastating news about her father's cancer. She hadn't wanted to accept it even going so far as to say he'd made it up—anything to say it wasn't true. She had heard of people getting sick and losing loved ones from the deadly disease, but it hadn't hit home for her until now. Her father had dealt with the illness before, and he hadn't let the family know. He must be dying. A feeling of dread washed over her. Sage closed the blinds in the window facing the busy cubicles outside her office. She knew she wasn't going to be able to help anyone for the next several days, perhaps even weeks, so she cleared her schedule. A soft knock came at the door, drawing her back from her thoughts.

"Yes," she answered.

Sarah came in and closed the door. Sage hadn't told anyone about her father yet. She was still gathering her head around the situation herself.

"Okay," Sarah said, taking a seat in front of her desk. "Tell me what Nick did? If he has done anything to hurt you, we'll kick his ass."

"Thanks," Sage said sadly, moving away from the window, taking a seat at her desk. "This has nothing to do with him. As a matter of fact, that was a one-time thing."

"Come on, chic-a-dee, don't leave me in a loopy-loopy. I want to know what happened."

"I had great sex with Mr. Wondaful," Sage reported as she looked up from a file she'd been reading. "I told him we wouldn't take it any farther. Hopefully, he is okay with that." Sage knew the man wasn't going to be thrilled about it. For goodness sake, she'd slipped out like a coward. It was only a matter of time before he confronted her.

"Sage, he's into you, and you are willing to pass him up?" Sarah asked, shaking her head in disappointment. "I know you are still having a hard time dealing with Luke's death, but you need to move on, honey. He isn't coming back. You must love again. You need to find a way to come to terms with his death. The only way to do that is to start dating. Open your heart up to someone else," she emphasized.

"Haven't I heard this before? How can you say that, Sarah?" Sage clenched her teeth, tears swelling in her eyes. She didn't know if they were for Luke or her dad, or for both.

Sarah placed a gentle hand on Sage's shoulder. "I want you to be happy, Sage. You haven't been in a long time. Really happy. I saw the way you and Nick looked at each other. There is no mistaking the passion between you two. Luke would want you to find love again. He wouldn't want you pining away. Your house is a shrine to Luke. Sage still have a lot of his stuff. I don't mean to sound cruel, honey. I love you. I look at you more like a sister than a friend."

Sage turned, giving her a hug. "I found out yesterday my father has cancer—colon cancer," she sighed heavily.

"Oh my God," Sarah said sadly. "I'm so sorry, Sage." She patted her back.

Sage and her dad were estranged, but now was the time for her to be with him. He was all she had left.

"When are you heading to Phoenix? I know you have a problem with him, but right now, he needs you," Sarah said.

I'm not sure when I'm leaving. I'm still trying to wrap my head around this. My dad dropped this on my aunt and me yesterday. I still can't believe he's been dealing with this, and he didn't tell anyone. He had it two years ago. It was in remission, but he had a check-up recently, and now it's back."

"You'll get through this—you and your family. He will survive this a second time, and it will be the last time in his life." Sarah spoke positively, hoping she was right. A lot of people lost their lives to cancer.

Sage raised her head, somewhat smiling. Her friend, her sister, was right there speaking words of encouragement. "Thanks, Sarah, I love you, chick. You have always been there for me when I need you."

"You do the same for me. That's what we do." Sarah pointed to her, then at herself.

"Yep," Sage smiled widely, feeling a little better.

Nick's mind wasn't focused on the meeting. He was totally preoccupied with Sage, replaying Friday night non-stop. The love they had made that night and early morning. The woman left him early Saturday morning as if nothing had happened between them. What they shared wasn't a one-time thing, but she acted like it was—slipping out of the house without a word. He was still angry at her. He hadn't gone to see her yet, giving her a bit of space. Maybe she needed that to see where her head was at with him. After all, she was afraid even though she claimed she wasn't.

This was new territory for her with a different man. She felt so good next to him. The love they'd made was extraordinary. Being with her was something he hadn't experienced with any other woman. The way her body naturally responded to him, and the way he responded to her instantly, making him want to give her all of him completely. They fit like the moon and the stars in the night sky. They fit together like two missing pieces of a puzzle becoming whole.

He was so lost in his thoughts that he didn't hear it when Paul announced the meeting was adjourned. He sat, inactive, in the chair, with his arms resting on the armrests, and his hands in front of him, touching at the fingertips. Paul tapped his shoulders.

"Yes, that sounds great," he said, coming back to reality.

Paul laughed, shaking his head. "Man, she has your nose wide open. The meeting is over. You were so zoned out," Paul said, packing up his briefcase. "The entire meeting."

"Sorry, I heard some of it," Nick smiled, standing. "Did anyone notice I was out of it?"

"Not really, Nick-O. They were more like you, wondering when the meeting would be over. Probably wishing you all had 'wrap it up' tattooed on your foreheads. Don't worry about it. Staci took notes for you." He picked up his briefcase. "You want to go to your office and tell me what's going on?"

"Sure," Nick sighed loudly.

"Hold all his calls, Staci, unless it's Sage," Paul instructed as he went into

Nick's office. "Now, what's going on with you and her?"

Nick sat in his seat, looking at Paul perplexed because he didn't know how he was going to get the woman he was falling for to be his. She gave her body to him freely, and now she wanted nothing.

"She doesn't want to have anything to do with me. She's afraid of me... her feelings for me. She stayed the night with me on Friday."

"What I saw on Friday night was bound to hit the bed-sheets and continue Saturday. I told you she liked you. Well, more than likes you," Paul grinned. "You slept together."

"Sage doesn't want anything from me. Nothing is what she's offering. She snuck out Saturday morning without waking me. Like a scared little girl. I woke to find her speeding off in a cab. I guess she does see me as a father figure in some way." He pushed up from the chair in frustration, moving toward the window.

"Wow, you really did a number on her," Paul noted with laughter.

Nick turned to look at him. "This isn't funny, man. I'm glad you find my situation funny. Ha, ha, ha, the joke's on me for falling for a woman who sees me like a daddy."

"I'm not making fun of you, Nick-O. It's obvious she cares a whole lot more than she wants to, and she doesn't see you like a daddy. If that were the case, she wouldn't have anything to do with you, much less have slept with you. She pulled a tip-toe move on you. Think about it."

"Yeah, I have. I haven't spoken to Sage since she ran out on me on Saturday. I'm trying to give her the space she needs to figure out her feelings."

"You shouldn't give her space. My advice is to strike while the fire is hot. Go after her, Nick. As you said, she's scared."

"I will. I need to make a few calls." Nick indicated urgency, looking at his wristwatch. He had a meeting with Gaines and Blackwell at three, so he had time to go see her.

"I'm on my way out. Talk to you later," Paul said and left.

After making a few calls, Nick left the office. He would go to Sage. He wasn't sure if it was such a good idea to go to her office, but he was willing to take a chance. He wasn't going to sit back and let her get away. Paul was right—strike while the iron was hot.

Nick arrived at BPCS twenty minutes later. He wasn't sure if Sage was in, or if she was, would she see him? It was a risk he was willing to take. He parked his Jaguar and walked slowly, rehearsing what he would say to her. He took the elevator to her department. When he arrived, he happened to run into Sarah.

"Nick," she smiled, surprised to see him. "Hello, you here to see Sage?" That was obvious. She was glad he was. Her best friend needed this type of excitement in her life. She observed the women gawking over him—eyelashes batting flirtatiously. He was a handsome specimen.

"Hi, Sarah. Yes, is she in?" he asked, looking around, noticing the women staring at him. He was used to the attention from women, but there was only one woman's attention he wanted.

"Sure, she's in her office. I'll walk you over," she offered. She hoped Sage wouldn't be too mad at her for escorting him to her office. She knocked on her door lightly.

"Auntie, I know. I'm going to talk to Lora after I get home today. I'm going to head out to see him as soon as possible. I'll have to speak to Martin about giving my caseload to some of my coworkers." Sage heard a soft knock coming from her door. She glanced up to find Sarah.

"Aunt Katie, I'll talk to you later. I must go. I love you." She hung up the phone, waving Sarah in, not realizing she had someone else with her.

Sage stood when she saw Nick standing at her door with Sarah. She took off her glasses, placing them on her desk. She wanted to leave her own office. What was he doing coming to her workplace unannounced? This wasn't acceptable on any level. This was her workplace and she didn't want her private life in the office, though he wasn't a part of her life, and she wasn't asking him to be either.

"Isn't this a surprise? Nick's here," Sarah disclosed.

"Fiddlesticks," Sage cried in annoyance. Sarah was behaving like she had won a grand prize or something. "I can see that, Sarah."

Nick smiled at the word 'fiddlesticks.' He thought it was cute the way she used it. He could see she was angry with him, and he found her reaction to his presence cute. But this was on her. Showing up unannounced was the repercussion of leaving without even a good-bye. Her running out on him as if nothing had happened—as if he hadn't mattered. Which he hoped he did. It would hurt like hell if he didn't matter. He was falling fast for her.

"So, I'll just leave you two alone," Sarah grinned, closing the door.

"Nick, what the hell!" Sage walked from behind her desk, heels clicking on the floor.

Nick strolled over to her, keeping eye contact. She was doing her best to intimidate him, but it wasn't working. In fact, she was turning him on. She was wearing a yellow pantsuit that fit her hips and flared loose at the legs complemented by white opened-toed heels, and a low-cut silky white top. She wore conservative jewelry—a small white pearl necklace with earrings to match. Her hair was in a high ponytail with several loose strands. She smelled of an enchanting vanilla perfume. She was a beautiful ray of sunshine. Nick wanted nothing more than to lift her off her feet, bring her close to his hard body, and wipe that fuming expression away entirely.

"I came to see you, baby." He cuddled her face gently. "I'm mad at you."

Sage couldn't tell he was upset with her. Her eyes fluttered at his touch. His hand felt good against her skin. She hadn't consciously responded to his touch—her body was betraying her. She cursed silently, recalling her guilt of sleeping together. She tried to get out of his grasp but couldn't. She was trapped.

He stood directly in front of her, pinning her in with both hands on her desk. He stared into her confused eyes; a smile touched the corners of his mouth. He knew she had feelings for him, and she wanted to keep them hidden.

"Sage, you left me without so much as a word Saturday morning. I was hurt. You ran out like what we shared was nothing— that it meant nothing to you. I know you saw me come outside to stop you." He continued to stare into her eyes.

"Of course, I saw you, Nickolas," she said, still trying to get out of his reach. *Good Lord, must you stand this close to me? Fiddlesticks!* What did he expect her to do? She told him that it was a one-time thing they'd shared, but here he was standing there, looking so goddamn hot. Freaking Mr. Wondaful in his black, tailored suit, white dress shirt, and burgundy silk tie. On his wrist was his stunning Rolex. His perfect hair was in place as always, and he smelled of a woodsy type of cologne. He was good enough to eat. Sex appeal exuded from the man. His hard body was blanketing hers, making desire build up fast inside of her.

"Nick, stop," she whimpered softly. "What we shared was lust and sex. That's all it was to me. My love died two years ago. Don't you get that?" she cried.

"Sage, love, I know you desire this as much as I." He groaned, moving close to her ear, muttering in French. He began to kiss her earlobe, taking his tongue tracing her ear, taking her lobe again. He pulled her off the desk, lifting her close to him, her feet dangling off the floor. "Sweetheart, I ache for you," he said softly in her ear.

"Just stop, Nick," she snarled, feeling the physical response he'd created, wishing he didn't affect her or her body. No number of long showers would get rid of him. But she needed to avoid him. She wasn't going to give her heart to another man. It would only end with her suffering. "I want nothing to do with you. Why can't you leave me alone? I left that morning hoping you would get it. We come from two different worlds." She squirmed to get away from him. "I don't want to get involved with you. We had sex. Okay, great sex. I owe you a dinner date. That's it."

He gazed into her eyes. She looked away from him. Her mouth said no, but her body was giving off signals all on its own. She couldn't deny it. 'Us,' for long.

"Why would you tease me like that?" he asked, turning her face back in his view, taking her lips, kissing them gently, causing her body to relax against him.

She began to kiss him back greedily as he did her. Their tongues danced and glided together in a scorching, lusty rhythm. Her head swirled, and her heart flickered for this beautiful man, as he continued to subdue her body wholly with the mind-blowing kiss they shared.

Nick had to pull back from her. Lord knew he didn't want to. He watched her for several moments. She wanted him. He rested against her desk, bringing her between his strong legs. She twisted away from him.

"Don't, sweetheart," he exclaimed, taking his large hand moving her face back. "Look at me," he asked in a hoarse tone. "Yes, this is happening. It's real, Sage." He nibbled at the corners of her mouth.

She wasn't about to be one of those women he bought his expensive gifts for, and then be tossed away like trash. She had her dignity. She had made love with him, and that was all she needed. She wished her body would respect her wishes—comply and behave.

"You aren't my type, and I'm most certainly not yours," she gestured with both hands. "I prefer men of a darker hue, and I certainly don't want a man much older than me," Sage said, hoping to hurt his feelings. Maybe then he would go. And stay away this time.

"Sage, no matter what hue you or I am, we both feel something for each other. I know what I feel when I'm with you." His hand touched her cheek. He wanted to say it was love but didn't want to risk losing her altogether. She tried to hurt his feelings bringing up their age difference and skin tone. Preferable, she didn't want a man of his color, but fate said differently. She may have been with darker hues in the past, but now she was with a much lighter tone.

"Yeah, lust, Nick. Lust. That's the feeling. I lust for things all the damn time. We had sex. How many times do I need to say it? Now that is over. You need to let it go," she reiterated, trying to move away.

Nick's hold tightened around her waist. He saw a future for them. He'd claimed her and her beautiful body two nights ago. He began to trace the outline of her face with his large index finger, and then traced the outline of her full lips, causing a soft whimper to escape her. He kissed her briefly, causing her mouth to open for him, but he didn't take her offer. He brushed her face tenderly.

Sage was disappointed when he didn't kiss her. She shied away from him as he followed her with his hot blue gaze. She moved away from him when they heard a knock at her door. *Saved in the nick of time,* she thought.

"Don't be so thankful to get away from me, Sage," he spoke as she strolled away from him, watching her body movements, wishing they were alone in his bedroom.

She didn't respond to his comment. She opened her door to find Cindy. Fiddlesticks! She knew Cindy would want to know what was going on between her and Nick. "Hi, Cid." She moved aside to allow her to enter.

"Hey Sage," she answered, stepping inside her office, surprised to see Nick.

"Hello, Cindy," Nick said with a smile. "How's it going at MCC?"

"Hi Nickolas, it's going really well. We raised so much money on Friday night," she declared radiantly. "I see my friend and my favorite donor have hit it off. You two

figuring out where to go for your hot date?"
She zoomed in on Sage.

"Nick was on his way out," Sage said,
moving toward Nick, motioning with her
hand to show him out of her office, and
hopefully out of her life. But somehow, she
knew that wasn't the end of it.

He leaned down, uttering French in her
ear, causing her body to jolt with pleasure.
"Sage, you did want to go out this Saturday,
right?" he asked, then moved close to her
ear again. "Our conversation is far from
over," he murmured. He had to move
quickly. Strike while the iron was hot, he
thought.

"Sure, Nickolas," she breathed, casting
him a frown as they walked toward the door
together.

"Until Saturday night, sweetheart," Nick
said then kissed her cheek before leaving.

Cindy stood with her mouth open in
shock. She was extremely astounded.

"You gonna tell me what I just walked in
on?" she asked, grabbing Sage's arm,
pulling her to a seat in front of her desk.

"Cid, you didn't walk in on anything
'cause nothing happened." Well, that wasn't
fully true, but Cindy didn't need to know
that. She missed the lip action between her
and Nick. The lip-action Sage shouldn't
have indulged in. She still loved Luke, and
her body wouldn't behave. Perhaps, she
needed to tell it what a *shallow, arrogant*

bastard he was. Maybe a gazillion times a day.

"Be real, Sage," Cindy said. She remembered how Sage had acted on Friday night at the auction. Nick had her totally rattled. And she'd left with him Friday night to remove the cobwebs. Sarah had told her about the cobweb part. "The man just kissed you on the cheek, calling you his sweetheart. Now, I know a man doesn't do all that for nothing. It's something. And you wouldn't allow it either."

"I'm not getting involved with a womanizer. For all I know, his wife left him because he cheated on her. Did you read what happened? The man almost killed another guy, and he only got a slap on the wrist. Money can buy freedom," she returned, moving behind her desk. "I shouldn't have allowed myself to fall prey to him."

"I'm sure there is a good explanation for what happened. He's too kind. He gives to charities. My charity for one. Everything on the internet isn't true, and you know that."

"I'm not getting hurt by him," Sage countered defensively. "He's been with too many women this year alone. He buys them expensive gifts when he's done with them. What kind of bullshit is that? He's a player, and I'm not about to fall victim to him or his shenanigans. So, can we drop it?"

"Okay, Sage. Let me know how that date goes." Cindy smiled like the Cheshire cat.

"Whatever," Sage said, shaking her head. Fiddlesticks! She did have a date with him on Saturday. She moaned, dropping her head on her desk, recalling her conversation with her father yesterday. There wouldn't be a date, thankfully. Not because of her father's sickness, but because she wouldn't have to see him.

"What is it?" Cindy asked.

"I found out my dad has colon cancer. I told Sarah about it earlier." She raised her head off her desk.

"Sorry to hear that, sweetie." Cindy got up from the chair, stroking her shoulder. "Aren't you going to be with him? I know you told me how you felt about him. He's your father."

"Yeah, I know, and I'm going to go be with him through this. At least for a little while—my sister and me." Sage thought about her father, wishing it was only a dream. She still loved her father, no matter how hard she tried to distance herself from him.

"Your father is going to beat this. I'll keep you all in my prayers. Let's go get lunch. I came to take you and Sarah both," Cindy said, trying to get her mind off things.

"Okay, sure, let me get ready while you go get her," Sage said, tidying up her desk.

"Sure thing, we'll meet you in the parking garage." She was out the door on her way to get Sarah.

Sage sat thinking about Nickolas Brimmer. He wasn't a good fit for her. He came with too much mess attached. Then her mind went to Luke. He was the love of her life for the past six years, and for three of them, she'd been his wife. He—her husband—killed on their third-year anniversary. She had always regretted that night. Admitting the pregnancy and abortion had sparked a very heated conversation between them. One that ended with a loss of life, pain, and suffering. And Nick wanted her to involve herself in him. Not happening. She had one date with him, and that would be the end of it. She got up from her desk and headed out the door.

Chapter 12

Max was on a plane, thinking of ways to open communications with her. Ever since he'd seen her running from the building that day, he'd wanted her. She was the most beautiful woman he'd ever laid eyes on. Max had tried to get more information out of Nick about her, but Nick hadn't given Max any. More than likely, Nick wanted her himself. But he was way too old for her. Max, on the other hand, was her peer.

He'd managed to learn that Sage had taken in Gloria's young daughter. What was her name again? Oh, that's right, Nicki. He'd noticed the little girl at the MCC gala. Max didn't want to be tied down with someone's brat, but if he got the chance to be with Sage, he was willing to make an exception. He did that with Gloria until she got pregnant and wanted to have it.

There was information on the internet about the auction at MCC. It showed Nick and her together, and they somehow seemed intimate. Was this a new fling for him? The post read, *"Nickolas Brimmer on the Hunt Again."* He only used women. He never wanted anything serious with them, excluding the marriage he had once had. Nick had played the field since his divorce. Max wasn't about to let Nick defile Sage, making her one of the expensive hoes he threw away when he was done with them.

Max understood Nick's motives—he'd caught his ex-wife fucking a man in his bed. He didn't trust women any more than he could see them. However, his woman Sage wasn't going to be on Nick's menu. Max had to do something to get Nick out of the picture. And he had. He'd made sure Sage read the post written about her and Nick. That would get him into her life after Nick was out.

He had a wicked smile on his face as he sent the post to her anonymously. She would think a jilted woman had sent it. Max sat beside her now, wanting to touch her. She smelled so good, like fruits and wild-flowers. Her curly black hair was tied up in a high ponytail and swayed when she moved her head gracefully. She had on a brown, short-sleeved floral top with a blue skirt. It stopped a bit up her thighs. On her feet were a pair of brown loafers. What lay between her legs was pure pleasure. There was no doubt about that. His eyes rolled shut, thinking about tasting her.

On Wednesday morning, Sage was on a plane heading to Phoenix to be with her dad. Martin had given her all the time off she needed. Her aunt would keep Nicki until she returned home, which she was very grateful for.

Sage prayed her father would pull through. In fact, she'd been praying hard to the universe these days, for a miracle. Her sister Lora had arrived in Phoenix Monday morning. Sage was seated next to a guy who couldn't seem to keep his eyes off her. She opened her laptop and began to read some of her emails. She saw a photo of her and Nick from a post someone had sent to her. She suspected it was from one of the women he had broken up with. It read: *"Nickolas Brimmer on the Hunt Again."* She closed her eyes, wishing it wasn't her in the photo. God, if only she had done the right thing. She had slept with the man. The best love-making of her life. A terrible mistake on her part.

Sage recollected how he'd wormed his way in her world, looking at her across the way at MCC with those sexy ocean-blue eyes. *Shallow, arrogant bastard.* If only she had been smart, but she'd listened to her body. The damn thing seemed to want her mouth and legs open for him. Her body wanted Nick.

The bastard would only hurt her if she allowed him in her life. That's what he did to women. His ex-wife didn't want him. He had beat a man almost to death. She should be running scared of him. If she were smart, she would be away from him. No date was essential. She smiled, rationalizing she didn't have to go out with him Saturday—or ever. She opened her eyes to find the guy next to her, still eyeing her like a creep.

"Is there something I can help you with?" she asked, wanting to know what his problem was.

"I noticed that's you next to the man in the picture. My name is Maxwell Turner," he extended his hand to her.

"Sage," she said, shaking his hand, momentarily.

It felt so wonderful holding her hand for only a brief moment. If only he could bring it up to his mouth to kiss, taking each finger into his mouth, sucking them one by one. "Is he your boyfriend? He seems kinda old for you." He smiled, showing a small gap between his uneven, white teeth.

"Not that it is any of your business, but the man in the photo isn't my boyfriend."

The man sitting next to her wasn't bad-looking. He was attractive with a black hair cut in a preppy style, and his beard matched his hair. He had round gray eyes and was probably six feet. He had a runner's form.

"I only presumed because he was standing way too close." He shrugged his shoulders.

She looked at the photo again. Anyone would think he was her boyfriend the way they were standing. The man was close enough to kiss her. He was making moves on her in public. At the time, she hadn't realized it because she was hypnotized by him. *Goddammit! He isn't my boyfriend,* she thought.

"He's too old for me like you said." She smiled slightly. She deleted the email of her and Nick, continuing to check her other emails.

"So, you headed to Phoenix or another stop when we land?"

Max knew she was going to Phoenix to be with her father. He'd eavesdropped on a conversation she had with Parker the day before. Max had been conveniently in the hallway. It was his lucky day.

She glanced at him peculiarly. He was getting a bit too personal. "I'm going to see my father. What about you?" she queried, noticing he was dressed like a businessman.

"I have business in Phoenix. I'm looking to acquire some art."

He also knew she fancied good art. It was another way into her life.

"Oh, you are a collector or an artist?" She was intrigued.

"I'm both. That's why I was looking at you. You have great bone structure. I would love to paint you," he said, gazing at her.

Sage blushed at his compliment. She patted her face, grinning. "Thank you."

"Is it possible you and I could get drinks while in Phoenix?" he asked.

"I don't think I'll have the time. My father has cancer. That's why I'm heading there." She turned away sadly, looking at her laptop.

"I'm sorry, Sage. I hope he gets better." He touched her arm, sympathetically.

"We are all hoping, wishing, and praying," she sighed.

"Well, perhaps I could take you to an art gallery to cheer you up. I'll be in Phoenix for a few weeks. I'm sure you'll get away for a little while. You should see some of Phoenix while you are there." He smiled sheepishly, eager she would accept his offer. He expected he wasn't coming off too anxious for her.

She thought for a moment before answering. He seemed like a good enough guy. And she loved art. She would need some time away from the center while they performed the surgery. She needed to keep her mind off Nickolas Brimmer as well. It was a risky move, but art was most definitely something she loved.

"Okay, maybe. Once I'm settled in." She moved a strand of hair away from her face.

"I'll give you my business card." Max was glad he'd had them printed up. It made it appear he was an authentic art collector.

Sage took the card, placing it inside her laptop case. "Thanks, Max. Sorry, you said your name is Maxwell, right?"

"Yes, but you can call me Max. All my friends do." He was fond of the way she'd shortened his name, making it come off her tongue so personally. Like they'd known each other a long while. "What treatment center will he be in?"

"Barridge Cancer Treatment Center. I'm meeting my family there soon as I get off the plane," she explained, looking at her cell phone. She had a missed call. She unlocked and saw the missed call was from Nick. "Excuse me a moment." She listened to the voicemail he left.

Hi sweetheart, I wish you had told me about your dad. I found out from Parker. We have more in common than you think. Call me as soon as you get this. I miss you.

The message sounded as though he thought they were a couple. They weren't. Sage was supposed to go out with him on Saturday, and that plan had changed. She was going to call and cancel when she was in Phoenix. Since Parker informed him of her whereabouts, there was no need to call him.

"Was it bad news?" Max asked.

"You could say that. Someone left me a message I hadn't planned on hearing from."

"Oh, it's good I'm here to cheer you up," he smiled broadly, making a funny face.

She giggled loudly. Some of the passengers looked their way.

Nick wondered why Sage hadn't bothered to tell him her father was sick. He had come to see her on Monday afternoon, and she hadn't mentioned it. He knew what it was like to have a parent suffering from cancer. He'd lost his mother to the lethal disease. Still, he couldn't understand why she was so willing to dismiss what had happened between them when he couldn't seem to forget their night together. It was etched so deeply in his mind that it invaded his dreams—her beautiful, naked body obeying his every command. He woke up with an erection each time, then took a cold shower to calm his body. He had better stop thinking about her now before he needed another cooldown. His phone buzzed, bringing him back to the moment.

"Yes, Staci," he answered, pressing the button.

"Mr. Royce Pierson is here to see you."

"Thanks, send him in, Staci."

"Sure, Mr. Brimmer," she complied, releasing the button.

"What brings you to our neck of the woods?" Nick asked, standing, reaching across his desk to shake his hand.

"Just checking in. What's up with you?" Royce inquired, taking a seat.

"I'm well. How about you? You still have the same girlfriend?"

"Yeah, things with Alexis are going well. I really like her. I hear you are in love, my friend. She has you whipped." He laughed.

Nick chuckled. "I see you have been talking to our buddy Paul. Yes, I have strong feelings for her. I'm still figuring us out. She doesn't want to give us a chance."

"Why is that?"

"She's scared of me. The way we are when we are together." Nick propped his feet on his desk. "I'm trying to get her to change her mind. I think a lot of it has to do with her husband."

"Have you thought about telling her what happened in your marriage? I'm sure she's read what the internet has said about you. Have you seen the latest post? You are with her, but the headline is making you out to be a player. Imagine that, Nickolas Brimmer, a player," Royce joked, laughing. He knew his best friend was far from that.

Nick hadn't gone onto social media looking for any news about him. He presumed the vultures had stopped posting about him. His life wasn't full of glamour. In fact, he thought he was boring. He'd read a recent post about him and Sage. Damn. She must have seen it. He cursed aloud.

"The public loves dirty gossip. Nobody wants to hear the truth. They slandered my name after my divorce, making me out to be the bad guy." He ran his hands over his head. "I know Sage has seen this," Nick said, handing Royce a bottle of water. Another reason for her not to call him.

"Thanks, Nick. You know how these rags are. They twist things around. You need to tell her about your past."

"Yeah, I know I should. Do you remember what happened? I mean, I don't want to make her afraid of me that way."

Nick didn't know how he would tell her the truth about his past. He was ashamed of what he had done to the poor man. He could be behind bars for what he had done. He was indebted he wasn't.

Royce noticed Nick contemplating the idea of telling her. "Man, just get it over with and let the chips fall where they may. Stalling isn't going to work. Thanks again for the water. Nick, if you care that much about her, tell her. I'm going to go pay Paul a visit before I head out. Think about what I said."

"I will." Nick got to his feet. "I just hope she doesn't run away from me totally when I tell her the truth."

"She won't." He smiled, heading to the door. "According to Paul, you both have it pretty bad for each other."

"Bye, Roy." Nick smiled, waving him out the door. Royce laughed.

Sage was a little tired after the plane ride to Phoenix. She went to her father's house to freshen up before going to the cancer treatment center. Max had been a good companion on the plane after all. He had kept her mind off her present situation, talking about art, music, theater, and ballet. She couldn't believe they had so much in common and was feeling better about spending time with him tomorrow.

She and Luke had shared some of those same things. Like art and music. Lucas was a sports nut, also, which found her learning the games. Basketball and football were his top two. She looked forward to the outing tomorrow with Max. Her dad would be in recovery around that time, so it would be perfect timing for her to get away. She planned on spending time with her sister and father after their meeting with the doctor today. She prayed his surgery went well. She and her sister would get together tonight to catch up on girl talk and old times.

She took a cab to the center around 10:00 a.m. Phoenix was a scorcher with the hot, muggy air. Sage was glad she had put on a pink summer dress that stopped right above the knees with flip-flops. Her long, curly hair was in a high ponytail. She wore only a touch of makeup, accenting her eyes with eyeliner and lip gloss. When she arrived at the center, she looked up at the large structure for a few seconds. She prayed the place could heal her father of his cancer. The inside of the facility wasn't at all how she'd pictured it. It didn't resemble any hospital she'd been inside of. However, the place was a treatment center. It looked like an oversized living room with nice furnishings, large flat-screen TVs, beautiful artworks, and sculptures. The flooring was made of mosaic tiles, with a large chandelier hanging in the center of the high ceilings. This was only the receptionist area, so the rest of the place had to be better than this. She was impressed with the ambiance.

She checked her cell and saw there was another missed call from Nick. He was a very persistent man. She didn't anticipate giving into him no matter how he persisted. Sage deleted the message, not bothering to listen to it, and dialed her sister.

"Hi Lor, I'm in the reception area. At least, I think I'm in the right place," she said, looking around. There were a few others in the area drinking coffee or tea, reading books and magazines. It was like something from an old English movie.

Lora laughed at her comment because she thought the place was extravagant, too. "I'm on my way to you. Dad can't wait to see you."

"Okay," she said, ending the call waiting on her sister. This was the first time she would be in the room with her father without hating him. Several minutes later, her sister appeared in the reception area.

"It's good to see you, Sage," Lora greeted with a warm smile as she hugged Sage.

"I'm excited to see you." She released her, looking her over. "You look wonderful."

"You don't look bad yourself," Lora teased. "Come on, let me take you to our Daddy," she said, holding her hand, swinging it back and forth.

"Does he really want to see me, Lora?" Sage paused, chewing her bottom lip. She'd treated her dad awfully for a long time. She'd been playing the 'what if' game for a while, even with her husband's death. If her father had kept the information from their mother, she would be alive. Her dad was selfish. He could have taken what he had done to his grave. It was his choice to cheat on her. She knew her mother worked long hours. She didn't spend enough time with them. However, that wasn't an excuse for him to cheat. She was sure her father was very lacking in that situation. Parker reminded her that her father had always been there in her and her sister's lives. Her mother was always making excuses for why she couldn't be there. She was hoping one day that would change. But it wouldn't happen after she died in the car crash. That was another reason she hated her dad back then. He had taken that away from her. Hope.

"Yes, he wants to see his favorite girl." Lora touched Sage's nose favorably. She saw a worried look on her sister's face. "Sage, he's going to be alright. We will have more time with him." She placed her arm around her sister's waist.

Sage smiled at her dimly. "I'm praying we do, Lora."

Lora hugged her. "Come on and see Dad. He's really missed his little girl."

Sage stood in the doorway of her father's room as her heart pounded hard in her chest. The thought of losing him was surreal. Tears swam in her eyes. She wanted him to be there when she married again and had children someday.

Wait, married again, with children. I can't even birth them.

She didn't know where that had come from. Lord knew she hadn't been thinking about it either. Her emotions were making her think crazy thoughts. She had a daughter. Nicki. She would adopt her eventually. She walked into the room, advancing toward her daddy, who had tears in his eyes. They embraced each other. It was a very tearful reunion. They released each other, smiling, taking a seat on the sofa. Lora left them alone to talk.

"This place is so nice," Sage said, touching the sofa.

"Yes, I guess they want to make people like me as comfortable as possible." He touched her face, making sure she was real. "I'm so glad I have both my daughters here with me. Baby-girl, I know you and I have a long way to go before you can forgive me."

"Listen, Daddy, I need to forgive you. I'm sorry it took me knowing I might lose you to realize it." Tears rolled down her face. "I love you, Daddy, and I don't want you to die," she cried. "We've lost so much time that we can't get back. I was stubborn and angry. I shouldn't have been angry with you, but her," she sobbed.

Cooper pulled her in for a hug to comfort her. This was his baby-girl, his favorite. He loved both his daughters dearly, but Sage was his pick. Lora was her mother's. He was still shocked she was here with him. He prayed the surgery would be a successful one. He wanted to make up for the time lost between them. He wanted to get to know Nicki. He wanted to be there for her when she remarried and had children of her own just as he'd been there for Lora.

"I love you more. Let's let the past go and move forward with the present." He kissed the top of her head. "I'm not going to die. I'm going to fight this hard. We'll get through this. I can't wait to hang out with both my daughters in three weeks or so. You are staying for the next three weeks?" he asked with uncertainty.

"Yes, Daddy, I'll be here. Aunt Katie and Nicki may come for a quick visit." She released him, smiling into his green eyes. She hadn't realized she missed her daddy so much. His green eyes smiled back into hers. It was good to have him back.

"I look forward to their visit. I can't wait to see that little girl of yours again." Cooper was glad his daughter was open for change in her life. Luke had been the love of her life for a while. Now she had Nicki, and with any luck, she'd find another man to give her heart to.

Chapter 13

A week later, Sage went out on another adventure with Max. She enjoyed the preoccupation while her dad was in recovery. She'd been able to clear her mind for a short period of time and not focus on the worst-case scenario about her dad and from thinking about Nick.

She thought about Nick too much as it was, so she'd decided to hang out with Max again. She didn't want to call it a date because in her mind it wasn't. They were two people hanging out and enjoying each other's company. She didn't want her dad or sister thinking it was a date either.

Her father's surgery had gone as well as expected. Everyone was thankful for that. He was recovering and still wasn't his old self yet. Sage left Lora and her dad home on a Sunday afternoon playing Uno. They both were skeptical about Max because she'd met him on the plane. However, she was going out with a guy for the second time. It was a day date, so they assumed he was harmless.

Sage wanted to take in some of the sights, and Max was good to his word, taking her to one of the local museums, where she admired the contemporary art exhibit.

Max had been so pleased Sage accepted another date with him, thinking it could be the beginning of a new future for them both. He'd made sure everything was perfect. And it had been. Just watching her beautiful face light up in sheer happiness was satisfaction for him. She wasn't at all he expected—she was down to earth and wasn't into material things like he thought.

He tried to buy her expensive jewelry when they were sightseeing, which she declined. Sage had offered to pay for her own lunch, but he wasn't going to allow her to do that. What type of man would he be if he had allowed her to pay? She was everything he could ever want in a woman. Max watched her as she studied the painting.

"Max," she called, trying to get his attention.

"Sorry," he babbled, coming back to the moment.

"I asked what you thought about the painting?" Her eyes sparkled with glee. "You do as I do when studying a painting," she said with a look of amusement. "I understand. These paintings all around us

237

can take you there." She glimpsed around at more paintings.

"Yes, I agree." He caressed the side of her face.

Max wasn't speaking of the paintings. She stepped away a little, and Max was disappointed. It made him feel unwanted. All this time, he'd been showing her how much he cared about her. Why else would he be spending this precious time with her? Her rejection of his touch enraged him. The blood in his veins ran hotter as the muscle above one of his eyes twitched a little. Sage didn't see the almost invisible twitching. If she knew what cruelty he was capable of, she wouldn't have objected to his touch.

Sage trusted she hadn't offended him, however, didn't appreciate his presumptuous behavior. She only wanted to be his friend and had made it clear to him that this wasn't a date. She learned that he was a resident of Breckville Towers. What were the odds that he lived in the same building as Nick and Parker? She hated that he lived in the same building as Nick. Nick already thought their relationship was more because they'd slept together.

"Hey, I'm sorry. I didn't mean to overstep my boundaries," Max said calmly, wanting to squeeze her long neck until she begged him to touch her.

"Okay," she acknowledged, coming to her senses. "I can only be friends with you. I don't want you to get the wrong impression, that's all."

"No, I understand. I get it. I respect your wishes."

Max smiled only to please her and put her mind at ease, wishing he could show how he felt for her. He didn't want friendship—he wanted her entirely.

After the museum, Max took Sage back to her dad's house. He had hoped they would spend more time together, but she couldn't. She wanted to be with her dad and sister, and he understood that. When she got back home to Bayville, he was going to make it his business to consume more of her time.

Sage walked into the house, closing the door behind her. She found her sister in the living room.

"So, how was your date with plane guy?" Lora asked.

"It wasn't a date, Lor," Sage answered, digging into the popcorn.

"I hope plane guy knows that," Lora said. She didn't like plane guy. There was something about his eyes—the way he'd stared at her sister. It wasn't a normal stare of a guy who wants a woman; there was something else.

"As a matter of fact, I made that clear today. He tried to overstep by buying me expensive jewelry and touching me, but I put him in his place in a hurry. I already have a guy who thinks he's my man."

"What?" she coughed, almost choking on popcorn. "What guy?" she demanded.

Sage was so pissed at herself for letting it slip. *Awe Fiddlesticks!* She didn't want to talk about Nick. The man had been calling her non-stop since she's been in Phoenix. He wouldn't take the hint to leave her alone. She was thankful she wasn't in Bayville and have to deal with him right now. Now, she had to deal with her nosey sister.

"It's nothing," Sage said, shaking her head, shrugging her shoulders.

"Oh, girl, please, I know you. I recall your first kindergarten crush. You haven't been interested in a man in a long while. I'm glad you are. Tell me about the guy who believes he's your man." A smile spread across her pretty face.

Sage had set herself up to be grilled by her sister, and now she would have to answer for it.

"I'm waiting."

"I know," she answered with a sigh. She may as well confide in her about Nick. "I met Nickolas Brimmer at the beach over a month ago. Well, at MCC first, then the beach. He's a womanizer—a shallow, arrogant bastard. He was married five years ago then his wife divorced him. The man also beat a man almost to death, and the judge only gave him probation. That's what money can buy the rich."

Lora could tell whoever Nickolas Brimmer was, her sister really cared for him. She hoped none of the bad she was hearing was true. "How do you know he's a womanizer or a shallow, arrogant bastard? How do you know he beat a man nearly to death?"

"It's on the internet. I didn't ask him per se," Sage answered, rolling her eyes. She really didn't want to know. Deep down, she wanted it not to be true.

"You know you can't believe everything the net has to say about anybody. They are usually half-truths or no truths at all. Why don't you ask him about his past?"

"I don't want to get involved with him, Lora. I don't have time for him. I have Nicki now. No room for a man, and certainly not Nick."

"Okay, so Nick and Nicki could be in your life together. They have similar names. It must be a sign from the universe," Lora offered, clapping her hands together, with a stupid grin on her face.

"Whatever, Lor. I'm going to go check on daddy." Sage got up from the couch.

"Okay, but I'm going to get to the bottom of this," she assured. She knew her little sister was still in love with Luke, but she was willing to bet this Nickolas guy would help ease her pain.

Sage went upstairs to her dad's bedroom and knocked lightly on the door. When she didn't receive an answer, she entered.

"Daddy?" she called softly.

"Hi, baby-girl," he answered. "Come on and have a seat." He smiled weakly. He'd been thinking about his late wife and the heated argument they'd had right before she drove off. He should have tried harder to stop her from leaving. If he had, she would still be alive.

Deborah always had an excuse for not spending time with her family. That's how Cooper saw it. He believed the girls saw it that way as well. They were all deprived of her love and attention.

"How are you feeling, daddy? You need me to get you anything?" she questioned, taking a seat near his bedside.

"No, baby. I'm okay for now. I was just thinking about your mother. I miss her still," he spoke thickly. "I wish I had stopped her that day. I regret not having tried harder for my girls. I know it was entirely my fault." He looked away from her.

Deborah seemed to care a lot more about her patients than her family. Sage had sometimes complained to her mother about not being there for them. She knew it wasn't her daddy's fault her mother died. She blamed him all those years until now. She was truly mad at her mother. She decided to get behind the wheel of a car angry then lost her life in the process. She was a medical professional; she should have known better, or at least have thought about her children. Deborah shouldn't have been so self-centered no matter how hurt she was.

"It wasn't your fault, Daddy." Sage leaned closer, taking his hand.

"I did an awful thing to your mother, my wife—the love of my life. I'm ashamed of it. I confessed my infidelity to her. It was only one time, and it cost me dearly. I should have kept it to myself, and she would be alive." He breathed.

"I feel the same way about my husband's death, Daddy. If I hadn't told him about the abortion, he would be alive. I miss him, too," she confessed with teary eyes. "If only I had kept my mouth shut. My husband, my best friend, would be here by my side. It hurts so much, Daddy," she cried.

"Awe, baby," he said, sitting up slightly, wanting to hug his baby-girl.

Cooper didn't know his daughter had been pregnant. He didn't know why she would have an abortion. He didn't like seeing her in pain. He prayed that she would find love again. He and Luke had met several times, and Cooper understood Luke was a good man. He wasn't a saint as his daughter may think because he too had confided to him about his relationship with Sage. His only regret was that they didn't spend enough time together. Luke was the son he never had.

"Sage, why did you have an abortion?" he asked after she calmed down.

"It was way before I met Luke. It was Parker's baby. I told Luke about it, and that's why we ended up in the car crash. He hated me after that. I saw it in his eyes," she sniffled. "We tried to have a baby, but we weren't successful."

"One thing I know my son-in-law didn't do was hate you. That man loved you so much, sweetie. When we did talk, he couldn't wait to have children with you. I wanted grandkids too. His eyes beamed every time he talked about you. I'm not just saying these things. We met in secret and talked on the phone. I'm glad we did." He smiled. "It wasn't your fault, Sage."

"I wish I could believe that—really believe that. I'm glad you two met as well." She cuddled his hand. "I saw the two of you once. It was a year or so before the crash. I knew he probably wanted to get to know you regardless of what my feelings were at the time. I'm truly glad he got to know you a little." She kissed the palm of his hand, then gave him a warm hug.

"Daddy, it wasn't your fault either." She stroked his hand. "I know you and Mommy had problems in your marriage. I know she didn't spend enough time with any of us, and that was her loss, not ours. We both need to move on from our past somehow. Maybe we can do it together."

"Yes, baby-girl. I'll try if you try." He brought her in for another hug.

"Of course, Daddy," she replied happily.

Nick was in his penthouse, thinking about Sage. Jazz music flowed through the room as he studied the paintings, he had done of her. He had added a new one to his collection. It was a painting of her standing in the garden at his house. Painting Sage was the only peace he had, knowing she didn't want him. She hadn't returned any of his phone calls and he had left many voicemails, hoping she would.

It'd been almost a month since he'd last seen her—it might as well have been eons. It felt like a piece of him was missing. The main piece. He didn't know when he had fallen in love with her. Perhaps, he spent too much time gawking at the paintings in his studio. He couldn't forget the night or the morning they'd shared together before she'd run out of his arms and out of his life.

Paul and Royce had suggested that he go to Phoenix and show her he wasn't giving up on her, but he hadn't made up his mind to do so. He realized for sure Sage had feelings for him. Hell, it was hard not to notice. Her body seemed to respond to his slightest touch and obeyed his will. A smile eased across his lips, thinking about how he excited her. She was trying to resist him but couldn't. He covered the painting and left the room. He picked up the phone in his office, dialing Royce's number.

"Roy, I need to borrow your jet. I'm heading to Phoenix," he said with a grin.

"Bout damn time. I'll make sure the pilot knows you are heading his way soon."

"Thanks, man, I owe you."

"Nah, we bros. Go be with your woman."

"Will do. Talk to you later." Nick hung up, getting ready to head out of the city. He ran into Max in the hallway.

"Where are you going in a hurry?" Max asked.

"I have some important business to take care of. Be back as soon as I can," he added, walking past him.

"You be careful, Nick," Max warned, heading back to his apartment.

Max had a feeling Nick was on his way to see her. Sage. His woman. His beloved. He had to do something about it. He had come back from Phoenix two weeks ago because she said she needed time to be with her family. Now, Nick was trying to move in on her and take advantage. Nick wasn't the right man for her. Why couldn't he see that? Sage deserved a man like him, not someone she had to take care of in ten years. He had to get her to see he was her soulmate—her one true love.

Nick had arrived in Phoenix around five that evening. He had gotten her father's address from Parker. He was rehearsing what he would say when he arrived at her father's door unannounced as he drove the rental Lexus. He had done that once before, showed up without letting her know. *"Second time is a charm,"* he mumbled.

However, it had been her not returning his phone calls that had worried him. He wanted to be there for her if she needed him. Her not returning his calls made things impossible for him. He also needed to tell her about his past and what had gone wrong. No matter the cost, he anticipated she would be understanding and see he wasn't a bad man. He had been in a bad situation.

It took him thirty minutes to arrive at her father's two-story home in the suburbs. Nick sat in the car for several minutes before he walked to the door.

Lora heard a car pull up in the driveway.

"Daddy, are you expecting anyone?" she questioned, heading to the foyer.

"No, sweetie," he answered.

The doorbell rang as Lora peeped through the peephole in the door. *Who's that?* she wondered. What she saw was a tall, handsome, sexy white male standing at her daddy's door. *It must be a friend of Daddy's coming to check on him,* she thought before deciding to open the door.

"Hello, are you here to see my Daddy?" Lora asked with a half-smile.

"No, not quite." Nick smiled brightly; he could tell she was Sage's sister by the resemblance. "I'm here to see Sage. She isn't expecting me. Is she here? Is she alright?" he asked, concerned.

Lora was surprised to see Nick in the flesh. And oh boy, his flesh was well-built. Her sister was in for a shocker. Lora could see why Sage cared for the man. He had a muscular body with dreamy blue eyes and had come all this way to see her. Wow. She was right all along. Her sister was withholding a whole lot of information.

"You are Nickolas?" Lora inquired with a grinned. This was a first for Sage—seeing a man of her dad's complexion. Her sister had always preferred the brathers—until now.

"Yes, I am." He was pleased she knew who he was. *Sage told her sister about me,* he mused. He might have a chance to win her over.

"My name is Lora." She stepped aside to allow him entry. "My sister and dad are this way. He's recovering from surgery." She closed the door lightly.

"Yes, I know. I hope he feels better soon." He stopped talking when he came into the living room and saw her.

"Sage, look who's here for you," she declared. "Nickolas came all the way from Bayville to make sure you were okay."

Sage froze for an instant.

"Daddy, this is Nickolas Brimmer." Lora introduced him to their dad because Sage hadn't made it her business to do so. She was still sitting next to their daddy in her frozen state. *Shocked. As. Hell.* As if she had forgotten who he was. *Nice, little sister,* Lora thought.

"Good to meet you." Nick walked over to Cooper and extended his hand. He hadn't known Sage's father was Caucasian. He could see where she got her emerald eyes from.

"Same here," Cooper said, shaking his hand briefly. "Have a seat," Cooper offered. Cooper looked him over briefly, noticing he was much older than his daughter. He had to be in his late thirties, early forties.

"Hi, sweetheart," Nick clamored to, taking a seat next to her.

"Hello Nickolas," Sage responded, fuming at him for a moment then turned her eyes on her sister. She noticed Lora sitting across from them with a quirky smirk on her face. She could tell she was amused.

"I didn't know my daughter was dating," Cooper said, looking toward them.

"Daddy, I'm not. I met Nick at the beach over a month or so ago. He won a charity auction I was in. I'm sorry, Nick, about not attending the date." She peered at him for a moment before looking back at the TV.

"Auction?" Cooper gasped, surprised.

"It was for a good cause, Daddy. Cindy needed me, so I offered my help," she stated, still watching the TV show. She had her daddy and the man she desired sitting next to her. *What? Desired him? Fiddlesticks!* she deliberated.

Cooper knew it was more than that. He could sense his daughter was into him by her body language. It was more than his daughter was willing to admit. He wanted her dating, but someone closer to her own age—like plane guy. His daughter didn't usually date guys of his complexion, so this was new, as well.

"What do you do for a living, Nick?" Cooper asked.

"I buy companies and invest in them," he responded, looking at Sage. He hoped she wasn't too upset with him for showing up like this, but she'd given him no choice.

"So, you are well-off?" Cooper probed.

This was the first time in a long time he could drill someone his daughter was interested in. Cooper hadn't done that since she could date at sixteen. He was finding it enjoyable to see him squirm.

"Yes, I'm well-established, thanks to God. I had an uncle to look up to, and he taught me how to be a success. I invest in all types of businesses, from corporations to small businesses. I also have investments in technologies." He hoped this was good enough for her father because he wasn't about to let Sage go whether Cooper approved of him or not.

"Sounds interesting. You have any other family?" Cooper asked.

"No, unfortunately, my mother and father are deceased, and so is my uncle. I have two close friends I consider family. They are also business partners of mine."

Sage didn't know he had no other family. She felt bad for him because she had close family and good friends in her life. She was truly blessed.

"Nick, you really care about my little sister?" Lora questioned him, smiling at her. She knew he had to, to come all this way to see her.

"With all my heart," he confessed, looking at Lora, then staring at Sage, who wasn't paying him any attention. She was more interested in the TV show and her Cherry Coke.

Okay, it was time she and Nick took this outside. She couldn't take it anymore. The two of them questioning him like they were a couple.

"Nick, it's time you and I talk." She stood, and so did he.

"It was nice meeting you, Cooper. Hopefully, this isn't our last encounter." Nick gazed down at the woman he loved.

"I'm sure it's not," Cooper admitted, watching his daughter. "Maybe next time we could talk longer."

"I'd like that," Nick said, smiling.

Lora got up and walked with Sage. "I like him, and I know you do, also. I think even Daddy does," she whispered in Sage's ear. "Well, Nick, it was great meeting you. Come back soon." She left the pair at the foyer.

"I can't believe you're here," Sage said, not concealing her anger.

"Let's get in the car, sweetheart, so we won't make a scene." He took hold of her hand, leading her to his rental. He thought she would resist, but she didn't. He opened the door for her. She sank into the seat with ease.

"To answer your question, I came here to see you. You haven't answered any of my phone calls." He touched her face softly. "Baby, I was worried."

"Nick, you aren't my man. We—you and I aren't a couple," she said, waving her hands objectively before speaking. "However, you made it appear that we are in front of my father and sister. You come here taking the role that I haven't extended to you." She pursed her lips, running her tongue over her top lip. "You and I aren't dating." She shook her head at him.

Nick didn't respond at first. He sat, looking at her profile for a moment before getting out of the car. Scene or no scene, he rounded her side, opened the door, pulling her from the seat. Positioning her on the door, he pinned her in with his hands resting on the hood. She was doing her best to hide her emotions, but he could tell it was a facade. She was looking away from him to avoid his gaze, biting her bottom lip. She knew it was a turn-on for him. Her body was pressed against his with no space. She had on a blue sundress with spaghetti straps that stopped halfway up her pretty thighs. It was as if she had known to put it on for him.

Sage could smell his cologne; it was tickling her nose. His blue stare was edging into her skin. She wanted to get away, but him being so close made it difficult to resist him. He had on a blue short-sleeve cotton shirt showcasing his sexy muscular arms. The dark blue jeans fit the lower half of his body perfectly. This was the first time she'd seen him dressed casually.

Nick lowered his head to her ear. "Sage," he growled her name. He raised his head to eye her again. She wouldn't meet his gaze. He lowered his head and drawled her name again, saying something in French.

A tiny sexual sound escaped her lips. She swallowed hard. He pressed his lips against her ear, whispering her name seductively. For a minute, she thought her panties were wet. *Wait, they are wet. Not again. Fiddlesticks!*

"Sage," he repeated in a hoarse tone. "Could you please look at me, and tell me you don't want me? I'll go away, and I won't bother you anymore." He placed a soft kiss on her ear, moving away, wanting to stare into her beautiful eyes. But her eyes were elsewhere.

"Nick, let me go," she pleaded. If she looked into his eyes, he would know her truth.

Nick took one hand off the hood and gently turned her face toward his. Her eyes were on his blue shirt. He began to pepper tiny kisses at the corner of her sweet mouth. "Sage," he continued, peppering kisses on both sides of her cheeks. He kissed her other ear, sucking her earlobe between his full lips, releasing it when he heard a soft sound escape her lips.

"Look at me, sweetheart."

"Nickolas, please," she begged. "What are you doing to me? I was fine with the way my life was, and now you come here confusing me. I want to go back inside."

"What you want frightens you, my love. Sage, baby, I won't hurt you. I'm afraid. I've been hurt before. I gave my heart away to a woman and had it ripped out of my chest. Baby, don't run from this. From us."

Nick wasn't going to allow her to escape him. He would do whatever it took to persuade her they belonged together. He wrapped his arm around her waist, lifting her off her feet. Sage looked into his eyes. He kissed her gently. She parted her mouth, allowing him admission. His tongue went into her mouth instantly, tasting her sweet, hot juices. She moaned softly as their tongues tangled and mingled together. When he heard her soft moans, he pulled away, staring into her eyes. She tried to turn away again, but he stopped her by placing his hand on her chin.

"You skipped out on our date." He caressed her chin. "I'm here to collect." He smiled when she giggled, lightening the mood. She was ticklish under her chin.

"No, I didn't. I had good reason to. I'm here in hot, muggy Phoenix. You were in Bayville." She touched the sides of his jaws.

He was pleased she touched him, showing her affection for him. "Okay, but now I'm here where you are. When can I collect?" he asked, kissing her lips.

She shied away from him like a schoolgirl, which he thought was cute. "Tomorrow evening, around seven."

"Okay, it's a date, baby." He planted her feet back on the ground, walking her back to the front door. "I've had you outside your father's house long enough." He stroked her face, leaning forward, kissing her mouth. "I'll see you tomorrow at seven."

Nick kissed her once again before getting inside the rental. Once Sage was inside the house, he pulled away. He wore a genuine smile knowing he would have the woman of his dreams.

Chapter 14

Sage had spoken to her aunt and Nicki earlier. She missed them both. She updated her aunt on her father's recovery, which was going well. She couldn't wait for them to come visit. Sage hadn't told her aunt about her date with Nick because she didn't want her to make a big deal about it, because it wasn't.

She was getting ready for her date with Mr. Wondaful. She and her sister had gone out shopping to find the right outfit earlier that day. What she brought from home wasn't sexy date wear. She chose to keep it simple though. She still wasn't sure Nick was the man she should be spending time with, but he did spend big bucks for her. It was only right that she played her part, making sure he had a good time. However, that didn't mean she should sleep with him again. Luke came across her mind. Guilt washed over her in that instant.

"I'm sorry baby, but you aren't here." She blew air from her lips, thinking what if it was a huge mistake going out with Nick.

She heard a knock at her door.

"Come on in, Lor," she yelled.

"All sookie sookie, you look marvelous, Sage. I knew that dress was made for you," she said ecstatically.

Sage had on a fitted burgundy dress that came up around her neck. The back-out dress exposed her butterfly tattoo at the small of her back that she'd had done in college. Sarah had one in the same place. It was a symbol of their sisterhood and a drunken night of partying. Sage wore a pair of two-inch, open-toed black heels, with little diamond-like studs on the back. On her wrist was a maroon pearl-like bracelet with little diamond studs. The fashion jewelry matched the ring on her middle finger and earrings. Her curly, long, charcoal back-length hair hung freely except one side that was pinned away from her face with a pretty silver clip. Her face makeup was light—some shimmer brownish eye shadow and outlined with black liner and mascara. Her lips shimmered with a reddish-brown lipstick.

"You don't think this is overdoing it?" she asked Lora.

"With the amount of money, he dropped at the auction to take you out, he deserves the best." She moved beside her sister, admiring her closer. "You are gorgeous."

"Thanks, Lor, and so are you." Sage looked at her sister. "Thanks for your help. This dress is a knock-out on me," she bragged, running her hands over the soft material.

"I know my stuff," Lora said, snapping her fingers, boasting with laughter. "They don't call me Dr. Tate for nothing."

Sage laughed. "No, they don't, big sis." She lifted her silver clutch from the bed.

They left the bedroom when the doorbell rang. Sage's anxieties filled her body now. She was about to be alone with the man who had the power to make her body behave as if she were his woman—which wasn't true. She was Lucas Luke Sullivan's wife. Sage was still feeling uncomfortable for having slept with Nick.

Nick was talking to Cooper when the ladies arrived downstairs. The pair were sharing a funny joke. When Nick saw Sage, he was hypnotized by her beauty. He strolled over to Sage, not taking his eyes off her.

"You look amazing, sweetheart." He took hold of her hand, kissing her palm.

"You look handsome," she grinned.

Nick wore a navy-blue dress shirt with a charcoal tie, a pair of charcoal slacks with black dress shoes. And he smelled good— good enough to eat.

"Okay, you two. Enough with the goo-goo eyes," Lora said.

"I'll see you later, Daddy," Sage said, giving him a hug and kiss on the cheek.

"You have a good time, baby-girl. And you take care of my daughter," Cooper warned, eyeballing Nick.

"Of course, I will. I'll guard her with my life." He drew Sage to his side. "Are you ready, Sage?"

"Yes, let's go," she replied, leading him out of the room.

"Have fun, and don't be out too late, young lady," her sister teased.

"See you later, sis," Sage responded as she and Nick walked out.

Nick led her to his rental. He didn't open the door immediately—he was adoring her from head to toe. She was so beautiful—his beautiful goddess. He couldn't wait to get her naked again. He touched the side of her face with his hand, placing a gentle kiss on her lips.

"Do you know how much I want you?" he murmured in her ear, kissing her lobe. "I'll show you later," he groaned, deeply, "if you allow me to."

Her body did what it always did when it came to him. Her hormones got away from her, making her lose control—making her want to do things to him that she shouldn't, knowing what the outcome would be. He wasn't the kind of man who stuck around. If she wasn't careful, she could fall in love with him. *You know he'll hurt you. Cause he's a shallow, arrogant bastard,* she reminded herself.

Nick stepped away from her, his eyes consumed with so much passion for her. He caressed her lips delicately with the tip of his finger. He wanted to kiss her again but didn't. He had to keep to a schedule because he was flying her out of the city. He wanted this to be a night they would never forget. He opened the door for her, allowing her to slip inside.

"I promise not to speed, love." He put the car into reverse, heading to their first destination.

Sage sat comfortably in the seat, wondering where he was taking her. They had already passed several nice restaurants, none of which pleased him, she guessed. He continued to drive until they reached an airport.

"Nick," she coiled toward him, "where are we going?" she questioned, biting on her lower lip timidly.

"Don't worry, Sage, I promise you are in good hands. I have a surprise for you. Do you like surprises?" He touched her thigh, running his hand up and down the soft flesh.

"Yes," she hissed.

"Good," he said, getting out of the car, and opening her door. They were at a private airport. She noticed several private planes in hangars.

"Nickolas, you own a jet?" she inquired, gazing up at him.

"No, not yet, but it's in the works. I have it on borrowed time. A good friend loaned it to me. You okay with flying?" He took hold of her hand, walking her to the plane.

"Yes, I'm okay with it." Her heels clicked on the concrete as they walked. "Nick, you do realize we are going on this date because you won me at the auction?" Her heart still belonged to one man—Luke.

"Really, Sage, you want to go there?" He stopped them dead in their tracks. "You know that we mean something to each other, no matter how you try to run away from it. All I have to do is touch you. Like this," he mumbled, pulling her close to him, gliding his hands up and down her spine, causing her to tremble at his touch. "You can't run from me tonight. You are all mine." He kissed her lips briefly, then took hold of her waist, guiding her to the jet. Before they spoke again, they were buckled into their seats, alongside each other.

"Where are we headed?" she questioned excitedly.

A pleasant flight attendant handed them a glass of wine.

"It's a surprise, sweetheart. That's what I have in store for you tonight." He kissed her cheek.

"I really love surprises just so you know," she said with a grin. "Are you really trying to spoil a girl?" she asked.

"Yes, I plan to spoil only one girl, and her name is Sage Sullivan." He cupped her chin, staring at her lovely face.

"Good, I love it." She brushed his jaw.

They arrived at Montgomery Field within an hour and fifteen minutes. A black limo waited for them. Sage's eyes gleamed with enjoyment. She couldn't wait to see the next surprise. She had no expectations of any kind, apart from spending time with this dazzling, exciting man seated next to her, and find out who he really was.

Nick finally told her where the plane had landed before they drove past a sign that revealed all. They were in San Diego. She was ecstatic. She hadn't been to San Diego before—that pleased him. He would give her a short tour of Ocean Beach before they dined. Ocean Beach was where a few of his properties were located. He'd grownup there.

"I want to show you this beautiful, small community. I hope you like it," he said, gaping into her eyes yet again.

"I don't think you have anything to worry about, Nick. This whole trip is a big surprise to me," she pointed out, gaily. "I've never been on a date with a guy who flies me by private aircraft to have dinner."

"Good. I'm the first and last." He stroked her thigh, tenderly.

Sage looked out of the window, enjoying all the wonderful scenery. She was like a little girl in a candy store. Excitement filled her eyes. She liked to travel to new places and discover new things. She and Luke did that often when he could get away from work.

Sadness ran through her momentarily as she thought about Luke. She felt guilty again, being with Nick. The universe must be playing a sick game with her, making her have these feelings for a man who could probably care less about her. All the other women in his past were all the proof she needed. Yet, she couldn't seem to bring herself to stay away from him.

Nick noticed her mind was elsewhere. She was his tonight, and he wouldn't allow room for anything else. He moved closer to her and draped his arms around her waist. He inhaled the citrus scent of her hair. "You smell enchanting." He took his hand and moved her hair off her shoulder and began to softly kiss down her neck. She moaned. He moved back to her ear, nibbling at her earlobe. She closed her eyes and tipped her head to the side. Nick ran his hands through her silky, curly hair. He placed more kisses down the length of her neck. "Sage," he grunted her name, "I'm falling for you, sweetheart."

Sage's eyes popped open—she came back to her senses, straightening up, and moved away from him. There was no way he could be falling in love with her. They had met almost two months ago, and Sage didn't believe in love at first sight. Not anymore. She didn't reply to what he said, she only glanced out the window. Moments later, the limo was parking. She was relieved because she didn't want to get into a deep conversation. She wanted to avoid that at all costs. She also wanted to avoid being photographed with him again, so she best be on her guard.

The driver got out of the limo and opened the door. Nick helped her out as he instructed the driver to return in two hours.

"This is beautiful, Nick." Sage took him by the hand smiling up at him.

"Yes, this view is very beautiful," he replied, smoothing the sides of her face.

She blushed.

"Well, where are you taking me first?" she queried, enthusiastically.

"I see someone is very excited," he said, draping his arm around her waist and ushering her away.

One of the first places he took her was on Newport Avenue. It had some of the finest antiques and collectibles. Nick bought Sage a stunning bracelet. It had little hearts and odd-shaped stones, dangling from the gold chain. She thought it was too expensive—he purchased the jewelry despite her objection. It was his way of making sure a woman felt good after he eventually dumped her like old trash. She had to remember not to get too attached to him.

The pair visited a boutique store. The lovely dresses on display in the windows drew them in. Sage tried on a few of the dresses. Nick gave his approval on the ones he preferred. He intended to spoil her.

Sage didn't think highly of him going over her head and purchasing things for her. She knew he wasn't going to be with her long anyhow. So, why was he pretending?

"You have got to stop, Nickolas. Don't buy me anything else. I mean it." She narrowed her eyes at him. She hoped to God no one was lurking around to take pictures of them. It was quite a shock that someone had photographed them at the auction in Bayville. She hadn't realized he was one of Bayville's celebrities. There was a lot she still didn't know about him.

"This is part of the surprise. I thought you loved surprises."

"Let's go, Nickolas," she demanded in a soft whine.

"Okay, we'll go." He took the bags from the counter, thanking the cashier, and they left the shop.

"Nick, what do you expect me to give you? Is it sex you want?" she asked as they walked down the sidewalk. "We've already done that. You don't have to buy your way to my pussy."

In the past, that's what he'd done—bought his way into a woman's bed. To hear her say it was hurtful. She meant more than that to him. "I'm not asking for sex. I want more from you. Much more," he declared seriously. "I've told you that before I want us to be in a serious relationship."

"I don't want that. I haven't been in a serious relationship since Luke," she explained sadly. "He was the love of my life." She didn't want to continue this conversation.

"I know that, sweetheart. I'm not rushing you. I can wait for you. I'm a patient man."

"Let's go, Nick." She wasn't considering any kind of a relationship with him. He was too old, and she preferred men with darker complexions. Why had the universe dealt this hand to her? Well, she wasn't going to accept it. Return to sender.

"You can't run away this time. I have you all to myself. I'm not ready to leave, and neither are you. You're upset. I didn't mean to upset you. I was only surprising you. I won't buy you anything else tonight. Except, dinner. The limo is waiting for us."

Hand in hand Nick and Sage walked back to the limo. Nick handed the driver the bags and gave him instructions for their next destination.

In the car, Sage was quiet. This, whatever it was, was going to stay in San Diego. Luke was the only man she intended to give her heart to. She wasn't going to forget him. Let some other man move in and make her forget him. No. She wasn't going to stand for it. Not that she would allow Mr. Wondaful the chance 'cause using women was his objective. And there was a picture of her with him on the net. *"Oh gwad, not me too. Awe fiddlesticks!"* she thought.

"Sage, baby. You're torturing me. Please talk to me," Nick begged, stroking her hand. He hadn't meant to upset her. That was the last thing he wanted to do.

"I have nothing to say to you. I want to go home." She furrowed her lips. "I don't want to be near you anymore." Her eyes burned through him.

Suddenly, he pulled her onto his lap. He positioned her face in his hands, slanting down, staring into her eyes—a smile across his full lips. "You don't want to be near me?" he asked, running his hand through her hair. He drew her closer and inhaled her fruity scent. "I most definitely want to be near you, love." His mouth claimed hers in a deep kiss.

She tried to hit him, but he immobilized her hands with his large one and continued to kiss her. She stopped resisting and melted against his muscular chest. He let go of her hands.

She couldn't fight him anymore. She wanted this. She wanted him to take her in the back of the limo. Fuck her wildly. Was she wrong for thinking such dirty thoughts? She wanted pleasure and passion. She wanted a man to want her as much as she did him. She wanted Nickolas Brimmer.

Sage unbuttoned three buttons on his dress shirt, then ran her hands over his chest. She felt the rock-hard muscles on his chest and abs. Her hands began to run freely in his thick black hair. It felt good, touching him like that. His creamy skin next to her mocha skin. He groaned every time her hands touched him. He cupped her breasts and began to massage them. The dress she wore exposed her cleavage.

Sage moaned softly. The kiss was growing wilder. More urgent. He was aware he couldn't take her in the back of a limo. There wasn't enough room for what he wanted to do to her. He drew away and placed her back on the seat, buttoning up his shirt.

She straightened up her dress, then coiled away shyly, avoiding his lustful stare.

"Baby, we only kissed and touched each other. There is no need to shy away from me. We've seen each other naked. Remember?" He ran his index finger up her thigh. "I enjoyed every moment of it. I had to stop myself before I got out of control. Trust me, it took all my willpower to stop." He buttoned up the last button. "Are you hungry?" he inquired.

"Yes," she stated softly. "For you," she murmured under her breath and continued peeking out the window. Sage had a hunger only he could cure, but she kept that to herself.

"I know this great little restaurant here in Ocean Beach. I think you'll enjoy it."

Nick watched her, however, her attention wasn't on him. He took hold of her hand. She turned, staring into his ocean blue eyes. They seemed to glow. Nickolas broke the stare. She continued to enjoy the scenery out the window. He let down the divider and gave the driver different instructions, then closed it, giving them privacy. He wanted to go ahead with dinner because he didn't know how much longer he would be able to keep from having her in the back of the limo.

"What I said earlier about me falling for you, I meant it. From the first time I saw you, I recognized you were special. Sage, I understand you love your husband. Give me a chance to show you we belong together. Please, don't push me away," he confessed, as he traced the butterfly tattoo with his finger.

Every burning touch of his fingertips was making her body respond. Sage tried hard to resist him, but her body seemed to be controlled by him as usual. Betraying her, revealing what she didn't want him to know.

Nick wasn't going to give up easily. He moved close to her, leaving no space between them. She could feel him against her. His body heat was tickling her skin. She didn't dare turn around, for if she did, she would be staring right into his gorgeous face.

"Baby," he said close to her ear, tugging at her earlobe with his mouth. "Sage," he whispered deeply. "Sweetheart," he breathed, resting the side of his face against hers.

"Nickolas!" She finally turned to him.

"Don't you feel it, baby?" He angled down, so his face was in her sights.

"No, what?" she denied with a slight whimper in her voice.

"Feel this," he groaned, capturing her mouth with his own. His mouth claimed hers in a zealous kiss. She tried to move away from him, but she was pinned against the door. His mouth ventured from her lips to her collarbones, placing soft, sweet kisses. Nick trailed down to her neck, tasting her with mouth and tongue, then he proceeded to her breasts, kissing her cleavage. He had to have—they were so plump and gorgeous just sitting there waiting to be touched by him. He pulled her off the door then untied the dress. Her beautiful breasts set, pointing right at him, ready for him to devour. He stared at them with hungry eyes. His mouth watered for the taste of them. He groaned before he took the large brown bud into his mouth. Sage moaned loudly as soon as he took her nipple between his lips. Her body was in a hot tizzy. Lust ripped through her like a mighty wind. Her head fell back as she cried his name softly.

Nickolas held her breasts captive in his large hands. He teased her beautiful nipples. He licked, teethed, and suckled her breasts, giving her pure pleasure. Back and forth, he teased both breasts with his hot mouth. He flickered his tongue over her breasts, using his hands to massage them delicately.

She felt her body awakening from a siesta. Her core was burning hot. She continued to moan his name. Her hands were in his hair. He ran his tongue down to her belly button, creating a burning blaze with his tongue. He planted tiny kisses on her belly. Then his tongue traveled back up to her throat.

"I want you, Sage. I want to be inside you so badly," he whispered, as he ran his tongue over her ear. "I want to explore your entire body," he muttered. "Not here."

She opened her eyes. The look in his eyes matched hers—raw desire. She lost control again. Sage sat next to him, feeling embarrassed. She felt awkwardly bare in front of him, even though only her breasts were exposed. She began to tie her dress.

He reached to help her, but she dismissed his helping hand. She tied the dress and scooted away from him to put space between them. She was satisfied when the limo came to a halt.

Chapter 15

The limo pulled up in front of the Port Rose restaurant. The lighting was soft, creating a romantic ambiance. Sage was relieved because she didn't need her picture taken with Nick. Maybe that had been a one-time thing because so far, she hadn't noticed anyone lurking with a camera. It might have been a Bayville thing. The maître d' seated them at a table decorated with flowers and lit candles on a red tablecloth. Nick pulled out Sage's chair for her to sit, then he took his seat.

"This place is really nice, Nick," Sage noted, looking around. She hoped there wasn't anyone in here who recognized him. They were now in a private space.

Nick watched her. She didn't seem at ease. "Sage," he called her name in a low, deep whisper. "You don't want to be here with me?" he asked, leaning forward, touching her cheek.

"Nick, must you touch me in public? I wish you wouldn't," she requested as her eyes scanned the area.

"You saw the photo of us from the auction." He drew a deep breath, sighing heavily. He didn't care who understood he was with her. He didn't like the damn headline. He didn't want her to think he was a player—he was a good man in the wrong relationships.

Too many wrong relationships even though he had each of them investigated. Nick was with her now—the right one. She'd come into his world unexpectedly. He wasn't looking for love, and yet, it seemed to have found him. He didn't want to ruin their night together with truths. Not that he didn't want to tell her everything. He wanted their night to be perfect. And it would be. "Sage, there are no reporters here. It's a very private restaurant. I promise. It's only you and me."

"Besides all these other guests," she smiled, feeling a little better. "I didn't know you lived in the public eye until I saw that picture and headline. I was on my way to see my father. To top it all off, one of your women sent it to me personally." She thought it was a scorned woman who'd sent her the email. She didn't need that kind of drama period.

"What?" he asked her, surprised. "Sure, I'm in the public eye at times, but I'm not important to reporters anymore. I'm boring except when they want to make-up a lot of lies about me. Like that awful headline you saw of us." He took her hand. "I don't have any women. The only woman I'm interested in is here with me. Why didn't you tell me when you first received it?"

Nick didn't like that someone was interfering with them. Every relationship he had ended on a good note, except his marriage. Well, at least, he thought they had. He hadn't had any problems dating. He hoped he didn't now because he would protect her.

"I didn't think it mattered, and you aren't my man. You are free to date other women just as I'm free, if I wanted, to date other men. Which I don't want to date, so that we both are clear," she clarified.

The server came back with the bottle of Opus One wine Nick had ordered, interrupting their conversation. The server poured a little into Nick's glass first and waited for his approval. Nick tasted the wine like an expert and nodded to the server to pour. He filled both glasses, placed the bottle on the table, and left.

The muscles in Nick's jaw spasmed as he watched Sage. He had a tendency to get jealous when it came to her. He had hoped to alleviate that awful emotion after what happened with his ex-wife. He never wanted to be at the point of almost killing someone ever again. The fact that she expected they were free to see other people, made the green-eyed monster appear. He had hoped they would be exclusive, once past the dead husband issue. In her mind, she was probably still married, even though she didn't wear the ring. He was curious when she'd stopped wearing it.

Sage picked up her glass. She noticed Nick eyeing her with creased brows. She perceived it had to do with her last remarks. She had to set boundaries with him, even if her body didn't want to. "Are you going to drink the wine?" she asked, holding the wine glass, trying to change the subject.

"Sage, I'm not a man who shares a woman," he admitted. "The women I've dated knew that about me. When I'm with someone, it's that person and me only," he said, moving toward her, stroking her hand. "I only want you. I choose to be with only you." He kissed her hand, then picked up the wine glass. "To you and me," he toasted, staring into her eyes. He could only pray that he had his jealousy under control. They touched glasses, taking a sip.

"Mum, this is really good," Sage said, taking another sip.

"I'm glad you like it. I wasn't sure, but I see you have an expensive pallet," he quipped.

"Whatever," she wiggled her nose at him, laughing. "I love Cherry Coke and Cheetos Puffs. Now that's a sophisticated pallet." She was spirited; the mood had changed from the previous conversation.

"Duly noted, sweetheart," he chuckled. "But on the other matter, Sage, please let me know about anything out of the ordinary. I need to know, baby," he said sincerely.

"Okay, Nick," she agreed, picking up the menu. "I'm starving."

"Then let me feed my baby." He smiled, lifting the menu from the table.

The server had come to take their order and refill their wine glasses. Nick and Sage sat comfortably, waiting for their dinner.

"So, I'll tell you a little about me first," he replied, sipping the wine, "then you can tell me a little about you."

"I never said I would kiss and tell." She sipped her wine, gazing into his eyes.

"It's only fair, love. I'll start. I was born in San Diego. I grew up here in Ocean Beach. I love to surf whenever I get the chance. I went to college to study art, but I ended up working for my uncle. I changed my major to business and painted in my spare time—mostly landscapes and buildings. When I'm inspired, I paint different things. I'll show you some of my artwork on our next date. My uncle owned Paradise Shores Hotels. I inherited the chain after he died."

Nick loved how easy it was for him to talk to Sage. She sat listening to his every word. It had never been easy to talk to his ex. She would always butt in or start an argument for no reason. It was invigorating to have a woman who respected him finally.

"My uncle was one of the few good people I loved in my life. He died seven years ago. I have a business partner and friend named Paul Writhers, whom you've met. He is like a brother to me and has been my best friend for twenty years. We've been in business together for about the same amount of time.

Royce Pierceton is another good friend. I met him at a business convention years ago and invested in new technologies. Paul and I both did. I've known Roy for fifteen years." He picked up his wine, taking a drink. "There is a guy about your age I've known since he was seventeen. His parents work a lot. They still do. They didn't seem to have time for him, so I've been a mentor to him. He's like a nephew to me. He's an artist. I've been trying to get him to show off his artwork."

"Wow, a man of many talents. It's good to be of service to people, especially the ones who need it."

She thought about Nicki. Sage was pleased she'd made the right choice to be in Nicki's life. She prayed she would be a good parent to her. She wasn't trying to replace her mother because no one could do that. Even after Sage had lost her mother, her aunt couldn't replace her, but she could help ease her pain.

"I love art. I used to go to art galleries quite often. I recently went to an exhibit in Phoenix. I didn't know you held that talent," she smiled broadly. "Did you paint any of the art that's in your building? There were some paintings in the apartment that Parker occupies that I simply loved."

"Yes, as a matter of fact, my mother has a few paintings hanging, and so do I. I just don't publicly acknowledge it."

"You sound like me. I don't publicly acknowledge my writing. I especially loved the painting of the mother and child," she said, sipping her wine.

"Thank you, but I can't take credit for that one. It's one of my mother's. I really love that one the most. It's a painting of the two of us." His lips curved into a smile.

"It's simply beautiful. They all are wonderful. So, which talent do you prefer surfing, painting, or businessman?"

"Painting." He set his glass down. "My mother loved to paint. She was very talented. She also taught children at a community center. Painting was her joy. Well, besides yours truly," he boasted with a crooked grin.

"Yeah, I can see you being spoiled," she jested. "Maybe next time you'll show me some of your work."

"Yes, I'll show you which ones are mine," he said with sadness.

"You still miss her—your mother." She caressed his jaw. "I still miss my mom too. She was killed in a car crash years ago. I was sixteen."

"Sorry to hear that, baby." He kissed the palm of her hand. *Wow, her mom and husband both killed in tragic accidents,* he thought.

"How did your mom die?" she queried.

Sage felt her phone vibrate. She hoped everything was alright at home. "Hold that thought." She opened her bag to see who it was. Nothing important. "Sorry." She resumed listening to him.

"Her name was Megan Brimmer, and she had breast cancer. She passed away when I was twenty-three. I know what you are going through, so if you ever want to talk to me about it, I'm here for you.

Cancer, it is a terrible disease," he confessed, looking downward, remembering his mother's pain and battle with the awful killer. Sage petted his jaw with compassion. He resumed talking to her.

"My father died from a massive heart attack. I was thirty when he died. I wasn't close to him, only by name. He was a marine who served his country and stayed gone a lot, but I had my dad's older brother, Uncle Simon. He taught me all I know. My mom had a sister, but she died when I was a kid. I have no other living relatives, which is hardest for me around holidays."

She saw the sorrow in his eyes. It pained her to see it there. It must be tough being alone in the world with no family. At least he had two good friends and the guy he mentored. He had to be his friend, too. Sage softly kissed on Nick's hand.

"I can recall when I lost my mother, it hurt like hell. I blamed my daddy for her death for a long time, until recently. I thought I would lose him." She stopped talking, drinking her wine, fighting back tears. She was so thankful he was recovering well.

Sage was opening-up to him. Nick was pleased she was finding it easy to talk to him. "Why did you blame him?" he asked.

Sage set her glass down and met Nick's eyes. "He cheated on her. She was so upset that she took off in her car and killed herself. I thought it was his fault until I realized why I blamed him. I even hated him for it. My mother spent most of her time working—it was always patients before family," Sage said sadly.

Nick took her hand, kissing it tenderly. "He took away your hope."

"Yes, that's why I hated and blamed him for so long." She pulled away, picking up her wine glass. She noticed she was telling him things about herself that she shared with only those closest to her. Thankfully, she felt her phone vibrate again. She looked at it a second time. She wondered why he was texting her.

"Nick, how old are you?" she asked bluntly, changing the topic.

"Wow, really, sweetheart?" he laughed. "Do I look that old? What are you trying to say? Huh, baby?" He caressed her cheek with the backside of his hand.

Nick perceived she was getting uncomfortable talking about herself and had changed the subject. He wondered who was texting her. He didn't want to pry, but she'd received messages back-to-back. He recognized from her expression as she read the texts they weren't from family.

"No, silly," she giggled. "I'm twenty-six. See, I told you my age, and women don't usually do that." She took another sip of her wine. "You are a very handsome, sexy man," she added to put his mind at ease because truthfully, his age didn't matter—it was an excuse on her part.

He already thought he was too old for her, but he wasn't going to allow her to get away either. He had already claimed her, and he would do so again later.

"I'm thirty-nine, love. I know that sounds old for you. You called me a father figure, and you didn't need a daddy." He simpered, resting back in his chair comfortably.

"Sorry, I said that. You're not so bad." She cuddled his hand playfully. "Thirteen years apart. I thought you were in your late thirties. Like I said, sexy," she admitted, biting her lip seductively.

"Stop with the teasing unless you want me to take that sweet, pretty mouth of yours." He reached under the table, nuzzling her thigh.

"You're so bad," she hummed, shaking her index finger at him playfully.

They ate their meal, continuing to discover things about each other. They already realized they had some music in common. She was even surprised he liked old-school rap. They enjoyed comedy and mystery movies. He confessed that he had several paintings of her in his studio and promised he would show her when she came over for a visit. She told him how she became a fan of basketball and football, which he was a fan of, too. She discussed that he and her late husband were the only souls who knew about her writing. He assured her writing secret would be safe with him. He volunteered to read them if she permitted him to. He wanted to learn more about her husband, but she shut down. She recounted she stopped wearing her wedding ring at the beginning of spring. It was going to be tough to get her to move past her husband. However, he would wait for her because he recognized she was the one for him.

After their romantic dinner, they went to Ocean Beach Pier. It was a favorite stop for fishermen and surfers. Nick had spent a great deal of his time there in his teen years. He would sometimes take his uncle's yacht out. Now, he had a much bigger, faster yacht. Nick helped her aboard and headed out for a cruise.

The ocean air was cool and refreshing on the water. It was lit up by the light of the Moon and the stars. It was extremely magical and romantic. Sage was daydreaming... well... night-dreaming, when Nickolas interrupted her thoughts. She was standing near the railing, looking out at the ocean.

"Yes, Nickolas?" she spun around, giving him her undivided attention.

"You like the open water?" he questioned, slowing the boat down. He had been watching her the entire time and saw she was enjoying it. You could hear the water splashing softly against the boat.

"It's nice out here. I haven't been out here in a long while. I forgot how peaceful it was." She turned back around, absorbing the view, pushing a memory away of Luke.

Nick moved and stood directly behind her. He placed a hand on either side of her on the rail, then lowered his head and inhaled the aroma of her hair. "Would you love to come back here with me?" he asked, close to her ear.

Sage could barely breathe. His closeness was very distracting. She wanted to step away, but she was trapped. All she thought about was going below deck and making love.

She swallowed hard. "Nick, you're standing too close to me."

"I'm not close enough, Sage." He released the railing, pulling her close to his large frame. He wrapped one arm around her slender waist. She pressed her body against him. She could feel his erection pressing into her. He brushed her hair to the side, partially exposing her neck. He pressed his lips against her neck. Sage let out a tiny whimper. He began to pepper tiny kisses down the length of her neck.

"Don't start this again, Nickolas. You never finish what you start. I don't want to be left hot and bothered again," she moaned feverishly.

He spun her around swiftly. Sage's breath caught in her throat for a second. He saw a look of amusement on her face.

"It happened twice in the limo. Remember? If you're too old to handle a young, vibrant girl like me, let me know. I'll get you some Viagra pills or whatever is hot on the market for your dysfunction," she teased. "I'm sure my sister, Dr. Tate, would help you out if needed." She smiled wickedly.

Nick had a look on his face she hadn't seen before. His irises darkened to a deeper shade—deep sea blue. He was ravenous for her.

"Trust me, sweetheart, I don't need Viagra, or any other drug, to get me going." He took her hand and placed it on his crotch. He was long, hard, and thick for her. He stared into her eyes. "Do I need Dr. Tate to prescribe those blue pills or what?" He smiled at her, mischievously.

She cleared her throat, then wet her lips. "No," she answered timidly. She tried to shift away, but his hands blocked her in.

"No shying away from me now, love. You said I don't follow through." He pulled her close to him, tilting her head up to meet his hungry gape. "I'm going to prove to you I don't need Viagra." He took her by the hand, then led her to the lower level of the yacht. Once down below, he showed her to a nice size bed.

"I have a question for you." He held her face, caressing it fondly. "Do you mean for this to happen again? You and I making love?" He kissed the corners of her mouth.

"A trillion times, yes," she moaned with pleasure.

Maxwell couldn't believe it when he'd followed them to the Port Rose. His woman was on a date with the man he thought was his friend. Apparently, Nick wasn't his

286

friend. He was at the table with his woman. Sage was the most beautiful woman in the room, and Max couldn't be with her. He could only worship her from afar.

At first, he thought she caught sight of him, but she hadn't. His eyes twitched with an evil glare as he watched. He should have been thanking his lucky stars she hadn't. He had been spying on her. Before he left Bayville, he learned from Nick that he was taking her to San Diego. It was like pulling teeth trying to get information out of him. He made sure he followed them everywhere he could go without being spotted. It really irked him seeing Nick acting like a love-sick puppy over her. What Nick didn't know was that she was his. His beloved Sage. He would eventually let him know that. He didn't want to kill Nick, but if he had to, he would. Friend or not, Max wasn't about to let Nick take Sage from him.

He watched as she let him touch her so wantonly. His hands caressed her soft face, and then her hand touched his thigh. He wanted to rip Nick's head off for fondling her. Didn't he know she was too young for him? She was almost young enough to be his daughter. His hands pulsated, wanting to snatch her away from him, but he didn't want to scare her away. He had been texting her, but she wouldn't respond to his messages. She was too busy looking in Nick's eyes. He cursed harshly and continued to stalk her until dinner came to an end. He paid his check, hurrying out the door, making sure he wasn't seen. He followed the limo to Ocean Beach Pier. To his dissatisfaction, he couldn't follow any farther. He didn't want to risk being seen by Nick. But when he got the chance, he would let her know how he really felt about her.

When Sage and Nick returned to Phoenix, she decided to spend the night at Nick's hotel. He didn't want to have it any other way, and neither did she. She hadn't realized how much Nick meant to her. She didn't know how much she missed being in the arms of a loving man.

Sage was still scared because of Nick's past—the way he treated women. She prayed he wouldn't do her the same way. She was risking her heart. She didn't want it stomped on by him or anyone. She lay in bed next to him, listening to his breathing. He was snoring and sleeping so peacefully. She realized she slept peacefully—no dreams about her accident with her husband. She wished they could remain like this, lying next to each other, enjoying the sweet sounds of his breath, his large arm wrapped around her small waist. She felt protected in his arms. He moved slightly, tightening the hold on her.

Nick woke to have her lying in his arms. He tightened his hold on her because he wasn't about to let her leave again. He was on cloud nine with the woman he loved.

Yes, he could utterly admit it without doubt. He was in love with her and had been from the moment he first saw her. She was the one he wanted to marry and have his children with. He wanted her and Nicki. He knew she would adopt her, and he wanted that, also. He wanted them to be his family.

Her body was pressed up against him. He wanted her all over again. She moaned, pressing her rounded ass against his erection. He ran his hand up and down her beautiful naked body. She twisted, turning toward him, smiling. She was the most beautiful woman he had ever had—his goddess. The bright smile on her face was priceless, and he was the one who'd put it there. He pulled her on top of him, moving her curly mane away from her face. He kissed her so passionately it caused her to sigh and say his name.

"I need you inside me," she moaned softly. She reached for his shaft, sitting on it, filling herself up. She moved and rolled on him slowly at first, then picked up the paced, rolling her butt and hips, gripping him tightly. She cooed his name as she rode him. He moved with her, giving her more of what she wanted. He felt her hold on him, causing him to almost release, but didn't. He wanted them to release together, and they did a few minutes later. She lay on top of him, panting, trying to get her breath. He caressed the softness of her back, trying to calm his breathing. There was no way he would let her walk away from him. Age be damned—she was his and his alone.

Max arrived back in Phoenix two hours before Nick and Sage. Good thing his parents had two private jets. He was in his hotel room, waiting on Sage to return his text messages. The only thing for him to do now was to confront her about her affair with his so-called friend. He didn't understand why Sage would do this. Didn't they have a great time together? Holding hands and kissing as they took in the sights together. She acted like she enjoyed being his girl. He was pissed off to the highest pisstivitives. His feet pressed the luxurious carpet back and forth. Max headed for the door. When he reached for the handle, he shook his head, realizing it was a bad idea. He wanted to leave his room and go down the hall to confront them. However, he had to play it cool. He had to remain in the shadows for now if he wanted his relationship with her to work.

Max had to think of a plan to get Nick out of the picture for good. When he arrived back in Bayville, he would make sure that happened. Out of all the women in the world he could have had, it had to be her. Nick had been granted entrance into her beautiful temple—his beloved-beautiful temple.

"You will pay dearly, Nick. That's a promise," he vowed, looking out the window of his hotel room. He picked up his phone to see if he'd received any text messages from Sage. Nothing. He threw the phone against the wall. Luckily for him, he'd purchased a heavy-duty cover that protected from shock and water.

Chapter 16

Sage had promised Nick she would contact him after she returned from Phoenix two weeks before. Another week had gone by and she still hadn't called him. What happened between them almost a month ago would stay in San Diego as would the night in Phoenix in his hotel room.

Sage had clued-in Lora and her dad about her surprised trip to San Diego for dinner. Lora wanted full details about her night, however Sage didn't give her any. Lora could only guess what happened and her dad, also. It must have gone well because she hadn't bothered to come home until the next morning. Still, she'd had time to compose herself and realize it was all a huge mistake. She wasn't in any position to be in a relationship with Nick.

That's what he wanted from her. Love, honesty, trust...the total commitment. But she had that with Luke and had lost big time. It was taken from her so quickly. It was a pain she never wanted to experience again. She had true love once, no matter what had happened between her and Nick. *Oh yeah, lust.* That's what happened between them. If she kept telling herself that, it just may be true. Luke was her true love, who was taken away from her by death. It was an evil thing that interrupted their lives, leaving her alone and him gone. She hated it. What's more, she felt she had betrayed him by sleeping with Nick on more than one occasion. Her weak flesh took over every time she encountered him, but it wouldn't happen again. Come hell or high water, she would make sure of it.

Her thoughts were interrupted when she heard a knock coming from her office door. She looked up and saw Sarah standing in her doorway.

"Wow, chick-a-dee, what is going on with you?" Sarah asked, closing the door behind her. "Work can't be that bad. I made sure I had people on your top priority cases." Sarah made herself comfortable in a seat in front of her desk.

Sage ran her hand over the bridge of her nose, sighing heavily. "It's not work." She pressed her lips together, closing her eyes briefly. "I have to end this lustful escapade with Nick. He claims he wants a relationship with me." She opened her desk, taking out a small bag of Cheetos Puffs. "You want some?" she offered to Sarah.

"No, you need those more than I do. But you can't eat away your problem. You must deal with it. Not that Nick is a problem," she clarified.

"That man is a shallow, arrogant bastard." Sage grimaced, chewing her Cheeto angrily. "I don't know why I allowed myself to get involved in clearing the cobwebs," she sighed, pointing downward.

Sarah erupted into laughter, shaking her head. "Chick, you needed it cleared," she said, continuing to laugh. "But was he any good?" she asked with a grin.

"Yah, the man was better than good," she indicated, chewing on another puff. "I'm gonna need a Cherry Coke."

"White-boy got the skills," Sarah laughed. "White-man," she corrected. "Sage, let's face it. He's the only man who's made you want to have sex. How does he make you feel? Is there an emotional connection there?"

Sage rolled her eyes, digging into her bag, retrieving another puff. There wasn't anything emotional except lust. "Yeah, lust. I don't want to be with him. I had my fun with him. We've both had our fun. You know, when I was in Phoenix he showed up. I couldn't believe it. He had the nerve to show up at my dad's house uninvited to collect on that goddamn dinner-date," she said, licking the tip of her finger. "He took me to San Diego by private jet. Can you believe that?" she reported, shaking her head.

"Wait, the man flew you to dinner?" Sarah leaned close to the desk. "Do tell chick. I know you had a grand ole time." She batted her eyes gleefully. "And he got to meet your daddy and sister in the process."

"Whatever, it doesn't matter that he met my daddy and sister. So, he's met Auntie and Nicki," she spat. "He's a show-off. That's what that whole night was about."

In Sage's mind, that's what it was about. She didn't want to think about what happened—that she was possibly in love with him. She'd rather stay delusional about that night and blame it on lust.

"Like I've said before, and I'll say it again, Nickolas Brimmer is a shallow, arrogant bastard. I don't want him anywhere near me or Nicki. Men like him think they can have anything they want. He can't have the total package. I let him sample the goods but that's it," she added, frowning.

Sarah examined her friend. Sage had feelings for the shallow, arrogant bastard whether she wanted to admit it or not.

"Sage, you have more than lustful feelings for him. You care about him, don't you?" she hinted, leaning back in her chair.

"I. Do. Not!" Sage exclaimed with resentment. "I need a Cherry Coke to wash down the puffs."

Sage wasn't going to admit she cared about him, or anything else. It was pure lust between her and him.

"Okay," Sarah said as she stood. She knew the conversation was incomplete, but it wasn't over. She had a feeling Nick wouldn't say it was over with her best friend. A smile appeared on her lips. She would love to be a fly on the wall listening to their conversation. She could imagine all the lame excuses Sage would come up with.

"What are you smiling about?" Sage questioned arching her brow.

"Nothing chic-a-dee," she stated, following her out of the door.

Nick was waiting for any implication from Sage that she wanted to be in a committed relationship with him, however not a word from her. She remained silent. She'd been back in the city for a while. A month since their night together was advancing. That night was rooted deep in his mind. It kept him up at night, thinking about the love they shared. He had a feeling she didn't want a relationship with him. Why else wouldn't she want to see him when she got back? She intended for it to be over. She even went as far as to say they were free to see other people.

The thought of another man touching her, angered him. His mind was murky with primitive thoughts, forbidding her to stay away from whoever was interested in her. He didn't believe she was seeing anyone—at least he didn't think she was.

Nick wasn't about to call it quits. He believed Sage loved him. She might be confused because of her feelings for her late husband. He could understand that, but her wanting to shove him away wasn't logical. He pushed up from his desk, furiously. *"Sweetheart, I won't let you go. You're mine,"* he mumbled. He stared out of his office window with his hands resting above his head. His phone buzzed, bringing him back from his thoughts.

"Yes, Staci," he answered.

"Mr. Pierceton is here to see you," she replied.

"Thanks, Staci. You can send him in."

"What's up, buddy?" Roy asked with a grin.

"Work," Nick said, taking a seat behind his desk. "Have a seat."

"Why didn't you come to Vegas with me and Paul last week?" he asked taking a seat. "We had a blast. Got into some trouble. The good kind, I mean," he added with a chuckle.

"I had things to do. I wouldn't have been fun to be around," Nick said, resting back in his chair.

"I thought you fixed things between you and your woman. Wasn't she flabbergasted with you flying her privately to dinner?" he asked.

"Yeah, so much Sage hasn't tried to contact me since she came back to Bayville three weeks ago. I don't know what to make of things with her. One minute I think I'm making progress, and the next I'm being put in The Father Figure Zone." His lips curled into a wide smile. "Oh, she's also called me a shallow, arrogant, bastard."

"The what zone?" Roy asked, laughing. "She said all of that... you, a shallow, arrogant bastard?" he snickered.

"Hell, that's the excuse she uses to keep me at bay." He grinned. "Which won't stop me."

"Have you confessed what happened in your marriage? What caused your violent rage? And don't forget about all the relationships you've had since your divorce. The woman is probably afraid to be with a guy like you," he said. "I'm willing to bet she's read what the net has to say about you or maybe she had someone investigate you—her detective boyfriend—and has drawn her own conclusion about you.

"He isn't her boyfriend," Nick cleared up, eyes blazed with anger. "She made that cockamamie story up to keep me at bay. As you can see, that isn't working. I know I need to talk to her about my ex-wife and all the bullshit that happened. Me, almost beating the poor guy to death. And I haven't been with that many women," Nick finished defensively.

"Don't get upset with me," Royce replied. "Come on, Nick, you think she hasn't counted?" He shook his head at him. "Take my advice and talk to her."

"I will do that. We need to talk to each other about our pasts. She hasn't revealed anything to me about her husband. As far as I know he's St. Luke. He was a good husband to her."

"So, you are up against a Saint?"

"Something like that. He even did some work on several mergers for this company—she's aware of it. We spoke only when it came to mergers, but he seemed like a good guy then. All about business. He was great at his job."

"You two would have gotten along great outside of business then," he jested.

Nick could honestly say they probably would have been friends if they had taken the time to know one another. He was glad that hadn't happened because he probably wouldn't be with the woman he was in love with now. That's if the woman he loved accepted him into her life.

"Yeah, I believe so," Nick responded. "How's your love life?"

"My love life is just peachy. I'm not in love like you are, but I'm not trying to be either. I don't want the unexpected to happen just yet," Royce answered.

"You can't control what's meant to happen." Nick stood.

"Perhaps, but I'm going to steer clear as long as I can. I'm going to head out. Talk to your woman, buddy," Royce reiterated before leaving.

"I know, Roy. I got this." Nick spoke confidently, but he wasn't. He was afraid of Sage ultimately rejecting him.

"Okay, later then," he said, exiting his office.

Nick took a seat at his desk. How was he going to convince the woman he loved to take a chance on him? He knew he had to get her alone where there weren't any distractions. Where she didn't have a place to run except into his strong arms. No matter how she denied her feelings for him, he knew differently. She lost control just as he did when the two of them were together. *"Alone,"* he whispered. *"I have to get her alone."*

The sun was setting beautifully on a balmy evening in Bayville. Sage went to the Angelonia Art Gallery after work to see an exhibit.

The gallery wasn't as crowded, which was a good thing for Max. He didn't like being in a large crowd. He felt trapped around a lot of people. He had followed Sage to the gallery. This was a great opportunity for him. He had called her a few times since she'd been back. The purpose of the calls wasn't to speak with her, it was to hear her voice. After a few moments of silence, Sage would hang up which really upset Max. It made him feel as though he didn't matter to her. At the moment, though, it gave him great pleasure watching her as she examined each painting in the exhibit. It seemed as though she could see into the artist's eyes as she studied each painting—feel what each artist meant to say with his or her work. His hands itched to run over her frame. She wore a pink pant-suit—or was it rosy? Who cared? All he knew was that he wanted to touch her beautiful body. Every night, he'd dreamed of making love to her since he'd first seen her running from the building where he lived.

Sage could have sworn for a moment she was being watched but she didn't see anyone. There were only a few people in the gallery. She turned around, looking at a painting of a black woman singing, with her head upward, that held her attention before being spooked.

She thought about Nick revealing he could paint. It must be nice to inherit such a wonderful gift from your mother. The only thing she'd inherited from her mother was her looks. Her aunt and sister would argue differently about that because they said she got her stubborn streak from her mother. She wished things had been different between her and her mother. Her eyes brightened when she noticed the next painting.

Max was so busy gawking at Sage, she'd almost caught him. Good thing he could move quickly. He wasn't old and run-down like Nick. He wished she would see that Nick wasn't the right guy for her. Or maybe she already had. Nick hadn't been in the picture since her return from Phoenix. He was pleased about that. Max had called Nick to meet him at the gallery, pretending it had to do with his art show. He noticed she had moved on to some of the sculptures. This was it. No more hiding in the shadows.

"Hi Sage," Max said, coming up beside her. "I thought that was you."

Sage was startled to find Maxwell Turner standing next to her. She wasn't in the mood for company and wished he would leave her alone. She had come to the gallery to clear her head and to relax. That wasn't going to happen with Mr. Creepy around.

Fiddlesticks! Freaking creep!

"Hello Maxwell," she replied dryly.

Okay she doesn't seem too thrilled to see me. "How have you been? How's your dad?" he asked as if concerned for her father. His only concern was for her, he could care less about her father.

"I'm good and so is my dad." She looked at him sideways, then resumed looking at the sculpture.

"When did you get back?" he asked as if he didn't know. He was testing her to see if she would tell him the truth.

"Oh, about a month. I'm trying to relax," she declared, praying he would get a clue and leave. *For goodness sakes! Just* leave *already!*

Great, she didn't lie to me. "Mind if I tag along with you? I would love to have some company. *Please don't say no. I don't know if I can take it if you turn me down, beloved,*" he spoke inaudibly.

"Sure, why not," Sage said with a sigh of regret. It was the last thing she wanted—to spend time with Max.

"Remember the last time we were in an art gallery together?" he asked.

"Sure do," she remarked, walking slowly. *Wish I hadn't gone anywhere with you, Creepville!*

"I did try calling you while you were in Phoenix. I guess you were too busy taking care of your dad."

"Yep," she uttered, stopping at a huge sculpture.

Her first lie. "*Why would you lie to me, beloved? I would never do that to you. I know you were too busy with Nick. I know he had his hands all over you,*" Max said to himself. He had to stop thinking about Nick groping her. He was becoming angry. His left eye jerked and his hands formed two fists. He felt like hitting something or someone.

Sage caught Max's strange behavior.

"Maxwell, I think I'm going to head out now. I have to pick up my daughter," she said, reaching into her purse to retrieve her keys.

"No, don't go," he pleaded. "I thought we would catch up a minute."

"Sorry, but I have to go. Like I said, I have to pick up my daughter."

"I didn't know you had a child." He acted as though he didn't know about Gloria's child—Sage claiming her like she was hers.

"Yeah, I do now, so I'll see you around," she excused herself curtly. *Creepville*!

"Perhaps, we can go out some other time," he said, hopefully.

"I don't think that's a good idea. I'm not interested in dating. Sorry," she said, walking away from him, praying he got the hint.

"We can be friends, then," he added, moving alongside of her. "Grab coffee sometime soon."

Fiddlesticks! This fool won't take me letting him down easily.

"Maybe, but right now I'm in a hurry. Bye, Maxwell." She scampered off.

"That nut-job wouldn't take no for an answer. Thank God I didn't respond to his

304

texts or calls when I was in Phoenix," she mumbled, heading to her car.

Nick couldn't believe it when he saw Sage darting away from Max so quickly. It was her. She'd been back in the city and this was who she spent time with. *Fucking unbelievable.* He came to the gallery to meet Max about exhibiting his art here. He couldn't believe it when he received the call less than twenty minutes ago. He motioned over to Max after Sage left.

"What's up, Max?" he asked, looking at him intensely.

"I was waiting on you to show up, but I was also enjoying a day out with my girl. She had to take off to pick up Nicki," Max lied. He could see Nick didn't like what he was hearing.

The corners of Nick's eyes crinkled, with his large arms folded across his chest. Probably to keep from laying him on his ass. "What do you mean, your girl?" he queried.

"She doesn't want anyone to know about us yet. You know, her still being in mourning over her husband and all. She wants us to be under wraps," he lied again knowing this would set Nick off.

Nick couldn't believe she would keep that from him, then he remembered her saying they could see other people. *Damn, didn't know she was serious.* He ran his hand over the back of his neck, massaging the pulsating pain.

"You alright, Nick?" Max asked. *This guy is so gullible.* "You want to hang for the game on Thursday night?"

"No, thanks. I must go. I have an appointment. We'll do this another time," he disclosed, moving away from Max before he knocked the fucking grin off his face. But he realized it wasn't Max's fault—it was his own. He got involved with another woman who hurt him. How could he have been so stupid? He'd let his guard down with her. She possessed his heart. He got into his car, slamming the door. "Fuck! Fuck! Fuck!" He hit the steering wheel with his fists. He deserved answers from her, and he would get them as soon as he calmed down.

Parker had been watching Maxwell Turner for some time. He knew about his shady past—always getting off scot free. If not for his parents, he would have been behind bars. His juvenile record had been sealed but there were crimes he had committed against young women after he'd turned 18. All of those had been somehow dismissed or paid off. None of the girls had wanted to press charges or testify. This time Max was obsessing over the wrong woman— Parker's friend. He would do whatever it took to make sure the psycho was behind bars before someone ended up dead, if not already. Parker's gut told him Max had killed Gloria Fulton, leaving her daughter motherless—and the woman was two months pregnant. No doubt the baby was his. It really angered Parker that the piece of shit was still free.

Parker sat behind his desk at the department, thumbing through the casefile, puzzled by the facts in each case. Some of the cases had hard facts but nothing stuck. He leaned back in his chair, looking up at the ceiling in thinking mode. His mind was all over the place when he heard a tap at his office door—Corbin Lester was standing in his doorway.

Lester had been on the police force for two years before Parker came back to Bayville. He should have been promoted to detective second grade before Parker. He'd been at the department longer and possessed more knowledge and skill in his opinion. He wasn't a fan of Parker Richards. Fact was, he hated Richards. He was a cocky SOB sometimes—always showing him up whenever he was in his presence, which was rare. Corbin only came to Parker's office to see if he could get information about the Gloria Fulton case. Other than that, he wouldn't come to him for shit.

"How's it going, Richards?" he asked, moving closer to his desk.

Parker was perplexed by the intrusion. What the hell was he up to?

"You tell me—you are in my office," Parker countered.

"I was going over a case of mine, and I wanted your help with something." Corbin sat, pulling his chair close to Parker's desk. He didn't need Parker's help—he needed to see the file on Gloria Fulton.

"You want my help?" Parker asked in disbelief. Corbin never asked anyone for help and Parker found out the man resented him for having been promoted to detective second grade. Parker was suspicious of Corbin's reasons for asking for help.

"I know I wasn't a fan when you were promoted, but I can see why the captain gave it to you. You are a fucking great cop," Corbin complimented. Of course, he didn't mean a thing he'd said. He had to do it to get information for his friend Max Turner. Corbin didn't understand why he was working for the pervert Turner again. He knew he shouldn't be mixed up with a loose cannon like him. The man wasn't wrapped too tight. Maybe his parents dropped him as a baby or something. But either way, the stupid fuck didn't have all his senses.

Parker didn't believe a word Corbin was saying because since he'd been promoted, this guy was always looking for a reason to nitpick his decisions. He wasn't buying his good cop routine. Didn't he know they were a part of the same brotherhood? No need to kiss-ass now.

"Okay Lester, I'm all ears. What can I help you with?" he asked, closing the folder and placing it in a desk drawer. He distinguished Lester trying to peer at the file before covering it.

Fuck! The bastard moved the folder Corbin was trying to snoop in. This was a waste of his fucking time—he could have been doing something enjoyable on a Saturday afternoon. Maybe hanging out at a bar downtown drinking and enjoying the attention of women.

Corbin discussed a case that involved a woman's husband stealing funds from a company he worked for. "He must have done something awful to the woman for her to go there," he acknowledged.

"Usually, women stick by their criminal partners," Parker answered, rubbing his eyelid.

"Thanks for your expertise on this, Richards." Corbin stood, stretching. "I'll let you know how it all plays out."

"You didn't need my expertise on this, but you do that. I'd like to know what happens. Hey, close the door. Thanks," Parker said, opening the drawer and retrieving the file.

"No prob, boss," Corbin said, glancing at him furiously when Parker wasn't looking.

"Fucking prick," Parker enunciated, looking up from his case, wondering what he was after.

"Knock, knock," a man around the same height and build as Parker opened his door.

"What's up, Scott?" Parker said with a sigh. "Man, I thought you were that prick coming back in my office."

"No way could I pass for detective thinks-he-knows-everything," he chuckled, walking into Parker's office. Scott Castonburgh had been Parker's partner as long as he'd been a part of BVPD. "What did he want anyway?"

"He wanted my help on one of his cases," Parker replied, leaning back in his chair. "Which I find odd. The man can't stand the sight of me."

"That is strange. He's probably up to something. What? I don't know. Better watch your back, partner," Scott warned. "Turner has been up to no good again. He's been following Sage more than usual. The tracker picked him up at her job around 1 p.m. then at an art gallery, and at the gym. Later at her aunt's house. You think we need to warn her?"

"No, I don't want to worry her. That's why we are looking out for her and Nicki," he said. "I think our detective thinks-he-knows-everything was trying to get a glimpse at the Gloria Fulton file I had out earlier. I put it out of the way when he came into my office. I think those two might know each other. Maybe that's why the prick came into my office."

"Could be. I'll get on it—see how those two are connected." Scott moved to the door.

"Thanks for doing this, partner," Parker said.

"No prob, man. You would do the same for me. I'll let you know what I find out." He left his office.

Parker picked up the case file, hoping he was doing the right thing, not telling Sage about Turner.

Chapter 17

Katie was putting the finishing touches on the strawberry shortcake while Cooper was making a salad for Saturday brunch. It was one of Sage's and Cooper's favorite desserts. Cooper had come into town yesterday. He was almost back to his old self and had changed a lot of his lifestyle habits—he wanted to stick around a while. Cooper wanted to see his baby-girl happily married with children.

"Coop, I made something special just for you. I hope you like it," Katie said. "I think I put my foot into this Saturday brunch," she said with a hoarse laugh.

"I know you did, Kat. You always know how to cook it up," he said. "I can't wait to dig in."

"Honey, you best trust and believe. My momma taught me everything I know. I tried to teach your daughter, but Sage isn't good in the kitchen. That girl... that girl," she said, shaking her head with a grin on her pretty face. "She can make sandwiches and soup from a can. Those are a few of her specialties."

They both laughed.

"I know my baby-girl can't cook. I remember when the girls were around twelve and fifteen, they made me a Father's Day dinner. Now Lora's fried chicken was good. Sage's mac and cheese was terrible. You could probably glue two sheets of paper together with it." He chuckled. "Hell, use it for sheetrock."

Katie laughed until tears were in her eyes. "What did you do with the mac and cheese?"

"Too bad we didn't have a dog at the time, but I managed to ball most of it up in a napkin. I pretended it was the best meal I had ever had—and it was." Cooper smiled, remembering how lucky he'd been to have his two beautiful girls cooking especially for him. He was grateful he and Deborah had them.

Katie looked at Cooper—he was happy. She was glad to see him looking well again.

"Cooper, have you made your peace with my sister's death?" Katie asked.

"Yes, I think I have. I beat myself up for a long time over something I couldn't control. Sage made me realize I couldn't change what happened. True forgiveness is letting go of something and moving forward with your life. I was stuck in the past, drowning in misery. I've decided to live. I hope my daughter can forgive herself. She blames herself for Luke's death. Did you know about the baby she aborted when she was dating Parker?"

"No, she didn't tell me that," Katie said.

"She told Luke the night of the accident. That's why she blames herself," he replied. "But it's not her fault. I hope she realizes that."

"I didn't know about any of this. I guess she wanted it that way. I'm joyful you two are talking again, and closer than you've ever been before. Sage confided in you about something so personal—something she hadn't told me."

That was huge for Cooper. He finally had his daughter back in his life. Katie had wanted to see that happen for a very long time—her niece coming to her senses.

"Perhaps, you should talk to her about it again. See if she is trying to let go of the past as you have. Make sure she knows she has you to come to if she needs to talk about it again."

Cooper nodded in agreement, placing the salad on the countertop. He didn't need Katie to tell him what he already knew. He guessed it was her motherly instinct. She had been Sage's mother for the past twelve years and still counting.

Sage and Nicki had arrived at her aunt's at 11:45 a.m. She was cheery; her father was back in Bayville for a visit, and he was better. It was a week before August, and he would return to work. Cooper wanted to spend as much time with the daughter he'd been estranged from for so long.

"Tell me, what's become of you and this Nick guy? I thought he would be here with you or wasn't it genuine between you two?" Cooper could only hope because he would prefer Sage dated someone closer to her own age.

Sage cringed before speaking of Nick. She didn't know what to say. She was supposed to have contacted him when she returned to Bayville but hadn't. She thought for sure he would call her—no phone calls. No texts. No emails. Not a damn thing. The man had stopped talking to her since she'd come back to Bayville. It could be that he'd found a new interest. The thought of that tugged at her heart. It'd been a month and no word from him. It hurt. She hated herself for the unwelcoming feeling he seemed to cause her. She tried not to think about him most days, but it hadn't worked. There was a little problem that had developed from their fun escapades.

"I don't know, Daddy," she said, batting back tears. "I've tried not to think about that man. He's a shallow, arrogant bastard. I hate him," she cried.

Sage was pregnant with Nick's baby. It happened the second time they had sex. How could she be pregnant with this man's child, and she wasn't able to get pregnant with Luke's baby? Nick must have had great little swimmers. The little suckers must have a little gym installed somewhere. The universe had a way of making things complicated. Nick was not the man Sage wanted to spend her life with. They had used protection, and she was still pregnant. Funny how life could catch you off guard.

Her father turned toward her, hearing the pain in her voice. His daughter had feelings for this guy. A much older guy and he'd better get used to the idea of Nick in her life if that was a possibility. Cooper placed a hand on her shoulder and squeezed it gently.

"Sage, it sounds like you care about this man. Do you?" he asked.

"I don't know, Daddy," she expressed. "I don't want these feelings for him. He's been with too many women since his divorce. Nick ends a relationship by giving women expensive gifts. I don't know why I allowed myself to get involved with a man like that. I should have known better, Daddy. I was a fool," she said with glassy eyes.

Her father pulled her into his embrace. He was glad he could be there for his baby-girl, but he was mad at Nickolas Brimmer for causing his baby-girl pain. *What did she call him? Awe, shallow, arrogant bastard.* If he could see him now, he would make him feel the pain his daughter was feeling.

"I'm pregnant," she whispered.

Had he heard her right? His daughter pregnant? He released her and stared at her. "Did I hear you correctly?" he asked, caressing her cheek. "You're having a baby?"

"Yes, Daddy." She smiled somewhat. Sage thought she couldn't have children. She hadn't even realized she missed her monthly visitor until two weeks ago. There was no need to track it as she hadn't been intimately involved with anyone after Luke's death. However, it was too late.

"You're ecstatic, right?" He continued to gaze into her eyes, shocked by his daughter's pregnancy.

"Of course, Daddy, I'm happy about the baby. I thought I couldn't have children. I know you and Luke had to talk about us giving you grandkids." She sniffed. "After the crash, I didn't go see a specialist. I didn't see the point of it. I lost Luke."

"We did," her dad conceded. "He was happy. He wanted children badly, but he found out he couldn't give you babies."

Fiddlesticks! What? She shot up from the chair. Luke had never communicated that to her. All this time she thought it was she who couldn't get pregnant. *Lucas Luke Sullivan,* she scolded silently.

"I didn't know he couldn't have children, Daddy. He never told me that. I thought it was me." She sighed, remembering a conversation she and her husband had.

"We'll both see a specialist to find out which one of us can't have children," Luke said, pulling his wife close. *"I love you no matter what. You hear me, sweetheart?"* He kissed her mouth.

"I feel the same way, Luke. But I want to have our babies," she cried, sadly. *"I think it's me, and I'm sorry, Lucas."*

"Baby, it might be me. I want the same thing, but if it's not in the cards for us, we have each other, and we can adopt. Don't worry, everything will be alright."

"I'm sorry he didn't tell you. He probably would have, but his life was taken too soon." Cooper took hold of Sage's hand, stroking it gently.

"How long did he know he couldn't have children?" she asked.

"I imagined it was a few weeks before the car crash. We talked about three weeks before your anniversary. He was grateful to be your husband. You made him feel like a blessed man. I could see and hear it in his voice every time I saw or spoke to him."

Sage didn't know they'd kept in constant contact. She felt a bit jealous because her father knew more than she did. Her husband never confided he couldn't have children. He should have told her, and maybe things wouldn't have been so disastrous for them. Luke wasn't perfect, but he came close.

"We argued that night. He was mad at me because I confessed that I had been pregnant once with Parker's baby years ago. But deep down, he was mad because he couldn't give me what I wanted. What Parker had done all those years ago." She took a seat next to her father. "I wouldn't have blamed him. I wish he had told me."

"Sage, you can't continue to dwell on the past, sweetie. You must let it go, so you can grow. You had three wonderful married years with your husband. Some people don't get that. You were blessed, and God has another plan for you. All three of you," he added with a grin.

Sage laid her head on her father's shoulders, thanking the universe she had him in her life.

"When are you going to tell everyone else about your surprise?" he asked with a grin.

"Oh, I don't know." She looked up at him, grinning. "But you are the first."

Sage hadn't given Nick any sign she wanted him to be a part of her and Nicki's lives. But he had given that up after a month had passed. Of course, he was hurt. He was more than that. He was furious with her, and there was nothing he could do about it. She had made it clear he meant nothing to her. His pain ran heart-deep.

Most days, his mind was preoccupied with her. Nights were the toughest. He needed her next to him. He missed her scent, touch, and taste. He missed her face, her eyes, and her smile. He missed the way her hips and ass swayed when she walked. When she laughed, her whole face lit up with joy. He missed the sound of her voice.

Nick had been miserable when he learned Max was with her. Max had told him he met her on the plane to Phoenix to meet his parents. That didn't sound like a woman who was still grieving for her husband. But what did he know, he had made love to her twice, breaking down her defenses. Max said they had hit it off, and they took in the sights of the city. They had remained in contact. Now he comprehended it was Max texting her when they were on their dinner date. After finding that out, there was no need for them to talk. He had his answers. *"I guess I was too old for you,"* he spoke, glancing at a painting of her, touching his swollen member. The one he had painted of her in the nude. It was perfect.

His beautiful goddess. Well, that wasn't true. She was no longer his. He needed to go out for a while. It was a Saturday night, and he didn't have a damn thing to do. It would help him get her out of his system if he found someone else to vent his frustrations out on. He covered the painting, walking out of the room, banging the door shut. He turned on a mix of old-school 60s-80s music he loved. 'I think I'm Out of Your Life' came through the waves. The irony of the song. He laughed, running his hands over his face. He glanced at the clock in the hallway—it was 7:30. He picked up his cell phone to call Paul. He needed to get out of the penthouse.

"Hey what's up, Nick-O?" Paul asked.

"Oh, I need to get wasted where I can't feel my face. What do you have in mind, unless you have plans already?"

"Bout damn time you get out of your funk. I'm driving. You need to get hammered."

"Shit-faced, totally. Meet you downstairs in twenty minutes," Nick replied.

Nick was on his way out of the building when he saw Max. He speculated if he was on his way to see Sage. No, he wasn't going to dwell on him or her. He had plans to get wasted tonight and wasn't about to waste his time thinking about her, or what Max was doing with her, or to her.

"Hey Nick, where are you off to?" Max grinned.

"Out with Paul. About to get drunk. What about you?" He didn't want to know. He was being friendly. After all, he had been a mentor to him. He didn't want to be an asshole.

"Going to check up on my girl. I plan on taking her out dancing later," he answered with a glimmer in his eyes. "I can't believe a woman like her would go for me. I have big plans for the two of us. Marriage may even be in the cards for us." He was lying through his front-gap teeth. She hadn't been in contact with him. He'd been spying on her daily, making idiotic plans in his dumb head. However, gullible Nick didn't know that. Max laughed to himself. All Nick had to do was go see her, but Max was glad Nick had given up on her, leaving hope for him.

Nick regarded that Max hadn't pointed out Nicki in his plans. Didn't he know Sage was a package-deal?

"Don't forget to include Nicki into your plans because Sage is the kid's mother now. Anyone can see she loves that little girl as if she were her own child," he commented.

Nick could see that Max wasn't interested in Nicki. *And this was the guy who she had chosen to spend time with? Un-fucking believable*, Nick thought.

"Sure, I know to include the brat. Kids love me," he lied, knowing full well he didn't care or want children. However, it appeared as if the brat was like an unwanted puppy, he couldn't get rid of. So, again he found he had to make an exception with her because he was determined to have Sage. She wouldn't have to worry about anything. She would be at his beck and call, taking care of him, fulfilling all his needs—that would be her only job. As a matter of fact, he wanted that with Gloria, but the bitch had to get pregnant. He was so close to having her as his prized possession. Now he was making the same plans for Sage. His new beloved.

"I have some plans of my own, so if you'll excuse me, I'm off," Nick said, sulking away.

"Okay," Max yelled after him, giggling.

Nick climbed into Paul's BMW.

"What's going on? I saw you talking to the weirdo," Paul said.

"Max was gloating about his relationship with Sage," Nick said, closing the door. "Says he's taking her out dancing. He also mentioned he planned on marrying her, but he doesn't want Nicki as part of the deal." Nick frowned. "I just don't understand why Sage would be into a guy like Max, but apparently she is."

Paul put the car in reverse, backing out of a parking space. "You gotta be kidding?" he said, putting the car into drive, speeding out of the garage. Paul watched Nick for a second, then turned his eyes back on the street. "I wouldn't believe anything that guy says. Remember when his folks first moved into our rental property Ashton-View Hills seven years ago? I told you that guy was missing some screws before he started sniffing up behind you like he needed a daddy. I don't think Sage is into him at all. When did they started dating?"

"Max said he started dating her when he was in Phoenix. He was on the plane with her, heading to see his parents. They hit it off on a plane ride. I saw her walking away from him at Angelonia Art Gallery several weeks ago, which confirmed he was seeing her. I couldn't believe it when I saw them together. She made time to see him but didn't want to see or call me to tell me she didn't want a relationship. That's how little she thinks of yours truly. Un-fucking-believable!"

Fifteen minutes later, Paul pulled into the Knights Jive Club. It was a good place for Nick to drown out his pain for a little while. He hoped Nick would change his mind and talk to Sage before it was too late. *Stop being stubborn, thinking the worst. No matter what he thinks he saw that day at the gallery, it couldn't be true. Nor all the crap Turner was mouthing off about.*

When they were inside, they found two vacant seats at the bar. Parker was at the bar having drinks with Scott.

"Well, look who it is," Paul spoke with a grin. "Our favorite detective. How's it going on a Saturday night?" he asked.

"It's going, man. Taking time off to hang with my partner. This is Scott Castonburgh. Scott, this is Paul Writhers and Nickolas Brimmer," Parker introduced.

"How's it going fellows?" Scott asked, raising his glass to them, taking a drink. Scott knew of them because of the party Parker had thrown to get to know some of the neighbors.

"Not good for my friend here. That's why we're out. He needs to drown his sorrows," Paul said, hitting him on the back.

"In that case, bartender," Scott yelled, getting the bartender's attention, "set my new friends up with whatever they are having."

"Bourbon," Nick said.

"Make that two," Paul said.

"What's going on, Nick?" Parker asked, taking a drink of his whiskey.

"Women," he mumbled in agitation, not saying anything else.

"My friend here says Sage is dating some other guy, and he spoke of marriage," Paul answered for Nick.

Parker's eyes bulged from in their sockets. He knew damn well that couldn't be true. "Wait, not my friend Sage," he said skeptically. "As far as I know, Sage isn't dating anyone. I'm pretty sure if she were, Sarah and Cindy would know. Who's the guy claiming he's dating her or even speaking of marrying her?" he asked.

"He got his information from an unreliable source," Paul said. "I've been trying to get him to talk to her and assume nothing."

Scott was looking between everyone, drinking his whiskey. This was getting more fascinating by the minute. "Who's the source?" Scott asked.

"Maxwell Turner," Nick said. "He couldn't wait to tell me. It's like the man knew Sage and I were seeing each other. He told me once he was interested in her and looks like he got his shot. The bastard!"

Parker and Scott looked at one another. They didn't believe that. Not this obsessive, fucking no-good bastard.

"You mean to tell me Sage is supposed to be dating this guy Turner?" Parker questioned, shaking his head, not believing a word. "I find that highly unlikely. We've have had this suma-bitch under surveillance for a while now."

"Yeah, we've been watching him. He's at his apartment now," Scott said.

"Why are you watching him?" he asked.

"I can't say, Nick. It has to do with a case," Parker said. He weighed if he should tell Nick about the situation even though he and Sage weren't together.

"You think we should tell him since he's been watching her? And it's obvious he cares about her deeply," Scott mumbled to Parker.

Parker thought for a moment. Sage might be in danger now that the bastard was spewing lies, one of them that she was dating him. And he was planning a marriage in his stupid, fucked-up head. Parker turned his attention to Nick. "We need to talk, but not here. Give me a time and place to discuss this matter privately."

"I'm free tomorrow," Nick said, sobering up a little. "Come by my apartment around noon."

"Will do." He nodded his head.

Nick knew whatever Parker had to tell him was bad. Sage wasn't dating Max or anyone else for all that mattered. It was a sick, twisted fantasy of Turner's. He had to have it all wrong from what Parker and his partner had said.

Turner was stalking her. He recalled the memory of them at the gallery. Sage was probably walking away, furious with him. Nick had let his jealousy distort the image. He cursed himself. Nick perceived he had to speak to her after his conversation with Parker tomorrow.

Chapter 18

On Sunday morning, Sage and Nicki went to the community center to offer a helping hand. Sage let Nicki see a counselor before heading to the garden. She wanted her daughter to talk to someone. Sage felt this would help her cope with any issues she was dealing with.

Sage was in the rec room, reading to some of the smaller children. She chose the book "*The Invisible String*" because it dealt with kids being apart from the people they loved. It was a great message for anyone, including herself. Love was the everlasting connection that binds us all.

She had been receiving phone calls from Nick but hadn't wanted to speak to or see him. Why did he want to talk to her now? She'd been back in Bayville for over a month, and he hadn't bothered calling. Now all of a sudden, he wanted to talk. What was up with him anyway?

Sage finished reading the story, and Cindy came over to join her.

"Okay, children, thank Ms. Sage for reading this awesome book to you all," Cindy said with a bright smile.

"Thanks, Ms. Sage," all the kids responded in unison.

"You all are very welcome," Sage said with a warm smile. "Now you all enjoy the rest of your day."

"You too," some of the kids hollered joyfully.

"You all go find Ms. Gertie. She will give you all a treat for being so good," Cindy directed. The children ran off to find Ms. Gertie.

"Okay, let's go to my office and talk." Cindy grabbed Sage by the hand, leading her to her office.

"So, tell me what's been happening?" Cindy asked, taking a seat at her desk.

Sage sat biting her lower lip, not responding right away.

"It can't be that bad," Cindy said.

"No," Sage agreed.

She'd been receiving strange phone calls. They'd started when she returned to Bayville, but they'd recently stopped. She prayed that was true. Nick had told her to give him a call if anything out of the ordinary happened, but they weren't together. It probably had nothing to do with him anyway.

"Okay, what I want to know is, when are you going to talk to Nickolas? I know you care about him just as he cares about you," Cindy said. "He asked how you were doing the last time he stopped by three weeks ago. I think he was hoping to see you."

"I hope you told him I'm not his concern. He shouldn't be asking about me. I haven't heard from him since I've been back. I suspected he's moved on." Sage struggled to keep back the tears.

"You can tell me what's wrong," Cindy said, noticing the tears in Sage's eyes.

"Nothing is wrong. I hate Nickolas Brimmer. I wish I hadn't met the man," she lashed out, tears rolling down her cheeks.

Cindy took some tissues from the box, handing them to her. "Something is going on, honey," she said softly. "Did he do something to hurt you?"

Sage couldn't tell her about the baby. She wasn't ready for anyone to know. She had told her father, just not any of the girls. She was carrying a man's child who didn't give a damn about her. He had taken what he wanted and left her alone. But she should have known it would happen. All she had to do was examine his past.

"I'd rather let sleeping dogs lie." She took the tissue, cleaning her face. "Have you heard from Sarah?" she asked, changing the subject.

"Yeah, a few days ago. She and Parker are in love bliss. Something I wish I had," she said with a sigh.

"What about Paul Writhers? He asked about you the night of the auction. Are you two seeing each other?" Sage asked, intrigued.

"We went out on a couple of dates, but then he backed off. I haven't heard from him since."

Sage could see Cindy was hurt. "So, he's like his best friend—use women and toss them to the side like trash," Sage said with anger.

"No, I don't think so. He was a gentleman with me. We didn't have sex or anything. I don't know, maybe I wasn't his type."

"Cid, you are a beautiful woman. Don't you dare, for one measly minute, think it was you. It was him. Men like Paul and Nick flock together. They get what they want and move on," she replied.

Sage thought about the baby she was carrying. She wasn't sure when or how she was going to tell Nick. Surely, he would welcome their child even though he'd walked away from her. Surely, he wouldn't do that to a child. Nicki opened the door to Cindy's office, interrupting her thoughts.

"I'm all done, Ms. Sage." Nicki skipped over to her.

"Okay, lovebug," Sage said, getting up from the chair.

"Thanks, Sage," Cindy said. "And thank you, little missy. Did you have fun helping in the garden?"

"I did," she exclaimed with laughter. "I want to do it the next time we come back. Can I, Ms. Sage?"

"Sure, if it's alright with, Ms. Cindy." Sage touched her nose.

"You know I love helping hands," Cindy said, smiling.

"Well, there you go, lovebug. You can help in the garden next time."

"Yippie!"

"We are going to head out. I'll talk to you later, Cid. You take care of yourself," Sage exclaimed.

"You do the same."

After Sage spoke with the counselor regarding Nicki, they left the community center and headed to Sarah's.

"Ms. Sage, why hasn't Nick come to see us? I thought you were happy he was your prince."

Sage stopped at a red light. She knew Nicki was bound to ask questions about him. She seemed so sure he was a match for her. She had rehearsed what she would say. Truth of the matter was, she wasn't sure of anything when it came to Nickolas Brimmer.

"Lovebug, Nick and I are friends. You know, sometimes friends don't see each other, and that's okay. He was my prince for that one night."

"I really like him," Nicki said, gazing out the window, disappointedly.

"Oh, sweetie." Sage glanced at Nicki, then back at the street. "Sometimes, adults are only meant to be friends."

"I know," she replied, turning to look at Sage.

Nicki wanted Nick to be her daddy. She hadn't had a father in her life except for her mother's boyfriends, who'd never been that nice to her.

"I wish he would be my daddy," she said sadly. "He's nice," she sighed, turning to look out the window.

Sage could understand her wanting Nick to be her daddy. He had been nice to her, but it took more than being nice to be a father to a child. Nicki didn't understand that.

"Nicki, are you still pleased to have me as a parent?" Sage asked as she pulled up in front of Sarah's house.

"Yes," she answered, nodding her head with a smile. "I'm glad. You're like a mother to me. That's why I call you Ms. Sage," she beamed happily.

"I'm glad, too," Sage said, parking the car. "Now, let's go see Auntie Sarah." She got out of the car, rounding the passenger side to get Nicki out. Sarah was in the middle of cleaning when they knocked on the door.

"Sorry to interrupt you, chick," Sage apologized, giving her a hug.

"Not a problem," Sarah said, hugging her back. "Hey, Nicki." She smiled warmly, patting her on the shoulder.

"Hi, Auntie Sarah," Nicki greeted.

"You two come on in. I am in the process of cleaning up a bit." She moved aside, allowing them to enter.

"Chic-a-dee, I need my entire house cleaned," Sage complained.

Sarah closed the door leading them to the kitchen area. "You want something to drink? I do have Cherry Coke, your fav," she grinned.

"*No, I better not,*" Sage said to herself, remembering she had to eat and drink better for the sake of her baby. "Water is fine." She took a seat at the counter.

"I have something special for you, cutie." She took hold of Nicki's hand, leading her to the table. Sarah took two peanut butter cookies from a container, placed them on a small plate with a glass of OJ, and gave them to Nicki.

"Thanks a bunch, Auntie Sarah," Nicki sang happily, accepting the snack.

"You're welcome, baby. Be a good girl while I talk to your Ms. Sage." She patted the top of Nicki's head.

"Okay," Nicki answered, chewing on the cookie.

Sage sat at the counter, waiting on Sarah to join her. She was deep in thought when Sarah handed her the water sitting across from her.

"You look like you have a lot on your mind, chic-a-dee. You want to talk about it?" she asked, sipping on a glass of water.

She hadn't told Cindy about the baby, but she had confided in Sarah years ago about the same situation. This time she was mature and would love and cherish the life that was growing inside of her. She needed to talk to someone about it.

"I'm pregnant," she whispered, taking a drink of water, waiting on Sarah to respond.

"You're pregnant? I can't believe it. Congrats, chick. Wait, you are happy about the baby?" she questioned, thinking about the last time Sage had been pregnant. She was frightened to death for her friend.

"Yes, I'm tickled-pink, Sarah. I want the baby. I don't know if Nick would want it, or if he even wants children. I haven't been in contact with him since I got back from Phoenix, and he hasn't tried to communicate with me. Nick is probably doing what he does best—using another woman to get what he wants."

"You have to talk to him, Sage." Sarah reached across the counter, taking her hand. After Parker filled her in last night on what happened, they needed to talk. He told her to keep their conversation private. It was a part of a police investigation. "I know you are upset with him, but for the baby's sake, talk to him." She released her hand, drinking her water.

"And how do you suggest I tell a man who doesn't want to have anything to do with me that I'm pregnant? Just blurt it out? I haven't figured out how to tell him yet. Oh, I know, 'We haven't seen each other since Phoenix, but by the way, I'm two months pregnant.' What if he denies the baby is his?" she cried softly.

"Yes, you tell him like that. I don't believe he'll flake on his child. You don't believe that either. You are afraid of him and the way he makes you feel. The night of the auction, I saw the way you behaved around him. I could have sworn I saw love growing between you two that night." She smiled.

"That's not true," Sage exclaimed. She looked over at Nicki, who was flipping through the TV channels. "I love Luke. I'm in love with Luke. Not Nick! He's such a player. He's been with too many women. The internet doesn't paint him as a good guy either. He's a shallow, arrogant bastard. Maybe I do want him to reject the baby like he's done me. Nicki just asked me about that man. She wants him to be her daddy," she whispered.

"Oh, Sage," Sarah said, getting up from her seat, moving next to her, comforting her.

Sarah understood her friend cared more for Nick than she was sharing with her. Nick just may be the man to be Nicki's dad if given a chance to prove himself. Sage may be in love with him. From what Parker told her, Nick was in love with her.

"You and Nick need to talk," she stressed, caressing her back. "From what you are saying, neither one of you have talked to one another. There isn't any closure. You are both stubborn—communication is the key."

Sage knew all that Sarah said was true. She and Nick needed to open communication. It had to start with her since she was pregnant.

Sage and Sarah talked about other topics for a while before Sage decided it was time to leave.

"Nicki and I should head home. It's been a long morning for us. I'll see you tomorrow at work. Tell Park I said hello."

"I will, and you take care of yourself. Have you been to the doctor?" she inquired.

"Yes, I have. Everything is good so far." Sage smiled, genuinely. "I've been taking horse-sized vitamin pills, which I hate, but I take them for the little one." She rubbed her belly.

"Good, who else knows besides me?" she whispered.

"My daddy knows, and now you, so don't go spilling the beans just yet." Sage laughed but was serious, also. They both moved near Nicki.

"I won't. Your secret is safe with me, chic-a-dee."

"We're going to get out of your hair. You need to get back to your Sunday chores. Come on, Nicki, it's time to say bye to Auntie Sarah." She took hold of her hand.

"Okay. Bye, Auntie Sarah."

"See you later, sweetie." She patted Nicki on the back lightly.

Sarah met Parker at his place after finishing her chores. She couldn't get over the fact that Turner had made up that mess about Sage and boasted to Nickolas they were dating. The fool even thought he had a chance at marrying her best friend. She was glad Parker and Scott were looking out for Sage's well-being. Someone like Turner could be dangerous. She hoped Sage would communicate with Nick about the baby soon.

"Baby, do you think Nick will speak to Sage today?" Sarah asked, looking up at Parker as they sat snuggled on the sofa.

"Yes, I told him everything he needed to hear. He's going to take the necessary measures to help keep her safe, as well. I hope Sage is willing to talk to him. Nick told me she hasn't wanted anything to do with him since she came back from Phoenix."

"That's not true," Sarah said, looking at him. "Sage thinks Nick isn't interested in her. They are both making assumptions. I've told her to communicate with Nickolas. She really needs to more now than ever." She thought about the baby Sage was carrying.

"What do you mean by that?" Parker asked, eyeing her.

"I meant, she needs to stop pretending there isn't anything between them when there is."

There's a small human developing, she thought. She couldn't tell Parker about the baby.

"Sage is afraid of Nickolas's past—what happened in his marriage and the things the internet said about him. I know she's in love with him. You remember the night of the auction—they looked like two people in love."

"Yeah, I remember her behavior toward him," Parker laughed. "She was acting like she didn't want anything to do with him, but we both know it wasn't true," he said, placing a tender kiss on her lips. "I was even her fake boyfriend the night of the cocktail party." He grinned.

"She didn't tell me that," she giggled. "Our girl really tried to stay away from him, but what's meant to happen will be." She kissed him firmly on the lips.

"I agree, baby," Parker said, nibbling the corners of her lips. "Those two will come around sooner than you think if Nick has anything to say about it," he said, between nibbling kisses. "I bet he's on his way to see her."

"You're probably right, baby. Now let's take this to the bedroom," Sarah moaned softly.

"Yes ma'am," he agreed, scooping her off the sofa, heading to the bedroom.

Sage had to do some soul searching. She decided to drop Nicki off at her aunt's house for a little while and went to the cemetery to visit her husband and mother's graves. She hadn't been to the cemetery in a long time or made peace with their deaths. She thought if she visited their graves and talked openly, it would help her. It was a long shot, but she figured it might do her some good. Sage picked up flowers for the graves before going to the cemetery.

"Mommy, I miss you so very much. I wish you were here," Sage said as she placed the flowers on the grave. "I love you, Mommy. The thing is, I love Daddy, too. I know you did as well. I pushed him away and blamed him for you dying. But I know he didn't kill you—it was the car crash. Why did you do it, Mommy? Why did you drive that night? I wished you had listened to Daddy and not gotten behind the wheel. I know he hurt you deeply, but you hurt me, Mom—you left Lora and me. We didn't have enough time together. I know I wasn't your favorite. I know you loved me. I wish you were here, Mommy," she whimpered, taking a tissue from her pocket, wiping her nose. "I was hoping you would stop spending so much time with your patients and be there for me—for all of us—more. We really missed you when you were at work. I know Daddy missed you most of all. I blamed him all those years when it was you, I should have blamed. You took away my hope when you died. I hoped you would be in my life more. On some strange level, I thought by holding onto you, I still had that hope. I know I didn't, and I don't now. I forgive you, Mommy. I love you." Sage hugged the gravestone, then stood up, wiping her eyes as she headed to Luke's grave.

A dread came over her. She didn't want to go to his grave. However, she knew she needed to.

This was the third time Sage had come to Luke's gravesite. The first two times, she wasn't ready to let go. She still wasn't certain she could. Sage laid the flowers on his grave as tears fell uncontrollably from her eyes. She tried not to think about that tragic night, however she couldn't help it.

"Luke, you know I love you. I will always love you. You were taken away from me too soon. I miss you so much," she wept. "My heart aches for you. I wish I could take back everything. I should have kept that damn secret from you. I would have you with me if I had. Do you know how many times I dream about you, baby? About us? It's too painful at times."

She began to think about Nick. "But when I was with Nickolas Brimmer, it hurt less. The times I slept with him, I rested peacefully. Nightmares didn't invade my dreams. I'm pregnant, Luke," Sage sniveled, caressing her belly. "He doesn't know yet. I don't know if he will even accept this child.

Why didn't you tell me you couldn't have children, sweetie? I wouldn't have blamed you. We could have adopted as we planned to if it didn't work out for us. I'm going to adopt this beautiful little girl named Nicole-Marie Fulton. You would love her as much as I do. Luke." She said his name in a soft whisper, eyes flooded with tears.

"I have to move on, baby. I need to let you go. I think I'm in love with Nick. The man I'm pregnant by. I know he has moved on with someone else, but I need to let you go for myself. I have moved on with my life. I've been at a standstill. I love you, and I always will, my love." Sage stood, wiping her eyes with her heart feeling a little lighter. "Goodbye."

Nick had been trying to contact Sage all morning, but she hadn't responded. He went to the park to clear his head and figure out what he would say to convince Sage she was the right woman for him, and he was the right man for her. With Turner's obsession with her, he needed to come up with a solution quickly. He was on a park bench with dark shades on when he noticed Nicki and Katie walking his way.

"Hi Nick, how are you?" Katie asked.

"Hello, Katie," he answered, removing his shades. "I'm well. Hi, Nicki," he greeted happily.

"Hey, Nick," she said, looking at some kids kicking around a ball with their parents.

"You enjoying this beautiful morning?" he asked. "You're welcome to sit with me," he offered, motioning with his hand.

"Okay, thanks," Katie said, taking a seat. Nicki took a seat next to her aunt, placing her ball down on her lap.

"We were playing with her ball, but I got tired and needed to rest for a spell."

"Nicki, would you like to kick the ball around with me?" Nick offered, looking at her. "If it's okay with your Aunt?" he asked, looking at Katie.

"It's okay by me," Katie grinned, looking at Nicki. "Well, Nicki?"

"Sure, if Nick wants to." She got up from the bench with the ball.

"Of course, sweetie, I want to," he said, reaching for her hand.

"I thought you liked my Ms. Sage, Nick," Nicki said as they walked. "Isn't she beautiful? She was your princess that night. She said you only wanted to be her friend, and that's why you haven't come to see us—that friends don't see each other all the time."

Nick couldn't believe Nicki was asking about Sage and him. She sounded so mature for her age. She obviously wanted them together. He wished Ms. Sage wanted that, too. He had to be careful how he responded to Nicki because he didn't want to get her hopes up thinking he and Sage would be more. He wasn't sure if he still had a shot with Sage.

Nick stopped walking, bending down to be level with her. "Nicki, I like Ms. Sage. You're right, she's the most beautiful princess in the world to me. But sometimes adults can only be friends, sweetheart."

"Ms. Sage said that, too," she voiced with sadness.

Nick lifted her head. "Hey, sweetie, that doesn't mean I can't show you how to kick a ball around, or anything else you want to do that's fun. You will need to get Ms. Sage's permission though." He touched her nose playfully.

Nicki eyed him with a big smile. She still supposed there was a chance he would be her daddy. "Come on, Nick, let's kick the ball around." She tugged at his hand.

"Okay, sweetie," he said.

Katie dialed Sage's number. She wanted her to know Nick was spending time with Nicki. Katie didn't consider Nick was anything but a good guy. Her niece had a problem with that being true. She could also understand her niece not believing. She didn't want to get hurt.

"Hi Sugar, guess who Nicki and I ran into?" she asked.

"Hello, Auntie, and who?" Sage asked.

"Nick," she stated, waiting on her to respond.

"Where are you and Nicki?" she asked curiously.

"We're at the park. She's playing kickball with Nick as we speak. He's really good with her. Sage, the man offered to play with her. I don't understand why you pulled away from him," her aunt said.

Sage had had plenty of reasons. Obviously, he wasn't the kind of man who stuck around for a long time, not to mention his shaky past. Now she needed to find a way to tell him about their baby, regardless of anything else. Would he be thrilled about her unexpected pregnancy as much as she was?

"So, he's good with Nicki. That doesn't mean he's good enough for me to bring into our lives. Listen, Auntie, I know you mean well, but let me figure this out," she sighed.

"Okay, Sug, I'll see you later."

"Later, Auntie."

Nick was in his car, debating if he should get out and knock on Sage's door. He had made a huge mistake not coming to her in the first place. How could he have been so blind? He believed Max and his lies. If it hadn't been for Parker, he would still be in the dark about everything.

Parker had told him Max had been following Sage for a while now. He'd also clued Nick in on the women that have gone missing who were involved with Turner. Nick needed to show Sage how much she meant to him, and he could be trusted with her life. She was very important to him, and so was Nicki. He wanted to marry her one day soon. He had to fix their relationship if he could even call it that—technically they weren't in a relationship.

If he wanted the answers to his questions, he needed to get out of the car. He stepped onto the front porch, pausing. *"Okay, here goes,"* he spoke aloud, ringing the doorbell. When he didn't get an immediate response, he knocked. He wasn't going to go away—he needed the answers.

Sage heard her doorbell ring. She looked at the clock, it read 9:30 p.m. She climbed out of bed, picking up her robe. Nicki was asleep in her bed. She closed the door lightly, hoping not to wake her.

Sage hurried to the door, praying whoever it was wouldn't wake Nicki. Her heart skipped a beat when she looked through the peephole and saw Nick. She hadn't expected him to be on the other side of her door, banging like the police. She had to compose herself because she wasn't ready to face him yet. He had already given her aunt and Nicki hope they would be together and that had upset her. She needed time to think. Shallow. Arrogant. Bastard. What gave him the right to come to her place unannounced like the freaking cops? *"Fiddlesticks,"* she said in a soft, angry murmur.

Come on, baby, open the door. His knocks became harder.

She couldn't believe he would knock on her door like he was out of his ever-loving mind. His knocks became harder. She yanked the door halfway open, looking at him angrily.

"What is your problem?" she asked, with the door half-cracked.

"We need to talk, Sage. I'm not leaving until we do." He stood bolstered against the door. "I've been trying to reach out to you all day. You've been avoiding me."

"I don't want to talk to you. It's late, and I'm about to go to bed. I have work in the morning." She pretended to yawn.

"Baby, please," he begged. "I've missed you." He touched her cheek.

"Nick, I..." she paused, staring up at him.

She began to look him over more closely. He hadn't shaved, and his hair wasn't neatly laid on his head. His blue eyes looked tired. The wrinkle lines around his eyes were more evident than usual. He had a blue t-shirt with white basketball trunks on. On his feet were a pair of gym shoes. This was the first time he didn't look well put together. He looked vulnerable.

"Nick," she spoke softly. She opened the door to step outside on the deck and looked in the direction of a neighbor's house.

"Sweetheart, I'm a mess without you. Can't you see that?" He turned her face to meet his stare. "Let me come inside. I need you, Sage."

Seeing her standing there, looking so beautiful, made him forget why he was there. His beautiful goddess. He truly missed everything about her. He ran a hand over his unshaven jaw, watching her. He couldn't read her at the moment. She stood there looking so titillating and intoxicating at the same time and had no idea how much power she had over him. She had on a black, thigh-high nightgown with its matching robe. Her polished brown toes were bare. Her curls framed her oval face beautifully. Without warning, he snatched her up against him.

"Nickolas, no," she rebuked mildly, pulling away from him.

It felt really good to be against him like that. He smelled of sweat with a hint of musk. However, that didn't stop her from wanting him.

"You and I haven't spoken to each other in over two months now, and you have the audacity to be around my child today. What was that all about anyway? Then you come here now telling me you miss me. I don't believe you."

"Sage, love, I'm sorry. I'll explain if you allow me to come in."

She had to hear what excuse he had to offer. Besides, this was a good enough time to tell him about the baby.

"Okay, sure," she said, biting her lower lip. Being this close was stirring up her already rampant hormones. He had been the only man to make her body respond so chaotically.

Before he released her, he took her mouth hungrily. He missed her perfect mouth and groaned as he kissed her lips, savoring the sweet pleasure they offered. She parted her mouth, giving him entry. He took her up on her delicious offer. He opened her front door, closing it behind him with his foot. He positioned her against the door, settling her feet on the floor then deepened the kiss, obliging them both of the intensifying explosions. He pinned her there with both hands, continuing to assault her mouth. They groaned and moaned from the heated kiss.

Sage stepped forward, touching his jaw, caressing him, enjoying the roughness of his unshaven face. It was a new, exciting experience for her. She had never felt his face unshaven before. It felt like a long torture session ending—her touching him like that. She didn't know how much she'd really missed him until that instant.

Nick towed her closer, lifting her off her feet, sampling every inch of her beautiful mouth; a mouth he'd been longing for. It felt like it had been a century since he'd tasted it.

God, he couldn't get enough of his beautiful goddess. She had to know she belonged to him. No other man was meant to have her. They were put together by the universe. Perhaps her husband may have had a hand in it, as well. Luke wouldn't want her to be on this earth alone. Nick knew if the circumstances were reversed, he wouldn't want her to go through life alone.

His hand began to travel underneath her nightgown. When she rebuked his hand and pushed away from him, a part of him went numb.

She allowed herself to get carried away by the fiery kiss. Her body always behaved poorly in his presence—offering her up like a sacrifice. She thought she should feel guilty for allowing it but didn't. Could it be her husband wasn't perfect, as she'd made him out to be? That was no longer true. She thought she was the one who'd kept a secret when it was them both.

Her Luke should have been honest with her. She assumed it was her fault he died because of her secret. It weighed so heavily on her heart each day until her father told her about her husband's secret. Though she felt a little better after visiting his grave, maybe she could love another man, completely. However, she knew this had to stop. She hadn't seen or heard from him. Yet, her body had no shame. *Freaking Mr. Wondaful.* She pushed at his chest, so he would stop, and he did.

Nick looked into her yearning eyes. She wanted him, but she pushed him away. It hurt to know she rejected him still.

Chapter 19

Nick watched Sage for a moment. He wanted her to be his wife. They loved some of the same things, had laughed together, and enjoyed each other's company. She possessed human qualities his first wife hadn't like faithfulness, loyalty, and honesty. Sage was the woman he wanted to marry. But how was he going to convince her she was the only woman for him and that she was meant to be with him?

They'd found each other at the right time and place. Yes, she'd loved a man once before and lost him. However, she was a new chapter for him. He was no longer afraid to commit to a woman. He didn't need short-term relationships. Nick was a new chapter for her, too, helping to heal her broken heart. He would be the mender that made her heart whole again.

Sage could feel her barricades coming down. In the past weeks, Sage had more feelings for him. For so long she'd been in denial of her feelings for Nick for fear of it not being real. Fear was one of the reasons she hadn't contacted Nick when she got home from Phoenix. She wasn't ready to let another man get into her heart only to have it ripped to pieces. She didn't trust him because of his past. Even now, she didn't trust herself when it came to him.

"Nick, follow me," she mouthed. He took hold of her hand. She led him into her living room, where they sat. "Tell me why you have come here," she asked.

"Sweetheart, I wanted to come to you when you first got back. I asked you to contact me if you wanted us to move forward. You didn't, so I accepted you didn't want to have anything else to do with me. I love you, Sage. I'm in love with you. There are some things I have to tell you, and I hope you don't walk away from me afterward." Nick ran his hands over his messy raven hair.

"You know I was married five years ago. The marriage lasted two years. I thought I was in love with her. I hadn't suspected before we were married, she flirted and spoke inappropriately with other men. My friends warned me about her, but I didn't listen. I met Daisy Winters at a Millionaires' Conference one year before I married her."

"Is there really such a thing? A Millionaires' Conference," Sage asked cynically.

"Yes, my love, there is." He smiled, kissing the palm of her hand. He'd known

Sage wasn't the type of woman to go after a man's bank account from the beginning.

"Daisy voiced all the things I wanted to hear. She was looking for love and wanted a family. She presented herself as a successful, wealthy interior designer. In the beginning, we wanted some of the same things, but she was telling me what I wanted to hear. I didn't see her lies or deceit. She was a decorator, but not a millionaire. Truth is, I wouldn't have cared about that anyway. Daisy came to the conference to attract a sucker like me. She was very beautiful and cunning.

Fast forward, we were married in a short time. It wasn't until after we were married, her true nature started to show. Two years into our marriage, I had to go to a conference out of town. Paul and I got as far as the airport when I realized I'd forgotten some important documents for the meeting. We went back to the apartment—Paul waited for me curbside so we could save time. I let myself into the apartment, and I heard Daisy upstairs. For a minute, I thought she was in trouble, but when I heard the words, I knew better.

I got to the bedroom door and found her in bed with another man. I lost it. I was so angry, and out of control, I nearly beat the man to death. If it hadn't been for Paul, I would have killed him. The judge gave me one year' probation, and I had to go through an anger management program. When the guy recovered, he sued me and won, which I didn't care about. I had to pay five million dollars, and I would have given more. I'm ashamed of what I did."

Sage felt sympathy for him. He had been dealt a bad hand with his ex-wife. She didn't know how she would have reacted in the same situation.

"It's okay, Nick. I understand."

She hadn't understood at first. She'd assumed the worse because of the many women he had been with. She'd misjudged him.

"No, it's not okay. I could have killed him. My jealous rage could have killed him. You must know when I saw you with Maxwell Turner at the art gallery, I was jealous. I thought you were seeing him—he told me you were. I wasn't going to allow myself to get caught up in jealousy again. Not that kind, anyway. Trust me, it would've been that kind."

"Wait, Max told you he and I were dating?" *Bleh.* She felt sick and placed her hand over her belly.

"Yes," he said, facing her.

He recognized it was a lie when he saw the expression on her face—absolute revulsion. Turner had convinced Nick, and now he was mad at himself. He had lost time to fix what was broken between them because of Max.

"Baby, I'm sorry. He made it seem so real. He said you were dating and that he planned to marry you. The thought of that being true tore at my insides."

"*Eek*," Sage disputed, looking at him in shock, covering her mouth with her hand. He had to be following her. The thought of that scared her.

"I've never dated Max. When I was in Phoenix, we went sightseeing together and to an art gallery. He wanted more from me, but I told him we could only be friends. The night you and I went out together, he was texting me, but I ignored him. I thought he would get the message that I wanted nothing to do with him. Then he ambushed me at the art gallery here. He was still trying to pursue me. I felt something was off about him that day. I want nothing to do with him. He's a fool-creep, a pile of nasty horse manure. He's someone I wish I had never met."

The thought of that man following her was unnerving.

"I'm so sorry for thinking otherwise," he pulled her into his embrace, held her close, and kissed her forehead.

"Nick, I have something to tell you. It may come as a shock because it shocked me." She raised her head from his chest, sitting up straight.

He gazed at her, wondering what she was about to say.

"I'm two months pregnant. Well, almost three." She spoke bluntly, running her hands over her hair.

Nick sat speechless for a moment. *She's pregnant?* He continued to stare at her as if he didn't know what she was saying. The news had rendered him mute. She prayed he wanted the baby but couldn't tell by his expression.

Nick was flying high at that second with the idea of being a father. It was so surreal. Nick stood and brought her up with him, spinning her around.

"Nickolas," she giggled joyfully. "Put me down."

He stopped, placing her feet on the floor and patted her belly. She wasn't showing yet, but their baby was growing inside her.

"I'm going to be a father," he cheered.

"Yes, I thought you wouldn't want the baby. I guessed you didn't want me either."

Sage shied away from him. He wasn't a shallow, arrogant bastard after all. He was a decent man. She had him figured wrong. He was the man she had fallen in love with.

"Sweetheart, I've wanted you from the first time I saw you. I don't want to be with anyone except you. You are my one and only forever. I want our baby, too. I've always wanted children."

Nick kissed her longingly on the mouth, then pulled away from her. They needed to discuss Maxwell Turner. He wasn't going to leave her alone for another second.

"We need to talk about Turner," he declared, leading her back to the couch. "He's the guy I had been a mentor too. The one I told you about. I had no idea how messed up in the head he was. I'm so sorry. I hadn't been there to protect you," he said, kissing her forehead. "But I'm here now, love."

"I had no clue he was following me. I received some strange phone calls, but they have stopped. I know it was him since he told you that hogwash. You have nothing to apologize for. It's not your fault he's an insane person," she insured."

Nick had asked her to tell him if she received anything out of the ordinary, but he wouldn't dwell on that now. She was with him.

"Parker has been looking out for you. He and Detective Scott Castonburg. Do you know Parker's partner?" he asked.

"Yeah, I know of Scott. He's been Parker's partner for two years, I think. I don't understand why Park didn't tell me this."

"He didn't want to worry you. And, it has to do with the murder of Nicki's mother. Max is somehow tied to this case. Parker gave me some brief details. I'm spending the night with you, and I don't want to hear any objections." He stroked her cheek gently.

She wouldn't give him any either. She would feel safe if he stayed.

"I have no problem with you staying here tonight."

"Good," he approved, kissing her forehead. "I want you and Nicki to come live with me at the house on the outskirts of the city. I want you both safe."

Again, she didn't mind. It would only be until Maxwell was no longer a threat to her or her unborn child and Nicki.

"Okay, Nick," she agreed, kissing him.

He was surprised at her boldness to kiss him. He shouldn't be, but it was refreshing to know she cared about him. Even if she wasn't over her husband, Nick would have a special place in her heart soon.

The next morning, Sage woke at six a.m. Nicki was in her bed asleep because she'd had another nightmare. Like the last nightmare, Nicki didn't confide in her. Since this was her second nightmare, she may have to see a child psychiatrist on a regular basis. Preferably, someone at MCC.

Sage eased out of bed, not waking Nicki. She went to the guest room to peek in on Nick, but he wasn't there. When she went downstairs, she heard the TV playing the morning news in the living room. The weather lady said it would be in the low eighties today. She noticed Nick lying on his back asleep with his arm draped over his forehead. He was shirtless and Sage could see the muscles in his chest contract. She was tempted to caress them but didn't. He looked so peaceful lying there. She moved closer, then stroked his jaw. He grabbed her.

"Fiddlesticks, Nick," she yelped.

He wore a boyish grin, dragging her on top of him as he sat up straight, bringing her with him. He positioned her on his lap, running his hand up her smooth thighs. He drew her close to him, staring into her eyes, then placed his hands on her cheeks, smoothing her lips with his thumbs. He lowered his head and grazed her lips with his own.

"How are you this morning?" he asked, releasing her face.

"I'm doing okay. I thought you were going to sleep in the guest room. Was it uncomfortable for you?" she asked concerned. She wouldn't have agreed to him staying over if it was going to interfere with his sleep.

"I was a bit restless for a while, so I came downstairs to watch some TV, but apparently it was watching me," he replied, trying to assure her he was okay.

He was restless because of Turner. He was a threat to her, and Nick felt the urgency to rectify the problem quickly. He didn't want anything happening to his family. Nick couldn't be with them all the time and decided to hire a bodyguard for Sage and Nicki. He hoped Sage would go along with it.

"Baby, how would you feel if I hired a bodyguard to watch out for you? I'm not able to be with you at all times, and I feel a guard would keep you, Nicki, and the baby well-protected."

She wasn't keen on the idea that she needed someone watching out for her twenty-four-seven because of that nut-cake Maxwell Turner. She felt it unfair her privacy had been compromised. Sage hadn't led that buffoon on in any way, but he had it in his tiny head that she was dating him. Hell, he thought that she was his girlfriend in his dweeb-mind, no telling what else he thought about her. How twisted was that? It was all her fault. If she hadn't indulged the fool-creep on the plane that day, he wouldn't be obsessed with her. Never in a million years would she presume anyone would be obsessed with her. It was crazy.

"No, I don't want anyone invading my private life." She ran her hand through her messy hair. "I hate that this idiot has put me in a situation where I need someone to watch my back at all times. It's ridiculous. I've never hated anyone in my life before, but this guy has put me in that position," she admitted with weeping eyes. "I'm afraid..." she said, cutting her words short, covering her face with her hands. Tears rolled down her cheeks.

Nick pulled her close to his chest, making her feel protected because she was. He would do everything in his power to make sure of it. Seeing the tears stream down her face made him want to go over to Max's apartment and brutally hurt him. If he could get away with it, he would. He didn't like the fact that she was afraid of this fucking dickweed. Guys like Turner had delusional jealousy toward their target. He interpreted Sage's kindness as something romantic. Sage wasn't interested in the likes of him. Nick was still angry at himself for believing she was involved with Turner—the woman he had gotten to know. He should have known.

"It's okay, baby. I promise you're safe. I won't allow that bastard to get near you or Nicki." He stroked her head, kissing her. He held onto her closely, wanting to comfort her and dissipate all her fears. The only way to do that was to get rid of Maxwell Turner permanently.

Sage knew she was protected as she laid against Nick's strong chest, but he wouldn't be there for her all the time, therefore she needed a bodyguard. She loathed the idea of her privacy being invaded but knew it was necessary. She raised her head to meet his stare.

"I do need someone to look out for me when I'm not with you. So, yes, my darling to the guard." She cuddled his jaw.

He was appreciative she'd approved of the bodyguard, but even if she wasn't on-board, it wasn't an option to not have one. She was carrying his baby, and he wanted them safe. He took hold of her cheeks, placing a soft kiss on her lips. He was about to deepen it, but he heard Nicki calling for Sage. They pulled apart, getting to their feet. Nick grabbed his shirt, putting it on quickly. Nicki came over to the two of them, rubbing the sleep from her eyes.

"Hey, lovebug, did you sleep okay in my room?" Sage asked, taking hold of her small hand.

"Mm-hmm," she said, muffled. "I just didn't know where you were when I woke up." She hugged Sage's leg.

"Awe, lovebug, I wouldn't leave you alone. I love you very much." She stroked her back, lovingly.

"Good morning, Nick," she said, moving away from Sage.

"Hi, sweetie pie," he answered, lifting her off the floor. "How would you like for you and Ms. Sage to come stay with me for a little while?"

She looked at Sage for approval and got it. "That would be okay," she said, placing her little hand on his jaw. "Are you and Ms.

Sage girlfriend and boyfriend now?" she asked innocently.

"Come on, Nicki," Sage announced, taking her from Nick's arms. "It's time for breakfast," she said, placing her feet on the floor. "What would you like?"

Nick was disappointed Sage hadn't answered Nicki's question. He wanted to say they were, but he knew she wasn't ready for that type of commitment from him yet, though she was carrying his baby, and it seemed like the perfect choice. But he realized she loved and cared a great deal for her late husband. Surely, she would make room for him to take up a portion of her heart because he wasn't about to let her go—no matter what. His thoughts were interrupted when she roped her arms around his waist. He turned around, gathering her into his arms.

"Is that coffee I smell?" he queried.

"Yes, I made it just for you. The baby and I can't have that for breakfast," she said. "I'm going to have toast and fruit. You want breakfast? Not sure how long you were intending on staying. I know you have a corporation to run." She batted her eyes up at him cheerfully.

"Of course, I do, however, you, him or her," he said, caressing her belly, "and Nicki are my top priority. I don't want you making excuses not to come to me or contact me with anything, Sage. You are the most important people in my life," he explained with emphasis, hauling her into his arms. "Thanks for the coffee."

Sage was glad to hear him admit that. At first, she was afraid to give herself to him and with good reason, because she didn't know what she was getting herself into until now. She could honestly say she was blissful again. She hoped it didn't fade away because Maxwell was there to throw stumbling blocks in their way. He had already tried to split them apart. Lord only knew what he was capable of doing. She prayed Parker and Scott put him behind bars if he had anything to do with the death of Nicki's mother. The evil that people do was petrifying. There are good people in the world too, and she had opened her heart to him.

"So, you told him about the baby?" Sarah asked, sitting in front of Sage's desk.

"Yes, I admitted about the baby, but you are not going to believe how I told him," she said.

"Oh," Sarah said, leaning slightly forward. "How did you tell him?"

"First off, let me tell you that I have a bodyguard now. I have a car to take me to work and Nicki to school. I will be guarded twenty-four-seven until I'm in the presence of my man. I hate the fact that my privacy has been invaded. Nicki and I live with Nick for the time being."

Sarah sat paralyzed for a moment. She heard her best friend say, 'my man,' which she thought she'd never hear again. *And now, she's living with him. Oh, and she has a bodyguard. Wonder if he's fine. Cindy needs a good man in her life*, she thought to herself.

"Wow, all this happened yesterday," she stated questionably. "Why do you need a guard?" she frowned. She knew Parker and Scott were looking out for her.

"Okay, now for the rest of it. Maxwell Turner has been following me around, and I had no clue. Parker understood, and he didn't even bother to tell me. I can't believe he wouldn't tell me. That fool-creep Maxwell told Nick I was basically his girlfriend. I couldn't believe the BS when Nick told me. Parker and Scott have him under surveillance. Nick told me he might be tied into the murder of Nicki's mother. If he killed that little girl's mother, I'll be sick. I talked to the bastard, and I went sightseeing with him and to an art gallery," she cried.

"It's not your fault if this low-down-rascal did murder her mother. You aren't guilty of anything but being friendly. There's nothing wrong with being friendly." She got up from the seat, moving beside Sage, rubbing her shoulders.

"Thanks, Sarah. I don't know why I always get the short end of the stick. Doesn't the universe want me to be happy?"

"Sure, it does. You have two wonderful people in your life, and you have a baby coming. You're blessed to have them all. You found true love again, which I had my doubts about for a while. You have blossomed beautifully, Sage. Happiness looks perfect on you. You're going to get through this. You have a man in your life and family and friends. How about that."

"Yes, I know." Sage looked at her grinning. "That's a huge win."

She was in a great place with Nick. This was the time to tell him she was in love with him but was afraid to jinx their new-found relationship by telling him. What if it doesn't work out? What if he was used to being with different women and couldn't get used to being with just one? What if? She was still playing that ridiculous game.

"I had come to a complete stop with my life until Nicki and Nick came into it, making it move again. I'm grateful for that. I'm also grateful for my family and friends, nagging me, telling me I needed to move on and live."

"Chic-a-dee, I remember when you chewed me out for saying you need to give love a do-over again. I'm so glad you took my advice," Sarah said.

"Yeah, you and me both. Good thing I listened."

"Parker and Scott are going to put that fool-creep behind bars soon, especially if he's a murderer. I guess he had his reasons for not telling you," Sarah assured.

Truth was, Sarah knew Parker hadn't wanted to scare Sage to death by telling her she had a stalker.

"Maybe, I guess he did. You grill him good when you get home." She laughed.

"You better believe it, Chick," Sarah said grinning.

"Okay, enough about my life. How are things in the world of Sarah J. Crawford and Parker Richards?"

Sarah blushed. "Things are going really well. I hope neither of us messes this up. We are both prone to relationships not ending well." She half-heartedly smiled.

"I think you two found each other in the nick of time."

"Only time will tell. I look forward to finding out though. Tell me, is the guard cute? Cindy could use a good man in her life right about now," Sarah said as she headed for the door.

Sage leaned back in her seat with a wide grin on her face indicating he was handsome.

"Yes, the man is fine with a capital F," she bragged. "I'll introduce him to you later.

If I didn't have a man, he would be right up my alley." She giggled.

"That hot, huh?" Sarah laughed.

"Oh yeah."

"We better get busy introducing Cindy first. Hey, don't go anywhere alone," Sarah warned, turning around, looking at her seriously, changing the subject. "Never underestimate an insane person like him."

"I'll be careful. I promise. Nick has me well-protected."

Sage walked to Sarah and cuddled her. She prayed it was enough to keep her from the likes of Maxwell Turner. She was afraid but wouldn't let Sarah know that. She didn't want her worrying over her.

"I'll talk to you later."

Sage went back to her desk, staring out at downtown Bayville, her thoughts on her aunt and sister. She had to tell them she was expecting. Cindy needed to be told, as well. She couldn't wait to see the expressions on their faces. She placed her hand on her belly.

"You are truly loved, my beautiful baby," Sage whispered. She leaned forward, put on her glasses, and got back to work.

Chapter 20

Sage was at the office finishing up last-minute paperwork giving Nick some alone time with Nicki. He took her to Angelonia Art Gallery because he knew she loved to paint. She was pretty good for a child her age. He wanted to expose her to as much art as possible.

"So, Nicki," Nick turned, looking down at her. "Are you enjoying this?"

"Yes, very much," she grinned. "My favorite thing so far is that one." She pointed at a magnificent sculpture. "My mommy loved to paint. She promised we would go to an art gallery, but we never got the chance to go," she said, sadly.

Nick caressed her small hand, sympathetically. "I'm sorry, sweetheart," he said, gazing down at her. "I bet your mom taught you everything she knew about painting."

"Mum-mmh, she was teaching me about lines and compositions. I miss her, but I miss her less when I'm with you and Ms. Sage," she spoke joyfully.

"I'm happy too, sweetie," he said with a grin. "I'm honored to be a part of your life. I can continue to teach you everything I know about painting."

"Thanks, Nick," Nicki said, hugging his leg.

"You're welcome, sweetheart," he said, picking her up, cradling her for a moment before they walked to admire another painting.

"This is so great," Nicki said, looking at a painting with many varieties of colors and tones. "I want to be an artist when I grow up," she acknowledged with excitement. "I also want to be a social worker like Ms. Sage. She helps so many children. She's sort of like a superhero."

Nick was impressed Nicki thought of Sage as a superhero because in a way, she was saving the lives of children who needed her.

"That's so nice of you to think of her that way. I think she's a superhero, as well. You can be anything you want when you grow up. Don't let anyone tell you differently." He patted her head lightly.

"Oh, I won't," she assured him.

"How about we continue viewing the gallery another day, and we go get some ice cream before heading home?" He shifted toward her slightly.

"Hooray!" she said with excitement.

"Okay, then it's settled. But don't tell Ms. Sage we had ice cream before dinner." Nick took her hand and led her out of the gallery.

"Oh, I won't," she agreed happily.

Later that evening, Sage joined Nick and Nicki at Cape Diego Pizzeria.

"So, how were your adventures today?" Sage asked, looking between the pair, taking a bite of her pizza.

"We had a great time," Nicki answered gaily. "We went to the art gallery, then we went and got ice cream. Oops," she said, covering her mouth, looking at Nick for a moment. "I wasn't supposed to tell you we had ice cream before dinner. Then we went to the toy store. I'll show you what I got once we get home," she said, biting into her pizza.

"It's okay, Nicki. I don't think Ms. Sage minded that we had dessert first," he winked at her. "See, we both had a perfect day together," he focused his attention on Sage. "And you were worried I couldn't handle a few hours with her," he admitted, taking a drink of his soda.

"I had faith in you, baby." She squeezed his hand. "I'm pleased you and Nicki got along well. After all, you need the experience."

They both decided not to tell Nicki about the baby yet. Sage thought it would be best to wait a little while.

Nick caressed her hand, acknowledging her last statement. He would do his best to be a good father to his unborn baby and Nicki. If it wasn't for his uncle being in his life, he wouldn't have had a father. He owed everything to his uncle.

"Good," he acknowledged, biting into a slice of pizza. "I think all three of us should take a trip together. Somewhere near a beach and loads of sunshine," he said, placing the pizza on his plate, taking a drink from his soda. He belched. "Excuse me."

Nicki giggled at him. Nick touched her nose playfully.

"I think that's a great idea. Do we get to choose?" Sage asked, pointing at herself and Nicki.

"Sure, baby. Wherever my lovely ladies want to go," he guaranteed.

"Okay, we'll have to think long and hard about it," she admitted, tugging on Nicki's ponytail. "We'll give you an answer in a few days." Sage smiled.

Max was frustrated after the failed attempts to get near Sage. He had followed her bodyguard to the pizzeria. There was no sense of him staying there. He couldn't get near his beloved.

He went home to come up with a plan. He was in his office on the internet, searching for ways to dispose of a body. His head throbbed from his search. Rubbing his temples, he clicked on another webpage with disappointment. He couldn't let this come back on him. This was the only option he had to get rid of Nick. It was Nick's fault he had to go to these lengths. He hired the bodyguards, keeping him from taking her. They were around twenty-four-seven. He imagined they even ate and used the bathroom with them to keep him away. It was so pathetic the lengths Nick went to keep him away.

Max couldn't break back into her house again because someone was there as well. So pathetic. He pushed up from the office chair, taking his bottle of whiskey with him. He hoped the whiskey would help his aching head. Looking out the window, Max noticed the copper and his girlfriend heading into the building. The pair was making his stomach churn. A malicious grin formed across his dry, cracked lips, as he remembered his old pal who'd assisted him in the past. Well, he wasn't his old pal—more like an acquaintance.

Max moved away from the window to make a phone call. He wasn't going to get his hands dirty with this. Come to think about it, he might not be able to pull the trigger himself. Nick was like an old uncle to him or an older big brother. Shame he had to get rid of him, but he wasn't giving

Max any choice. He picked up his cell phone and dialed a number.

"Hello," a deep voice answered. "This better be good. Interrupting my goddamn sleep."

"Good to hear your voice, too, old pal," Max said.

In truth, these two weren't pals at all— they were frenemies at best.

"I be goddamn, Maxwell Turner."

He sat up on the old brown couch, rubbing the sleep from his round, beady eyes. "I haven't heard from you since I helped you with that other problem you had. What's been up with you?"

"Nothing much," Max replied, scratching his beard. "I met a girl, and I'm planning on asking her to marry me soon. I must get rid of the boyfriend first. That's why I'm calling you old pal of mine. I need your help on this one. You still take those requests? I know this is short notice and all, but I could really use your help on this. Unless you don't do this type of thing anymore."

Max ran his hand over his preppy hair then picked up the bottle, taking a drink.

"Sure, old bud. I'm still in the business," Jacob Holden affirmed, sitting completely straight.

Jacob had better listen to the shit-for-brains. He hadn't had the pleasure of killing anyone in over two months. He had an itch that needed satisfying. He craved the smell of blood spilling from a victim. He was more twisted than his acquaintance Max. He took pleasure in imposing pain on someone and watching them die. He was a professional killer who didn't give a damn about anyone but himself. He liked his whores and whatever alcohol he was consuming that day or night. He and Max knew each other through an old friend of his in the police department. They'd gone to the same high school together and got into plenty of trouble. Turner and Holden didn't get along well.

"When do you want this to go down?" he asked.

"You have any plans for tomorrow? That's how fast I want this to go down." Max pressed his index fingertip down on the bottle, then picked it up, taking a drink.

"Fuck, this is gonna cost you a whole lot more," Holden said, swallowing the last of the vodka, then poured more into the glass.

"Money isn't an issue. I need to know if you can handle this by the end of the week without doubt. I need this taken care of, and I don't want it to come back on me. I need this done right," Max said, taking another swig of the whiskey.

"Hell, I've never botched a job. I've never had a mutherfucking problem in the past," he snarled in anger.

"Okay, calm down, old pal. I'm just double-checking. This woman is very

"Yes, I did." She flashed a grin. "You need us, Sugar, and I'm here as long as needed. I'm glad Cooper is here, too."

"Me too. Nicki is in for a good surprise," Sage said, moving her hair away from her face."

Nate came into the kitchen, speaking to them, as he poured himself a cup of strong black coffee. "Sage, you feeling alright?" he asked.

"As best as I know how, Nate. Have you heard from Parker this morning? Anything new?" She hoped.

"Nothing new. Same intel as yesterday," he replied, sipping his coffee. "Maybe he'll call later with better news."

"I sure hope so," Sage replied.

"I'll see you later. I have to check on the other guards," he added, heading out with his coffee in hand. He and Cooper spoke briefly.

Cooper walked into the kitchen. He hugged Sage before heading to the coffee.

"You sleep alright, Daddy?" she asked.

"Yes, baby-girl. Like a log. I didn't realize I was so exhausted yesterday."

He took a seat beside her, taking a sip of his black coffee. He could tell she had been restless, which was understandable.

"Nicki hasn't come downstairs yet? he asked.

"Nope, she'll be down any minute now," Sage ensured, rubbing his arm.

"Cooper, how was your flight?" Katie asked.

"It wasn't bad. I arrived about fifteen minutes to eight. Made it here at 9:15 p.m., I think," he replied, rubbing his eye.

"You are taking care of yourself, right?" Katie inquired.

"Of course, Kat." He smiled. He was happy he had a concerned family in his life. He was blessed. Nicki walked into the kitchen, yawning and rubbing her eyes, unaware of her aunt and grandpa. When she opened her eyes focusing, she jumped up and down happily. Sage was thrilled that Nicki was genuinely amazed. Her daughter needed this. Sage walked over to her.

"Well, it looks like my baby is happy her two favorite people are here for breakfast." She kissed her head.

"Granddaddy, you're here." She hurried to hug him.

"Yes, baby-girl," he said, picking her up, hugging her. "I missed you, too. Were you behaving like a sweet princess?" he asked, planting her in a seat next to him.

"Yes sir," she answered, nodding her head. "Just ask Ms. Sage and Aunt Katie."

"Oh, I believe you have," he pulled her cheek lightly, smiling down at her.

"Breakfast is served," Katie announced, setting platters down on the kitchen table. She prepared eggs, fresh, cut fruits, and pancakes.

"Wow, Aunt Katie," Nicki said, jovially, "I wish you could live with us."

"Hey," Sage broke in laughter, "You don't like my cooking, sweetie?"

"Sorry, Ms. Sage but Auntie cooks the best foods."

"I agree, baby-girl," Cooper acknowledged, rising from the seat, helping Nicki off the seat at the counter.

"I see y'all making assumptions I can't cook." Sage stood with her hands about her waist.

"Sage," her aunt said with a wide smile, "you're good at certain dishes you prepare. Like grilled cheese. That's one of your talents in the kitchen."

"I won't argue with y'all because Nick loves my food," she bragged.

"We know," her aunt placed her hand over her belly.

They all laughed except Nicki.

"What's so funny, Ms. Sage?" Nicki asked, innocently.

"Your aunt is talking about me not being such a great cook." She patted her back.

"Oh," Nicki sang happily. "But I said it in a much nicer way, right, Ms. Sage?"

Everyone burst into laughter again, including Nicki.

Parker called Sage later on that day to update her. Unfortunately, there wasn't anything to report differently. He wished there were, but he hadn't come up with any more leads.

He was angry with himself because he kept coming up with dead ends. Bringing his work home hadn't worked either. The Captain wanted them to find Nick quickly. He demanded results. His boss's boss was on his Captain's case hard, looking for progress. The Captain put more people on the case to assist. Nick had people in high places.

Parker hadn't realized Nick knew so many powerful people. He sat at the desk in the borrowed apartment with the file on Gloria Fulton. His gut screamed Max somehow fit into her murder. Either he killed her and her unborn child, or he had someone else to do it. The craze-bastard had been stalking Sage, which was why they believed she was in grave danger. He even admitted his plans to Nick. He wanted to marry her. And God only knew what else he had planned in his tiny brain. The bastard was sick. How could anyone murder a pregnant woman? He closed his eyes momentarily, then glanced down at the file still in his thoughts when his cell rang. The caller ID indicated it was Cooper. He hesitated before answering the call.

"Hello," he spoke, wiping his tired eyes.

"Hey Parker," Cooper said, walking out onto the patio. "I want to know what your efforts are to find my future son-in-law.

442

Sage isn't doing well. She's good at pretending, but I know my daughter. I'm worried about her."

"I'm doing my best to locate him. I understand this is tough on her. You don't need to remind me. I've been working around the clock. Both Scott and me. And other officers. This case is at the top of everyone's list. I can't give you the information—just know this is a top priority." He glowered, scratching the tip of his nose. Cooper acted as if he wasn't doing his job. He remembered back in the day Cooper didn't care for him. He thought he was trouble. He was, but only with the girls.

"Okay, Parker," he stated, watching a guard patrolling the grounds. "My daughter has had enough heartbreak and pain caused by the men in her life she loved, including me. You catch my drift?" He wanted Parker to know he understood what happened years ago between him and his daughter. "So, I hope you find him alive. She couldn't bear another death," he emphasized.

He figured Sage must have told Cooper about what happened in her past with him. But no, his friend didn't need another tragedy. "I'll make sure we bring Nick back to her alive." He prayed that God was listening, or his angels were. He hadn't gone to church in a very long time.

"I'm glad you know what's at stake," he said. "It was good Nick hired the bodyguards for her protection. But he failed to protect himself in all this."

"Nick didn't anticipate Turner making him the target. None of us did. Turner's sights were always on Sage. Goes to show the lengths this bastard's willing to take to have her. I gotta go, Cooper. Know that I'm working very hard to find Nick," he added right before disconnecting the call. As soon as he ended the call with Cooper, he received another call. He glanced at the caller ID. It read Blackwell Corporation. He took a seat at his desk.

"Hello," he answered, waiting on the person to respond.

"Well, Detective, have you located Nickolas yet?" a man with an airy voice asked.

"Who am I speaking with?" Parker asked.

"This is James Blackwell. You interviewed me when Nick went missing Wednesday night. I'm checking in to see if you have made any progress in locating him. I've known Nick for quite some time now."

"Mr. Blackwell, I can't disclose any information about the case. My partner and I are working hard to find Nick. He means a great deal to us."

"You know he's expecting a child," Blackwell informed. "It would be a shame if that child grew up without his father."

"I know that, and we're doing our best to find him." He didn't appreciate Blackwell coming at him as if he answered to him. He already had to deal with many others concerning Nick. Hell, his boss was on his ass hard, chewing what little he had left. "Mr. Blackwell, are you sure you didn't see anything unusual other than the blue Ford?" he questioned.

"No, sorry, but that's all I remember that stuck out like it didn't belong there. It was an old, rinky-dinky truck. One that looked like a late 80s model."

"I have to get back to work," he said, rubbing the back of his neck.

"Sure, Detective. Let me know if you need anything to help find Nick. I mean that," he ensured.

"Will do, sir. And thanks," he added, ending the call. Parker grabbed his gun and put it on as he thought about Nick. They had become friends in such a short time. He prayed he didn't let Nick down nor Sage. He had to find him. "God, please give me a sign where to look," he pleaded. He locked his desk, walking out the door.

The following day, Sage and Nicki were very surprised when her father brought home two unexpected guests—Lora and her

445

son BJ. Her father hadn't specified that they were coming for a visit. She was so lucky to have them all there. She really needed a diversion from her reality. Nick could be badly hurt or even dead. Her mind was running on so many terrible thoughts. Lora and her son being there was a huge help.

"I can't believe that you're here," Sage said, embracing her sister. "And you little mister have grown," she said, releasing her sister, embracing her nephew.

"I'm seven years old, Aunt Sage," her nephew said, grinning. His eyes wandered over to Nicki.

"This is your cousin, Nicki," Sage said to BJ. "This is your cousin BJ, Nicki," Sage introduced.

"Hey, you wanna check out my room? Ms. Sage and Nick bought me a lot of awesome stuff," she suggested with excitement. "We can play a lot of games if you want."

"Sure," he agreed. The pair took off, upstairs.

"No running upstairs, you two," Sage called.

"Okay, Ms. Sage," Nicki hollered back.

"I see those two will get along great," Lora said, interlocking her arm with her sister's.

"Yep, two peas in a pod," Sage said with laughter.

"Yeah, until one of them aggravates the other," their dad added. "I'm going to head to the library to catch up on some reading and let you girls reconnect awhile," he said, disappearing from the room.

Lora and Sage went to sit in the garden. Lora noticed the bodyguards walking the perimeter of the property, but she was watching Nate.

"I see you have eye-candy watching your every move," Lora giggled.

"Whatever," Sage said, joyfully pinching her sister.

"Ouch," Lora squealed.

"Nate is here to protect and serve, nothing more."

"I know. I'm only teasing you, Sage." She wanted to distract her sister as much as possible. "He used to be your type back in the day."

"Don't I know it, but don't say that to Nick. We've discussed Mr. Nate already." Sage's mind was on the man she loved. Praying he would be alright." Tears gleamed in her eyes. She'd lost count of how many times she'd cried.

Lora caressed her back lovingly. "So, what news have you heard about my brother-in-law?"

"So far nothing good, but Parker and Scott are working on finding him. I'm keeping the faith that they will bring my man back to me alive," she breathed. "He's not your brother-in-law until he puts a ring on this finger."

"Of course, Nick will put a ring on that finger. I believe Parker will bring him back to you alive, little sister," she affirmed, continuing to stroke her back gently. "Parker won't let you down. If anyone can find him, it's most definitely Park." She prayed she wasn't wrong.

"Hey, who's watching my little niece?" Sage asked, wiping her eyes, changing the subject. "I know Ben can't watch her while he's working."

"Oh, we have a nanny who takes care of the kids from time to time. She's great with them. That's one of the reasons I'm interested in working part-time."

"She's an old lady nanny? You don't want some young, good-looking woman around your husband. I don't care how trustworthy he is," Sage said.

"No, Mrs. Carrington is a sixty-year-old lady, whom I trust."

"Good."

"Hello, ladies," Nate said with a smile.

"Hi, Nate. Let me introduce you to my big sister Lora. She and her son are visiting me," she introduced gaily.

"Nice to meet you, Lora," he greeted, extending his hand to her.

"Same here, Nate," Lora grinned, accepting his hand, shaking it. "My sister is happy to have you protecting and serving her," she expressed, teasingly.

Sage pinched her side.

"Ouch," Lora gulped, looking at her sister.

"Nate, is everything alright?" Sage asked.

"Yes, don't worry. We have everything under control here, I promise," he reassured. "I'm heading inside for a moment. The other guards are checking the grounds as we speak. Again, don't worry, Sage—we're keeping you all safe. Be back shortly," he said, walking away.

"Wow ," Lora emphasized, watching after him.

"You need to stop," Sage replied with laughter.

"I'm married, Sage, not blind," she affirmed, tapping her shoulder, happily.

There were still no new updates concerning Nick. He'd been missing since Wednesday night—it was now Saturday evening. The longer he went missing, the less likely he would be found alive. It frightened Sage to her very core. *"God, please let Nick be alright,"* she prayed, kneeling. *"My children and I love him and need him more than you. You have plenty of angels—you have Luke, and my mommy Just please spare him. I don't know if I could survive without him."* She sniffed. *"Please grant me this favor."* Sage headed downstairs and found Lora, Cindy, and Sarah talking on the patio.

Sarah suggested they have a girls' night out to get Sage's mind off things.

"Come on, Sage, I think it would be good for you to go out for a little fun with your girls. And sister, of course," Sarah voiced, looking at Lora with a bright smile.

"I think that's a great idea, sis," Lora said, kneeling in front of her sister, stroking her hand.

"I don't know. I think I should be here in case Parker has some news for me," Sage looked around at everyone.

"Sage, you can go out for a bit. Parker will call you on your cell if something comes up," Sarah insisted, touching her back. "You won't miss his call."

"Hey, it's okay. We're here," Lora said, caressing her back. "We'll make sure you keep tabs on your phone. That way, you won't miss a call."

"Let's all go out, Sage," Cindy said. "It'll help ease your mind to see other things and do something different. How can you turn down a fun time with the three of us?" she smiled, looking at Sarah and Lora.

"Huh-uh, I agree with Cid," Sarah acknowledged, hoping to help change Sage's mind.

Sage didn't see what difference it would make to hang out with them. She wouldn't have fun because her mind would be on the man she loved. But she obliged them to keep them from worrying about her.

"Sure, but it won't be fun for me," she said glumly. "I won't be any fun to be around until my love returns to me alive. I'll stay out no more than two hours—that's it," They gave her a group hug.

Later on that night, Sage ended up at a club with her friends and sister. The kids were home with their dad. Nate accompanied them to the club. It was non-negotiable. The four of them found a booth near the back. Club Latey was where Sage's aunt occasionally sang. It was a nice jazz spot with live music on Saturday nights.

As soon as they were seated, the server came to the booth.

"What can I get for you lovely ladies?" he asked.

"Well, handsome, I'll have a vodka with pineapple juice on the rocks," Sarah said.

"And I'll have an apple martini," Lora stated.

"Make that two apple martinis," Cindy added. "Sage, what are you having?" Cindy asked, nudging Sage's elbow.

"Oh," Sage said, coming back to reality. "I'll have cranberry juice with no ice, thanks."

"Okay, ladies, I'll be back shortly with your drinks."

"Aren't you glad we got you out of the house?" Lora asked.

"I guess," Sage answered, doubtfully.

She wished she had remained home. It wasn't the time for her to adventure out when her man was still missing. The sound of laughter, dishes clinking, and people talking faded into the background as she became more and more consumed with worry about Nick. God, why had she said yes to them? At least she could be in her own bedroom to cry. She batted back her tears hard.

"Hey, look who's performing tonight," Sarah said, pointing at the stage. They knew Sage's aunt would be there, but she didn't.

Sage's eyes followed Sarah's finger. When she saw her aunt, Sage's face beamed with joy. She hadn't heard her sing in a while. The last time was earlier that year at one of her aunt's friend's birthday party.

"Thanks, you guys," she said, looking at each one of them. Her aunt blew her a kiss. She dedicated the first song to Sage. It was entitled "Dear to My Heart." After three additional songs, Katie took a fifteen-minute break and joined the ladies at their table.

"I'm so proud to see you all, especially you, Sug." She touched Sage's back lightly. "Are you having a good time?"

The server interrupted their conversation. "Sorry, ladies, but here are your drinks. "Ms. Katie, you want anything before you head back on the stage?" he asked.

"No, my break will be up in a few, but thanks, Marco."

"Let me know if you all want to order anything from the dinner menu. The kitchen closes at 11:30 p. m."

"I think drinks will be fine," Lora said. "Thank you."

"I'm okay, Auntie," Sage said, resuming their conversation. "I didn't expect to see you performing tonight. Thank you for your dedication. You sang beautifully. It was a refreshing surprise. I haven't heard you sing in a while."

"I'm happy you enjoyed it. Thanks, girls, for getting her out of the house for a little while." She hugged Sage briefly before going back to the stage. I have to get back to work. I'm glad to see you all out together."

After Katie's last set, the girls said their goodbyes and headed home. Sage hadn't heard from Parker. It was so frustrating not knowing if Nick was okay. She knew she was in for another restless night.

They followed Nate to the black Suburban with black tinted windows. In the SUV, the girls talked to one another about work, politics, and their relationships. Cindy stayed out of the relationship-topic because she wasn't sure about her and Paul. She noticed Sage had been quieter than usual.

"Hey, you good?" Cindy asked.

"Yeah, I'm okay. Just wish Parker would call me with some good news."

Cindy wished the same thing. She hated to see Sage go through this feeling completely helpless. She prayed Parker would phone soon with great news—that he was home safe and sound.

"He will," Cindy encouraged, holding her hand.

Chapter 25

Parker pulled the plug on the outside surveillance of Turner. He'd concluded that Lester compromised the operation by letting Turner in on what little information he knew. It wasn't much but enough to make Turner paranoid and stay put.

Turner was definitely spooked—the guy had been looking out his window every five minutes, anxious about something, since Thursday evening. Parker used two of his best detectives to review video footage hoping it would lead to something. Scott was busy investigating other possible leads. Parker asked Nate to help him out by keeping an eye on Turner. Nate was willing to help, making sure Sage and Nicki were both safe. Of course, Parker wanted the same thing. She had her dad, sister, and nephew at the house. Before Nate instructed the bodyguards, he updated Sage on the information Parker had given him.

Parker went back to the station, waiting on word from Nate on Turner's move. Unlocking his desk drawer, he took the case file out and stared at a picture of Gloria's dead body. Parker set the picture on his desk, and moved through the folder, looking for any clue he might have overlooked that would give him a lead on Nick's whereabouts. Not finding anything new, he set Gloria's file aside and took out the file on Turner.

Parker studied the file, focusing on Turner's previous victims. Max had never been charged, and Parker found this dumbfounding—he couldn't be that clever. Parker knew that for a fact because Lester was his inside help. Scott had done some digging on Turner, Lester, and Holden. He discovered that all three men had known each other since high school. Corbin must have covered up information that could have closed some of the cases concerning other girls Turner had been associated with.

Parker kept thumbing through the files for a few minutes before walking to the window, watching Bayville at its busiest hour of the night on a weekend. You could smell many of the local eateries and hear music off in the distant. There were couples casually walking in the well-lit park nearby.

He looked past the park at one of the tallest buildings in Bayville—Nick and Paul's building. It was lit up magnificently. He had to find Nick before Turner had someone do something awful to him. He didn't want to say kill him because Sage had been through enough, losing the people she loved. Parker would turn this around and put the sick son-of-a-bastard behind bars.

Parker moved away from the window, gathering up the information on Turner to return it to the file, when he stumbled across a picture he hadn't noticed before. It was a picture of an old warehouse out on Callipillar Road.

The warehouse was about twenty or thirty minutes from the city. He knew about the place because it used to be an old furniture warehouse and had employed one thousand people back in the day, including him. It was his first job. He worked there after school sometimes. It shut down a few years after he left for college. Nobody understood why the place went out of business. People said it was because the owners got bored with it.

Maybe God had answered his prayers. He called Scott to let him know he might have a lead and was on his way to the warehouse. He would call him to let him know if it was a dead-end or not. It would be truly destiny at work if this was where Nick was being held.

Holden went to check on his guest. It was a Saturday night, and Turner still hadn't shown up. He wished the psycho bastard wouldn't show, so he could get on with his business. If it hadn't been for

Lester, he would have done what he wanted to do by now and gotten rid of the evidence. But he had to be a loyal friend to Lester. In actuality, Lester was the only one Jacob had, so he couldn't mess that up. He walked down the stairs, heading to Brimmer, kicking garbage out of his way.

Nick slowly raised his head when he heard the man walking around the warehouse, making a lot of noise. Nick moaned. His head was still pounding, feeling like he had been in the ring with a heavyweight boxer. He wished this lunatic would get on with whatever he was going to do. If he meant to kill him, he wished he would do it—not play goddamn games. But the devil-eyed bastard better make sure he was dead. If not, Nick would get his revenge on both men—show them he wasn't a man to be fucked with.

Jacob moved to where Nick was restrained. Standing still, he watched him for several seconds like a wolf about to attack its prey. He only had a short time left before he could go to work on him—cutting away at his flesh, making him holler out in agony.

This was his gruesome compulsion. He had endured pain all his life. He didn't have anyone to show him how to love. His father only taught him how to hunt, hurt, and dish out pain. He had no mother. His father said she took off because she didn't want him. He hated his father to his very core and dreamed of the day when he would kill him. When that day had come, what a great feeling it was. To torture, and finally kill the person who had been beating him, cutting away at his body, making him do gruesome things to others.

It was in his DNA to be evil. 'Evil is what evil does,' was his father's saying and now his own. If it hadn't been for Lester, he wouldn't have anyone in the world. Their bond grew stronger after Lester had assisted him in burying his father's body. To this day, no one knew what had happened to his father.

"Well, somebody really adores you up there." He pointed toward the high ceilings with his crooked thumb. "I talked with an old pal of mine a day or so ago, who's an old pal to your friend Turner. Thanks to my pal, you get to live until Sunday at 1:00 a.m. If you're wondering why I haven't done anything drastic, that's the reason." His evil smile accentuated his thin mouth. "But that's about to change."

Nick eyed him, wanting to smack the insane grin off his damn face. The ropes around his hands burned when he tried working his hands loose. *Too damn tight.* The imbecile made sure he couldn't get loose. He had to give him credit for his craftsmanship. It was probably the only thing he was good at.

"Why don't you come over and untie me, so I can inflict pain on you? Maybe kill you," Nick growled. "I think that would be befitting for a guy like you. How many have you killed and gotten away with? Ten. Thirty. Fifty." He counted, trying to get a reaction—to unnerve him.

"You must think I'm a real idiot to think I would admit something like that to you." His lips drew back in a sneer. "People pay a pretty penny for the work I do." Jacob rubbed his crooked thumb against two of his fingers on his left hand. "I assure you, I'm the best at what I do. I've been doing it since I was thirteen. I helped my old man on his many late-night kills if you know what I mean." The evil grin slithered across his thin lips again.

Nick couldn't believe the fool was blurting out about his past. What type of man would teach his son appalling shit like that? To harm another person and to behave like nothing was wrong with it—the evil-sick-fucked-all-the-way-up kind.

"Sorry you had a rough upbringing," Nick said, sympathetically, trying to get on his good side—eager he would continue to be open with him. This guy had every excuse in the book to be a monster. His insane-normal was created by his insane father. When Nick had learned that he was going to be a father, he was excited. It was the best news Sage could possibly give. He couldn't wait to hold his child, protect him or her from danger. Yet a lot of people who had children didn't deserve them. It sickened him to know a man, who was supposed to be a father, created this crazed-monster that sat before him.

Jacob took a knife from his back pocket. "Let me demonstrate what my old man taught me," he grinned evilly, moving the knife across Nick's face, applying pressure.

Blood began to run down Nick's face. Jacob was ravenous for more. He moved the knife to Nick's chest, slicing him, causing blood to spill. The blood ran down Nick's chest like a waterfall. Jacob inhaled hard, smelling the fresh blood. He had to get a grip because he couldn't begin his evil desires. He wiped his blade on Nick's shirt.

"Can't wait to get into my fun and games," he laughed, walking away.

Nick wasn't about to give the lunatic the satisfaction. He only grunted when Jacob was inflicting pain. He knew the wound on his chest needed stitches. It was still bleeding. Hopefully, it would stop soon.

Parker killed the engine and rolled silently into the alley at the abandoned old warehouse. He stepped from his vehicle, closing the door softly. The windows were dirty and difficult to see through, but he saw the blue Ford pick-up through the window closest to the large bay doors. It was the same truck caught on camera, leaving Nick's building. The very one Blackwell described.

Lights filtered through the slime of the windows, so Parker knew someone was inside. He went to the other window and saw Nick tied to a chair. The perp was sitting on what looked like a milk crate. Parker's phone vibrated in his pocket. He stepped away from the window and took cover in some shrubs nearby.

"Hello."

"Man, I've been trying to reach you for the past fifteen minutes. Scott said you got a lead. Something about a warehouse," Nate said.

"Yeah, that's right. I'm here now, and Nick is here." Parker heard a car pulling up and watched from his vantage point.

"Turner has left his place. Not sure where he's headed. Wait..." he said, glancing at the building. "...he just turned off at a warehouse." Nate continued to drive past the warehouse, not wanting to spook Turner.

"That's Turner getting out of the car. You call Scott and give him the coordinates. I'm going to see if I can get inside." Parker instructed after Turner was in the building.

"Okay, I'm on it. You be careful, Parker," Nate cautioned.

"I will," he inclined, ending the call, moving towards one of the windows.

Max opened the door to the warehouse. Holden immediately jumped from the crate, drawing his gun, aiming it at Max.

"Whoa, whoa," Max said, closing the door with one hand and waving the other at him. "No need to aim that thing at me. I'm here on business," he conveyed.

"You should have called first. I didn't think you'd be here so soon. Hell, I didn't think you'd show at all—you complaining about being watched. I've been itching to get on with what I want to do with him. I can't wait to hear his first scream," he said with a deadly look, "and see the first drops of blood hitting the floor."

"You're a sick fuck," Max said. "Well, that's gonna take a while. I have until Sunday at 1:00 a.m., remember? And it's Saturday evening." He gave Jacob an icy stare.

"Little shit! No need to remind me. If it hadn't been for Lest, you wouldn't be here," Jacob said, tucking his gun in the front of his pants.

"I see your boss has arrived," Nick said, smiling.

Holden yanked Nick by the head. "Listen, you suitcoat asshole," he growled. "This little shit isn't my boss. I'm doing a friend a favor by letting him be here. That means I'm doing your stupid ass a favor too. Giving your ass more time on this earth. You will be dying soon enough." Jacob released him, punching him in the gut, applying pressure on the wound he had caused earlier.

Nick coughed from the blow to the stomach. The wound on his chest was oozing again.

"Have your little fucking reunion, but Sunday 1:00 a.m., I want you gone. You got that?" he shouted at Turner. "Little ungrateful shit," he mumbled.

"Yeah, yeah, yeah," he said, clapping his hands together. "I got it, boss," Turner said, taking a seat in front of Nick.

"Now see, that's more like it," Jacob addressed, looking at Nick. "I told you he wasn't my boss." He whistled, walking away from them, heading back upstairs.

"I see you are getting along with Holden nicely," Turner said.

"Whatever, Max," Nick expressed, still trying to catch his breath. "My woman wants nothing to do with you. Even after you have this sick-crazed-lunatic kill me, Sage won't have you."

"See, that's where you're wrong." Max's face reddened with anger. "She will have me. I'll be there to comfort her and take care of her. And those brats, too, even though I don't care for the little snots. But I'm willing to do whatever it takes to be with the woman I love," he proclaimed, placing a hand over his heart.

"Where did I fail you as a friend and mentor? How did I miss all the signs?" Nick asked. "I thought you were my friend. I went out of my way to help you. I wanted to help get your art career established. I had no idea how sick you are. I thought of you like a nephew."

"You were good to me, Nick. You were more of a parent then my biological parents. I've always respected you." He ran his hands over his preppy hair. "We just want the same woman, which I think you're too damn old to have to begin with. You should have left her alone. You're more like a daddy symbol, not a boyfriend. You should have left that role to me. I am her peer. You use women, and when you are done, you get rid of them buying them off like cheap whores. I won't allow that to happen to her. You don't deserve Sage. I'll protect my beloved from you."

He thinks he's more deserving of Sage than me. This bastard is on crack or something. Sure, he's been with different women in the past. And he gave them nice parting gifts. They were only after his wallet most of the time. I have finally found the love of my life. And this old fuck thinks he's worthy of her, Max thought.

"You listen up," Nick paused, "You insane fuck, Sage doesn't want you. It doesn't matter how old I am. We love each other. We are going to have a baby together and adopt Nicki. I'll say this again, and maybe it will stick in that fucked-up brain of yours: She doesn't want you. She hates you. You are the gum that's attached to a shoe. The one who doesn't want to take no for an answer. You make her skin crawl. The thought of you being with her is totally hideous. She doesn't want or need your motherfucking protection," Nick said loudly, staring at him lividly.

Max rose from the crate and marched to Nick. He hit his jaw then massaged his hand. "You hard-head moron," he scorned. Nick's head went to the side briefly before he spat blood from his mouth with a grin on his face.

"You think this shit is funny?" Max asked, hitting Nick's jaw again with the same fist. The force of the second blow dropped Max to his knees in pain.

Nick grinned through bloody lips. He still couldn't get himself loose from the restraints.

"I have to admit, you had me fooled at first, thinking she was your girlfriend. I let my jealousy get the best of me. I was the fool believing your lies," Nick conceded.

"You made it so easy for me, Nick. I followed you to Phoenix when you went after her. I kept my eyes on you the whole time except when I couldn't. I wanted to hurt you for defiling her. But I have someone better at this than I am. You know what Holden plans on doing to you?" Max asked, standing, rubbing his hand.

Nick already presumed what the imbecile wanted to do. He wanted to torture him. The crazed-bastard had been abused by his father. Jacob was fulfilling the family legacy.

"There's no need to tell me," Nick replied, watching him with red eyes. "That fucked-up bastard and you are made from the same cloth. Two insane pea-brains."

"Nope, Holden is way more fucked-up than me. I'm going to tell you anyway." Max moved beside Nick, pulling his head back with the hand that wasn't pulsing. "First, he's going to stick you in several parts of your body with a screwdriver. Next, he'll make it seem like he's finished, only to put more teeny-tiny holes into you. He'll also pull some teeth from your mouth. Second, he'll take some plyers and take your fingernails off, and then he'll cut some fingers," he said, as he cracked-up. "Third, he'll slice you up into pieces, burning your body, so no one will be able to recognize you. Oh, I won't be here, of course. I'll be preparing to see my beloved. There's a lot more I left out. I want you to be surprised. I don't want to take the fun out of the foreplay."

Max turned around because he thought he heard a noise, then realized it was Holden making all the racket upstairs—probably getting his tools ready for Nick.

Nate parked his jeep out of sight and joined Parker near a broken window. Parker could see Turner on the floor as if squirming in pain. It appeared he hurt his hand against Nick's face. He saw Nick smirking at him. He noticed Nick's bloody, swollen face and his bloody ripped shirt. There were probably more wounds, but from where he was, he couldn't tell.

"Glad to see you here," he whispered.

"Figured you need back-up until your partner and friends in blue show up," Nate said, unholstering his gun.

Nate and Parker move silently and quickly, approaching an entrance near the back. Parker opened the door slowly, glancing inside.

"It's the assembly room," he mumbled. "It's clear."

They moved inside the room, quietly watching their surroundings, making sure they didn't bump into anything. The warehouse was still filled with a bunch of junk.

Nate closed the door without making any noise. "You been here before?" he asked.

"Yep, use to work here back in the day. The money wasn't bad either. Especially for a teenage boy."

They moved to a door with a window. Parker knew the next room was the packaging room. He opened the door and didn't see anyone inside. There was nothing but old large boxes, dust cloths, old chairs, and broken tables. The pair moved into the room, looking around.

"Why did they close this old place down?" Nate whispered, ducking down beside him near large boxes that were stacked up shabbily so they both were hidden.

"Not sure. I went off to college. Came back, and the place was out of business. Rumor has it that the people who owned it got bored with it. Closed it down," he said, stepping toward the entry, looking out. He could see Turner talking to Nick.

"On my count. We move in on three," he whispered about to make a move until he saw Lester enter the warehouse. "Shit, now why is this guy here?" he mouthed, stooping back down beside Nate.

"What guy?," Nate asked.

"Lester," he announced, taking another quick peek.

Corbin entered the building with his gun drawn and a brown bag in the other hand. He was a cop after all. He didn't want to run into any kind of problem he wasn't anticipating. When he saw Max talking to Brimmer, he lowered his weapon, putting it back into his holster.

Turner didn't expect to see him here. Holden had to drag him into their situation.

"What's in the sack?" Max asked, nearing him.

"I should be asking what happened to your hand," he stated, looking at his swollen, black and blue knuckles.

"Nothing I couldn't handle," he said, trying to get a look inside the bag. "I see you and Holden are about to have a party without me."

"I'm only here because Jacob needed some supplies," he said, maneuvering toward the staircase. He would prefer if Turner went on about his business, which was using Brimmer as a punching bag.

"Count me in on this little shindig," Max said, following him upstairs.

"'Bout fucking time you showed up, Lest. Thought I was gonna starve to death," Jacob exaggerated, putting the hatchet down. "I didn't know you invited a third wheel," he said, looking at Turner.

"Why wouldn't he invite me? If it wasn't for me, neither one of you would be here, nor have stacks in your bank accounts."

"Okay, you have money, little shit. We get it," Holden said. "You're the one who needs us," he bragged, pointing his index finger and crooked thumb at him as if they were a loaded gun.

"Stop the bullshit," Lester addressed, placing the bag on the wobbly table. "Enough with the cattishness. There's plenty for us all."

He pulled out cold cuts, white sandwich bread, two bags of plain potato chips, roasted nuts, and a twenty-four pack of beer.

"You two still act the same way you used to when we hung together. Time can't change some things."

"Guess not," Turner agreed.

"Can't wait to dig in," Holden said, grabbing the chip bag, ripping it open. "Thanks, Lest, I owe you, pal."

Jacob retrieved a beer from the pack, wolfed down a couple of handfuls of chips, taking a swallow of beer, washing down chips.

"Damn, slow down, Jacob, before you choke to death," Lester said with a slight grin. "The food won't grow legs and run," he joked.

"Yeah," Turner chimed sourly, opening a package of turkey breast slices. "No class whatsoever," he taunted.

"I haven't eaten since Thursday night. Ran out of Vodka. Killed the rest of my whiskey about an hour ago. And it's Saturday night. Thanks to you, shit-for-brains," he replied, looking at Turner. "If it hadn't been for your perverted ass, I would have this job done. Not involve ole Lest here. And on my way back to where I belong. But you want to spend time with Brimmer. I see he roughed your hand pretty good."

"His face met my fist a few times," Max moved beside him, with dark eyes. "Don't mistake me for a softy, moron. I'd kick your ass."

"Gibberish, shit-for-brains. We know the kind of ass-kicking you do, and it doesn't involve men."

"Now, dip-shits, I suggest you stop with the foolery because you have unfinished business." Lester stared out the window at Brimmer for a second. "Max, you have another situation with Richards to worry about. And you both have this situation to worry about in the next room. They have reported him missing. I've seen his face plastered on all the news channels. You both better be on your best behavior or trouble will find you. There's only so much I can do to protect either one of you."

"I didn't invite you here," Turner said, then looked in Holden's direction. "You brought him in."

"Naw shit-head, this your fault. You wanted more time with your friend out there. Involving ole Lest here. I could have done my business if it weren't for you."

"Knock it off," Lester said, "I'm here on my own. I had to see what you two were up to. When I saw the news report of the missing businessman, I knew it had to be the two of you. So, you both need to eat and shut the fuck up, and get on with whatever this is here," he said, staring out at Brimmer once more.

"You right, bro," Holden said. "Listen up, Turner. You handle your business tonight. No need waiting on Sunday, but I'm keeping my extra cash for this job. Since his handsome face is splashed on the news, we can't take any chances."

"You're right," Max said. "I'm almost done with him. Keep the money.

"Good, we can move forward. With any luck, no problems between you two," Lester said.

Chapter 26

When Parker realized the perps were occupied eating and talking, he and Nate took the advantage to untie Nick.

"You don't know how great it is to see you both," Nick implied. "How's Sage?"

"Worried about you," Parker stated. "Other than that, she's okay. I'm gonna head upstairs—you two stay here."

"There's no way I'm going to let you enter a room outnumbered," Nate said. "I'm coming with you."

"Count me in," Nick claimed, grabbing a broken two-by-four. He was in pain, but that didn't bother him. He wanted to get the bastards with every inch of his being. Pain wasn't an option.

"Okay, but we move in on my mark. And thanks."

Fifteen minutes went by before Turner stood to go downstairs. "I'm about to say my goodbyes to Nick. I'll see you two never," he voiced, moving near the door.

"Good doing business with you, Turner," Holden said.

"Stay out of trouble," Lester said, looking at him. "Remember that other thing you are involved in."

"*Ack*, I remember. I'm not looking for any more trouble. See you around," he said, backing out of the room, shutting the door. When he came down the stairs, he realized he had found trouble, facing him with a deadly gaze, and his friends upstairs had no clue.

Parker and the guys were about to move upstairs when they heard the door open and saw Turner walking downstairs.

"Well, well, well," Nick said. "Nice to see you again, but under better circumstances." He laid the two-by-four down, clutching Turner by the collar, hitting him in the gut. "Now you know how it feels to get sucker-punched."

Turner dropped to the floor, coughing, holding his stomach.

"Nick, keep an eye on this one while we head upstairs," Parker advised. He had a feeling Nick wouldn't mind.

"My pleasure," Nick said, picking Turner up by the collar, dragging him across the room out of sight. When they were out the way, Nick pulled Max's head back.

"Look at me, you piece of shit," he mumbled. "You thought you had the whole thing figured out. But my girlfriend's friend had you figured. They had been watching you when I had no idea. You will be going to jail for a good long time."

"That's where you're wrong, asshole," Max snapped, holding his stomach. "All I have to do is make a phone call to my parents like I've done in the past. They usually come through for the son they never wanted," he stated with bared teeth.

"I doubt they can help you out this time. You've been caught in action. My soon to be fiancé isn't your beloved anything. Sage is mine, as I've told you before. I protect what's mine. You spineless rat." Nick gripped Max's head hard. "Sage and the baby she's carrying belong to me. Of course, you knew that already," he whispered. "You will never come near her or my children. If so, consider yourself dead. And that's a promise I'm prepared to make a reality. You will never hurt another woman again. You spoiled rich brat." He punched him in the face, rendering him unconscious.

Nick heard the sirens approaching, which meant he was leaving this place soon to be with the woman he loved.

Nick was taken to the hospital after he gave his statement to BVPD. The doctor said he had a concussion and two broken ribs and would recover in no time. He laid in the hospital bed, counting the minutes before Sage would be in his arms. Parker and Nate reassured him one of them would bring Sage to the hospital. It was the only reason he went straight to the hospital as they advised him to.

He eased out of bed to check his coat pocket. Yes, it was still there. He took it, easing back to the bed, opening the ring box. He glanced at it with half-lidded eyes. Pleasure emerged on his face. As he gazed upon the flawless diamond, he found himself getting sleepy. He closed the box, tucking it underneath the covers, drifting off to sleep.

When Sage arrived, she took the elevator to the floor Nick was on. She stopped at the nurse's station, inquiring about him. The nurse told her he had been sedated, so he wouldn't be talking much and directed her to his room.

Once there, she opened the door and saw the man she loved, bruised up. She had moist eyes as she went to his bedside. His face was swollen, and she noticed that his chest was bandaged, which meant he had broken ribs. She held her head upward, thanking God he was okay, then touched her belly whispering, "Daddy's gonna be just fine." She took hold of his large hand and softly kissed his palm. She was so thankful God allowed Parker and Nate to get to him in time.

Nick began to stir when he felt her kiss. He smiled, opening his eyes. "Hi baby," he spoke groggily.

Sage stood, cuddling him. "I thought I was going to lose you. I was so scared, my darling." She sniffled, raising her head, gazing into his eyes.

"Never, sweetheart," he affirmed, stroking her back lovingly. "I'm not going anywhere. You're my world. I'm glad the idiots took me. I don't know what I would've done if it had been you, my goddess. I love you so much," he grunted because she was positioned on his aching chest. But he held her there a few minutes. "Baby, my ribs hurt," he sighed sleepily.

"I'm sorry, Mr. Wondaful." She moved away from him, taking a seat at his bedside. "I love you, Nick," she said, cuddling his jaw. She realized he had fallen asleep. The drugs had kicked in.

A few days later, Sage had planned a surprise welcome home party for Nick. Everyone who was close family and friends was at the house. Sage and Nate left to pick him up.

"I never got the chance to thank you, Nate," she commented, looking at him with her shades on. "If it hadn't been for your help, I wouldn't have him back. I'm grateful to both of you. Thank you."

"I'm glad I could help—no need to thank me. I know I was a pain to have around all the time," he said, making a stop at a red light.

"Blah, blah, blah." She made a face, then burst into laughter, and so did he.

"Wow," he said, taking off after the light changed to green. "That bad, hm-mm." He smirked.

"Not too bad. You have loosened-up a bit since we first met. It was like pulling teeth though," she confessed.

"Sorry about that, but I had to focus on my job, which was protecting you," he replied.

Nate was pleased everything had worked out for them both. Those sadistic lunatics were going to chop Nick up into pieces and burn his body from what Parker told him.

They pulled up at the hospital about fifteen minutes later. Sage walked hurriedly to Nick's room. She couldn't wait to have him home. And boy was he in for a surprise when he found his family and friends there.

"Hey, slow down," Nate said, walking swiftly beside her.

"You can't keep up," she bantered. "Am I walking too fast for a strong guy like you?"

"Nope, not at all," he said, opening the door to Nick's room. However, Nick wasn't there.

"I know he told me he was being discharged today," she said, looking around the room puzzled. "It's October 29th?" she questioned, looking at Nate. She glanced at her phone to make sure.

"Yes, that's correct. Maybe they took him for some tests or something. I'll go check," Nate said, leaving the room. He knew Sage was in for a big special surprise she hadn't seen coming.

Sage took a seat next to the bed, wondering where Nick was. She went to the closet to look for his belongings. There wasn't anything there. Confused, she closed the door, moving back to the chair, and sat waiting on Nate. When the door to the hospital room opened a few moments later, it wasn't Nate but Nick. She went to him immediately, standing on her toes, wrapping her arms around his neck.

"Where were you?" she breathed against his chest.

"I was waiting for you to arrive." He held her close, stroking her hair. "I'm fine, baby. I'm not going anywhere," he promised, kissing the top of her head.

She released his neck, looking up at him. "So, where were you? Did they need to run more tests? I was worried."

"No, they didn't. I'm fine. No need to worry, sweetheart."

Nick drew her away from the door, showing her to the seat next to the bed.

"I've been rehearsing how and where I would propose to you for a little while now," he said, staring into her eyes. "Wondering if you would accept my marriage proposal, I asked your dad for your hand, and he was okay with it. I was shocked." He cracked a smile. "I also asked him if you were ready to marry again. I saw the look on your face at your house when Nicki asked if I was your boyfriend. You avoided answering her. You act as if total commitment frightened you."

"Nick, I'm--" her words were interrupted by him. He kissed her lips gently before speaking.

"I know you didn't see yourself being with a man like me, but thankfully, the universe knew you were meant for me." He took the black box from his pocket. "Sage Sullivan, will you do me the honor of being my wife, my beautiful goddess?" he requested on bended knee.

Sage's eyes grew wide as the letter O formed on her lips. Her eyes were watery, watching the man she loved on one knee with an exquisite diamond ring. And he had gotten her father's permission to marry her. That had to have taken some courage because she knew her father didn't approve of Nick. He hadn't come out and said it, but she knew. She was glad her father gave him his blessing.

"Well, my beautiful emerald-eyed goddess, will you?" he queried.

"Yes, a trillion times, yes, Mr. Wondaful!" she sang, jubilantly, getting up from the chair, wrapping her arms around his neck.

Nick grunted softly.

"I'm sorry, baby," she released his neck, remembering his ribs were healing.

"I'm okay." He took the ring from the box and placed it on her finger. He stood up, bringing her with him. He thought for a moment she would say no. But he should have known his beautiful goddess would accept his proposal. He pulled her close and kissed her zealously. They kissed until the door swung open. It was Parker and Nate.

"I take it the bride-to-be said yes," Parker said with a wide grin.

"Yes, she did," Nick answered, kissing her lips softly.

"Congrats, you two," Nate said.

"Let's go," Parker said, everyone is waiting."

"I'm glad it took an auction and a risk to bring you into my life," she whispered.

"Me too, my love. Me too," he repeated.

Nick and Sage stared at one another, knowing they had found what was missing in their lives. It was an amazing feeling to find someone who completed your heart. All because they both decided to take a risk on each other and love.

Maxwell Turner was behind bars. He thought his parents could work their magic to get him off, but they couldn't pay anyone off this time. He had been connected to the murder of too many women. Their beloved-lunatic would have justice served for some of his present and past crimes. He wouldn't have a trial because his attorney cut a deal.

Parker and Scott connected him with other women. They contacted some of the victims' relatives. The paintings of the many different women in his apartment and the painting of Gloria helped their cases. He had some of Gloria's work stashed at his place, connecting him to her. Her initials were on her work. GF was her signature. That's what gave them away. The deal with the District Attorney removed the death penalty from the table, to life without the possibility of parole if Max told them where some of the bodies were. No one had a clue how deranged he was. Not even his parents realized he was capable of such horror.

Jacob Holden was brought up on kidnapping and attempted murder charges. They also connected and charged him with some of Turner's victims. His trial was set for the following summer. Nick would have to testify to help put him behind bars.

Corbin Lester was arrested for aiding and abetting both Turner and Holden. He was also accused of extortion because of the large sums of money Turner paid him. His trial was set around the same time as Holden's.

It was December 17th on a nice, warm Saturday afternoon. Christmas wasn't too far away. Christmas in Bayville was such a magical time of year. Everywhere you looked, you saw beautiful decorations. The city took Christmas seriously. Maybe more seriously than other cities or countries. It was Sage's favorite time of the year. If it could stay like this all year round, it would be heavenly. People seemed better and in happier spirits. She loved everything about the holidays. Sage and her aunt had their little traditions baking cookies and cream-filled pies for Santa. She loved licking the spoons and talking with her aunt. The whole house was decorated beautifully and smelled like Christmas cookies.

She and Nick decided to have a party in honor of their daughter. They were married in a secret ceremony at the courthouse but would marry again with a big church wedding after the baby was born. They officially adopted Nicki two weeks before the courthouse marriage and wanted to surprise her with a party celebration. Nicki stayed the night at Aunt Katie's. They would be arriving around 2:30 p.m.

Sage moved around the kitchen, preparing different platters. She didn't want to hire a catering service because it was an intimate gathering. There would only be close family and friends, and she didn't mind putting the special event together.

"Sage," Nick said, going to her aid. "I told you not to do too much. We could have hired a catering company," he fussed, rubbing her five-month pregnant belly.

"Baby, it's only a veggie platter," she sighed, pinching his jaw. "I can handle these platters." She looked around the kitchen, proud she had done a terrific job. Everything was set perfect. "You don't need to worry. I'm not even that big yet. When I blow up like a big old basketball, then you must be protective of your wife," she said, heading to the punch bowl.

"Baby, I don't want anything happening to you or our unborn child," he said sincerely. "And everything looks great!"

"The doctor gave us a good clean bill of health," she said, brushing her hand across her belly. "And it's okay for me to do things around the house that aren't strenuous. It's even okay for me to exercise, sweetie." She stopped mixing the punch bowl when he took her hand, drawing her close to his body.

"I've never told you this, but I've always wanted a large family," he commented, kissing her glossy pink lips.

"Wait," she said, "how many children are you talking about?"

"Six," he professed, kissing her mouth lovingly. "So," he said between kisses. "We. Better. Get started. As soon as you are well enough." He cracked a boyish smile.

"How about we have one more, and we discuss the other three later." She caressed his chest.

"Deal," he chuckled with laughter.

Later, the house was filled with close family and friends. Sage, Lora, Sarah, and Cindy were in the library. Sage was showing them a copy of her recently published book, "*Happenings on Castleberry Road.*" It was her first novel to be published and happened to be the one that Nick had read. Sage had landed a writing contract, and her other stories were well on their way to being published as well. It was still all new and exciting for her.

"I can't believe you never mentioned to any of us you're a writer," her sister said with pride.

"Sage," Sarah said, excitably, "this is amazing." She held the autographed copy Sage had given her.

"Yes, chick," Cindy said, running her hands over the cover. "Wonderful."

"Thanks, ladies. If it hadn't been for Nick, I wouldn't have published it. He's the reason I went after my dream. I was scared at first. I can finally admit that. I'm really in a very glorious place with my life," she said, honestly.

"Looks like you both rubbed off on each other. He just had an art exhibit at Angelonia Gallery three weeks ago," Sarah said. "And his work is brilliant. When are you doing your book tour?"

"Right now, my focus is on my baby." She ran her hand over her stomach. "Nicki and my new husband," she told them happily.

They all looked at her shell-shocked.

"When did this happen?" Lora asked. "I thought we would be bridesmaids."

"You all still will be. We had to get married in order to adopt Nicki officially." She smiled.

"That's great," Lora said, hugging her. "I know Nicki's happy to have you both. The surprised look on her face when she entered the house was priceless. I hear she had a hand in putting you two together."

They all laughed.

"Yes, you could say she played cupid for us. She got her wish. She's very happy. She has a new mommy and daddy, and a new baby brother on the way."

"I'm glad they caught the bastard who murdered her mother and her unborn child," Sarah said. "I know her mother would approve of you and Nick adopting her little girl."

"Yes, I think so, too," Sage said. "I'm so glad fool-creep will be behind bars for a long time. And his friends will go to trial next summer. I hope justice is served on a platter for them both."

"So, it's a boy," Cindy chimed, changing the conversation to a lighter topic. She was the only one who caught Sage's remark. It was a day of love and joyfulness.

"Affirmative, the doctor told us a few weeks ago. I'm so glad all of you are here with me celebrating this wonderful occasion with us. Let's get to the party. Okay, ladies, group hug," Sage said, smiling at all of them.

Sage went to the kitchen, grabbing a meat platter from the counter. When she came into the room, her family and friends were engaged in lively conversation. She also noticed Cindy and Paul talking. She was glad now that both her best friends had men in their lives they loved. And the men loved them back just as much. They all would be happily married with children soon.

Nick was talking to some of the guys when he spotted his pregnant wife walking out with a platter. He immediately went to help her.

"Sweetheart, you shouldn't be carrying this," he protested, taking the platter from her. "I'm here to do that." He placed the platter on one of the tables.

"Baby, it wasn't heavy. We discussed this earlier. You act like it weighed thirty pounds." She looked up at him, amused, kissing his jaw.

"I don't care if it's lite. You have your husband for that. I don't mind spoiling you." He kissed her lips.

"Let the man spoil you, Sug. He's only looking out for you." Katie radiated, coming up beside them.

"Thanks for your support, Katie." He kissed her cheek. "My wife thinks she's superwoman sometimes." He smiled, towing Sage into his embrace.

"Mommy, Granddaddy said he was going to teach me how to be a good stockbroker," Nicki said, skipping over to her parents. Sage and Nick loved the fact that their beautiful daughter started calling them mommy and daddy.

"Oh, he did, huh? Your granddaddy is the best teacher I know, lovebug." She caressed Nicki's cheek, looking in her father's direction. He was conversing with Parker and Scott.

"Daddy, can you take me to your office, so I can see what you do?" She looked up at Nick. They had painting in common. He would make sure she followed her dreams. When she was older, she would be just as good as he or better at painting.

Nick picked up their daughter. "Sure, baby. I'll let you be my little assistant."

"Hooray!" She hugged his neck. "I'm really happy about my party," she beamed, looking at them. "And I have the bestest parents. Can I get a cupcake now, Daddy?

I'm hungry for one," she said, rubbing her belly.

"We are extremely happy you're our daughter," Sage said, and Nick agreed by patting Nicki's cheek.

"You have to eat first. Then we can both have a cupcake and all the sweets we want," he said, tugging her nose playfully. "I'll fix us a plate."

He and Sage looked at one another briefly and smiled. They were extremely happy for the first time. They had the family they'd always wanted. It wasn't too risky to love again after all!